OF
ARAGON

OF
ARAGON

CAROLINE WILLCOCKS

atmosphere press

For John, Tom, Claire, Jenny and Jimmy with love.

CHAPTER

1

Dear daughter, my Alice, I write this for you in the second year of our glorious Queen Elizabeth's reign, long may she live. Although Alice, I must tell you that her mother was not always kind to me, although she said I sang like an angel. Those fine ladies often had sharp tongues. What could I do? I shrugged my shoulders and smiled, because that is the lot of servants. Although I was their equal, I knew I could never tell her so.

But that's half way into my story, and I must start at the beginning. I tell you, I have served six queens and known eight. I remember our most beloved Queen, Katherine of Aragon, when she was still young, with a complexion like a rose. I remember that King Henry loved her dearly and carried her favours at the joust. And her, well, he was the love of her life, more fool her. Queens love like us ordinary women, but their hearts are private, guarded by royal protocol. I have seen what has happened in their privy chambers, heard their tears, watched when they thought no one was looking. I have tales to tell, and now I am nearing the end of my life, I will set them down for you. Us small people, we leave such a fleeting footstep in time, but I will not let my memories die with me.

It is up to you, Alice, to pass these stories on to your children. They will know the truth, and although it will no longer matter, it should make them proud.

What I tell you must stay close within our family for now, dear Alice. It would still be too dangerous for you to share my strange story with anyone else. Remember to keep this document safe, at the bottom of your oak linen chest, where no one else will see it. If the truth is known, even now, it would threaten both your and my lives. You are the apple of my eye, my golden lass, and I would never bring harm upon your head. The truth, for now, must remain secret.

I was born in London in 1510, I'm told. We were never sure about the date. My father and mother lived in three rooms in an old house within the City of London walls. We shared it with five other families. They called it 'pestering', changing the old dwellings into homes, not for one, but many poor families. My father worked as a cook for a wealthy cloth merchant who lived in one of the houses clinging to London Bridge. We didn't see him very much. He would sleep often at his master's house so that he was at hand to prepare the breakfast in the morning. My mother Joan had also worked as a serving maid until she fell pregnant with twins – me and my brother. She was small, and round and dark haired. I still remember her warm arms, and the yeasty scent of the bread she used to bake every morning. She wore a grey worsted gown and a white coif over her hair. I loved her so much.

But the person that I looked up to most during my childhood was my brother, Will. We were twins, although you never would have believed it. Will was tall, with dark curly hair and brown eyes that twinkled with mischief. Me, I was thin, and small with hair the colour of rust and small blue eyes that looked piercingly into the faces of the people I met.

"It's as if you want to look into their souls, Kat," my mother would say. "Look down, my daughter. Respect your elders." But I couldn't. I wanted to find out about people. I

2

have always been curious, eager to learn. I wanted to know how others lived their lives; were they all as ordinary and dull as ours? I remember Mistress Stabb, who lived on the top floor. I looked into her black eyes, and her wizened face, and knew immediately that she was different. She saw things that other people didn't. She was a widow whose husband had died, leaving her a small portion to live on. Sometimes she would hurry out, carrying a large bag. But many people visited her. I would hang out of our window and watch them coming and going. They would come looking anxious, their souls unquiet. Later, they would leave, their faces either joyful or wet with tears. What was it that she was practising on the floor above us?

One day Will and me crept up to her chamber. Our mother was at the market and she had left us with a loaf of bread to eat and some small ale. We had strict instructions to mind the fire which flickered in the corner of our little hall. But we were bored, and tired of gazing out of the window. We saw one woman leave, looking around as she went to check no one had seen her.

"So what did Mistress Stabb do to her?" Will laughed. "She looks as sour as a lemon!"

"Maybe she cursed her," I suggested, "or conjured up a demon in front of her!"

Will shook his head. "No, she's just a sad old sow, gossiping with women who have nothing better to do."

I sat up straight. "Don't you talk about her like that, Will! We're told to respect our elders. I think she is very mysterious. She could be a witch!"

"A witch?" he scoffed at me. "I'll wager she's no more than an idle old woman who drinks too much ale." His eyes twinkled as he spoke, and he turned and started to tickle me hard. I fought him off, strongly, and hit him on the side of his head.

"Stop! Stop! God's wounds, you are strong sister," he gasped. "Stronger than you look!"

"That'll teach you not to respect women," I crowed. "I tell

you, she is a woman of magic. She casts spells and sees the future!"

"So why can't she cast a spell to live in a palace then? Come to think of it, Kat, we could ask her to cast a spell for us so that we can live in a palace, and have lots of money, and let Father and Mother move back to the country away from this hole!"

"Maybe she could," I said. "I know the priest would say it is a sin, but if it's for good, what is the harm?"

"Those priests, they like to frighten us," Will laughed. "But I'm not scared of them. They milk the poor, those clerics. Look at Cardinal Wolsey, with his palaces and his mistress! Some priest he is."

I nodded. "Yes, I heard the bawdy songs from the alehouse last night. That butcher's boy is the talk of the town, acting like royalty now he is the king's Lord Chancellor."

"I'll not let him dictate what I will do," Will declared. "You know, Kat, there are people now who say priests aren't needed to know what God wants. All you need to do is read the Bible." He fell silent, maybe reflecting that neither of us could read.

"Tell me Kat, do you really believe Mistress Stabb is a witch?"

"Yes, indeed I do," I answered. "And you know me, I notice everything!"

"Let's go and see!" Will said boldly. "We can bring her our morning loaf, as a gift, and ask her to tell our future." He held his hand out to me. "Come Kat, let us find our destiny!"

I jumped up. I have always been told I am as bold as a boy. Maybe it didn't always serve me well, but I was determined not to let this chance go by. Will might have changed his mind by tomorrow, and it wasn't long till our mother would be back.

Carrying the bread wrapped in a linen cloth, I followed Will up the small twisting staircase. It didn't smell good, with stale odours of rancid meat and sweat lingering in the air. Our mother kept our chambers as clean and sweet as she could.

Every summer she would go with us to gather cowslips and daisies from the fields outside the city to dry and mix in with the rushes for the floor. But here it was dark, and the air was trapped. Will turned back.

"Should we go back, Kat?" he asked. "I would be a poor brother if I allowed you to be frighted out of your wits."

"Keep going," I insisted, pushing him up the stairs. We got to a door, old and heavy, scarred with many pits and stains. "Here, let's knock!" Trembling, I knocked on the door. It echoed emptily, but nothing happened. We waited, and then I knocked again. Will started to pull me from the door, but as I turned the door started to creak open.

In the doorway stood an old woman, maybe about forty years. She was smiling broadly, although she had no teeth to show, and her face was wrinkled from the sun.

"Come in my dears," she croaked. "I've been expecting you."

I turned to Will. "See? I was right!"

"Right about what, my sweeting?" Mistress Stabb whispered, her eyes crinkling up in merriment. "I think I know."

By then we were both shaking, but it was too late. She gestured for us to come into the room, and you know us two, we were brought up to respect our elders. I held out the bread to her.

"We brought you a gift, Mistress, our mother's bread," I stammered, holding it out to her.

"Why thank you sweeting. I accept your gift with a glad heart," the old woman said. "Now tell me what you want from me."

"Well, er, I have a touch of the ague," said Will, "maybe a poultice or something?"

She laughed heartily. "Come and sit down by the fire, my sweetings. You are both fine, healthy children, you have no ague. But – I can tell you. You both have footsteps into the future that will lead you in ways you could never imagine.

Look into the flames of my fire, look at the pictures they make. Look at the dreams that will come true, my dears."

We stared intently into the fire. At first the flame flickered hesitantly. Then it seemed to form into a high tower, and a handsome keep. Men were mounting horses. Suddenly, the old woman's voice became loud and shrill. She pointed at Will.

"You, my boy, will serve the greatest in the land, the very greatest! You will marry royal blood. You will live in palaces, you will hunt with the hounds, and sometimes the hare. But, my boy, you will die in your own bed. I can tell you that now."

"Why thank you mistress," Will joked. But his face was white. "You have the gift to speak to my heart's wishes! I think this is dreaming, not reality."

"Ah yes, my boy, it is a dream. But dreams come true my dear, dreams come true," she whispered, smiling. I shifted impatiently.

"What about me, Mistress Stabb?" I demanded. "You have given Will his royal future. What about mine? Am I just going to be a serving lass?"

Her face darkened. "Look back at the fire now, sweeting. It is your turn." The fire flickered again. The tower was still there but surrounded by beautiful ladies in a garden. I looked at one, all fair and golden, and then she melted into another, a dark French beauty. She melted again, as woman after woman appeared in the flames.

"My sweeting, you will be a serving maid," she said flatly. I sighed, disappointed. "But I hear music around you. You will be the heart of royalty! You will hear secrets. You will know what no one else knows. And yes, you will die in your bed. You and your brother here, your lives are linked. Whenever you are parted, you will find each other again."

I said crossly, "But what do you mean? The heart of royalty! How could I ever be that? And how could Will marry royalty? We are simple children. We do not have connections at court!" I was beginning to agree with Will, that she was just a silly old woman.

"Aye, well, young lady, just wait and see. I can tell you this, foundling, there is much about your story that you do not know..."

The door slammed, and my mother stormed in.

"Stop this nonsense at once! Mistress Stabb, I have kept a quiet tongue in my head about your doings up here. But you must not involve my children! If you meddle again, I will make a complaint against you!." She took there, her legs apart, glaring at the old woman.

Mistress Stabb drew herself up to her full height. Suddenly she looked menacing, and I was afraid for my mother. The old woman's dark eyes were piercing as she stared her in the face.

"Mistress Cooke, I will leave well alone for now. But you know, and I know, that you will never report me. It would put you at too much risk. We both carry the deepest, darkest secret in our hearts, and were it to become known, you and your family would be in grave danger."

"You are talking with the faeries, Mistress Stabb, and you know it," my mother accused, her voice faltering. "Leave my children alone!" She picked up the linen cloth that the bread had been in and started twisting it in her hands.

"Make the truth your close friend, Mistress Cooke," advised the old woman, "or else you may find it betrays you. Now go and leave me to my necromancy!" She laughed loudly and led us to the door, virtually pushing us out. We were all shaking as we ran down the stairs to the safety of our chambers, now dark and without a fire.

"And I told you to mind that fire!" our mother snapped at us. "Promise me, children, that you will never visit Mistress Stabb again. She is a witch, and she is dangerous."

"But she knows something," I said. "She was talking about royalty. If she's a witch, then she knows. How can we be royal? We don't even know anyone at court." My mother's face clouded.

"Mind your tongue my girl! Do not speak of this. Do you

understand?" She said this so fiercely that I started to feel tears welling up in my eyes. Will saw, and came and put his arm around me.

"Mother, it was me that encouraged Kat to go up," he lied. "It is my fault. Beat me for it, not her."

"I've a good mind to beat you both!" she shouted.

"But the court," I protested, despite Will frowning at me. "What is it about the court and us? And it was me that decided to go to Mistress Stabb, not Will!"

Our mother sighed. "I will never get the truth out of you two," she said. "You always were like as one. One will always dissemble for the other. So I will punish you both. No going out for two days. You can stay in and help me keep these chambers sweet and clean."

I started to object, but she held her hand up. "It's for your own safety. I don't want you associating with that witch anymore. She brings danger for us."

"But... but... she said I might be a great man and work at court," Will muttered, his eyes downcast. I could see he had been excited by the witch's soothsaying, and did not want to let go of that dream of becoming a grand gentleman someday. I hugged him tightly to console him.

But then our mother said something that amazed us both. "If you want to know about royal connections, I have a sister, Meg. She was a laundress at the court. Not a great lady or a great gentleman! Just a laundress, washing and making her hands red raw for her betters. So don't go running away with the idea that you will ever have a royal connection. The only connection is through used cloths and stained sheets." I dropped my arms from around Will and turned to face her.

"But mother, why did you not tell us?" She stared me in the face, as if unsure of what to say. I noticed she still had the linen cloth in her hand, twisted to a rag.

"Meg and I don't get on. I haven't seen her for eight years," she said eventually. "Since you two were born I was too busy, and she wasn't bothered." She dropped the cloth.

"So that's it, you two. Forget it! Forget it all. And now you can remake that fire and get this chamber warm!" She bustled out of the door, leaving us to struggle silently with the fire. We were both shocked by this encounter. Our mother, the gentlest of women, had never spoken to us like that before, and we didn't like it.

We never spoke of Mistress Stabb again, and if we passed her on the stairs we would shrink into the wall, so that we didn't brush against her. She would smile, and continue on her way, knowing that we couldn't hurt her. But in our games, we played grand gentlemen, going on a hunt, with grand ladies riding white palfreys beside them. The truth, Mistress Stabb had lit a flame in us that would never be extinguished.

That January, we came to eight years of age, and we started to learn more of our responsibilities and tasks within our household. I didn't like this, as Will would sometimes go and help my father in the merchant's kitchen while I was expected to stay at home and learn how to spin, how to wash and clean. But I was boiling with ideas and hopes. I wanted to learn to read and write. I wanted to learn how to dance and play the lute. I had so many dreams then. But as it was, I learned how to scrub a linen sheet, how to remove a stain and how to spin a fine thread. I liked to help my mother, but it wasn't enough.

One day, in the middle of that cold January of 1518, my father came to the house, with Will tagging along behind. My father was a tall, dark man, with curly hair like Will. He had the same smiling eyes, but they were often tired. He worked so hard, and was only able to visit us once or twice a month.

I was delighted to see him.

"Father, Father, have you brought me a sweetmeat?" I cried. My father would often sneak out a tasty morsel from the meals he prepared for us to taste.

"Here you are sweetheart," he smiled, "some sugared almonds." He dropped a few into my outstretched hand and kissed me on the top of my head. Then he walked over to my mother and put his arm around her. I noticed that Will was watching him anxiously.

"Wife, I have news," he said, looking down into her eyes.

"Bad news?" she cried, fearing that her little world was in danger. She was often anxious, I'd noticed that.

"No, no. Good news. Good news for our family and for Will," he reassured her.

"For Will? Has he got a position with you Tom? That would be great fortune for our family. We might even be able to live somewhere else with two wages," my mother said excitedly.

My father paused. "Not with me, Joan. With a city lawyer."

"What? How do you know a city lawyer?" she questioned, starting to look anxious again.

"Hush, wife, listen. As you know, Will has been coming with me to my work in the kitchen. He's helped with the pots and turning the spit. He is a good lad." Our father smiled at Will, who looked nervously at our mother. "One evening my master's page went missing. In a fight somewhere no doubt. That boy is no good! Will was there in the kitchen and the master asked him to stand in as a page, as he had some important guests coming. Will was so excited, he said yes straight away! We had to get him into some clean clothes and wash his face. He scrubbed up well, didn't you my son?"

"Yes, I did!" Will looked more and more excited, although he kept glancing at our mother.

Our father continued. "One of the guests was a city lawyer and arranger – his name is Thomas Cromwell. I didn't know of him, but they say he's a coming man. He was taken with our son. He asked Will what he wanted to do in life, and what did Will do but come out with all this nonsense about being a fine gentleman and going hunting?" He smiled, but our mother glared at Will.

"Cromwell laughed and said in that case Will should come and work for him, because he planned to be a fine gentleman himself one day. It was a joke, or that was what I thought. I went back to the kitchen and busied myself with the fruit and sweetmeats. Will did not follow me back. I thought it was strange, but maybe the master had got him pouring wine I thought. Later that night, I was just cleaning up when Master Cromwell came down to my kitchen. 'Master Cooke,' he said, 'I'd like to take your boy into my household as a page. I think he will do well in my service'."

"But he is only eight!" our mother cried. "He is too young!"

"Old enough for the fine folks, they send their sons away at eight," my father replied levelly.

"And he said I would learn to read and write, to ride and even to speak Latin!" Will burst in, unable to control himself. "He will make me into a lawyer maybe!"

My mother wept, but Will and my father were determined. So, a few days later, with many tears, we said farewell to Will. He promised that he would visit and whispered in my ear. "I'll get a position for you when I can, Kat, I promise."

We didn't see him again that winter. I sometimes thought of running away from home to join him, but then that would leave my mother alone, and I couldn't do that. The hours passed, more slowly than ever. Hesitantly, the days started to lengthen, and the sun became stronger.

The sweating sickness was in the City. Every day, my mother would go to the market and come back with news of more poor souls who had succumbed. You know that it takes you so suddenly. One morning you are breaking your fast, planning to go to market, and by that evening you are dead. My mother learned that the gentry were leaving the city in droves, all heading for their country houses.

"The King and Queen have gone to Richmond!" she cried one day. "They will not be back in the city for months." When she went out now, she wound a handkerchief around her face. There was nothing more we could do. We were there, like all the working people, in the crowded and dirty streets of the capital.

One day my father came, looking grave. "My master is leaving London," he said. "He has told me to follow him to the country. He doesn't trust the country cooks."

"You can't go, Tom!" my mother cried. "What will become of us, without you? We will have no money to live on." I started to cry and clung to my father's legs.

"Don't go Father, I beg you. Don't go, don't go!" Tears were rushing down my face. My father detached himself gently from me.

"Sweetheart, I have to go. I am ordered by my master. I cannot lose this position, we would starve without it!" He turned to my mother, who by now was trembling and white with anxiety.

"Wife, do not disturb yourself. My master has given me six months' wages in advance. It is no use to me. What can I spend it on in the country? It is for you both. It will keep you going until the autumn, when everyone can return."

We had to let him go, although we felt we'd been deserted. What could he do? We were the servant class, at the mercy of our masters. Then, just a week later, my mother came running in with more news.

"Master Cromwell has gone to the country! I heard at the market. His house is empty now! Will must have gone with him." Later we heard that he had maybe gone to Rome, we didn't know why. We felt betrayed. We raged and cried. At least my father had told us. But what could Will do? Maybe later, when he had learned to write, he would send us a letter. For now, we did not know where he was, or where my father was. It was just the two of us, clinging together in the big old bed and trying to comfort each other.

The next day my mother came back from the market without vegetables. She was sweating heavily.

"Kat, I am so hot, and my head hurts. I was in the middle of the market, and suddenly the sweat was pouring off me. I had to turn back, I couldn't go on." Her face was wet, and she was trembling.

I was only eight, but I knew I had to grow up at that moment. I put my arm around her. I had no thought for my own safety. Yes, she had the sweats, but she was my mother! I was only a child. But how could I not take care of her? I knew that some people came through the sickness, and it was my job to make sure my mother did.

I put her to bed and washed her face to cool her down. She was so thirsty, and I kept bringing her small ale, but it did no good. She started raving, rolling from side to side in the bed.

"Kat, Kat, you're not my Kat," she called out.

"What do you mean, mother? I am your Kat. Don't upset yourself. I'm here." I spoke quickly, trying to dispel her delirious fancies. But she wouldn't stop.

"No, you have another destiny," she croaked, "you must find Meg, she will tell you.... Her voice tailed off, and her eyes closed. She was barely conscious and breathing heavily. I sponged her face again and held her hand. It was burning. I kept trying to talk to her, silly little memories of my childhood, but she didn't reply.

She never spoke again. I sat with her for what seemed ages, but was only an hour or two. Before the sun set, she was dead. I clutched her close and tried to slap her back into consciousness, but her face was bluish white, and the warmth was going from her. I flung myself over her body and sobbed. How could she leave me like this? With her passing, I felt completely alone, with no one to care for me. The intense grief was like waves, washing over me, knocking me over with its ferocity. I tried to make sense of it, and then I tried not to make sense of it. But it was no good. My mother was gone.

It must have been midnight when I stirred. Tired from weeping, I had slept for an hour or so. I sat up, rubbing my eyes. Yes, it was true, my mother was dead. But now, I had to think what to do. I was here on my own. How would I tell my Will and my father? How would I live without her? The world seemed to close in on me. For a moment I felt like what I was, a terrified child, shaking in the darkness.

Then something came over me, maybe my mother's spirit. I felt strength flooding into me. Somehow I had to carry on, I had to make my own way in the world now. I'd find my Will and my father, but they were in other households now. It was up to me.

CHAPTER

2

I slept fitfully beside my mother's body until the daylight came, hearing the sound of my own breathing, and not hers. As the sun's rays filtered weakly through the window, I knew then what I must do. Mother would not have approved, but I had to get help from someone. I washed my face and hands with the water my mother had brought in yesterday, took a sip of small ale and went to climb the stairs to Mistress Stabb's chamber.

When I knocked at the door, it fell open. I peered inside. Mistress Stabb was heating a small steaming pan on the fire.

"Come here child," she said. "This will calm your spirit." She picked up the pan and carefully poured the contents into a small tankard.

"No, I don't want that," I protested. "It could be poison." She laughed, and it was a kind of witch's laugh, cackling at my reluctance.

"It's only chamomile, my sweeting," she said. "It will soothe your troubled mind. I am not going to harm you. I'm here to help."

I took a wary sip and found the warmth quite comforting. It tasted of grass and fields, and sunshine. While I drank, she was watching me carefully. At last she said, "So, you are on your own now." I put down the drink.

"How did you know?" I demanded angrily.

She laughed again. "The pictures in the fire, my sweeting, they tell me much."

At that moment, I felt the tears well up in my eyes again. Another wave of grief overtook me, and I started to howl. Seeing this, she came to me and enfolded me in her arms. She hugged me tight while I cried, burying my head in her apron. I know my mother had warned me against her, but I had no one else, and she was there for me.

At last, she pulled back and wiped my eyes with a kerchief. I looked her in the face, and her eyes were kind.

"Now, my sweeting," she said, "we will work out what to do."

She set out her plan for me. I was so shocked, I just sat and listened numbly. First, we must arrange for my mother to be buried, as soon as possible. Mistress Stabb would talk to the gravediggers, and she could be buried that night. Whatever we did, Mistress Stabb said, we must not say it was the sweats that killed her. Otherwise we would be confined to the house for forty days, and that would hinder me in finding my destiny.

"My destiny?" I objected. "All I want is to be safe and with my father again."

"Ah, but you don't know where he is, do you sweeting?" she answered. "No, you must find your aunt Meg, who is a laundress at court. She will get you a position."

"How do you know all this, and yet you don't know where my father is? What kind of witch are you?" I shouted at her.

"One who respects destiny, and the fate that I see mapped out for you," she said calmly. "You must go to the court, there is no other choice for you."

My mind was whirling. I remembered my mother's last words, that I had another destiny. What did this mean? I had lost my mother, and now it seemed I was being pointed towards a path that had nothing to do with her, or my father.

What could Mistress Stabb see, and why was she not being clear with me? But when I taxed her with this, she shrugged her shoulders and smiled.

"I cannot tell you all sweeting, for that is for you to discover. What I can tell you is that your search will begin tomorrow, at dawn."

I led a small procession that night to the churchyard, where my mother was buried, in a spot underneath a small rose bush. The tears flowed down my face as I realised I would never see her again, until we were both in heaven. Until then, I would pray for her every day, that her sweet soul would ascend to Paradise.

Mistress Stabb had no time for tears. After I'd returned, she informed me that I would stay the night with her, ready to leave early in the morning. She had paid for me to ride with the King's Posts, on their regular route to Portsmouth.

"You are to leave them at Woking," she said. "The court is at Woking Palace now, keeping away from the sweats. That is where you should go to find your aunt."

"Why can't I just stay here?" I cried. "I can live here with you."

"No, you can't sweeting, the money will run out, and you will be begging on the streets. I tell you child, a much better fate awaits you."

"What money?" I asked. I hadn't thought of such things until now. I was a child, remember?

"I took your mother's purse when I was washing her body before we put her in her shroud. She had money that now belongs to you. I paid the messenger from that. Take the rest, you will need it." She held out my mother's battered leather purse to me, and my heart turned in my breast. How often had I seen my mother digging into it for the odd small coin she needed to buy flour, or a cabbage? But of course, my father had given her his wages for six months, so there should be enough in there to last some time.

And so, that morning, before the sun was properly up, I took my last look at my family's chambers, remembering all the laughter and love that had lived there. I took a small bag of clothes. A shift, my mother's kirtle, which I could shorten, a spare coif and some woollen stockings. I wore the faded green dress that my mother had given me last summer.

Mistress Stabb took me to the King's Posts, who were saddling up their horses, laden with saddlebags full of letters. They were big, burly men, wearing the King's livery, with hard, weatherbeaten faces.

"Here is your horse, mistress," one brown-haired man said to me, gesturing at an enormous black steed. My head barely reached the stirrups. I had no idea how I was going to control that massive beast.

"I can't ride," I admitted, blushing to the roots of my hair. What an idiot they must think me! But the man just laughed and swept me up in his arms.

"Then you'll have to ride pillion with me," he said. "My name is John, little mistress, and I reckon that by Woking, I'll have you riding!" He perched me at the back of the saddle, and then mounted himself. I put my arms around his chest and turned to say goodbye to Mistress Stabb. But she had gone already. Why had she not stayed, even for a moment? What was I doing, trusting her to sort out my life? I truly felt alone now, and realised that I could depend on no one. My fate, whatever it was, would be decided by me.

John, the King's Post, was a kindly man, and he coaxed me to sitting in front of him sometimes, learning to control his horse, Pegasus.

"In the stories, Pegasus was the messenger of the gods," John said, "and sometimes my Pegasus is the messenger of the King, who is a god among men." Pegasus was a huge, gentle animal, and he followed my orders to stop, walk, or even canter exactly.

"No galloping," said John, "this horse has got to get to

Portsmouth. We don't run them hard, they get tired, and then we'd lose time in the end." If John had an urgent message from the King, he told me, he would hire a different horse at each twenty mile stopping point, to allow him to go really fast. But he preferred Pegasus, who knew his master well, and was used to the route.

As we left London, I kept looking around curiously. Our mother had taken us to fields just outside the city, but I had never seen such stretches of countryside before. After a hard winter, the green shoots of wheat were peeping through the earth. The meadows were full of flowers, cowslips, daisies, buttercups, looking like a wonderful, embroidered cloak of colour. Standing knee deep in the grass, we saw cows lazily chewing the cud, enjoying the feel of the sun on their backs. There were gentle downs, where sheep roamed, nibbling at the short turf. Lambs were jumping and running everywhere, and it was hard not to feel my heart lift at these sights of spring.

I heard the ewes calling to their lambs in the evening as we neared a village. I was so tired, and as John lifted me down from the horse, my knees nearly buckled with tiredness.

"It's been a long day for a small mistress," he said. "Let us get some meat and drink, and then you can sleep with the maids tonight. There will be space for a small one like you."

We sat in the inn, and one of the maids brought over two bowls of steaming pottage. I dug in my bag for my spoon and started to eat. John was already nearly halfway through his bowl. It was mainly vegetables and oats, but with a few slivers of bacon. It wasn't as good as my mother's, but to a hungry girl, it tasted wonderful. I realised I had not eaten a large meal since before my mother died. Digging my spoon in, I started shovelling the hot salty soup into my mouth. Then I ripped off a piece of bread and dipped it in the pottage, revelling in the pleasure of tasting and chewing, taking more and more until my stomach was full. We drank small ale, but afterwards John had a tankard of cider, which he allowed me to taste. It was bitter, to my mind, but strong and relaxing.

It wasn't long before I was lying on a pallet in the maid's chamber. There were two girls there, both a bit older than me. I felt hot, and one of the girls started to snore. But I was so tired, and I had not properly slept for two days. So it wasn't long after the candle was blown out that I was fast asleep.

I woke up to the sound of massed birdsong the next morning, quickly aware of the scratchy straw beneath me. The sun rose early in June, so it was already light. The maids had already risen, and I was on my own. I washed my face quickly and went downstairs, where John was waiting. We had a simple breakfast of bread and small ale, before he saddled up Pegasus, and we went on our way.

After many hours of riding, we came into Woking. It was a small place, with a grey old church, a market square, and some shabby looking wooden houses. John didn't stop. He had letters to deliver to the King, and he wanted to reach the palace before nightfall. He told me that he would sleep there before making his way to Portsmouth the next day. It might be that the King had messages for his naval commanders moored there in the Solent. As he told me this, I was suddenly reminded that even this friend would be moving on, and that I would be on my own. How would I find my aunt Meg, and would she take me in? What if she disowned me? My mother had said that they had not been friendly together, although I didn't know why. What had happened eight years ago that my mother had been so reluctant to talk about?

Pegasus was plodding on, his steady gait calming me. John had one arm around me, and with the other he was barely guiding the experienced horse. Pegasus knew his way along the path, that was clear. But after a few minutes, John ordered the horse to stop. Immediately he pulled up and stood still in the middle of the highway.

"Look, little mistress," John said. "This is the end of your journey. Woking Palace is ahead." I looked over the fields and saw a honey coloured building, quite large, but not as grand as Whitehall Palace in London. John pointed out the great hall, a large building in the middle of the palace. To each side there were smaller stone apartments, with a large kitchen a few yards away. At the front of the palace there was a garden with clipped hedges and laurel trees running down to a meadow in front of the river Wey. I could see fine ladies and gentlemen walking in the garden and hear the sound of their laughter carried by the warm breeze.

This was what I had dreamt of, and yet I was frightened. How could this be my world, a world where I could feel at home? I didn't know then that I was destined to spend many years in this world. Although it never felt like home, I became used to it, and felt comfortable with it.

The stables were at some distance from the main buildings. John dismounted, lifted me down, and left Pegasus with the stable boy.

"Come, little mistress," he told me. "Walk with me up to the main gateway." He strode quickly on, with me tumbling behind him, clutching my bag in my hand. Now he was within the royal palace, he was quick and business-like. I wondered if he had wanted to have a little girl tagging along with him and realised that by taking me, he had shown great kindness. A bit breathless, I called out to him.

"Thank you, John. If I can ever repay you for your aid, I will do so."

"No need, little mistress," he smiled. He looked at the gatehouse, with two liveried men standing each side. "Now, hold back while I speak to the guards."

"King's Post masters! I bring messages for his Grace!" One of the two men looked at him and nodded. It was clear that they knew each other. I stayed where I was, a few yards behind. They all ignored me.

"King's orders," the man in charge snapped. "You are to bring the messages to him immediately!"

John said, "I will do so presently, master. I must just find this young mistress's aunt. She is in the Queen's employ."

"No time for that!" the man rapped out. "The King wants to see you now. Leave her with us. We'll find her aunt."

"Very well." John shrugged and looked apologetically at me. "King's orders, little mistress," he said, "so I must go." He walked on, following the man in charge, who led him into the courtyard. I was left with the other man, who didn't look pleased to be saddled with a little girl. His oily face was wrinkled with a frown.

"So your aunt works for the Queen, does she now? And what does she do? Is she a lady in waiting?" He looked at my grubby gown and sniggered. "No, I thought not! What's her name?"

"Please sir, she is the Queen's laundress. Her name is Meg. I have important news for her."

"Queen's laundress?" he sneered. "There's no Queen's laundress here! Most of the staff stayed at Richmond. The Queen is using local staff here, less risk of the sweat."

"But... but... I was told she was working here," I stammered, tears springing into my eyes.

"Well, she isn't! So go and lose yourself girl. And don't come back!" He moved towards me menacingly, and I took to my heels and ran. I didn't know what I was doing, I just knew I had to get away from that horrible man and his leering face. I ran down, back towards the stables. Thankfully, when I looked back, I saw he hadn't followed me. I ran round the back of the stables so that I was out of view.

As I rounded the corner, I could see a high door set into the wall. This could be somewhere to hide, I thought. I opened the door and nearly fell into a large stack of hay. Nearby I could hear horses eating, crunching and snuffling. It was dark and smelled of flowers. I thought of my mother and the sweet daisies she picked. It felt like she was telling me to rest here, to stay safe among the scent of meadows.

I remembered what Mistress Stabb had told me. She'd told me to find my aunt here, at Woking Palace. So why had she lied? She had sent me far away from home, to a place where no one knew me, and I had no friends. Had she wished evil upon me? Or was she simply mistaken in her visions? I was troubled and disillusioned with her. For a few days I had thought she was showing me my destiny, but now I knew she had just been playing games.

I heard voices nearby. A man's voice, loud and hearty. He was speaking to a woman. Her voice was soft and slightly accented.

"Here she is, sweetheart," he said. "A white palfrey for you to ride on. She is mild as milk."

"My lord, you are so kind, thinking of me and our precious babe," she said, and I could hear the smile in her voice.

I crept to the inside door and opened it a crack. Hardly daring to breathe, I peeped out. I could see two rows of horses standing in their stalls, some of them eating hay. But it wasn't the horses that caught my attention.

Standing there was the most magnificent man I had ever seen. He was tall, taller than my father by far, and his shoulders were as broad as an ox. But his waist was neat, and his legs were muscled and taut. His hair was red-gold, cut short to his head, and he was clean-shaven. I gasped in awe, then pulled back, afraid that they had heard me. But the sound of horses eating filled the stables, and my little breaths had not disturbed them.

I knew, immediately, that this was King Henry. Who else but him was so tall, so commanding and handsome? And if his bearing did not tell me he was the monarch, then his clothes surely would. Despite the warm weather, he wore a black velvet coat studded with gold and lined with sable. Underneath there was a deep red doublet, emblazoned with pearls, diamonds and gold. At his neck there was a white silk shirt embroidered in black thread. His hose fitted tightly to his legs, their shape highlighted by bejewelled garters. To me, he looked like the sun, his majesty blazing so brightly.

I peeped a bit further round to see the woman he was talking to. Yes, surely, she must be the Queen! She was small in stature but dressed every bit as magnificently as he was. Her gown was of the finest blue brocaded damask, studded with pearls and sapphires. At the front of her gown, where her skirts parted, she wore a green front part, this time dotted with seed pearls and tiny golden flowers. She was not tight-laced, and I could see that her belly was round beneath her gown. A tiny frond of auburn hair curled out from under her English hood, like the ladies I had seen in the city, and her face was smooth and pink.

Somehow I felt drawn to this woman. She was not as impos-ing as the King, but I noticed the warmth of her smile as she looked up at him. She loved him dearly, I could see that. He was attentive to her, holding her arm and looking into her grey eyes.

"So, sweetheart, although you cannot hunt with me this summer, you can ride out and take the air. The scent of the fresh meadow herbs will help you and our baby to stay healthy until, God willing, you have a safe delivery of a son." He smiled at her, almost entreatingly, and she looked down for a moment. Then she glanced up at him again, and her lips tightened. I sensed that she was unhappy somehow, although being a child I had no idea why.

There was a noise of men running into the stable. The King turned, annoyed at being disturbed.

"What is it fellow, that makes you disturb me and my sweetheart in our conversations? I do not welcome interrup-tions when I am with the Queen." His voice became harder, more authoritative. The servant stood panting and trying to catch his breath.

"Haste, fellow! What interrupts our pleasant afternoon?" the King said.

The servant caught his breath and said apologetically.

"Your Grace, the Post is here. He has messages for you. Your orders were that you wanted to see him immediately he arrived."

The King nodded swiftly. "Yes, indeed! Lead me to him, fellow!" He turned to the Queen and bowed.

"My deepest apologies, sweetheart. It pains me to leave you, but I will visit you in your chamber this evening."

The Queen sank to her knees in a deep curtsey and murmured, "Thank you sire, I shall be pleased to entertain you."

The King moved to leave and paused at the outside door. "I will send your ladies to you, sweetheart. See you anon." He strode out, letting the door slam behind him.

The Queen looked after him for a moment, and then she moved towards the inner door, towards me. I was surprised to see her pick up her skirts and show a dainty foot, clothed in a blue leather riding boot.

"That man treats me like a fool! " she shouted. Suddenly, she kicked the door, and with not inconsiderable force. The door knocked into me, and I toppled over. I fell at her feet, shocked and afraid.

Queen Katherine looked every inch a queen as she examined me, as if I was a piece of rubbish at her feet. Her blue eyes pierced through me.

"Jesu, what brings you here, maid? As if I have not enough to bear, I find a foundling at my feet!" That stung me.

"I'm not a foundling," I shouted. "I had a mother, but she died! My father is with his master, I don't know where." I was angry, and the tears were welling up. I don't know how I had dared to speak to her like that, but her anger had released my own.

The Queen paused and looked down at me, shaking and trembling with tears. Her face softened.

"Do not be afraid, little maid," she said softly, and put her hand on my head. "I will not chide you. It is hard for a child to be parted from her mother." She looked very sad, and I wondered if she was thinking of her daughter, Princess Mary. I wondered how often she saw her. I knew that at some time the princess would be sent to live away from her mother. Royal children had their own households. They were too important to stay with their own mother. Immediately, I felt a warmth towards the Queen, who seemed only too human.

"I came here to find my aunt," I said, emboldened by her kindness. "Her name is Meg, she is a laundress in your household. I hoped she might find me a position."

"A position, little maid? I do not recall your aunt. Royal ladies have no reason to go to the laundry. She will be in London, with the rest of our staff. We have been travelling with only our closest servants." My face must have fallen because she knelt down and put both hands on my shoulders with her face even with mine.

"What is your name, little maid?" she demanded, "I will know with whom I am speaking."

"Kat, your Grace," I answered. "My family name is Cooke."

"So Kat, I will make you a position. Stay with me in the royal household. You can be my little maid of the chamber. Your duties will be to keep my sewing boxes tidy, to serve wine, and to sing with my ladies. In due course we will find your aunt, of that I am sure. " She straightened and stood up. "Come Kat, we will meet my ladies."

I could not take in what was happening. "Your Grace... why me?" I stammered. "Your Grace, I am dumbstruck." She laughed, a deep throaty laugh.

"Not so much that you can't speak well. I feel a tie to you Kat. Maybe we were born under the same star," she smiled. "I cannot explain it, but you feel so familiar to me. Come now, my ladies will be waiting for me. We will need to get you washed and find some clothes for you."

"I have clothes," I said indignantly, holding up my bag. The Queen laughed that throaty, warm laugh again.

"No, Kat," she said. "We will find you grander gowns. You are serving the Queen now."

She gestured to me to follow her out of the stable door.

Outside, there were three fine ladies, all waiting in the stable yard. They dazzled me with their fine silk gowns, and the jewels that hung around their necks. Even their gable hoods were studded with pearls.

Queen Katherine pulled me forward to face the ladies. Their faces were not welcoming. In fact, they looked at me as if I was the muck from the stables.

"Ladies, meet Kat!" The Queen announced. "From now on, she will be known as Mistress of the Pin Cushion."

"But your Grace, she is dirty!" a tall woman protested. She looked down her nose at me, gathering her skirts close around her. "Where did she come from? She is just a beggar!"

"Never mind that Elizabeth," the Queen said decisively. "She is here now! Take her to the maids and tell them to wash her and give her some clean clothes. There are some old linen smocks of mine, they will be long, but they will suffice. For now, she can wear her gown but she will need new clothes making."

And so I was taken into the Palace, past the guards who barely noticed me now that I was with the Queen. We went to the maids' quarters, where a flushed-looking girl welcomed me. I was stripped of my gown and my old smock, and then wiped down all over with rose water. It was cold, and I felt very vulnerable. But the maid was kindly and told me not to worry, the King insisted on cleanliness, and it wasn't as bad as it seemed. Soon I was standing in front of a large fire, with a clean smock which extended to my ankles, and some soft leather shoes. I put my spare gown from my bag over the top. For now that would do.

"Now, mistress, you must go to the Queen. She has asked for you to attend her in her chamber."

I followed the maid through many long corridors, past the Great Hall, with servants scurrying to carry in the dishes for the court's forthcoming supper. We eventually got to an embossed door with gold leaf initials, H and K intertwined.

"The Queen's Presence Chamber," the maid said and pushed me through the door. I was excited and very nervous. What was this new world I had entered?

The Presence Chamber was large, with tall windows that let in the late afternoon sunlight. It was like stepping into a magical glade. Every wall was covered with tapestries, glowing green and gold. There was a white deer running up a hill, away from the woods. Within the wood a goddess stood, with a company of ladies. Each had a silver bow and arrows. There were hounds running around their feet, so lifelike that I could almost see them coming to greet me. I stared, open-mouthed.

"Come here, Kat, and let me introduce my ladies," said the Queen. She had changed and was now wearing a scarlet velvet gown with a black front part, and black sleeves. The gown glowed with rubies. I hung back, afraid to approach her magnificence.

"Come child," she said. "You must curtsey to each lady as I introduce you."

And so I met the highest group of ladies to serve the Queen. To my childish eyes, there were so many of them, and they seemed so forbiddingly grand.

Maria, Lady Willoughby was always kind to me. She had long dark hair, which I would sometimes comb, and dark eyes. She was Spanish and had accompanied the Queen when she came to England. Maria had been friends with Katherine for years. She was with her when her first husband, the young Prince Arthur, died, and through the years afterwards when she was a young widow. Maria had just married herself now, to another courtier, Baron Willoughby. I thought she liked her husband, as she was always smiling. She had adopted English fashions and was always well-dressed. She felt the English cold, so her gowns were lined with fur, and she carried a small dog sometimes to warm her hands. She smelled of oranges and sandalwood, and I loved to sit next to her, basking in her perfume and her warm smile.

Lady Elizabeth Stafford was married to Richard Radcliffe, and she had three sons, all of whom lived in the country. Like her brother, the Duke of Buckingham, she had royal blood, although she never talked of it. She was a quiet, withdrawn woman, often to be found reading her Book of Hours. She was not kind or unkind – just indifferent.

Lady Elizabeth Boleyn was far from withdrawn. Of all the Queen's ladies, she was the most beautiful, with her white and rose complexion and green eyes. Her elegant hands were slim, and she showed them off by gesturing with them, often letting her rings catch the light. Men looked at her when she swept into the room. I was only a child, but I thought I would never be that kind of woman. I was too thin, and my hair was ginger rather than red. Indeed, Elizabeth Boleyn called me the Queen's ginger Kat! I knew she looked down on me. She was, of course, a Howard. That meant she was a member of one of the greatest families in the land, and she didn't welcome guttersnipes like me. They were the kind of family that liked to be different from others. Her husband, Thomas, was a diplomat and their daughters, Mary and Anne, were both ladies in waiting at the French court. Elizabeth would often boast about their immense learning and courtly skills.

"The French court is so very much more sophisticated than here," she would say. "They talk of all the latest questions of the hour. And the fashions! Would we were as elegant as the French!"

Sometimes, then, Katherine would look up from her sewing and cast a challenging look in Elizabeth Boleyn's direction.

"Elizabeth, none can match the discourse at the English court, for its piety and thoughtfulness," she would admonish her. "And as for the costumes, the English court is more magnificent than any! Look at me, ladies!" And she would stand up, with her red and gold silk gown billowing around her, her eyes twinkling and start to laugh. She knew that she was not lithe and slim like a young maid, but she was every inch a queen. She would stand there as if to say, "I am short, and my waist is stout, but I will always be beautiful!"

As I settled in, I found the Queen to be kind and a thoughtful mistress. I was homesick sometimes, missing my mother, but she seemed to sense when I was feeling sad and would give me a task to do, tidying up her silks or pouring wine. I would then be rewarded with a handful of the sweetmeats I loved. I thought of Will and my father often, but I had no idea where they were now. It felt as if all of my old life had vanished into thin air. The only link with the past I had was John, who I saw sometimes when he came on his regular journey with the post from London to Portsmouth. He was reassured that I was alright and finding my feet in my new life.

I was not the only child in the Queen's chamber. Her daughter, Princess Mary, would spend some of every day with her, and those were the times that the Queen smiled the most. She was just two years old, with reddish gold hair and a pink complexion. The Queen told me proudly that Mary was a very clever child, already learning her letters. Katherine's eyes would follow her little girl as she toddled around the chamber, petting Maria's little dog Señor, and sneaking bits of sweetmeats to share with him. Katherine had a monkey that was chained to a stand, for it could be vicious. Mary was scared of the monkey, as it had struck her once when she tried to hold its hand.

Usually, I stayed with the Queen until she retired to bed, when I would be sent away to sleep in the maids' dormitory. But one night she asked me to comb her hair before she put on her night cap. She had beautiful hair, real red, with golden highlights in it. I loved to comb it, it smelled so sweetly of roses. I stood there, with her sat in front of me, lulled by my regular movements of the comb. It was as if it was just the two of us there. The candles flickered, and the firelight cast shadows around the bedchamber. The ladies moved quietly, putting away the sewing and the books.

"Stay with me tonight Kat," the Queen said softly. "You other ladies go to your beds now." She spoke so quietly, but we all knew that it was an order. Scarcely pausing, the ladies curtsied and made to leave the room. They wanted to hasten to their husbands, who were waiting for them. I continued combing, hypnotised by my repeated actions, and the silky feel of her hair as it fell to her waist.

Outside, there was the sound of men's voices. Katherine started from her reverie and whispered an order. "Hence, child! Go from here!" But the door was already opening. I made for the large oak fourposter bed and dived into it, pulling the covers over myself. Who was this, and why were they visiting the Queen so late in the night?

It was dark and warm in the bed, and the sounds were muffled. At first I could hear Katherine talking softly with a man, but I couldn't hear what was said. Then Katherine raised her voice.

"Husband, you talk sweetly to me, but I cannot share your bed tonight, I am bearing our child." So it was the King she was talking to! I knew that he visited her chamber sometimes, but I had always been away before he arrived.

"Sweetheart, I do not wish to risk my most precious gifts, you and our child. I have not come to share your bed. I come to share news. I have been dining with Wolsey and the French ambassador. By heavens that man knows good wine!"

I could hear coldness enter the Queen's voice. As a Spanish princess, the French were to her old enemies. She didn't like the King entering into arrangements with them. She much preferred the Holy Roman Emperor, Charles, who as well as ruling over much of Spain and the Low Countries, happened to be her nephew.

"So husband, of what have you been talking?" she enquired icily. "It must have been great matters of state to entertain him privately."

"We are working to build our friendship with France," the

King said. "You will know, madam, that the King of France has a new baby son, born this year. Our daughter Mary will prove a fitting bride for him."

"What? She is but two years old!" the Queen cried. I could hear the anguish in her voice. Her darling daughter becoming almost a hostage to Spain's oldest enemy. It was too much to bear.

"Indeed, madam," the King replied brusquely. "And the Dauphin of France is but four months old. They will not be married for many years. But I intend to have them betrothed this year."

"Betrothed? How could you do this to me? Sire, you have heaped many troubles on my head, and I have borne them as a good wife should. Why even now, you are playing with Bessie Blount, dancing attendance on her as if you were a callow boy!"

"Mind your tongue, wife," Henry snapped. "As you know, I would not harm you nor our unborn child. But all kings have mistresses. And why should I ignore a lady's fine eyes, or dainty ankle, when they are offered to me as my right?"

"You are my husband!" Katherine responded. "Sometimes I think you care nothing for me." She spoke hoarsely, "And now you plan to take my dearest daughter from me and give her to those libertines, the French! I cannot believe that you could send her to such a fate!" I heard her rushing towards him and then a muffled slap. Was he hitting her? I tensed up under the bedclothes.

But it was the King who called out.

"Stop, Madam! Contain yourself." I peeped out from under the covers. He was leaning down over her, holding her by the wrists. I noticed his be-ringed hands, strong and white. His shirt was open, and I could see the golden hairs of his chest. Standing there, in control, he was a handsome man. He spoke to Katherine forcefully,

"Wife, you are with child. You have baseless fears and fancies, and I understand that. But you have always acted as a

Queen, and you will continue to do so. Our daughter will leave us one day, it is her destiny. Be grateful it is not Scotland she is going to!" He chuckled at his own wit. It was only five years since the Scots had been roundly defeated by the English at Flodden Field.

"Yes Sire, and I was Regent when we defeated them! You might remember that you were in France fighting the French. They were our enemies then!"

He sighed. "And now they are our friends. We fight, we make friends. It is the way of the world." He let go of her wrists and took her face in his hands.

"My Queen, we have been at war these days, but I want peace. Sweet Kate, show me you still love your Henry, your loyal heart."

"Yes sire," she answered softly. "You know that I love you. I will always love you. I am your Queen, and if you order it, I will always act as you desire."

He bent down and made to kiss her. She made no move away, and they moved together. I dived right down under the bedclothes, praying that they would not move in my direction. They were murmuring to each other and kissing. His voice was caressing,

"My sweet Kate, my love and my queen, what would I do without you? How would I rule this kingdom without you at my side?"

"My Lord, I love you dearly," she whispered. "At night I long for your touch. I want you to be close, to never let me go." With this, he took her in his arms and pressed her to him, his hands roaming down over her nightgown, following her hair down to her waist. She sighed deeply.

I was feeling more and more afraid. What would happen if Henry found me hiding in his wife's bed? Katherine had told me to leave, but there simply hadn't been time. What would I say, and how would I brave the displeasure of the King?

They moved together towards the bed. Henry was watching his wife, but Katherine had seen me.

"My Lord," she cried. "We cannot lie together; I would not be able to withstand your passion." She is clever, I thought, she can manage this lion tenderly. "See, I have a serving girl already abed, warming my place for me." She pulled back the covers and exposed me, shivering.

Henry looked shocked and then scowled at me. "Why did you not tell me wife? Why is this foundling in your bed?"

I hated being called that, and the anger rose in me. I don't know how I did it, but I sat up and said, "Your Grace, I am no foundling. My mother was a good woman and a true Christian!" I stared up at him defiantly. His eyes hardened, and his lips started to tremble. What had I done? Been disrespectful not only to my elders but to the King of all England. Quickly I bobbed a curtsey on the bed, but fell over back into the tangled sheets.

"I beg your pardon, your Grace. My mother would have been angry with me, for she was always telling me about disrespecting my elders and betters." I cast my eyes downwards, praying that he would forgive me.

Katherine intervened, "My Lord, she is a new little maid who is so handy around my chambers, and she is so small and dainty. See, she has spirit." A snort erupted from the King. I was alarmed, but then I realised he was laughing.

"Spirit she has indeed wife! Well, she is a comely little thing. You can keep her. But tell her that if she ever breathes a word of this night, I shall cut her ears off! Did you hear that wench?"

I nodded quickly. "Yes sir, I did! I promise I won't say a word."

The King swept out, still laughing, leaving the Queen looking pensive.

"Kat," she said, looking into my eyes. "If only you knew what queens have to endure!" She put her arms around me. "But now my little maid, it is time to sleep. Come, let us lie together."

And so we lay on her big soft bed, her arms around me. The embers of the fire flickered, and we slept.

CHAPTER

3

With the end of summer, the court moved back to Greenwich Palace, "the Palace of Placentia," as Queen Katherine called it. It was a pleasant place, still in the country, but near enough to the bustle of the City. As soon as I got there, I asked for my aunt Meg. But no one knew her. Maybe she was at Whitehall, they said. I should wait until the Court moved there. More in my mind was my father. I longed for him and wondered where he was. I knew his master lived in a fine house on London Bridge, but which one? There were many dwellings crowded together on both sides of the bridge. Then there was Will. Was he still in Rome? I had no idea.

Queen Katherine kept me busy. I did not have time to go in search of them. And I was growing to love her. Maybe she took the place of my mother, but I felt safe in her company. I was never so happy as when she bade me sleep in her chamber and it was just the two of us, safe and warm on the soft down mattress.

The Queen's belly was growing large, and she got tired more easily. Very often, she would beg me to go and fetch her kerchief, feed the monkey or play with Princess Mary. I was happy to help her. As the fall of the leaf came upon us, the Court became a bustle of seamstresses, tailors, nobles and ambassadors. Princess Mary's betrothal to the French prince was to happen on the 5th of October.

"But he's only a baby!" I said to Lady Maria Willoughby, "he can't even speak."

She laughed out loud. "Do you think, Kat, that is important? Of course not. The admiral of France is here to play his part."

But Princess Mary, although only two years old, was standing for herself. She was a clever child, and forward for her years. That didn't mean that she didn't fidget when she was being fitted for her cloth of gold betrothal gown! She was wanting to go and play with Lady Willoughby's dog, Señor, and wouldn't stand still for the seamstress. Every time the woman stopped to find a pin, Princess Mary would toddle off, calling the dog's name. Katherine watched her with pride, but her eyes were tired. After I chased her round her mother's chamber, catching her at last, Katherine gave her a none-too-gentle cuff around the ear.

"Mary, you are a Princess of England, behave like one!" Not that the Queen was ever angry with Princess Mary for long. She loved to sit and sing to her, and had started to teach her some letters. Typically kind, she had involved me in the lessons, knowing that I had not the skill to read. So, I was learning my ABC with a Princess! Of course I was six years older than her, and so I progressed more quickly. But then the Queen cleverly suggested that I help Princess Mary practice, ensuring that we both were sure of each separate letter before we moved on.

But on the 5th of October, I was near the back of the crowd of courtiers and servants in the Queen's great chamber while little Princess Mary waited on her own. Her cloth of gold gown gleamed and her red hair was partly covered by a bejewelled black velvet cap. She stood very still and straight, her tiny figure dwarfed by the enormous bulk of Cardinal Wolsey and Lord Bonivet, the tall Frenchman. Her proud mother and father watched as he slipped a tiny gold ring with a huge diamond onto her finger. Then it was their turn to vow that they would support the happy couple in the future. I know that Queen Katherine was not happy. But she did her duty, as she always did, and said that she accepted the match with great pleasure, and only a slightly strained smile.

As the formal ceremony ended, Princess Mary turned to Lord Bonivet.

"My Lord, are you the dolphin?" she asked imperiously. I noticed a murmur of laughter coming from the members of the court. We often called the Dauphin of France the Dolphin, but we didn't know that Princess Mary had picked that up.

"Are you the Dolphin?" she repeated, "if you are, I wish to kiss you!" With that, the laughter became widespread, and the King came and picked his daughter up in his arms.

"This girl, she is so learned, and she never cries," he boasted. "No, Princess, Lord Bonivet takes the place of your husband, the Dauphin. When he and you are grown, then will be the time for kissing!"

And so the following days went in a haze of parties and dancing, hosted by Cardinal Wolsey at York Place. Queen Katherine took to her chamber sometimes, bringing me with her. I wished I could join in with the fun, but it was my duty to stay with her. Sometimes we'd play cards, and sometimes she would ask me to sing. In the mornings, after Mass, she would question the ladies who had been at York Place the night before.

"And so, my Lord the King, with whom did he dance?" she demanded. Lady Willoughby looked a bit uncomfortable.

"With his sister, your Grace, as the first lady of the Court in your absence." But the Queen was not to be placated with this partial truth.

"And with who else?" she enquired icily. "Come, Maria, we know that the King dances with more than one lady."

Lady Willoughby reeled off a list of ladies who were part of the French delegation. "And then, your Grace, just for one dance or two, Elizabeth Blount."

"By my heart!" the Queen swore. "That wench again! How dare she, the little hussy?"

"Your Grace, be calm," Lady Willoughby entreated. "Give it time. Once you are delivered of a royal prince, you will be able to make her leave court. For now, you should rest."

Queen Katherine was prone to small outbursts of temper, like a spluttering pot, but she would always regain her composure quickly.

"You are right, Maria," she agreed and then laughed. "But she is not the problem, it is Sir Loyal Heart, the King! But still, I know he loves me."

"He does indeed, Madam. He asks for you every time he sees me," Lady Willoughby said.

"After all is said and done," mused Katherine, "I am his Queen, and nothing can change that, not ever!"

As the days of October passed, all the women of the household started to make preparations for the Queen's lying in. Fine ladies are not like us, they withdraw in the last month of pregnancy, away from the eyes of men. But it was the man servants that were involved right now, hanging rich tapestries on the walls of the lying in Chamber. These were all Biblical subjects to edify and encourage the Queen in her labour. Then her great bed was hung with purple cloth, as thin as tissue, billowing around the richly embroidered coverlet. A vast cradle was carried in, large enough for me to sleep in, and covered with a crimson cloth of estate. This was for the baby Prince or Princess, Lady Willoughby told me.

"But see, when the babe is not being viewed by the great of the land, he shall sleep in here," and she pointed to a much smaller crib that could be moved next to the Queen's bed. A birthing chair was brought in. I did not know then about birth, and I wondered about it. Why was there a hole in the seat? It looked uncomfortable to me. But when I asked, the ladies laughed and hushed me.

"These are not matters that should concern you, ginger Kat," said Lady Boleyn, who was speaking from experience, having born many children, although only three lived. She looked down her nose at me. "When the Queen is in her travail, you will have no place here, you are still a child. The Queen will have her experienced ladies around her, and the midwife." I was disturbed by this. I did not want to leave the Queen's side, knowing that without her, my treatment might not be gentle. I prayed that night that the Queen's delivery would be short, and that my time without her would only be a few days.

Still, the serving men brought in ever more items for the Queen's comfort. The floor was covered in rich, soft carpets, with large cushions being strewn all around. Tapestries were hung over every window but one, and beeswax candles were made ready to provide a warming light. Finally, with great care, some statues of the saints were carried in. There was Saint Margaret, Saint Anne, and of course the blessed Virgin Mary. The Queen would be able to turn to them in her pains and pray for their help, and for a safe delivery, as Saint Margaret was delivered from the stomach of the dragon.

It was early November, and about a month before her baby was due, that the Queen went to the church of the Observant Friars, next-door to Greenwich Palace, to ask God for his blessing for the birth. The King attended, and afterwards he led her back to her chamber, followed by a throng of courtiers. He paused at the door, bowed, and bent to kiss her hand.

"May God safely deliver you Madam," he prayed, "and return to you to me, my jewel." He turned and looked at all of us standing around, courtiers, servants and ladies. Then he spoke loudly and clearly, with a touch of impatience in his voice.

"And may God bring me that most precious jewel of

all, a son and heir for England!" The assembled company clapped heartily while the Queen put her hand over her belly. Everyone knew she had carried five babies, and only one had lived beyond two months. This most dutiful, most kind and graceful of women had failed so far in her most important duty, to produce a Prince of Wales. This time, she hoped, it would be different.

The Queen picked up her skirts and said, "Farewell your Grace, and to all my friends. Now Ladies, we must withdraw." She led a small procession of chosen ladies through the door, which shut gently behind them. Now what would I do? I watched the King and his nobles walking back, followed by their servants and pages. I did not want to go with them, but where should I be? My place was with the Queen and her ladies. I leant on the door. If I couldn't go inside I would just sit outside and wait. It felt the safest place to be.

I must have fallen asleep, for when I woke it was darkening. Suddenly the door I was leaning on opened, and I fell backwards into the birthing chamber. Lady Boleyn was standing there, holding the door and looking very annoyed.

"You! You are still here!" I cowered, fearing she would send me away. "I don't know why the Queen loves you, ginger Kat, but she will have you with her. We have protested, and told her that a maid has no place in a birthing chamber, but she will have her way! She says you warm her bed for her, and she cannot sleep without you!" My heart leapt.

"My lady, thank you! I will be a good maid, you'll see. I will do whatever you ask, so long as I can stay with the Queen!" Lady Boleyn frowned as she ushered me in.

"It's only till she starts her travail, ginger Kat! Once she is labouring, you will be out!"

The chamber was dark and warm, with firelight and candles flickering. Katherine lay on her bed, her red gold hair spread out on the pillow. She spied me coming towards her and held out her arms.

"My little Kat," she called. "Come to me and keep me warm, child." I ran to her and snuggled up against her. I didn't think I had been as happy for many months. Here was the love and tenderness that I had so much missed since my mother's death. I truly loved Queen Katherine, and she loved me. Yes, I was of no importance, a pet like her monkey to indulge and laugh at. But I knew that I meant more to her than that. And for the first time in my life, I felt that I was special.

I had never been in a birthing chamber before. Ordinary women like my mother kept working until the last moment. Most women went to their bedchamber, with their husband waiting anxiously outside and the midwife hurrying in to deliver the baby. This was very different. It was dream-like and dark, a sanctuary that smelled of the rose and almond oils the ladies rubbed onto the Queen's tight belly. We could not see the outside world, and so we turned to each other and the Queen.

The ladies were less grand now, they were wearing ordinary gowns, their jewels left behind. Lady Boleyn remembered her last lying in with her son George. She talked of the pains, and how she had been helped by praying to the blessed Virgin Mary. She remembered the kindly midwife telling her, "Hold your breath, and strain downwards, as though you are going to the stool." I sniggered at the thought of the dignified Lady Boleyn in the garderobe, but instead of slapping the side of my head she just laughed.

"You should not be listening to this ginger Kat, but now you have – take it and learn from it! It may help you when your time comes!" I looked down and smiled. I didn't intend to marry, I thought. I wanted to be with Queen Katherine all my life.

The day passed slowly. We played cards and sang together – gentle lullabies to soothe the baby within the Queen's womb. The baby liked that, and the Queen would let us feel its tiny feet kicking hard against her swollen belly. Sometimes, one of us would go to the door to take in some more food and drink for us all sent up from the kitchen. The Queen was eating fresh bread with honey and oranges. We had pottage sent in, and meat, which we ate hurriedly, not wanting to spend any time away from our mistress.

Every now and then, Queen Katherine would raise herself from her bed and walk slowly towards the figure of the Virgin Mary. With help from her ladies, she would kneel in front of our blessed Virgin and pray to her,

"Kind virgin of virgins, holy mother of God, be present on behalf of thy devoted handmaidens, thou art the benign assister of women in travail." She would continue for several minutes, finishing by crossing herself and holding out her arm for one of us to assist her up. We would all rush to help, eager to be the one to be closest to our Queen. Lady Willoughby and me were usually there, hovering around her in case she fell.

But then, later in the afternoon, when she struggled upright, she let out a cry. Clutching her belly, she wailed loudly. The other ladies, startled by the sudden noise, clustered around her. Lady Willoughby was already steering her to her bed.

"My Catalina, my dear lady, come, come!"

"Maria, it has started. My travail is here! But it is too early, too early!" Katherine was distraught, tears rolling down her face. She had had several early deliveries, and the babies had not survived. She cried out in pain again and sank onto the bed.

"My pains are coming. Maria, the babe is coming," she panted before crying out again as another wave of pain swept through her.

"Your Grace, Catalina, do not fear. We saw your child kicking. He is well and hearty," Lady Willoughby said, using the name she'd called Katherine during their childhood in Spain. She helped her back against the pillows and smoothed the covers over her.

Queen Katherine raised her head from the pillows and tried to speak, only to moan as another pain came over her.

She panted quickly, again and again. It was frightening to see her like this. But then she regained herself.

"Elizabeth, fetch me the Virgin's girdle, that she may protect my baby!"

"Yes madam!" Lady Boleyn turned to go and find the sacred relic that supported and protected women in childbirth.

Meanwhile, Lady Willoughby turned to me and said, "Kat, go and get the guards to fetch the midwife. Tell them to waste not one moment!" I hurried towards the door, my heart beating. It felt so sudden, and I was frightened for the Queen. I had never seen a woman in travail before. I got to the door, ducked under the tapestry covering it, and tumbled out in front of the two guards.

"Make haste! We need the midwife in here!" I shouted at them. Immediately they stood up straight.

"I will send a messenger to fetch the midwife," one of them said, walking briskly away. The other guard eyed me warily.

"I will go back to the Queen," I said, trying to sound older and calmer than I was.

"Wait, girl! Let me ask her ladies." He knocked loudly on the door.

"But I came from there! The Queen wants me!" I protested.

The door opened and Lady Boleyn stood there with the tapestry hanging behind her. I heard an anguished cry coming from inside. The guard looked down, embarrassed, caught his breath and then spoke.

"My lady, do you wish this girl to come into the Queen's chamber?"

Lady Boleyn replied immediately. "No, of course not! A birthing chamber is no place for a maid! Tell her to go and wait until she is sent for." The door slammed in our faces.

The guard turned to me, "You heard what she said, girl. Be off with you!"

I went, but only to the next door that led into another chamber, and one beyond that. The floor was strewn with rushes and sweet aromatic herbs. I might not be allowed inside, but I would not leave my Queen. I sat down in a corner, making myself comfortable on the rushes. I would keep watch for Queen Katherine and her baby.

Around half an hour later, I heard footsteps walking along through the next chamber. It was dimly lit, and hard to see who was coming. I could hear voices, a man and a woman. I shrank back into my corner. As they approached, I recognised a messenger. With him there was an older woman carrying a large bag. She was walking as swiftly as she could, but she was older, and was having to struggle to keep up. As they came up level with me I saw her face.

I let out a gasp. I couldn't believe it. The woman was Mistress Stabb, I was certain of it. I would never forget that face. She cast a quick glance in my direction, and our eyes met, but she didn't say anything. Just then, the inner door opened, and she swept inside.

I was amazed and confused. Was Mistress Stabb a midwife? But why hadn't she told me? Had she recognised me in that brief moment? What would she do now? She'd left me without a word when she took me to the King's Post. She'd misdirected me to a place where there was no sign of my aunt. Did she mean me harm? She was a witch, and perhaps she had put a spell on me, even maybe on the Queen. I was fearful now and crossed myself, muttering a prayer to the Virgin Mary.

I stayed there for maybe two hours, watching and listening to try to discover what was happening. At last the door opened, Mistress Stabb came out, quickly followed by a serving girl, carrying a bundle wrapped in linen. I stood up and caught at Mistress Stabb's arm.

"What are you doing here?" I demanded. "What brings you to the Queen?" She shook my hand off and gestured to the serving girl.

"Be off with you, wench! Dispose of that discreetly!" The serving girl nodded and ran down the corridor, clutching at her bundle. Mistress Stabb turned to me, her eyes glittering.

"Come, Kat, walk with me." She led me down the corridor.

"So, why are you here? And why did you lie to me?" I cried, my voice getting louder as I got more upset. Mistress Stabb looked towards the guards.

"Quiet girl! You will get yourself removed from the palace, and how will that help?" she hissed. I saw that her eyes were glittering not with evil, but with tears. We stopped some distance down.

"I am here because it is my lot in life to help women give birth. I am the midwife, and it was my duty to tell the Queen that her daughter, God rest her soul, is dead. She died as soon as she entered the world." I gasped, and Mistress Stabb wiped at her eyes with a handkerchief.

"There was a night like this eight years ago," she said, "but it ended very differently. I carry that night with me in my heart." I didn't know what she was talking about, it sounded like the ravings of a disordered mind. But now it struck me that the Queen's baby had died, and all her hopes had been dashed. That wrapped bundle the maid servant had been carrying was the baby's tiny body. I shuddered at the thought that such an innocent soul was now dead.

"But how is the Queen? Does she well? Let me go to her!" I cried. I must comfort the Queen and tell her not to worry, that there would be other children. I would comb her hair and sing her to sleep. I would pray with her for another baby. I didn't know then that there would be no more children for Queen Katherine. She was getting older, and as Lady Boleyn later told me, her courses did not come every month.

Mistress Stabb put her hand on my arm.

"In a moment, Kat, you can go to her. It is your fate to be with her. That's why I sent you to Woking Palace. It didn't matter whether your aunt was there or not." Mistress Stabb paused and blew her nose on the handkerchief.

"One day, you will find the secret of your birth," she said.

"When the time is right for you to know."

"What secret? Why do you keep talking about a right time? Tell me now, if you know it," I demanded angrily.

Mistress Stabb laughed tiredly. "It is not good for you to know it now, it will cause great danger. It is enough that you are where you should be."

I turned away and shouted at her. "Stop talking in these riddles, Mistress! I don't believe you. I'm going to the Queen!" With that I ran back down and beat on the door to be let in. Lady Boleyn answered, her face expressionless. She motioned me inside.

"Come in, ginger Kat. The Queen is asking for you."

CHAPTER

4

Daughter, you don't know what a court is like. I can tell you it is like a clear night when the stars sparkle and the moon is full. It is brilliant, shining and bathed in light. But then again, when clouds cover the sky, that is also the court. Clouds of sadness, suspicion and doubt, and no light to guide you home.

That was the court after Queen Katherine lost her baby. At the centre of it was her grief, her terrible grief. That night as she lay in her bed, the tears streaming down her face, she was inconsolable. She was a Queen under her grand cloth of estate, but she was also a mother who had lost a child. I crept up to the bed, where Maria, Lady Willoughby, was stroking Katherine's forehead.

"Catalina, Catalina, my dearest lady, there will be others. You are still young," she comforted, trying to soothe the Queen as if she was a sick child. The Queen still wept. Lady Willoughby pulled out a handkerchief and started to wipe away her tears. As she did, the Queen sat up in bed and caught sight of me.

"Kat! My little mistress of the pin cushion, come here beside me." Her voice was low, and she was trembling as she held out her hand to me. I climbed up into bed, and immediately she clung to me as if she were drowning and I was her rescuer. It was strange for me that I meant so much to her. She was surrounded by fine ladies, but she turned to me, an eight-year-old girl. There are so many reasons for that, I know now. But at that moment I think she saw in me the child that she could never have. Of course, she had Princess Mary and loved her dearly. But Princess Mary had her own governess, and her own rooms. She was of the blood royal, and she wouldn't be present at such scenes of birth and death, with all of their humanity and messiness. So, I think I took Princess Mary's place in the Queen's arms. I'm glad I gave her some comfort. I desperately wanted her to be happy again, but I was only a servant girl and it was beyond my power.

Those first few days, Queen Katherine was sombre. The birthing room, once so full of happy expectations and fear, was now a place of grief and stillness. We no longer sang, and when we played cards, it was dully and without zest. The Queen however, did continue to pray. She spent many hours on her knees in front of the Virgin Mary. But after a couple of days of weeping, she accepted the loss of her child.

She said to me, "It was God's will, Kat, that my daughter should rest in Paradise," she said softly. "She was baptised by the midwife as she was born, and so I know she is where all is well." I felt relief wash over me. We knew that unbaptised babies did not go to Heaven, but to limbo. But midwives had the permission of the church to baptise those babies who were near death, even as they were being born. Anything to save those poor innocents!

My mind returned to Mistress Stabb. How had she happened to be here, delivering the Queen's child?

"The midwife, is she experienced? How can you trust an ordinary woman off the street with your baby's soul?"

"My Kat, of course the midwife is experienced! Us women are at the point of gravest danger in childbirth, sometimes without the succour of God. I do not choose women who are not experienced, my child."

"So, Mistress Stabb?" I queried.

"You know her name, child! She is a midwife of many years standing. She is a widow, I believe, and has helped many women through their travails." The Queen looked down at her lap, the space where a baby daughter might have been. "But she is not my regular midwife. She attended me once before, about eight years ago, and then this time. But she has never delivered me of a live child, as did Mistress Williams." The Queen sighed. "Mistress Williams delivered me of a fine prince, my son Henry. He was a golden child! Some say I have not given the King a son, but I did give him a fine, healthy boy." She shook her head, "but then God took him after seven weeks." Tears rolled down her face.

I felt a surge of love for her. "I am sorry, your Grace, that someone as kind and good as you should suffer so!" She took my hand and kissed it.

"It is God's will, Kat. My little Henry is there in paradise with him." She wiped her eyes with a handkerchief. "And Mistress Williams was there two years ago for the birth of Princess Mary! She is our heir. And she is so forward for her age. We are blessed."

Princess Mary was allowed to see the Queen after a few days. She rushed into the chamber, bearing with her a hornbook to show her mother.

"See, Mother, Mother, I can read my letters," she boasted, bouncing up and down on the bed. She was getting very confident, especially now she was destined to marry the Dauphin and become Queen of France.

"Very good, Mary. But you must work hard. Now you and Kat here must start to learn to write those letters," the Queen said, stroking her daughter's head.

"But Kat makes me work," Mary protested, poking out her tongue at me. The Queen frowned.

"And very good too. She is a hard-working girl, and gives you a good example! Now stop that and behave like a royal princess. Anyone would think you were raised in the gutter!"

A bit like me, I thought. But I was pleased. During the Queen's confinement I had not taken part in any lessons, and I had missed them. Being honest, I did not enjoy always having to curtsey and be polite to Mary. Sometimes she was very cheeky, and I couldn't answer back. She was a princess, and I was only a servant, even though she was only two, and if she had been a neighbour's child I would have cuffed her across the head. But I was desperate to get back to learning how to write my letters.

Gradually the Queen recovered, and she took part as normal in the Christmas celebrations. At court, they exchange presents at the New Year. The Queen called me to her after mass and presented me with a small silver cup.

"For you, sweeting. May you drink long at my table." I was overwhelmed and stammered out my thanks. I had not thought that Queen Katherine would even think of me in the midst of all the feasting and dancing.

"You have done me good service Kat. I never forget my friends." She smiled and swept out to join the festivities, her green and gold skirt trailing behind her. I knew I must give her something, but how could I obtain a gift on this day? I had a little money left, but I couldn't leave the court on such a day. Then I had an idea. I was writing now, and very proud of myself. Princess Mary and I still practised our writing with the Queen. I was slightly ahead, but then, I was six years older than her. My progress was all due to the Queen's kindness and patience as a teacher. I would thank her for that, with the gift of a poem! I sought out Princess Mary's governess and begged her for a piece of parchment. She found one for me, grumbling at missing some of the fun in the grand hall. Then I sat down with my quill, and carefully, painstakingly, wrote a poem to the Queen. It wasn't much, but six months ago I had not been able to even write my name.

"On New Years Een

Kat loves my Queen."

I'd then finished it with a drawing of a tiny Queen riding a palfrey with a crown upon her head. I blew on it, impatient for it to dry, and then folded it and put it in the pouch that hung from my girdle.

Later that evening, I approached the Queen just as she retired to her chamber. She was pink from dancing, and her eyes were bright. She would not sleep for some time yet as she talked with her ladies about the events of the evening. I crept up to her and dropped a curtsey.

"Your Grace, I have a gift for you," I said boldly, as if I were giving her a golden goblet. I held out the paper to her. She reached and read it in a moment. She laughed softly and then folded the paper again and put it carefully down her bosom.

"Kat, my sweeting, your present pleases me much," she beamed at me. "Indeed, ladies, I esteem this present beyond all others, except for those from the King and the Princess." I noticed that Lady Boleyn looked annoyed at this. She had given the Queen a fine emerald brooch surrounded by diamonds, which had not received the same praise. I knew that some of the ladies didn't like me, but I was the Queen's favourite, so they kept their dislike masked.

That spring and summer, the court started to hum again with excitement. The French alliance was in place, and the talk was of celebrating it with a grand event. An event so magnificent that it would be talked about centuries after it took place! Lady Elizabeth Boleyn's husband, Sir Thomas Boleyn, was the ambassador to France, and he visited the Queen's presence chamber to give her the details of what was proposed.

Now, you know Queen Katherine didn't favour the French alliance at all. But she was every bit a Queen and listened with attention to Sir Thomas.

"Your Grace, the King and King Francis of France wish to meet as fellows. This meeting will bind our two nations together in amity and brotherhood." Sir Thomas was charming, easily versed in the art of gilding the black art of diplomacy with the gold of inspiration.

The Queen looked serious, but a small smile occasionally crossed her lips.

"*Fraternité* Sir Thomas?" she queried. "*Mais notre roi est tellement plus grand que François!*" Lady Willoughby had told me that when Queen Katherine came to England, she couldn't speak or understand French, but now she was fluent. Much of the court's culture, business and poetic love affairs was carried on in French. Queen Katherine was clever, and she wasn't going to be the dull Spanish lady on the edge of conversations! Oh no, she needed to know everything that was going on.

"Your Grace speaks well," Sir Thomas oiled. He was a handsome man in the prime of his life. Unlike his wife, he was dark with olive skin. His gown was of blue velvet, lined with fur, and his green doublet was slashed with silver. I noticed Lady Elizabeth Boleyn listening respectfully to her husband. Inside myself, I smiled. We heard all about the Boleyn family! How their daughters impressed the French King, Francis, and how Sir Thomas dined with him every month. More interesting though was to hear her tales of the family's life at Hever Castle, their home. I knew that Sir Thomas snored dreadfully and that his breath smelled in the morning. Looking at him now, with his fine silk shirt and his beard curled and oiled, it was hard to imagine his wife scolding him for keeping her awake at night with his snoring.

He told the Queen about the negotiations to arrange a meeting next year, in the summer of 1520.

"We will meet in Calais, where we will talk and joust and celebrate for two weeks," he said.

"Calais! But there is nothing there to house two courts!" the Queen objected. "We cannot meet the French King in cow sheds." She was exaggerating, but Sir Thomas acknowledged her point.

"Your Grace, Calais is English, and so we have the advantage." She nodded.

"Sir Thomas, I understand you. We must not give ground to the French. But Calais?"

"Your Grace, we will build a canvas palace fit for our great English King and Queen, and it will be more dazzling even than the sun! We are finding tent-makers and craftsmen to make our royal camp the most splendid that has ever been seen."

"So, tents," the Queen said flatly.

"Ah, but your Grace, such tents!" said Thomas Boleyn. "They will be connected together with galleries, and will form pavilions, which your Grace will find even more magnificent than your palace of Greenwich."

Queen Katherine looked doubtful, but Thomas Boleyn redoubled his efforts.

"Each pavilion will be dressed in blue and gold, or red and gold, topped with our Tudor colours of green and white. Inside, there will be grand tapestries, fine cloth wall hangings, and carpets. The tent poles will be fine carvings of lions, greyhounds and dragons, and will fly the King's standard. Your Grace, see, here are the plans." He offered her a sheaf of papers, which she took and studied for a while.

"So I will have my private apartments and my chamber, as here in Greenwich?" she queried, "and there will be accommodation for my ladies and my maids?"

"Oh yes indeed, your Grace. As Queen of England, you should have nothing less." He bowed, sensing that she was coming round to the idea. She raised her eyebrows but said little. After studying the plans for some time, she gave Sir Thomas permission to leave.

"Imagine, imagine!" Lady Boleyn exclaimed to me. "This time next year we will be meeting the greatest French nobility! You will meet my daughters, Kat! They are French mademoiselles now! You will learn much from them."

I was more excited by the thought of all the fine food that we would be eating, and the masques that would be taking place, which, according to Lady Boleyn, would be like visiting a strange, exotic faery land.

"There will be scenery that is so real, you will think you are in an enchanted forest, or King Arthur's castle!" she said. "There will be music and fine ladies and gallant knights speaking in poetry. It will be a different world."

I was very excited. I didn't know then that it wasn't just the entertainments and the feasting that would be unrivalled. Unknown to me, I was soon to learn something that changed my life. But for the time being, it was the preparations for this magnificent celebration that absorbed me and all of the Queen's household.

I was put to learn French with Princess Mary. After all, if she was going to be the Queen of France one day, she needed to learn the language. One day she drove the Queen mad by going around chanting a new French song, "Belle qui tiens ma vie," over and over again! Those Tudor girls, they were bright sparks, and by heavens they knew it. People think now of our good Queen Bess and say that Queen Mary was grim and gloomy beside her. But they didn't see them both as little girls. They were both fathered by a King who saw himself as only second to God. They both had intelligent, spirited mothers who loved to sing and dance. So, naturally, they were both brimming with life, wit and naughtiness.

Princess Mary loved Señor, Lady Maria Willoughby's dog. Lady Willoughby was this year pregnant with her first child, and loath to get up from her seat and play. But Señor and Princess Mary would run round and round the chamber, Mary dragging a ragged linen rag on a rope for the little dog to chase. Or she would dangle choice pieces of meat in front of Señor, teasing him until she eventually gave him the tasty morsel.

Queen Katherine would smile indulgently at her daughter, and Mary's laughter was welcome after the sad events of

November. But she wasn't allowed to run wild for long. Soon she would be sitting down, learning her letters, with me sitting beside her and the Queen directing us. There was also a governess, a Mistress Stapleton, who took us away and made us work very hard. But the Queen was with us whenever she could be. She rewarded good work with a sugared almond, and laziness with a little tap on the hand. I got many almonds and no taps, while Mary got many of both. Even at that age, she was a strong character, and not always inclined to do what others told her.

In those days the King still visited the Queen's chambers almost every day. He would come and call for music, or for some ladies to play cards with him. Then he and the Queen would sit together, a little away from the rest of us, and talk quietly. I knew they were talking of matters of state. King Henry respected his Queen and listened to her opinions. He knew that she took her role as anointed Queen very seriously, and that she always wanted to work for the good of England.

There was some merriment among the ladies when he appeared with a stubbly chin.

"Sweetheart, I am growing a beard," he told the Queen. "My brother King Francis and I have decided that we will neither of us shave until we are able to meet next year!" Queen Katherine looked at him and pulled a quizzical face at all of us ladies.

"Your Grace, you will be a long-beard, like an old man!" the Queen teased, "and I will not be able to get past your whiskers to kiss you!" We all laughed, and he looked a little taken aback. But he didn't give up his beard just then. Day by day his facial hair grew, and day by day the Queen made comments.

"I can see some grey in your beard, Your Grace," she remarked casually one afternoon. "How strange, as it does not show in your hair." On her face was a contented smile. She knew how to get rid of the beard. Our King saw himself as fit, healthy and young. And he was a magnificent man, no doubt about that. But there was also no doubt that his beard did have strands of grey in it. And he hated, above all, to be reminded that he was growing older.

The next day the beard was gone. The King told Queen Katherine that he had shaved it off for her sake and that he had told Francis he'd had to follow his wife's wishes. So, the Queen won that battle. But she wasn't going to be able to stop all the plans for the celebration of the English and French alliance, much as she would have liked to. For her, France was the enemy, and always would be so. As aunt of Charles, the Holy Roman Emperor, she naturally wished for an alliance between him and King Henry. But England was always teetering between two powers. Sometimes we were friends with the French; sometimes we were enemies.

So preparations continued within the Queen's household. All of her yeomen were to wear green coats, and orders for hundreds of yards of material were being sent out to the cloth merchants. But when the Queen saw the design for the coats, she wasn't pleased.

"These are too thin, they need a lining," she said, handing the parchment back to the tailor. "And they need to be full and broad. These are the men of Katherine of England. They must look rich and powerful!" So the tailor went back and produced another pattern which the Queen preferred, using white satin and green velvet. The footmen were to be even more colourful, with doublets of yellow velvet, orange boots, and black velvet cloaks. The household was full of men scurrying in with bolts of cloth for the Queen to look at, tailors taking measurements of the men, and horsemen discussing the decoration of the Queen's carriage and horses.

For me and Mary, it was like a magical land of glowing colours, jewels and anticipation. She, of course, was having gowns of state made, and even for me, there was a new gown in Tudor green. We rushed from chamber to chamber watching all of the preparations, giving our opinion as to the designs (and often being shooed out of the way or even cuffed on the head). It was such an exciting time.

The Queen was viewing material for her ceremonial gowns. Yards and yards of gold tissue and silver cloth embossed with damask gold were laid out in front of her. There were bolts of tilsent, a kind of silk, shot through with gold or silver thread. Crimson and blue tissue arrived, patterned with gold. Every time, the Queen would inspect them, pausing to rub a little between her thumb and index finger and then either nod or turn away.

We were in the middle of a session looking at cloth to make the ladies' dresses when a messenger came into the Queen's chamber. He bowed deeply to the Queen. She raised her head and waited for him to speak, not welcoming the interruption.

"Your Grace, there is a man at the gatehouse. He wishes to speak with a maid called..." he hesitated, checking his memory, "... Kat Cooke."

Queen Katherine looked at me, surprised. There was a murmur amongst the ladies. Who wants to see Kat Cooke, the foundling? Ginger Kat, who is skinny and small, and turned up out of nowhere? As for me, I had given up hope of returning to my old life months ago. It was now a year since I started in the Queen's household. I was excited to meet this man but scared too. Who was he? Was he anything to do with Mistress Stabb? I hoped not. I turned and looked at the Queen. What should I do?

"Go with him, Kat," the Queen said gently. "See who he is and what brings him to find you." She turned to the messenger. "Stay with her while she meets this man. If he is known to her, she may bring him into my outer chambers for some refreshment." The messenger nodded and waited as I got to my feet, stumbling on my skirt, and joined him at the door. I was in a fine green gown now, with a grey kirtle underneath, and my red hair was braided with ribbons. Although I was still small, every inch of me looked part of the court.

I followed the messenger through the many rooms that were situated beyond the Queen's chambers. People bustled continuously through these rooms, tradesmen bringing samples to show, courtiers, servants carrying wine and sweetmeats. The court was always busy, never still. At last we got to the great hall. I'd been running to keep up, and I felt breathless by now. My anxiety tightened my chest even further.

We went outside into the fresh air and strode through several courtyards, past stables and outhouses. At last we got to the gatehouse, with guards on either side. Standing just beside them, squinting against the sun, was a man with dark hair flecked with grey.

I knew him immediately. It was my father, Tom Cooke, standing there, looking uncertainly at me. I ran up to him and put my arms around him, hugging him again and again.

"Father, oh my father. I'm so happy to see you!" I cried, unable to believe it was him.

He held me close and said gruffly, "It's Kat. I almost didn't recognise you. You are a young lady now, and so tall!" He pulled back and viewed me up and down. I had grown a lot in the last year. In the Queen's household we ate well, and I was no longer a skinny waif. My clothes were good, and my body was scented with the perfumed oils we would all rub over ourselves to keep ourselves smelling sweet.

"I work for the Queen now," I told him proudly. I turned to the messenger. "This man is my father, and according to the Queen's command, he can come to her chambers for some refreshment." The messenger nodded and motioned for us to go forward.

I led my father across the courtyards, through the great hall, and the many chambers, one after the other. We made small talk about the weather and the midsummer's day celebrations that were coming up. At last we reached the door to the outer chambers of the Queen's quarters. I led him inside, to the presence chamber. The Queen was not there, but servants were coming and going, and I managed to catch one's eye and ask them to bring some bread and wine. We sat together on a bench beside one of the large tables used for whenever the Queen hosted a feast.

There was no one near us, and once we had our bread and wine, we were left alone. Now we could talk, and I could find out everything from my father. But first, I had to know if Will was alright.

"Where is Will? Have you seen him, father?" He shook his head sadly.

"No, Master Cromwell visits Italy often. I have not been able to find him at home." He brightened. "But I hear he is well, and I expect to see him soon."

"What happened, Father? When did you come back to London? I didn't know where you were." I became tearful as the memory of that terrible time returned to me. My father took a drink of his wine and reached over for my hand.

"As you know, Kat, I was in the country with my master. We had no word from London, but we didn't expect any either. Dear Joan was good at managing. I was certain you would both be alright." At this point his voice began to falter, and I saw the tears in his brown eyes. "I came back to London in the September and went straight to the house. I found another family living in our chambers. They told me the previous tenants had died. It was like I'd been punched in the stomach, such terrible pain. I ran from the house and all the way back to my master's house, crazy. I shut myself in the stable with the horse. Anything to get away! I was mad with grief, Kat, and guilt. Why had I left you both in the city? Why hadn't I stayed to protect you both, or die with you? For many months I wept every night. I could not bear to think of you both, my girls dead." He bent his head and the tears rolled down his cheeks.

"I tried several times to find Will, but he was always away

with Master Cromwell. At least I knew he was safely out of the way."

"Thank God he is safe," I breathed. "I did not know what had become of him. But father, how did you find me?" He smiled and kissed my hand.

"By God's good grace," he said, "and Mistress Stabb."

"Her! She's horrible!" I exclaimed.

"I know Joan didn't like her. But I thought she might know something about what had happened to you both. So on Mayday I went back to the house and knocked on her door. She asked me in and told me everything. How Joan had got sick and died. How you'd looked after her. Then how Mistress Stabb had got you a passage to Woking, where the court was, to find your aunt. She told me you couldn't find her but that you had been given a position at court. I couldn't believe it! My Kat! I was overjoyed to hear the news. My grief for Joan is great, but now I know you are alive and well, I thank God for his mercy!" We were both crying now, tears of grief for my mother and joy at finding one another. My father gulped a little more wine.

"Drink Kat," he urged, "do not let me sup alone." I took a small sip. It was sweet and raisiny, and much stronger than the small ale I was used to drinking. I took another sip, liking the warmth that spread through my body. It gave me courage to ask him the question that had puzzled me since my mother died.

"Father, what happened on the day I was born? When mother was dying, she raved, and she said that I wasn't her child. What did she mean?" My voice trembled as I looked at him. Now, at last, I would solve the mystery of my birth.

"Kat, you are her child, and mine – as Will is," he insisted. "You both fed from your sweet mother, slept in the same cradle, were carried in the same arms." But he would not meet my eyes.

"Father, Mistress Stabb also said something. I'm not your child, am I?" My father leant forward and crushed me in his arms. For a moment he clung to me, and then he pulled back.

"Kat, you are my child, and always will be! I am here to protect you and take care of you!" He paused and then said, very slowly and carefully, "But you were not my child at the beginning."

"What happened to me Father? I need to know!"

"On the day Will was born, Joan and I, we were so happy! A strong, lusty son! Joan was well and making plenty of good milk for him. I was a father, and I ran to my master to tell him the good news. He gave me the night off, and I returned home to find Joan happily sitting up in bed, feeding two babies. One, our dark-haired bonny boy, and one, a tiny red-haired scrap hardly clinging on to life. Joan's sister Meg was there, and a woman I did not know. She introduced herself as Mistress Stabb."

"Her!" I knew that she was behind all of this.

"She told us that a servant at court had had a baby, a month early. The poor girl was afraid she would lose her position and confided in Mistress Stabb. I found out then that she was a midwife. Well, Meg was there too, and Meg told the girl that her sister had just had a baby and could make room for another. Mistress Stabb said that she would take care of it all. The poor girl was so relieved that she wasn't going to get into trouble, she left the baby there and then."

"And that was me?" It started to make sense, but there were some things that still needed to be explained.

"Yes, it was you, sweet Kat, and we never regretted the day you became our daughter. Joan loved you so much. She had wanted a daughter, and now she had one, along with a fine son. God blessed us that night!"

"But Father, how did you manage? We were very poor." I remembered my mother, always trying to make our money last.

"Mistress Stabb helped us at first. She told us that the servant girl's mistress had given her some money for the baby

61

to be adopted. She gave us a little every now and then to help us out. And then, when there were some chambers vacant in the house that she lived in, she arranged for us to take them. She knew the landlord, and he charged a reasonable rent. But later your mother and Mistress Stabb fell out. Mistress Stabb is a strange woman, and your mother said she heard evil chantings coming from her chambers. Your mother was a religious woman, as you know."

Yes, I remembered our mother teaching us our prayers. The thought brought a fresh flood of grief to me. And then I realised that she wasn't my mother, and Tom wasn't my father. It seemed I had learnt nothing and lost the only family I had. I bowed my head and wept. My father (for I will always count him as such) took his kerchief and wiped my eyes.

"Kat, you are as much my daughter as Will is my son," he said gently. "You are my family, and I will look after you. Don't worry, I will never leave you again." I flung myself into his arms and hugged him, not wanting to let him go. After a few moments we pulled apart and laughed. We had so much to tell each other, and here we were wasting the time!

We talked until the light in the chamber became dim. Every now and then a lady would pass and look curiously at us, but pass on with just a smile in my direction. I realised the Queen had probably told them to give us peace together. Tom was willing to take me with him, back to his master's house, where there was a position for a maid. He was earning good money now, and he could afford to marry me well in a few years time to a boy with a trade. We would be happy, him and me. And soon we would see Will.

I told him about how the Queen had taken me in, and how she had looked after me. I boasted that I could now write my letters and speak a little French.

"And I can sing and play the lute!" I informed him proudly. He looked pleased and then a little downcast.

"You are doing very well at court, Kat. I want you with me,

but I can see that this is your home now. You are a fine lady."
I could see the pain in his eyes, and I blessed him for his kindness and sensitivity. My father was the best of men. He could see that I loved my life, and although he longed for me, he did not wish to take me away from where I was happy. I admitted that I would rather stay with the Queen now, but that I would see him whenever we had a day off. We agreed that we should not tell anyone about what had happened, it was too painful for us both.

Later, we spoke with the Queen herself, who told my father that he had a fine daughter and begged him to allow me to stay. He consented but said that he must make a contribution towards my keep.

"Nonsense Master Cooke! You have given me the greatest gift of all – your daughter! Bring me some sweetmeats when next you see her, that will be my price." As she said this, a great wave of love for her swept through my body. She was the kindest of women, and yet she understood pride. So she asked my father for sweetmeats, although the palace cooks made hundreds of them every day. That is why, my daughter, I loved her more than any of those who followed her. She was, and always will be, the dearest woman I served.

CHAPTER

5

King Henry paced the floor of the Queen's chamber, his face tense with anger. Meanwhile, Queen Katherine sat calmly, stitching one of the silk shirts he liked to wear. She was the Queen, but she said it was her prerogative to embroider her husband's shirts, as he would wish no other to do it. She was always the dutiful wife, even when she was challenging the King. As she spoke, her voice was steely:

"Your Grace does not treat me with the respect that I deserve. As your Queen, I should not be humiliated."

I buried my face in my sewing, but like the other ladies, I was listening intently. All of the court knew that the King had been showing off his illegitimate baby son, Henry Fitzroy. The result of his affair with Bessie Blount had been a lusty red-haired little boy, and King Henry was proud of him. It is said that he'd been telling courtiers that the baby proved he was able to sire a son. Of course, this meant that all blame for the royal couple having no legitimate son would fall on Katherine.

"You dandle this bastard on your knee as if he were your rightful heir. I have heard from all the court how you show him off," the Queen continued. "But you have an heir already, in the Princess Mary. You disrespect her and me, your wife, by this cruel action."

"I have waited long enough for a son!" the King snapped. "Had you provided me with one, Madam, then I would not need to make provision elsewhere."

"Make provision elsewhere? What do you mean? Princess Mary is your legitimate, true heir, born from me, your Queen. You could not supplant her for a whore's son?"

"I do not wish to do so Madam, but until I have a son, we cannot rest easy on our thrones. Pray that you will provide the Princess with a brother, even now as time goes on."

The Queen flinched at this, and I wanted to go to her and put my arms around her. He was cruel to blame her, and to comment on her age. We ladies knew that the Queen's courses were now only every few months, and she might not even have to strength to bear a healthy child again. But for her, Princess Mary was fit to rule any kingdom.

"My mother reigned as Queen of Castile." she pointed out. "Princess Mary has her blood, and my father's, the King of Aragon. From you, she has her intelligence and courage. She will make a fine queen."

The King shrugged his shoulders. "The English will not have a queen, I know that," he said off-handedly, trying to close down the conversation. But the Queen persisted.

"I have heard Princess Mary was left to one side while you were playing with this infant. Your Grace, the court is saying that devalues your royal line." She calmly stitched at the shirt on her lap, knowing that she had made a point. King Henry knew that if he was to try to make Henry Fitzroy his heir, he would face strong opposition, not only from his wife but from her allies at court.

"Sweetheart, I honour Princess Mary. She is betrothed to the Dauphin and will become Queen of France. My daughter will never lack for my respect and love." Katherine continued stitching.

"And now, my Queen, be merry!" King Henry's voice lifted. "We have so much to look forward to. As my Queen, you will be accorded great honour at our magnificent meeting with the French, and Princess Mary too. Together we will forge an amity between us and the French royal family. I need you there, my Queen. I need your experience and your skill. Say you will support me in this." His voice had softened now to an entreaty. Queen Katherine put down her sewing and looked levelly at her husband.

"Of course, I will support you, Sire, you are my husband and I will obey you. It is good to forge friendship. But let us not forget our other friend, Charles, the Holy Roman Emperor. We should meet him too, so that he knows we are still in concord."

"He is your nephew, Madam! Of course you are in concord with him!" King Henry laughed loudly, but then paused for a moment, thinking. "But you are right, Madam. It does no harm to strengthen old friendships. Yes, yes – maybe we should meet with him, if we have time." Queen Katherine bent to her sewing again, a smile on her lips.

"As you wish, Your Grace," she murmured. "Your statecraft is so far in advance of mine." The King puffed out his chest. Again, she had made him feel that he was the master in this relationship.

But as Lady Boleyn said to me later, "Better prepare for two great meetings now Kat. For we will be seeing the Holy Roman Emperor in the next year, for sure!"

Cardinal Wolsey was visiting the Queen at her chambers in Greenwich Palace. He was a big man with a red face, large white hands and a booming voice. We were all sewing when he was announced and immediately strode into the middle of the chamber, his red robes swirling about him. He bowed deeply to the Queen, who rose and held out her hand to him. At a nod from her, all of us ladies stood and curtseyed deeply. Not that we wanted to. Lady Willoughby was large with child, and Lady

Boleyn was reluctant to curtsy to the butcher's son, however exalted his office.

Courtesies over, we resumed our seats, and the Cardinal was invited to sit in a large wooden chair to the side of our group.

"Kat, fetch wine and sweet biscuits," the Queen ordered, and I scurried away to the kitchens. It was never easy to fetch things from the palace kitchen. First, I had to walk for five minutes to reach it, situated at some distance from the Queen's chambers. When I got there, the cooks were frantically busy preparing the food for the early evening meal. Great joints of meat were roasting, leavened bread was being baked, and the pastry cook was working on a grand artifice representing a bird in a nest. I was not altogether welcome and wished Queen Katherine had sent someone else. I stood there, uncertain of what to do.

In the end, one of the cooks took pity on me.

"Who are you?" he said, not unkindly.

"I'm Kat, one of the Queen's maids," I answered.

"You're the spit of King Harry, you know that? Are you another of his bastards, girl? Hard on the poor Queen."

"Indeed I am not!" I protested. "My mother died, and my father is a cook like you. I love and respect my Queen."

"Don't fret little maid, just making a joke. So what do you want?"

I answered with as much bravura as I could, "The Queen requests sweet wine and biscuits for the Cardinal."

"Does she indeed? What the Cardinal wants, he shall have! Go to the pastry cook, little maid, he will have some biscuits. Then take some of the wine put out on the side. We'll get some more from the cellar."

I hurried to collect the refreshments. Soon I was safely back on my way to the Queen's chamber. But the cook's joke stuck with me. Did I look like the King? Not really. I was small and scrawny, and he was tall and magnificent. Yes, I had red hair, like his. But his was reddish gold, whereas mine was more ginger. His skin was fair and white, almost like a lily, but mine was a little darker. If anything I looked more like the Queen, but that was probably just my imagination.

So suppose the King had got a servant girl pregnant? That would fit with the story my father had heard. A poor servant girl, taken advantage of by a powerful man, and then afraid for her job. Could that be the case? But then I thought of Henry Fitzroy, the King's bastard son, whom he carried around the court and lavished with jewels. King Henry had not disowned him. Indeed he had arranged for Bessie Blount, the child's mother, to be looked after and married well. Surely he would have done the same for the servant girl? Surely, I would be counted at least a minor lady at court, with my mother safely married off to a tradesman? I would not have been a foundling. It bothered me, that name. Foundling. It sounded like I had come about by witchcraft. Maybe Mistress Stabb had conjured me out of the flames of her fire? There would be spells she could cast that could make me look like anything she wanted. I shivered; this was an unsettling thought.

I dismissed that thought and walked into the Queen's chamber bearing the wine and biscuits triumphantly. The Queen and the Cardinal were sitting together now, deep in conversation. The Queen looked up at me, "Ah, Kat, what took you so long?" she said. "Pour the wine for the Cardinal, he will be thirsty".

"I'm sorry, madam," I poured out the wine and handed the Cardinal a full goblet. I placed the plate of sweet biscuits by his elbow. It was well known that the Cardinal had a sweet tooth. He took a gulp of wine and picked up a biscuit.

"Your Grace, we must not antagonise the French. Much as I honour and admire the Holy Roman Emperor, is it wise to plan to see him directly before our great meeting with the French King?" He dropped a crumb on his chin and brushed it away before smiling patronisingly at the Queen. Does he think she's stupid? I knew that she was as clever as any man, even the great Cardinal Wolsey. But she was a wise woman and pretended to be confused by men's matters.

"Cardinal, you must excuse me. My womanly longing to see my nephew, the Holy Roman Emperor, quite misled me! I do not meddle in policy, that is men's business." The Cardinal smiled forgivingly and patted the Queen's hand.

"Most understandable, Your Grace, that your heart has influenced your head. This is why it is best to leave such matters to your husband and his advisers." I fumed inwardly at the way he was treating her. But she simply smiled sweetly at him and turned to me.

"Kat, fill the Cardinal's goblet! He will be thirsty with all the work he has undertaken to make this grand meeting take place. I know my husband, the King, is sore beset with fears about the outcome."

"Your Grace?" Wolsey leaned forward. "Beset with fears?" he repeated, looking quizzically at the Queen.

"Indeed, he has confidence in his ministers, Cardinal, but he does not trust Francis, the French King." The Queen lowered her voice, as if speaking in confidence. "At night, when a husband talks to his wife, he talks of fears that he doesn't voice in public. Will Francis lead him into a trap? How can he, Henry, match the power of the French? What if Francis does not keep his side of the treaty? What can Henry, my husband, do to ensure there is not another French war?" She paused and looked down, smiling. "Of course, I may misremember his words, but he says you trust the French when you have the strength to make sure they do not renege."

Wolsey took another sip of wine. "Of course, Your Grace, the King is right. And England is a strong nation."

"Strong in all of Europe, with allies on either side," the Queen murmured, nodding her head. The Cardinal paused for a moment, tapping the fingers of one hand on the arm of his chair.

"The King must not feel himself at risk of betrayal. I must ensure that. When meeting with the French, he must be the strongest man at the table," he mused. "And mayhap the assurance of other allies would be a useful counterbalance." The Queen looked worriedly at him.

"My Lord Cardinal, as a simple woman, I do not know what is best. But I wish that you might advise as to how to assuage these fears of his. I cannot bear to see him anxious."

Cardinal Wolsey patted her hand again. "Do not fret yourself, Your Grace. We will ensure the King goes into this meeting as the great Harry that he is. Yes, we should inform our allies and reassure them about our aims. Maybe a quiet meeting with the Holy Roman Emperor on English soil? I am sure he would like to meet his aunt." Queen Katherine smiled at the Cardinal, her eyes shining upon him.

"Lord Cardinal, such a meeting would be dear to my heart, I can assure you! I simply wish to meet and talk with my sister's son, dear Charles. And I can rest safe in the knowledge that you, Cardinal, will be handling the business together with my husband, the King. England is fortunate indeed!"

Queen Katherine had a way with her, all her ladies knew it. She would pretend to be a silly woman, without knowledge of the world, although she was one of the most learned ladies I had ever met. Then she would persuade men to do what she wanted and make them believe it had been their idea all along. I couldn't help but smile at her cleverness.

The next day, King Henry and Cardinal Wolsey held a meeting in the Queen's chambers, discussing the plans for the wonderful tent city that would be built in the fields of France. The three of them sat late into the night, drinking wine and eating sugared almonds.

"Your Grace, I have sent a messenger to the Emperor, inviting him to England post haste," Cardinal Wolsey told him. "We have to leave for France very soon." King Henry took a large handful of almonds and thrust them into his mouth.

"Wolsey, as you know, I am determined to maintain my relationship with the Emperor. England will hold the balance of power between him and King Francis. But we must leave very soon for Calais. Emperor Charles may have to wait."

Queen Katherine looked distressed. She got out of her seat, moved toward the King and sank down in front of him in a deep curtsey.

"Your Majesty, I beg of you. Allow me to see my nephew in England, if only for a few short days!" She looked beseechingly at her husband, and he shifted uncomfortably in his seat before taking her by the hand and raising her up. As she returned to her seat, Wolsey hastened to ease the atmosphere.

"Sire, may I suggest we head for the south coast as planned? We shall see the Emperor there, or if not in Calais." Wolsey looked across at Queen Katherine, who merely bowed her head and smiled. But there was a determination behind that smile, I knew. She did not want to leave England before the Emperor Charles arrived. King Henry must meet with her nephew before he came under the spell of the French.

For the next week, Queen Katherine played a delaying game. She demanded that certain gowns be remade. The inner walls of the Queen's pavilion were suddenly wrong and needed to be redone. Then Princess Mary became sick, and as Queen Katherine told the King, "she needs to lie abed for a week to recover her strength."

Eventually, after the Queen had delayed for as long as she could, the whole court departed for Dover, travelling through Canterbury. I tell you, daughter, you have never seen a commotion like it. The King and his gentlemen riding on high heavy-hoofed chargers, the Queen in her litter, with ladies following on white palfreys. Princess Mary in her litter, with her governess and nursemaids. Then wagons and wagons trailing for miles behind the royal family and their attendants. Servants clinging onto the wagons, riding old nags, mules and even donkeys. Anywhere they stopped could expect every house, however humble, to be filled with people. Every morsel of food in the stores would be gone. Every tun of wine, every barrel of beer would be drunk. Then the supplies would run out, the houses would start to stink, and then the whole caravan would be on its way.

So it was that Emperor Charles landed at Dover only days before the King and Queen were due to leave for Calais. We were in Canterbury, at the house of the Abbot of the Augustinian Priory in that city, when a messenger arrived from Emperor Charles.

"I will fetch him here!" the King exclaimed. "Saddle up my horse." Queen Katherine was almost skipping with glee. She watched the King depart, then ran from the window to her women. She spent the rest of the day pacing her chamber, every now and then picking up her embroidery, taking a few stitches, then casting it down again.

"Ladies, let us dance!" she exclaimed. "Lady Boleyn, Lady Stafford! Kat and my maids! I want a Galliard! Lady Willoughby, fetch the lute!" Then her chamber would become a whirl of velvets, silks and sweet perfumes as the ladies danced and jumped with each other, laughing and singing. It was a true pastime with good company, in the very words of the merry song the King had written. He was one of the cleverest men in Christendom, daughter. Katherine was a match for him in almost every way. She was a diplomat, a war leader against the Scots, a linguist and a musician. She was already teaching me to play the lute, and I could play very well now. But, my daughter, the thing she lacked was a son. And for Henry's Queen, a son was the only thing that mattered in the end.

The Archbishop of Canterbury was to receive Charles, the Holy Roman Emperor, at Canterbury Cathedral with swirling incense and holy water. Queen Katherine would wait in the Archbishop's palace next door until the brief ceremony was over, and she could finally see her nephew.

As she dressed, she fussed over the details.

"This petticoat, is it too long?" she asked. "I cannot walk in it."

"Your Grace, let me tighten it here," Maria, Lady Willoughby soothed, and moved forward, placing her hands around the Queen's waist. "There, it is just the right length for your Grace. Don't forget you are in stockinged feet." Slowly, carefully, Lady Willoughby and Lady Stafford eased the Queen's gown over her head. I gasped; I had never seen anything so beautiful. It was in creamy cloth of gold, lined with violet velvet. Golden roses were embossed on the velvet, matching the shine of the outer gown.

"Don't stand there gaping like a fish Kat!" Queen Katherine snapped. "Fetch my hood, no, not the English one. I will wear the Spanish style." I rushed to do her bidding. She was nervous, I could see. Unlike some of the others, she did not normally take out her irritations on her maids.

"Come Kat, comb my hair," she called me, and as I went to her side, she touched my arm.

"I have waited for this day," she said, explaining. "My heart beats wilder than usual Kat."

I took her comb, made of ivory, inlaid with rubies, and started slowly to pull it through her hair, which, as usual was scented with rose oil. The Queen had beautiful hair, as full and silky as a young maid's. Although she was thirty-five years old and a little plumper than before, her face was unlined, her skin as white and pink as a sixteen year old's.

Queen Katherine knew how important it was for her to show her royal blood, her queenly position and her respect for both the Holy Roman Emperor and for her husband, the King of England. Although she usually favoured the English gable hood, which covered all of the hair, and cast a forbidding shadow over the face, at this crucial moment she decided against it. She would wear a Spanish-style headdress, made of black velvet powdered with diamonds and pearls, which allowed her hair to flow down her back, showing all of its magnificence. Why did she do that daughter? There were two reasons. First, she wanted to show respect to her nephew, who ruled Spain as part of his dominions. That was the diplomatic reason. But second, she wanted to remind her husband, the King, and his advisers that she was a daughter of Spain, and had powerful allies both inside and outside the court. I think then she was already feeling a little anxious about her position. Of course, none of us could have imagined what was to come, but with her headdress and her glorious hair, the Queen was telling King Henry that no mistress could supplant her in his affections.

Queen Katherine stood at the top of the stairs, waiting for her nephew, a golden, glowing queen at the height of her power and influence. But her face was strained. I watched alongside other maids and ladies as the great doors opened and a large group of Spanish courtiers appeared. Leading them was a young man, rather serious faced, with a good athletic figure and well-muscled legs. But what we all noticed first of all was his chin. It jutted out so strongly that it could not be ignored.

"The Hapsburg chin." Lady Boleyn whispered to me. "Many of them have it. Such a shame, it quite spoils his looks." I knew Lady Boleyn preferred the French king. After all, both her daughters were serving at his court, and her husband was ambassador there. She loved to share gossip that he'd passed on to her, including disparaging comments about the Holy Roman Emperor's chin. I turned away from her and watched the queen. As her nephew climbed the stairs she moved forward to greet him. She curtseyed deeply, and he took her by the hand. As he did so, her face crumpled and tears started to flow down her cheeks, shining like the pearls around her neck.

They embraced, and she cried out, "My Charles, my dear nephew. You are well come to England! My heart is easier due to your presence!" He stood back and bowed his head.

A little embarrassed, he said, "Dear Aunt, I have long

wished to meet you and to hear you bid me welcome. I bring you and your husband, King Henry, the amity and love of all my people." He had been Holy Roman Emperor but one year, but he was already courtly and serious in his demeanour.

"Come, Charles, to our chambers. There we will talk. We have some time before the state banquet. I have musicians ready, and the finest Rhenish wine." Queen Katherine ushered him away on his own, leading him to her chambers, where King Henry would join them. For an hour, the three of them were closeted alone in a conversation that, Queen Katherine said, was one of the most satisfying of her life. What did they talk of? Her sister Juana, and her parents Ferdinand and Isabella? Maybe for a while. But also, once the King had joined them, the conversation had turned to alliances, to trade, and treaties.

The three days that followed were so exciting. The court was full of Spanish gallants, oh so handsome, daughter! Even the older ladies were enchanted by their courtly manners and their compliments. One night the court danced until dawn, with the King and the Holy Roman Emperor leading the dancers. The Queen stayed until midnight, but then retired to bed. She gave us permission to go back to the dancing. Although I couldn't dance with the ladies and gentlemen of England and Spain, a group of servants were jumping and jigging in the outer chamber. I could dance a little now. A stately pavane was fairly easy, but a galliard got me out of breath. But I enjoyed myself so much on that night.

Later that night it was announced that we should call King Henry "Your Majesty" from now on, instead of "Your Grace." Lady Willoughby told me, "The Holy Roman Emperor is called Majesty, and the King liked the sound of it!" She laughed and patted her large belly. She would be away from court for the next few months, and I could tell she was looking forward to a break from all the scheming. "He's not going to be outmatched by the Emperor, now is he? Queen Katherine and I giggled until our sides split!" She turned to me and touched me warningly on the shoulder.

"Don't tell anyone I said that. The Queen will of course be using the King's new address. She follows him in whatever he wishes. She would not want him to know she found him at all laughable."

Next morning I was frowsty and slow. I stumbled when bringing the Queen her manchet bread, dropped it, and had to fetch some more. Señor, Lady Willoughby's dog, enjoyed an unexpected treat, wagging his tail as he devoured the bread. The Queen didn't reprimand me. I could tell by the smile on her face that she was well pleased with how the meeting was going. And, although both courts were due to cross the Channel shortly, she knew that Charles had got in first with her husband. And she knew, looking at her nephew, that although he may not be the most handsome of men, his seriousness and honesty had made an impression. He was not a game player like Francis. He did not want to get the better of Henry or show off his (considerable) power and influence. Rather, he wanted to do business, to cement family ties, and to establish himself upon the international stage. And in that, he had more than succeeded.

Chapter

6

I had been dazzled by the opulence and glamour of the meeting with the Spanish court, but that was as nothing compared to what was to follow. Those days when the English and the French Kings met as brothers were more dazzling than anything I have ever seen. Later, the meeting was called the Field of Cloth of Gold because the tented pavilions, the fine ladies and gentlemen, and even the horses were all emblazoned with gold. The centre of the field itself was set up as a tiltyard, where the English and the French could take each other on in the joust. It was situated between the English town of Guisnes, in Calais, and the French town of Ardres. Beyond the jousting field, the two courts spread out spectacularly in temporary cities so magnificent that men would talk about them so long as they lived. I can still remember it daughter, and it was the most marvellous spectacle I had ever seen.

The English palace had a timber frame, with canvas in between. But unless you touched it, you would not know it, daughter, because it was painted to look like fine white stone. There were many windows, each one glazed with the finest stained glass. I had never seen anything so magical as this white palace, with its glass sparkling and casting coloured light in the summer sun. But then the French made their pavilions from silks, satins and cloth of gold. But while the English were dazzled, they were also amused, as the French central pavilion, made entirely of cloth of gold, collapsed in a wind before the meeting even started. And the French, while they called our stained-glass windows a crystal palace, would also comment that our canvas walls were not as magnificent as theirs.

I remember the first day. I was with a group of maid servants. We had been given the afternoon off to watch this greatest of meetings. Each King rode to the central tiltyard, followed by hundreds of courtiers, footmen, and soldiers. King Henry's courtiers were all wearing cloth of gold, which sparkled in the sun. The French paused for a moment when they saw this, unsure as to whether what they saw was armour. I knew from what I had heard Queen Katherine say that King Henry and King Francis did not trust each other. Like King Henry, King Francis was concerned in case the whole event was a trap.

But no, all was peaceful. Once the French had realised that what they saw was gold and not fighting armour, they continued to ride forward. In the crowds we held our breath as the two kings rode up to each other, their massive steeds pawing the ground with their giant, feathered hooves. We watched the two men intently. I was only a child, but I knew England and France had been at war many times over the last few hundred years. Most of King Henry's lands in France had been long seized by the French, leaving only the territory around Calais. Would he accept that his French lands had gone? Would King Francis accept that Calais must, and would, remain English?

King Francis reached up and doffed his cap, followed a moment later by King Henry. Both men jumped down from their horses and moved together in an embrace. A loud cheer went up from both crowds of followers, followed by clapping. Some people were singing, others weeping with relief. Both kings waved to the ecstatic crowds and then walked arm in arm to a golden tent, where they were to have their first meeting.

As they left, the crowds started moving. Us maids linked arms and walked towards the central area. But people were going in all directions. They were looking for some good ale to celebrate the occasion, wine, sweetmeats and pies. One man pushed through us, and I was separated from the group. I was swept up, daughter, I didn't know where I was going. I was just excited to see all the sights, and to listen to the songs and music that filled the air. But then I found myself surrounded. I was much smaller than most of the crowd, and they pressed so hard around me that I couldn't see where I was going.

I made my hands into fists and started to push them into the backs of the crowd around me. One man turned round and swore at me.

"By Jesu little maid, mind your fists!" I looked up at him defiantly. He looked like a merchant, or maybe a lawyer. His figure was rounded, and his worsted doublet was straining around his chest.

"I couldn't see where I was going. You're all taller than me!" I protested. His face softened, and I saw he had kind brown eyes.

"Here, I have a page who can be your eyes. He is a little taller than you, and he can take you where you need to go, little maid." He turned around and pulled a boy back towards me. I saw a mop of unruly black curls, a ruddy face, and a figure that was taller than I remembered. Then I remembered....

For a moment I couldn't believe it. But then the boy saw me, and immediately he cried out.

"Kat! Oh my darling Kat! I thought I would never see you again!" He crushed me in his arms, oblivious to his companion, who was staring at us with interest and amusement.

"I see you know each other," he said, chuckling. "Well met, indeed! I must go and talk with my friends from France. Will, you stay with your friend Kat. Go round and see the sights

79

together. Come back to our tent by nightfall." He had an air of authority, but Will evidently felt at ease with him.

"Yes, Master Cromwell, I will," he said cheerfully. "Thank you sir!"

"And take care of little maid Kat! See she gets back to her tent before you return." He turned to me and bowed. "Thomas Cromwell, little maid. At your service." I bobbed him a curtsey. Little did I know then, daughter, how important this man would be in my life, and in Will's life. But my mind was full of all the questions I wanted to ask Will, and the news I wanted to tell him. So much to talk about and so much to see together! So I didn't look after the man as he pushed his way away from us, through the crowds.

Around the edge of the respective courts, there were many other tents, wagons and makeshift shelters. It seemed that the world and his wife had come to take part in this blazing magnificence. As well as the thousands of servants, cooks, armourers, horsemen, footmen and maids, there were merchants hoping to make contacts, country gentlemen wanting to get a toehold at court, artists, writers and above all, priests. Masses were said every day, both in the royal chambers and in the fields around the site. Then there were bishops, Archbishops and Cardinals. This meeting of royalty would not exclude the powerful princes of the church, all ennobled by the same church. Of course, in the days of Queen Katherine, the idea of an English church, separated from Rome, was unthought of. King Henry and Queen Katherine were considered the most pious monarchs in Europe.

But for me and Will, the most important thing was to find somewhere we could talk. I suddenly realised that he did not know that our mother was dead. The thought struck me like a blow.

"Mother is dead, Will. She died of the sweats," I cried. He turned and looked at me, his face white.

"I know Kat. I went back to the house. I heard a woman

had died, and I was afraid it was her. I knew if she was alive, she would have been there. I cried many nights for her." We continued together, momentarily silent in grief. At last, we got to an encampment of tents. Not cloth of gold tents, nor silken tents. Just plain tents of canvas and wood. It was quieter here and there weren't many people about. Will pulled me towards a large tent, pitched a little away from the others.

"This is Master Cromwell's tent," he said. "This is where we will sleep tonight. Sit down, sister, and we can talk."

I sat down on the grass outside. "But Will, I should just tell you, I'm not your sister!" Will dropped down on the grass beside me.

"What do you mean, Kat? We were in the same cradle, we were together all the time. We were two peas in a pod." He frowned, looking puzzled and a little uneasy. I leaned over and took his hand.

"Will, that is all true, but I was not born of our mother and father. I am a foundling, born of a servant girl." I told him all about what I'd learnt from our father, and from Mistress Stabb. He listened intently and then put his arm around me as we sat.

"We will always be two peas in a pod," he promised. "Now I have found you, I won't let you go." He picked a blade of grass and chewed it thoughtfully. "You remember Mistress Stabb? you remember she told me I would live in royal palaces and marry royal blood!" He laughed and looked at the tent. "This is no royal palace Kat, and while Master Cromwell is a clever man, he is not the King! She was a bit of a fraud, wasn't she?" Then he looked at me with that clear-eyed smile he had, and said, "I suppose I could always marry you, Kat."

I stammered a response, "No, we can't, it's not possible...."

Will interrupted, "Yes, it is possible, and it would be very nice, wouldn't it? Just like before."

I nodded and laughed. I knew it was a joke. Still I wanted to believe what Mistress Staff had told me. I hadn't told Will about what she'd said about my destiny. It felt fantastical and a bit silly. But still I couldn't help but wonder. I knew my mother had been a servant maid, but my father? Could it have been the King? Over the last year I'd been teased by the other maids about my likeness to Princess Mary. But that must be a coincidence, surely? If the King had fathered a child, he would have provided for it, and no one had provided for me. But suppose the servants had covered it all up, and he hadn't known? Could that explain his indifference to me?

I put those uneasy thoughts from my mind and turned to Will.

"So Will, tell me what you have been doing. Where have you been? You disappeared."

Will told me about his life with Thomas Cromwell, who had spent much of the last two years in Europe, doing business in Italy and France.

"*Je parle Francais*," Will boasted.

"*Moi aussi*," I teased him, and he smiled and hugged me tight.

"Oh my Kat, I'm so glad I found you!"

We talked for hours while the midsummer sun slowly set. Will told me about his adventures in Europe, and I told him about my service with Queen Katherine. I told him about my meeting with our father (I would always consider Tom my real father), and Will said we must meet him together. We laughed about our adventures in the past, we wept about our dearest mother, we hugged, and we laughed.

As the dusk drew in, Will took me back to the maids' tent on the outskirts of the English pavilions.

"Goodnight, Kat," he said. "I'll be at the tiltyard tomorrow. See you there."

"Yes, you will!" I knew that I could steal away in the afternoon. Almost all of the servants would be watching the jousts anyway.

For me, the whole seventeen days were like being at a never-ending fair, only more gorgeous and glamorous than any fair I had ever seen. And it was even more wonderful because I saw it all with Will. Master Cromwell was an indulgent master, and the Queen's ladies had forgotten about me, so we were able to spend much time together. Will's knowledge of French and his travels in Europe meant that he could point out many of the French retinue. And I could tell him all about the English ladies that surrounded Queen Katherine.

Of course, I didn't see much of Queen Katherine during those seventeen days. Her every movement was a piece of theatre and of statecraft. All of her most titled and influential ladies were around her. Servant maids like myself slept in the dormitory and helped to clean up. I was not near the Queen intimately at all during that time.

We did see her though, at her many appearances alongside the French queen. Queen Claude was very religious, as was Queen Katherine. But Queen Katherine was by far the more beautiful. Queen Claude was small and quite round in the last months of pregnancy. She had a hunched back, which made her seem yet smaller, and she had none of Queen Katherine's style. Yet she was loved by many and well known for her kindness towards her subjects. In contrast, her husband, King Francis, was flamboyant and handsome, known as a libertine. His clothes were rich, and they dripped with gemstones.

Will and I saw both queens sitting and watching the jousts and combats that ran almost every day of the meeting. They sat in chambers with full glass windows, with their ladies massed behind them. Princess Mary sat beside her mother, looking excited and fidgeting with her long silk sleeves. She looked so tiny on that massive oak throne.

"See Will, there is Lady Boleyn and Lady Stafford!" I pointed to the two ladies standing in the group behind Queen Katherine, both wearing gowns studded with gold. I saw that they looked tired and felt sorry for them. They had been on show for many days now.

"Ah, they are old women! There are finer ladies by far in

the French court!" Will claimed provocatively, looking at the svelte and stylish women who stood behind Queen Claude.

"No, we English are the most beautiful! Our rain and mist make our skin like milk!" I retorted, standing up for the ladies I knew, although I didn't really understand why. The only lady that was kind to me was Maria, Lady Willoughby, and she was with child and near her time.

Will shrugged. "Kat, I give way to you. And look Kat, at those two English beauties," Will pointed to the French court.

"They are all French," I said, shaking my head. Will laughed and pointed.

"Not these two ladies. They are Lady Boleyn's daughters. They've been learning the ways of the French court."

I looked where he was pointing. I saw two young women, both small-waisted and delicate-boned. But their colouring could not have been more different. One was pink and white, with tendrils of blonde hair showing against her hood – the very model of an English rose. But the other had dark hair from what I could see, creamy olive skin and large black eyes that sparkled dangerously.

"See, that is Mary Boleyn, the older daughter – with the golden hair. They say she is the mistress of King Francis," Will said, proudly showing that he was a man of the world.

"She is beautiful indeed," I agreed. "But the second daughter, is it Anne? She is not beautiful! Yes, her gown is elegant, and she bears herself well, but she is too dark! She is dark even for a French woman, with those large black eyes."

"Ah yes," said Will, "Mary is no doubt the prettier, but I have seen Anne hold a room in her hands, with her playful jesting and her flashing eyes. She will attract a husband, no doubt, although I hear she is not as free as Mary with her favours."

We saw both sisters later, strolling along in the grass, enjoying the midsummer air. Mary walked alone, occasionally glancing longingly towards the French royal pavilion.

"She's missing King Francis," said Will. "Can't get up to anything here, in the midst of all these people!"

Anne, though, was walking arm in arm with a young man. It seemed they were having a verbal duel, for he would say something, only for her to reply with a tart smile. Once, she tapped his chest with one long, slender finger. He answered her reproof with an embrace and we could both see that she was not unwilling to accept. No wonder, he was tall and slender, with brown curly hair. His doublet was of the finest dark blue velvet, shot through with silver, and his coat was black, slashed with green. He was one of the handsomest men I had ever seen!

"Look at Anne!" I exclaimed, "I thought you said she wasn't free with her favours?"

"He's her brother, Kat," Will explained. "He's George Boleyn. A pretty couple they make, eh?"

"I am an idiot! But he is close for a brother," I mused.

"Brothers and sisters can be close," Will said, closing his hand on mine. "I think we will always be in each other's hearts."

"But we are not brother and sister, Will. I am just a foundling," I said bluntly, and there was a long silence between us. I looked at Will, taller now than me, with the same kind face and laughing eyes that I remembered. I could not pretend that things hadn't changed, but how I wished that our connection would remain the same! But I was afraid he might not want that. I remembered he had joked that we could get married. But that was all it was, a joke. After all, what was I now? What was my background?

"Sister or no, you are closer to me than any other being alive," Will said. "We need to find out about your birth. You said mother had a sister at court, a laundress. Maybe she was your mother? We should look for her."

"Will, I've asked in every palace I've stayed in. I asked all the servants. Some of them say that they remember Meg, but that she's working elsewhere. Some have never heard of her.

I've tried to find her."

"I'll have a try," he said. "Master Cromwell knows lots of people, and has many contacts. They may be able to tell us something."

The weather broke after a few days, and the jousting was called off. It was too muddy and slippery for the horses. Will and I wondered what to do, but followed the crowd heading for the large golden tent.

"King Henry's challenged King Francis to a wrestling match!" a page told us. "You've got to see this! The queens are watching. But Queen Katherine looked none too happy about it. I'll wager she's worried King Henry will come off worst! But look at him, he's so large and strong. He will be the victor by God!"

We got into the tent and stood near the back.

"I can't see anything," I complained.

"Follow me," said Will, and he crouched and pushed through the crowd, weaving his way to the front. I held on tight to him, ignoring the odd curse and mis-aimed kick that came our way. After a few minutes we were right up at the front.

King Henry had stripped to his white silk shirt, which was open at the neck, showing the golden hairs on his chest. He was a large man, magnificent like a lion. King Francis was a hairsbreadth shorter and much thinner. His silk shirt hung loosely on him, his narrow wrists protruding from the cuffs, with dark hair showing against his pale skin.

I looked across to the grand gilded seats where the two queens were sitting. Queen Claude looked amused, her brown eyes darting all around the arena. Queen Katherine looked anxious, as the page had said. Looking at her, I knew that she would be afraid for King Henry's dignity, and hoping that he didn't make a fool of himself. I had learnt that although she loved the man, she was a realist about him. She knew he was vain and loved to be the centre of attention. And because she loved him, she didn't want him to fall flat on his face.

The tent was packed, and the ground shook with the repeated drumming of a small band of musicians. The kings faced each other at diagonal ends of the ring, with a small band of supporters behind them. A large red-faced man stood in the centre of the ring, beckoning the two kings to come and speak to him.

"That's Charles Brandon," I told Will. "He's King Henry's best friend. They grew up together."

Will nodded, watching the men conferring. Charles Brandon was negotiating the rules of the contest. I thought it must be hard for him trying to get two kings to obey rules like ordinary men. Eventually, both kings stood back while Brandon raised a handkerchief high above his head. For a moment he held it there, and then dropped it. The two kings moved towards each other, arms stretched out. The drumming became louder and more insistent.

Suddenly both men moved in on each other. The crowd started calling out.

"Come on King Hal! Throw the Frenchy!" The English in the crowd cried out. There was a thud as Francis landed on the floor, but he was up again in a moment and took Henry in an arm lock.

The French responded, "*Allez le roi roil François! Allez, allez allez!*"

"Beat him, Hal, beat him!" The crowds shouted their encouragement while the men rolled over and over on the floor. The cat calls got louder, reaching a crescendo of opposing chants. Even I, who had never seen wrestling before, was gripped. Of course, I wanted King Henry to win, and why shouldn't he? He was easily the heavier and stronger of the two men. But it was evenly matched, and neither of the men could pin the other to the floor. Charles Brandon jogged around the side of the men, ready to adjudicate, but he wasn't needed. These two were skilful and knew their sport. And every time one of

them was down, they sprang up again and pulled their oppo-
nent down. I glanced at Queen Katherine. She was smiling,
applauding, willing her man on. I knew that no one wanted
him to win more than she did. He was her King, her husband,
and she would support him to the death!

All at once it ended. Francis had Henry on the floor and
held him there. The French went mad, whooping and whis-
tling, shouting for *le roi François*. The English crowd went silent.
This was not how it was meant to work out. I knew the courtiers would be afraid of the mood King Henry would be in this
evening.

King Francis released him, and King Henry stood up. We
all held our breath. Then Henry clapped Francis on the back.

"Well won, *mon frére!* You had me there! I must learn the
Breton wrestling moves. Next year it will be a different story!"
Both men laughed uproariously and clasped each other in an
embrace. I could feel a collective sigh of relief coming from all
the ladies and gentlemen of the court. The King would blame
this on his Cornish wrestling training, not himself. That was
alright then.

And so the revels went on. Queen Katherine entertained
King Francis in her palatial chambers while King Henry visited Queen Claude. Both queens spent afternoons together
with their ladies, dancing and playing music. I was allowed
in, at the back of the crowds of ladies, but I played no part in
this great display. Any feelings I had of being ignored were
lightened, though, when I caught the eye of Queen Katherine.
She smiled at me and shrugged her shoulders. I knew that she
did not enjoy this at all, not least because she was having to
entertain the hated French. She beckoned me to her throne.

"Kat, tell the footmen to bring more wine. The flagons are
empty."

"Yes, Your Majesty." Queen Katherine now followed the
King's lead in her style of address.

"Oh, and Kat…"

"Your Grace?"

"Next month we will be in the dear palace of Placentia, Greenwich, and I will have you in my chamber again."

My heart leapt with joy. I had thought that after all this excitement, Queen Katherine might have forgotten about me. But no, she patted my shoulder quickly, and I felt the warmth of her hand. My beloved Queen Katherine still cared for me, a simple servant girl.

I remember so well the closing large mass of the event. It took place in the open air, in the tiltyard. It was June, and the weather was sweetly warm, but not yet so hot that the heavy court clothes were uncomfortable.

King Henry and Queen Katherine entered at one side of the yard, while at the same time King Francis and Queen Claude entered opposite them. Both couples processed to the centre, in front of all the courtiers, to kiss and greet each other. Queen Katherine wore a silver cloth gown embossed heavily with gold, and a Spanish headdress of black velvet dotted with golden and ruby pomegranates, while Queen Claude wore a French hood studded with pearls and a gown of blue velvet embossed with silver Fleur de Lys. Both couples were followed by gentlemen and ladies of the two courts. I saw Lady Boleyn with her husband, Sir Thomas. As English Ambassador to the French Court, he was presenting the couples to each other.

All around me, servants and sightseers were watching and waiting for the Mass to begin. People were talking, pointing out the courtiers that they knew or they worked for. The chat around me was in English, but I guessed the royal couples and the courtiers were speaking in French. Along with Princess Mary, I had started to learn the language, but I was not yet fluent. In any case, I couldn't hear what was being said, the noise around me was too great, but the couples seemed to be exchanging pleasantries, nodding and smiling at each other.

Cardinal Wolsey swept up towards the two couples, resplendent in red silk, with a great gold crucifix hanging on his chest. He didn't know it, but he was at the height of his power, and his influence spread far from England to France, Italy and Spain. He was holding a leather-bound copy of the gospel, which he offered to Queen Claude to kiss. She waved it aside, making way for *ma soeur* Queen Katherine. But Queen Katherine demurred and gestured to allow Queen Claude to go first. Queen Claude would not have it, and again gestured to Wolsey to present the gospel to Queen Katherine. Then both ladies laughed and, ignoring Wolsey, embraced and kissed each other, the gospel temporarily forgotten. The crowd chuckled and applauded in appreciation of the amicable solution to the problem.

As the Mass drew to its close, its quiet solemnity was broken by a couple of loud explosions. We all tensed, afraid that some attack was about to take place. Clouds of smoke billowed over the tiltyard, and through it we saw a gigantic dragon breathing fire down upon us. Some in the crowd panicked and tried to get out of the area, fearing that God himself had exercised his wrath on us. But others stood open-mouthed at the spectacle, gasping in amazement.

"It is a firework Kat!" Will cried. "It is the last English surprise! Well done King Hal and Queen Katherine! You did England proud!"

Of course, it was. King Henry had to have the last word. Francis may have bettered him in the wrestling, but our great King had, in the final ceremony, got his revenge. The French, first terrified and then amazed, clapped at the light in the sky.

"Bravo les Anglais!" the cry went up. King Henry smiled broadly and doffed his cap to the crowd. I noticed Queen Katherine stirring herself as if ready to leave. She was glad that the whole performance was nearly over. And while I was happy I would be back with her in her chamber, I was sad that this whole magical experience was coming to an end. It was about then that people, looking back on it, called it the Field of Cloth of Gold. And as such it stays in our history, forty years on, during the reign of King Henry's daughter Elizabeth.

I had very mixed feelings, daughter. This was the last day I would spend with Will, and I did not know when I would see him again. He reminded me so much of our mother, Joan. I'd cried more in these last two weeks for her loss, as had he. Together we had been able to grieve for this woman who had been more of a mother to me than ever my real mother had. Will and I had fallen into the old easy ways without thinking. I hadn't felt so relaxed for over two years. Although I knew he wasn't my brother, we still had that instinctive bond, a bond between two people that could never be broken. He had assured me that he would visit me, and at least I now knew where he was.

But to say goodbye to him just after we'd found each other! It was hard, so very hard. In him I had found a part of my past again, although it did not answer the questions I had about my origin. He had said he would look for Meg, the laundress who might have been my mother. But I didn't hold out much hopes of him finding her. She had left the court, no doubt, and no one knew where she was. She may even be dead, in which case my hopes of knowing who my real mother was would lie in the grave with her.

I cheered myself by thinking of the Queen. At last, after weeks of spectacular show, intrigue and courtesy, she would soon be back in her chambers. Back, with the familiar ritual of court life, so magnificent and splendid, but yet with the ability to withdraw into a private space where she was a woman as well as a queen. And I, just a servant girl, but one who had gained her affection, would be welcomed once again into her heart and her bed.

We returned to England, and for a short time all was calm. But it didn't take long for things to change. The Queen of England was shaking with anger, "Duke of Richmond!" She spat. "He has made his bastard son a duke!" The ladies who were in her chamber maintained a hushed silence. No one really knew what to say. We had just been informed that in a magnificent ceremony, the six-year-old Henry Fitzroy, King Henry's son by Bessie Blount, had been raised to the peerage.

"Sir Thomas More was there! I cannot believe it! And the Duke of Suffolk! I thought these men were my friends!"

"Your Majesty, it was the King's order. They had no choice." Lady Maria Willoughby tried to soothe the Queen's feelings.

"The King plots to replace Mary as his heir. I know it! He defies the rules of God! How can a bastard be favoured above a royal princess, born in holy wedlock?" She paced her chamber, with Lady Maria scuttling after her.

"Your Majesty, he cannot overturn the succession. He may favour the... the *boy*," said Lady Maria, uncertain of what to call the new Duke of Richmond. "But be of good cheer, the King knows the importance of legitimate rule. He would never overturn his legally born heir, never!"

Queen Katherine looked thoughtful. "You may be right, Maria. The King will always observe the rules. And then, the King will always make the rules."

It nagged at her for some days. She wanted to speak with the King, but he didn't visit her chambers.

"The King always has important business," she mused, "so let us have some important business here, tomorrow evening. Tell the ladies we will have a night of music and dancing! Maria, all my Spanish ladies will sing songs from our homeland, and tell the Boleyn ladies they must represent France. Then we will have compositions by the King, sung by all the ladies, accompanied by our musicians. Every lady must take part! Kat, I want you to play. You have a talent for music." She smiled broadly.

"If the Boleyns are here, then the King will be here," she murmured. Lady Anne Boleyn and her sister, Lady Mary Carey, were now part of the Queen's household. "Maria, will you ask your husband, Lord Willoughby, to inform the gentlemen of the King's household that they are welcome to join us tomorrow."

Lady Maria giggled. "Yes, my Catalina, I will do that. Now

Kat, we must tell the kitchens that we require extra sweet-meats and wine for tomorrow. And I will inform all the ladies in waiting that they are required to attend!"

The Queen's chambers were crowded, with the massed candles casting a warm glow on the crowd of gentlemen dressed in rich silks and velvets. I passed through the crowd, serving wine and bowls of dried, sugared apricots. Queen Katherine sat on the dais with her ladies behind her. The Queen wore tawny silk overlaid with a deep blue velvet gown, which blazed with diamonds. She watched intently as Lady Mary Carey walked in front of her, curtseyed deeply, and started to sing.

"Pastime, with good company," Lady Maria Willoughby whispered to me. "Good choice, the King's composition! Just wait and see now…"

Lady Mary was interrupted by a fanfare of trumpets. Suddenly, the crowd of gentlemen parted, each man bowing and moving back to form a passageway.

"The King! The King!" The whisper went up as King Henry strode into the chamber, followed by the Duke of Suffolk and the Duke of Northumberland. I had seen him often in the last years, but I never lost that feeling of awe when I cast eyes upon our ruling monarch. He and the Duke of Suffolk were the tallest men in the room, towering over the other gentlemen, and his legs were well-muscled and taut. He wore a gold doublet and a red velvet robe embossed with golden Tudor roses and the lion of England. I was of an age now to find him handsome. He was bearded now, and it suited him, and his blue eyes swept the room as if he was examining everyone present.

The Queen rose out of her chair and swept him a deep curtsey. He raised her up and walked with her to the dais. They seated themselves, and she turned to him.

"Your Majesty," she said. "You are very welcome tonight. We only lacked your presence to make this evening perfect. Lady Mary Carey was singing just now. Mary, continue!"

The King looked at Lady Mary, who cleared her throat,

looked over to the musicians, and started again. As the evening progressed, the Queen ensured that he had plenty of wine, fruit and nuts, beckoning me over every few minutes. Then it was my turn to play and sing, my first time in front of a large crowd of nobles. I was very nervous, but I sang well and true, and my fingers plucked the right notes on the lute. I noticed indulgent smiles among the courtiers. I was a bit of a curiosity, the foundling who could sing and play. After every song they all applauded, and Lady Willoughby called out for more. I loved the applause, feeling flushed with success. It seemed I had only been singing for a few minutes when I finished the last song. I curtseyed deeply to the crowd, who clapped loudly. Blushing, I retreated to the back of the dais, and the Queen signalled to the musicians to strike up a galliard, and everyone turned to take a partner for the dance. The King made to get out of his seat, but I noticed the Queen put her hand on his arm.

"Just one small thing, Your Majesty," she murmured, gesturing at me to withdraw. I knew what she was doing. She was fighting for her daughter's rights. With a mother's guile, she was charming him, smiling and laughing at his jokes. But she was deadly serious. She was ensuring that Princess Mary would not be supplanted by the King's bastard son. He stayed in conversation with her for a few minutes, and then she released him to go and dance with Lady Mary Carey. He almost ran towards the dancers, obviously relieved that she had not been angry with him. Queen Katherine leaned back in her seat and caught my eye. She smiled at me, a proud, triumphant smile.

Chapter

7

"My my, little maid, how you have grown. You are quite the fine lady now." John, the King's Post had delivered a message to Queen Katherine. He waited outside her privy chamber to find out if there was to be a reply. He looked me up and down with an appreciation that I had not noticed before.

"I nearly didn't recognise you," he said. True enough, we hadn't come across each other for over a year, and he could see a change in me. I was no longer the bedraggled little girl with the dirty, tear-stained face. Queen Katherine had taken me in, had wiped away my tears, and made a lady out of me.

I was fully fifteen years old, and my courses had started the year before. I was taller but still skinny. My skin was still as pale as milk, but my hair had grown thicker and was now a rich red gold, peeping out from my starched white linen coif. I spread the skirt of my fine black woollen gown and curtseyed merrily to John.

"Thank you, John. It is good to see you," I said graciously. It wasn't just my appearance that had changed. Seven years with Queen Katherine had meant that I could now speak French, Spanish and some Latin. I could play the virginals and the lute and dance with the best of them. Queen Katherine particularly enjoyed my singing and would demand it most afternoons. My mother would have been glad to know that I could sew a fine seam, spin, and make the silken shifts that all the ladies wore under their court gowns. I could read and write of course. My lessons with Princess Mary had meant that I could now help the Queen by reading out messages, and, if necessary, writing a reply from her dictation.

"Who would have thought you would have grown into such a beauty, Mistress Kat?" He took his cap off and held it in his hands.

"Did you ever find your aunt, Meg?" he asked. "I asked wherever I went. I heard tell of her working at Richmond Palace, but that was a while back. She got married, I was told."

"If she's no longer in royal service, then she could be any-where," I said. "Thank you, John, for trying." I moved away from him, but he called after me,

"Would you fancy a short walk to the stables when I have finished?" he asked. "You could see Pegasus. He will remember you, I swear." I flushed, feeling embarrassed. Why was John asking me to walk with him? He surely wasn't concerned about reuniting me with his horse Pegasus. On the odd occa-sions I had seen him before at court, he had nodded a greet-ing and then gone on his way. Did he, maybe, like me? The thought made me shudder, with him an old man and me only just fifteen.

"I will have to ask permission," I said, praying that Queen Katherine would not allow me to go. "You are so much older than me, John. I do not know if it would be fitting."

"You were not so worried when I first met you, Kat! I am just suggesting a short walk. I'm not going to abduct you!"

To my intense dismay, Queen Katherine nodded her con-sent immediately. She looked over at John standing in the doorway, the Queen's reply in his hand.

"I don't want to go, Your Majesty," I whispered. "He seems, um, interested in me."

Her blue eyes twinkled with fun. "So Kat, you have your first admirer," she said. "You are a young lady now, and fair enough, I think."

"But he's so old!" I protested, whispering to her hoarsely.

"I'll wager no more than five and twenty," Queen Katherine said. "Now, Kat, you are of a good age. Go and walk with him." For a moment I was annoyed with her. She believed that John would be a good match for me. That was all she thought I was fit for. I vowed that I would never marry such a man. Why should I leave this court, where I had plenty to eat, fine clothes and was learning so much? Being an ordinary wife paled in comparison.

Our walk to the stables was stiff and embarrassed, as it never had been before. John asked me about the Queen and my duties.

"So you can read and write Kat! You will make a good wife for some lucky man."

"Oh no, not me John. I want to stay with Queen Katherine! I am not made to be a wife." Indeed, the thought of living in a small house, cooking, brewing and cleaning, appalled me. I remembered my mother, Joan, struggling to do the washing, making her hands red raw with the harsh soap that was all we could afford. I remembered her stringing out our shifts on a pole she would hoist from the window out over the road and how her back would ache with all that labour. I did not want that for myself, not at all!

We reached the stable, and I reached up and petted Pegasus. He snuffled gently and pushed his nose against my hand.

"He's wanting an apple, Kat," John said. "Here, give this to him." He took a small red apple from his pocket and handed it to me. For a moment our hands touched, and I felt the tension in him.

"Here you are, Pegasus." I withdrew my hand and held the apple up to the horse's mouth. He closed his teeth over the apple, drew back, and started crunching it noisily.

"He remembers you Kat, but then who wouldn't?" John was smiling at me now, his face still kind but with a warmth I hadn't noticed before.

"I must go back to the Queen now," I said hurriedly. "It was good to see you John. Godspeed."

"I will ask for you the next time I bring messages. Maybe the Queen will allow you to take a longer walk with me?"

"I don't think so," I said, "she is very strict with us young girls."

He laughed. "And so she should be Kat! I will keep you in my thoughts and pray for your release from such a strict mistress!" And with that he put one foot in the stirrup and swung himself up and over Pegasus's broad back.

"Farewell Kat. Don't forget me!"

When I returned to the Queen's chambers, I expected her to cross-question me about what had occurred, but she was engaged in deep conversation with the King.

It was Lady Mary Carey who stopped me and took me aside. She had a goblet of wine in her hand, which she drained and put down on a table. I wished that she hadn't seen us walking out of the Queen's presence chamber. She was a sweet and kindly woman but the most eager of gossips, and her talk was often of sexual dalliance between the young men and women at the court. Lady Elizabeth Boleyn's eldest daughter, she'd joined Queen Katherine as a maid of honour the year after the Field of the Cloth of Gold. Recently she'd been joined by her sister, Lady Anne Boleyn, who was serious and rather reserved. No one could call Lady Carey reserved, however.

"So Kat, you have a follower now!" she teased. "Tell me, are his kisses sweet?" I blushed deep red, hating the thought of a man slobbering all over me.

"No, my lady! I have no interest in followers!" She smiled her generous, easy smile and put her finger to her red lips.

"Kat, you will learn about followers. Every maid has a follower, every lady has a lover." Mary smiled, her little pink tongue licking her lips as if she had been drinking cream.

"But Lady Carey, you cannot have a lover, you are wed, with one child and another on the way," I pointed out. This was forward of me, and I wouldn't have dared to say it to any of the other ladies, but Mary was different. She was always the first to laugh, the first to dance, and the last to complain. She treated me and the other maids like young sisters. She was never aware of her noble status.

She giggled and pushed me in the chest with her finger.

"You know who my lover is Kat," she whispered, "you're not a child anymore."

"I know what the ladies say," I answered, "but the Queen always tells us not to listen to gossip."

In truth, I had a suspicion, but I had never asked Lady Mary. To me, serving Queen Katherine was all I wanted. I was her little maid. I wanted nothing more than to be in her chamber with her, and sometimes to be allowed to share her bed. Maybe she was like a mother to me, having lost the mother that wasn't my mother, and having no idea about the mother who had actually born me. I had heard whispers that the King had enjoyed himself with Lady Mary, but I wanted to hear nothing that would damage the Queen.

"You know it is he," Mary whispered, looking over at the King, still deep in conversation with the Queen. "I love him, and he loves me."

"But you can't!" I was shocked. I did not expect this. Maybe the King admired Lady Mary, but love?

"I can. I have born him one daughter, Kat, and this baby is also his." A pink blush spread becomingly across her cheeks. She was looking as ripe and luscious as a peach, with her corn blonde hair escaping in tendrils around her hood and her belly swelling gently beneath her green gold gown.

"That cannot be, Lady Carey," I said stoutly. "Your children bear the name of Carey."

"The King would not bring dishonour on me," she stated

flatly. "I am married to a husband who is both kind and, er, accommodating. Any issue of mine will bear his name. This is how these things are arranged." She looked down at the floor, her hands twisting her skirt, and I could tell she wasn't happy about this. But then she brightened.

"I've known him for three years Kat. Oh, and I love him so much! He has worn my favour at the joust, although no one knew it was mine. He sends for me to his chamber whenever he is not with the Queen. He calls me his peach, and he loves me when I bear fruit."

"How can you?" I was angry. "You are betraying Queen Katherine, who has shown you nothing but kindness! She does not deserve this treachery!"

"Shshh, Kat, there's nothing like that. She knows about me, and she doesn't mind. Intimacy is not for older ladies. She is tired of the whole thing, he tells me, and she is glad that someone else can take on that burden." She looked at me with her blue eyes shining. "I would not hurt the Queen, and she knows that. I am no threat. Come drink some wine with me Kat. I want us to be friends."

"I can't drink with a lady. It isn't my place." Lady Mary Carey may be very friendly, but I knew there was a great divide between me and her. The only person that I did not feel that with was Queen Katherine, the greatest lady of all. But she was different, and the bond we had was special.

"Come to my chamber Kat. No one will miss us for half an hour. I need to talk. I can't talk to anyone round here except Anne, and she keeps telling me I am dishonouring the family." Her eyes filled with tears, and she looked at me beseechingly. "Please, Kat, I need a friend."

We walked swiftly out of the Queen's chamber and through the anterooms. The King and Queen were still talking, everyone else was playing cards or sewing desultorily. No one noticed our swift exit.

After five minutes of walking through room after room,

we climbed a little way up a winding staircase.

"Welcome to my chamber, Kat! It is small, but it is comfortable and close to the King's apartments." The walls were covered in fine tapestries, one showing the goddess Diana with her bow. It glowed green and gold in the warm light provided by a fire that had just been lit. Lady Mary shivered. "I feel the cold here in England. I long for the south." In the middle of the room was a vast oak tester bed, its columns carved with vines and grapes, with curtains of purple velvet.

Lady Mary waved her hand at the bed. "The King's present," she explained. "Before the birth of our daughter, Catherine." She walked over to a table beside the bed, where there was a flagon of wine and four goblets. She poured us both some wine.

"Kat, I know you love the Queen, and so do I. But she has not the strength for physical intimacy anymore. You must know that."

"I know that the King still comes to her bed," I said, but I also knew that for the past year, it had only been to sleep.

"You know, Kat, that they are not intimate," Lady Mary said. "All the ladies know. They see the sheets; they hear the sounds. I thought you knew that the King came to my bed. You must have done!"

I gulped at my wine. Now I came to think of it, I probably had known something was happening, I had just chosen to ignore it. Lady Mary sat on the settle beside the fire and gestured to me to sit beside her.

"The King first noticed me at York House three years ago when Cardinal Wolsey entertained the court. It was Shrove Tuesday I remember, and we were all making merry before the Lenten fast began. The King's sister, Mary Queen of France, had ordered some of us ladies to take part in an entertainment for that day. I remember the great chamber at York House, full of branches lit with tapers. It was like a magical forest. At one end was a wooden castle, the Château Vert, which we ladies had to defend with flowers."

I listened to her story. I had heard about this magnificent fantasy, but I hadn't seen it. I wished I'd been allowed to go, but I was only twelve at the time, and I was probably tending the fire in Queen Katherine's chamber, waiting for her to return.

Lady Mary's eyes moistened with tears. "We were playing the virtues. I remember the King's sister, the Queen of France, was Beauty, and I was Kindness. We had to defend the castle against the lords, who represented the virtues of chivalry. They were all disguised, and we had to pretend that we didn't know who they were!" She shrugged her shoulders.

"They were led by a lord called Ardent Desire, a tall, masked figure, who jumped up into the castle and took me prisoner. I still remember that thrill of his strong arms around me." She paused and looked into my eyes.

"You see, Kat, love is a wayward spirit, one cannot control it. I knew then that I loved the King, for it was he. He loves to disguise himself, but he is so tall he towers above all of the other lords. But, we have to pretend because it amuses him."

I drank some more wine. I was feeling a little tipsy by now. Warmed by the fire, I turned to Lady Mary.

"I am afraid of love," I said. "I am afraid to be hurt. Queen Katherine loves the King, I know that. So she will be hurt. How can love do this?" Lady Mary shook her golden head.

"Don't be afraid, Kat. Love is our natural and pure state. I cannot help my love for the King, and he cannot help his love for me. But we will do the Queen no harm, I promise you." Maybe love excused Mary and the King. But was it pure to love someone in secret, behind his wife's back?

"But three years you have loved! And why do you tell me now? I will have to talk with her. I cannot hide this."

"Yes you can!" Lady Anne Boleyn swept into the chamber, looking angrily at Lady Mary and myself. While Mary was fair and golden, Anne was dark, her body taut. And yet a spirit

burned through her that made her stand out against the softness of the firelight.

"You, Kat, must keep this to yourself. You are the Queen's
darling, and it would only hurt her dignity for you to bring it
to her attention!" she told me. Her dark eyes glittered as she
gazed at me.

"But if she knows already," I protested.

"She knows, and yet she doesn't know," Lady Anne said.
"She sees herself as the perfect Queen, and she is schooled in
ignoring what might spoil that. If you tell her, Kat, you will be
sorry. Yes, my sister's lover is the King, and he can dismiss you
in an instant, should she ask. You wouldn't want that, would
you?" I was a little afraid of Anne, and so I nodded quickly. I
shouldn't be meddling in these grand people's lives. It could
only cause me trouble.

"And you, Mary," Anne turned on her sister. "Why did you
tell Kat? You know she is close to the Queen. Do you want to
be shamed in front of Her Majesty? She could ask the King to
have you sent away, and then I would follow. Yes, the Queen is
old now, but he respects her. Your loose tongue lays us open to
dishonour." Her eyes flashed at her sister, and I could see why
some called her striking.

Lady Mary looked shamefaced. "I was teasing Kat about
her new follower. I was merry, and the afternoon was dull. It
just spilled out of me. I am sorry Kat."

"Sister, don't you see! You shouldn't be sorry to Kat, you
should be sorry to yourself and to our family! We all know,
and we all don't know. That way our honour is maintained.
You are with child, and Sir William Carey is the father. He
knows and he doesn't know. We have to maintain this, sister
– and our dignity." Lady Anne stood up tall, her body straight
and slender, and her face alight with intelligence. I realised I
was still sitting down and jumped up, bobbing her a curtsey.

Her face softened. "You're a bright girl, Kat, and you have a
lovely voice." Had she heard me sing? I knew Queen Katherine

liked my singing, but no one else had ever complimented me on it.

"How about you and me strike a bargain, Kat? I can teach you all the French songs and how to play them on the lute!" She looked at my black woollen gown. "And I can show you the fashions of France. I have a gown that would be so right for you. The sleeves are too short for me, but it would fit you like a glove, Kat. All you have to do is to be kind. The Queen is a proud woman. How would it be for her own little maid to shame her? Remember, she has not born the King a son, and any talk of love distresses her." She held out her hand to me, and I could smell violets, the scent almost breathing out of her body. She was offering me everything that the Queen did not: excitement, music development and fine cast-off gowns.

"Do we agree Kat? Shall I teach you to be a *mademoiselle*? You will be able to surprise Her Majesty with your attainments. And you shall attend on me, when the Queen does not need you. You will meet poets, warriors and great churchmen, and you will learn from them all. How does that seem to you Kat?"

I agreed immediately, all doubts had gone. The prospect held out by Anne was very exciting. I knew the Boleyn ladies were part of a younger group of courtiers who followed all the latest fashions, both in dress and in thought. I'd seen Harry Percy, the handsome Earl's son who they said had been in love with Anne before he was married off. I also knew of Thomas Wyatt, the poet who still nursed a regard for Anne. Queen Katherine was grand, but these people were just so glamorous. I was fifteen and hungry to be sophisticated like them.

I would never forget the kindness the Queen showed me, it was part of my life. But maybe because of that, I took it for granted. The Boleyn girls spoke to me more as a woman, and even an equal. They talked about men and sex. They showed me all of the latest fashions in music, dress, and lovers. I knew that if I wanted to develop my musical skills, to learn the latest forms, the Boleyns were the people who would help me. I wanted to see more of them, and I thought I could do that and keep my relationship with the Queen. As I said, I was only fifteen and very naïve.

So when I returned to her chamber, I did not mention my conversation with the Boleyn ladies to the Queen. I was glad that the King had gone, as it would have been difficult to look him in the face after what Mary had told me. The Queen was preparing for the late afternoon meal, held in the grand hall, with all the court watching her and the King. The ladies had already dressed her in her tawny silk gown over a kirtle of black silk, shot with gold. She called me to her.

"Kat, come! Comb my hair sweeting. It calms me." She looked upset, and I wondered what the King had been talking to her about. I took her comb and started rhythmically pulling it through her still lustrous hair. As I worked, I sang an old song that my mother had liked,

"I will give my love an apple without e'er a core
I will give my love a house without e'er a door
I will give my love a palace wherein she may be
And she may unlock it without e'er a key.

My head is the apple without e'er a core
My mind is the house without e'er a door
My heart is the palace wherein she may be
And she may unlock it without any key."

My voice and my combing bewitched the Queen, and she sat there for some minutes, her eyes misty and far away.

"He is going to send Princess Mary to Ludlow," she said at last, and I saw the tears gather in her eyes. "My dearest daughter is leaving Court." So that was what they had been talking of. No wonder the Queen looked pensive. She knew that royal children were sent away with their own households, but it was hard for her to part from her only daughter.

"I am sorry, Your Majesty," I said. "I know that you will miss her." She turned and looked at me.

"She is only nine," she said, as if she couldn't believe what was happening. "My heart bleeds to be without her at this tender age." I reached out my hand to hers. It wasn't allowed. Lady Boleyn would have been very annoyed. But I knew that there was tenderness between me and Queen Katherine when we were in private.

But then the woman became the Queen. "However, Ludlow is where the heir to the throne has been sent, through history, to establish a court for themselves. My first husband, Prince Arthur, had his court at Ludlow. It is a good sign. The King is recognising Princess Mary as his heir." And with that, she raised her hand away from mine. I once more became a servant.

"Braid my hair now, Kat, and then fetch the hood with the golden beading."

Truth to be told, I was not unhappy at Princess Mary's leaving for Ludlow. She was very much aware of her position and had teased me in ways that had made me unhappy. Sometimes, when we were learning together, she would pinch me when the Queen was not looking. I could not cry out, I was a maid, and she was a princess. I will always remember her ruddy face, grinning at me, daring me to cry out. Sometimes, though, I stuck my tongue out at her. That made me feel better, although Queen Katherine cuffed me once when she caught me.

Apart from the King, Queen Katherine loved Princess Mary the most in the world. Oh, she was strict with her, as she was with me, but for the Princess, and I must admit, for me, the Queen's reproofs were administered with love. Princess Mary's engagement to the Dauphin of France had long been cancelled as the English and the French fell out again. However, she had now been betrothed to Charles the Holy Roman Emperor, much to her mother's delight. Princess Mary was too young to marry and would spend the next few years at Ludlow, but that didn't stop her boasting about it.

"Call me Empress Mary!" she demanded. "Lie down in front of me and kiss my hem!" I would do so, but then secretly I would spit in her cup of small ale, an action that gave me much satisfaction. She didn't like it when ladies remarked on our likeness, which they sometimes did.

"Kat is just a milksop of a girl, so stringy and pale! She is a foundling, so what do you expect? But I am a Tudor princess, and I have my father's heart and my mother's beauty!" she cried out once. What could I do? She was right, and I knew that while Queen Katherine would be kind, she was always Mary's mother, for whom the Princess could do no wrong.

"Sometimes she looks through me as if I wasn't there," I complained to Will on one of our days together. We didn't see each other much, mainly on holy days when we were given some time off. He had grown into a tall, well-muscled youth. His hair was still curly and thick, and to me he looked very handsome. I was sure the maidservants where he worked would be paying him some attention!

"She is a princess, Kat, and you are a maid servant. It's the way of things, don't get upset about it," he reassured me. "But you are my princess, and always will be!"

I smiled and hugged him. He understood that the gap in my story, where my mother and father should be, made me unhappy. Every time I thought I might be closer to finding out who I was, doors seemed to close in my face.

"We never did find Meg, the laundress," I said. "She might have told me who I am."

"Hey, don't fret about that now. I have a surprise for you." He took my hand and pulled me along the street. We were heading for London Bridge, with its higgledy-piggledy houses and shops clinging on to its sides. It was early afternoon on a cold Candlemas day and the bridge was busy, with shopkeepers calling out, pie-sellers and innkeepers tempting us in to try their wares.

"Surprise? What surprise?"

"Ssh, you'll find out in a minute. Just follow me." He strode quickly ahead, with me almost falling over as I tried to keep up.

"Shut your eyes," he told me. "No peeping!"

Suddenly, I felt myself enveloped in a warm, strong embrace.

"My darling Kat," a man's voice said. A man's voice. It was Tom, Will's father. I struggled to think of him like that, because to me he was my father too.

"Jesu, how long has it been?" He stepped back and took my hands. "Look at you, with your long hair and your white hands. You are a young woman now Kat," he swore, looking me up and down. In truth, it had been about a year. It was difficult for servants like us to find the time to make visits. Will and I saw each other fairly often, as Master Cromwell was now employed by Cardinal Wolsey, and so they were both frequently at court. But it was harder to keep in touch with my father.

"Can I call you father?" I asked, wanting so desperately to hug him.

"Yes, I will always be your father Kat." He clasped me close. "Like I said to you, I may not be your sire, but I carried you when you were crying, I saw you as my own, I fed you, and put clothes on your back."

We spent the afternoon in the kitchen where my father worked. He made us pancakes, which we ate with honey and preserved fruits. We drank small ale as we talked, remembering the happy days when we were all together. I cried when we talked about my mother, remembering that terrible day when she died and I had been so alone. I still sometimes felt that bleak emptiness that had enveloped me then. In the course of one night, I had lost my mother through death, and then through an overturning of everything I had learnt about my origins. I was no longer Kat, the daughter of Joan and Tom, the sister of Will. I was a foundling, and the only people who had a clue about where I came from were Mistress Stabb and

Meg, the laundress. I knew that Mistress Stabb would not tell me, my only hope had been Meg. And after seven years at court I was no closer to finding her than I had been at the beginning.

I decided to try Mistress Stabb once more. I was not due back until late, so I had time to walk to the old tenements where we had lived so long ago. The streets seemed very dark and dirty to me after living in palaces surrounded by gardens and orchards. I walked as quickly as I could, afraid that I might be the target for thieves or worse. But it was quiet, and I reached our house without incident.

I looked up at the window that had once been ours and felt the tears spring into my eyes. It was that window I had looked out of when Joan, my adopted mother, had been dying. Further up, at the top of the building, was Mistress Stabb's window, glowing in the dark. She must be in and have candles and a fire going.

I pushed the outside door open and ran up the stairs, pausing for a moment outside our old door. I could hear a woman's voice talking soothingly to a child. I felt a wave of misery sweep me, thinking that this child had a mother and a place in the world, whereas I was from nowhere. Shaking myself, I climbed up the last flight of stairs to Mistress Stabb's apartment and knocked loudly at the door. I waited for a moment and then hammered at it as if I was trying to break it down.

"Wait a minute, wait a minute," the old woman protested. I heard the bolt being drawn back, and the door opened. There stood Mistress Stabb. She was older and more hunched than she had been before, and her face was grey.

"I knew you were coming," she said. "Now you're here, come in. Don't keep me waiting by the door." I followed her inside and waited while she settled herself in the fine oak chair she kept by the fireplace. "Sit," she ordered, pointing to a stool. I sat and then looked up at her, directly in her eyes.

"I want to know the truth, Mistress Stabb," I said. "My

father told me I wasn't his child, so whose child am I?"

She chuckled, and then brought up some phlegm, which she spat into a handkerchief. "He should not have told you. I am disappointed in him. He vowed to keep the secret." She glared at me. "So, he told you what he knew about Meg and me bringing you as a baby to Joan."

I leaned forward. "Yes, I know I am the child of a servant girl. Which servant girl? Was it Meg? And who was my father?"

Mistress Stabb took a deep draught from the cup that was on the floor beside her, then started to speak. "The servant girl wasn't Meg, my dear. Indeed, I can't even remember her name. 'Tis true that Joan and Tom were not your birth parents. But you'd guessed that anyway."

"So, who was my father?" I cried out, frustrated at her lack of cooperation.

"Kat, my dear, you know what courts are like. A servant girl falls pregnant. It is not the most surprising of events, especially in a court full of young men. Some of these girls were even taken on the dark stairways or in the shadow of the outer wall. Hard to see who is tupping you in those conditions." I lost my temper and got up,

"Mistress Stabb, you have teased me for years about my origins. Now you are simply making matters worse. You are saying that I am not the child of Tom and Joan, but giving me no idea of whose child I am. You're saying I belong to no one! You have no idea how painful that is to me."

Mistress Stabb started coughing again, and I waited patiently for her to finish. Eventually, she got up out of her chair and put her arm on my shoulder. "My dear Kat, do you still believe that I can see the future?"

I laughed contemptuously, "No, because you are a liar, and even if you do see the future, you do not tell the truth about it!"

She sighed. "So, you are angry. I understand that. But it seems to me that you do continue to believe a little. So, I will tell you something that will comfort you. Your origins will become clear to you, as they cannot be now."

"Why can't they?" I cried.

"Because, my dear, your life has to take a certain path before you learn anymore. But I swear to you, on my immortal soul, that you will find out the truth, and it will be at a time when it will not harm you." With that she started coughing again and sank down onto her chair.

"Go now, Kat. Go to your Queen and serve her well."

I returned to the Queen's night chamber around ten o'clock, finding her lying there in the great state bed, looking small in her white nightgown and cap.

"Come here Kat, sleep with me tonight," she said. "I need your warmth."

"Yes, Your Majesty." I bobbed a curtsey, took off my gown and hose, and loosed my hair. Standing there in my shift, I splashed my face with some water from the ewer, said my prayers quickly, and got into bed.

Queen Katherine gathered me to herself, putting her arms around me and letting my head rest on her soft bosom. Her scent was of the rose and almond oil she used on her hair. My heart was full of grief for my mother after an afternoon of reminiscing, and I felt the tears welling up in my eyes. Here I was being held by a mother, a kind and loving woman. But tonight, that didn't comfort me. I wanted *my* mother, whoever she was.

"Why Kat, you are crying! Don't cry sweeting. It will be alright." Queen Katherine took out a lace-edged handkerchief from her sleeve and wiped my eyes with it.

"It's just, you are so kind to me, just like a mother. But then I think I have no mother, and that makes me so sad," I whispered to her, my voice nasal with tears.

"Kat, I promise you, I will care for you like a mother," Queen Katherine said. "While I am alive, you will want for nothing. You will always be a maid of my bedchamber. You will have clothes, food in your belly, and even a little money to spend. Oh, and if that is not enough, we can find you a husband, if you want one."

"No! I don't!" I was indignant. Why would I want to go and serve a man when I could serve a Queen? I had been spoiled by my life at court and didn't want to be a skivvy to any man.

"Well, well, maybe you will change your mind, my dear. I would be loathe to lose you. You fill a space in my heart, Kat. I think of the babies I lost, that should have been in the royal nursery! I grieve for those children Kat, like you grieve for your mother. We don't know what they were like, how they would have loved us. You and me, we have grief in common sweeting."

"Do you think of them, your lost babies?" I asked. "Do you miss them?"

"Why yes, Kat. I cry inside for them every night. I am a mother of children, but they have been taken from me. I pray that I will see them again, but until then my body aches. You, dear Kat, ease that pain. God sent you to me, I am sure."

Queen Katherine folded me into her arms, and as the fire-light flickered, we slowly relaxed and fell into sleep. I sometimes wondered then what it would have been like to be her child. To have her love, which I knew I possessed, but also to have her respect. She loved me as a daughter, but only behind closed doors. In the court, I was just a skinny young maid, always at the back of the crowd.

CHAPTER

8

The Queen's household was busy preparing for Princess Mary's departure. New gowns were ordered, made up as the Queen decreed. Her lessons got longer and more concentrated. I was still with her, and we were learning Latin now. She would need the language to read the state documents that would now be sent to her. I learned alongside the Princess, and she was glad of the companionship, although she would never admit it. Together we would sing out the conjugations of verbs, starting with the verb to love.

"Amo, amas, amat, amamus, amatis, amant." Chanting it helped the memory, the Queen told us.

"Why do I love you, Kat, on some days and not on others?" Princess Mary asked. "Sometimes, you are very kind and help me with my learning, but sometimes with your common ways, you remind me that you are just a nobody and I'm a princess!" I would just smile patiently. She could be difficult, as all the maids knew.

But Princess Mary liked Lady Anne Boleyn. Sometimes, when we were sewing together, she would tell us stories of the French court, of the chivalrous knights and beautiful ladies that shone like stars around King Francis. In the mornings, after we had listened to a Bible reading, Lady Anne would discuss it with us. She, of course, knew Latin, and she explained some of the passages that we didn't understand. Then sometimes she would just laugh and sing some of the French chansons that sounded so exciting and somehow forbidden to two small girls. In truth, laughter wasn't something that was heard often in the Queen's chambers. Yes, they were calm, and the Queen's kindness was everywhere, but occasionally even Princess Mary found them a little dull. I found myself longing for a little excitement and imagining myself as one of the ladies so assiduously courted by the knights of old.

But the weeks were passing, and chests were being packed. Clothes, shoes, and plenty of fresh, clean linen. Jewellery and gowns of state. Books, and quills and ink. Then there were horses being groomed, ready to take the princess and her entourage to Ludlow. Huge carthorses were lined up to pull wagons full of tapestries and oak furniture, bedding and curtains. The Queen fretted about Princess Mary's health. It wasn't surprising, as the Queen's first husband, Prince Arthur, had died at Ludlow. They had only been married a few months, and I heard that they had not even been husband and wife in the true sense. A coughing sickness carried him off before he could claim his marital rights. Heir to the throne, he never became King, and so of course his brother Henry had succeeded and married Queen Katherine himself.

"Ludlow is not good for the health," she complained. "It is dark and damp. It rains there almost every day, when it doesn't snow!" But she knew that for Princess Mary to be acknowledged as the heir to Henry's throne, it was important for her to follow precedent. In the past, the Princes of Wales went to Ludlow to establish a separate court. And Princess Mary must do the same. So, the Queen insisted that a doctor and an apothecary should accompany the Princess, to protect her against ill health.

Her departure was choreographed, as always. King Henry

and Queen Katherine proceeded through the Great Hall of Greenwich Palace. Princess Mary, dressed in riding clothes, was waiting at the great door, dwarfed by the knot of people that surrounded her. Both King and Queen looked anxious. I wondered if the King really wanted Princess Mary to be his heir. He'd made it plain many times that the English would not take a woman to rule them. In sending Princess Mary to Ludlow, he was indicating that she was his heir, but he didn't look happy about it. His handsome face was frowning as he guided Queen Katherine through the ranks of courtiers all gathered to bid farewell to the young Princess. As ever, when they walked through the court, the crowd was like a wave from the sea, the sinking of heads, bowing and curtseying. Maybe, I thought, he will miss her. I wanted to think that, because a father's love is so important for a young girl.

The King and Queen came to a stop just before they reached the Princess, who swept them a deep curtsey.

"Your Majesties," she said in a small, clear voice. The King held out his heavily ringed hand. She bent and kissed it, then with a small panicky movement she pulled at her mother's hand before she had had a chance to extend it.

"Mother," she said, and I could hear she was near tears. She pressed Queen Katherine's hand to her lips, kissing it many times. But oh, the Queen, she was always a Queen. Gently, she withdrew her hand, patting Princess Mary on the shoulder as she did so. The King motioned for his daughter to stand up. His voice rang out across the hall.

"Fare thee well, daughter. Bring the splendour of our court to the Marches and show them the good governance of the Tudors!" Of course, Princess Mary wasn't actually going to rule anywhere, she had people to do that for her. But nothing could take away from the fact that this little girl was, from now on, the representative of Tudor power in the principality of Wales.

The Queen's voice was clear: "Go, daughter, my prayers go

with you. Remember, you are from great stock, from Kings of England and Castile. Do not let them down. Godspeed!"

Mary curtseyed again and left the hall with her retinue. The King and Queen proceeded after her to wave as they rode off.

Daughter, I didn't know then how much a mother loves her daughter. But you are the dearest angel in my life. I knew as soon as I had you that I would love you forever. And yes, I had to leave you sometimes. And that was the hardest thing I would ever do. But at that time, when I was fifteen years old, I had no idea of how strong a mother's love can be. So I didn't wonder at the Queen's calmness. I knew her as someone who would always do her duty in public. I tell you now, though, daughter, I never left you without the tears streaming down my face and my heart torn in two.

It was later that evening when the Queen started to cry. Sitting at her dressing table, in her nightgown, with the ladies moving about quietly, tidying the room. I was brushing her hair, which she liked; the room was dark and warm. She seemed calm, but then she raised her hand for me to stop. She turned her face up to me, and I noticed it was wet with tears.

"She's gone, Kat, she's gone," she whispered, and the tears came thick and fast, like a summer cloudburst.

"Your Majesty, don't cry, please don't cry," I begged. I hated to see her unhappy.

"I've lost her, my beautiful daughter. I've lost her!" She started to wail, and Lady Maria Willoughby hurried over.

"Your Majesty, you have not lost her," she soothed. "She will return for Christmas. You will see her again."

"She is delicate. She may sicken and die!" Queen Katherine was hysterical.

"God will watch over her, Your Majesty. Your prayers will keep our precious princess safe."

Lady Maria put her arm around the Queen and whispered to her, "Catalina, Catalina, do not distress yourself. Princess Mary is strong, like you. She will return to you, and you will watch as she becomes a great princess." The use of her child-hood name calmed the Queen. Lady Maria Willoughby was the only one allowed to do this, as they had grown up together in Spain. The Queen gulped like a child who was recovering from a tear storm.

"Yes, you are right, Maria." She wiped her eyes. Now she was the Queen again.

"Ladies, I wish you all to include Princess Mary in your prayers! Tonight, let us pray together!"

I wished now that Princess Mary had stayed at court. I had no one to take lessons with anymore, and my education had been forgotten about. Well, I was a servant maid, and my education had been to make learning easier for Princess Mary. Now she had gone, there was no point in me continuing. I prayed that the Queen might keep the tutors on for me, but of course, I was just a servant. I wondered whether I might get more chances to improve my skills with the Boleyns. I'd had a taste of learning, and I didn't want to lose it. Life started to drag. At night, I was often with the Queen as she clutched me to her in place of her lost babies. But in the day, I was no longer at her side. I spent more time with the ladies, fetching and carrying, playing cards when they needed an extra player. Sometimes, when I could snatch a few minutes, I would prac-tice new songs on my lute.

I was fascinated by the Boleyn girls. Maybe it was because they were less formal than the older ladies. Like me, they weren't part of the old aristocracy that could claim they descended from the royal Plantagenets who had ruled England for so long. Yes, I know I was a servant maid, and they were ladies, but like me, they didn't quite fit in. Queen Katherine was surprisingly kind to Lady Mary, who was taking her place in King Henry's bed. But the other ladies in waiting snubbed her, refusing to talk to her except whenever strictly neces-sary. There was no whiff of scandal about Lady Anne, but I could see she wasn't comfortable. Sometimes her intelligence proved a difficulty. The other women who served the Queen would voice their opinions on faith, music, or the latest fashion from France. Lady Anne would wince at some of their pronouncements. I knew she would have liked to challenge them and would no doubt have beaten them in any battle of wits. But she was junior to them and knew that would not be politic. So, she would press her lips tightly together and look down sullenly at the floor.

But oh! To me they also had a gloss and glamour about them that drew me like a moth to their brilliant flames. They were a splash of colour in staid and stately surroundings. They sang, they danced in the French fashion, and they talked, how they talked! When we were in Lady Mary's chamber there were no barriers between us, nothing that couldn't be said.

Lady Mary was big with child then, and she would often rest on the bed while I read passages from the chivalric romances that Lady Anne had introduced me to, and Lady Mary had enjoyed when she was at the French court. There were tales of knights who were madly in love with ladies, who were aloof and often in impregnable towers. These ladies might send a word, a fleeting smile, in the knights' direction. But they were cruelly unobtainable. However, in the end, as with all good stories, the ladies would be rescued by the knights, and love would conquer all.

Mary would lie there as I read, luxuriating in the story. Anne, on the other hand would be occupied, maybe writing notes in her book of hours, or composing a poem to share with the other ladies of the court. She was always busy, Anne.

"I have my parfit gentil knight," Mary boasted. "He would do anything for me." She stretched languorously on the bed. "Look what he has given me." She pulled out a long string of creamy white pearls that hung around her neck. "He says they are moons, but not as perfect as his little Mary moon, who shines on him during the night." Lady Anne looked crossly at her sister.

"But he doesn't visit you now, does he sister?" she said scathingly.

"He does not like to risk me or the babe, Anne, you know that. When I am with child, he will not be intimate, much as he would like to."

"So, he is in someone else's bed. I heard he was blowing kisses to Elizabeth Carew." Anne said. "Do you not care about that? Your perfect knight in another woman's bed?"

"You know he will come back to me, once the baby comes and I am churched," Mary said. "He always comes back, and I will be waiting."

"But how can you, sister? You say he loves you, but you accept him tupping other women. If he is your perfect knight, then he should stay faithful to you. I could not endure it."

"Queen Katherine endures it," said Mary. "It is the way of the court. Now he no longer is intimate with her, he visits me. Once I am with child, he visits Elizabeth Carew. But I tell you this Anne, he loves me, of that I am sure."

"How do you know?" Anne asked her sister quizzically. I held my breath. It seemed like the sisters had forgotten that I was there, book in hand, ready to continue with my reading.

"He tells me that I am his peach, his moon. He says that one day he will establish me in my own manor, and that he will visit me every night. He talks of growing old together."

"He is a man, Mary, and he lies. You are his mistress, and when he no longer wants you, he will drop you like a stone." Anne looked at her sister severely. "To keep a man, you have to marry. Nothing less will do."

"Nothing less than what?" A man's voice rang out. George Boleyn strode into the chamber, bringing a gust of fresh air with him, and the scent of grass and hounds. I guessed he had been hunting with some of the other courtiers. In looks, he was like Lady Anne, dark and fine-boned, but lithe and muscular. He wore a midnight blue doublet, slashed to reveal a white silk shirt beneath, with black hose and a black velvet cap.

Lady Anne's face warmed as she regarded her brother.

"Never you mind, George! Why do you always interrupt our conversations? We must have some privacy."

Lady Mary laughed and stretched out on the bed.

"George does not know the meaning of the word privacy! He will storm into our chamber when we are getting dressed just because he cannot wait to tell us the news. We are lucky he doesn't follow us into the garderobe."

"That is not true, and you know it, Mary!" George protested. "Come, little Kat, tell me what my sisters were talking about." I felt the eyes of all three on me and flushed. I was just a servant maid. If I told George what Anne and Mary were saying, then they could have me punished, and if I didn't then he could do the same.

"Just women's talk, my lord," I stammered. "Nothing important."

"That's right Kat!" Anne said. "He is just a great big bully, aren't you George?" Her eyes were teasing, sparkling like black diamonds. He walked towards her and picked her up, holding her aloft.

"Put me down George," she cried, but I noticed she was laughing.

"I won't, not till you tell me what you were talking about!"

"I will not do that! It is not your business!" she protested, raining blows upon his shoulders.

"Sister, stop! You have grown heavy! What is a poor man to do when his sister will not confide in him?"

"Anne was telling me that the only way to keep a man is to marry him," Mary interjected. "Although you are married to Lady Rochford George, and I do not see you keeping her."

George put Anne down suddenly, and she smoothed her hair and her skirts.

"That is true enough, Mary," George said. "I detest the woman. I ask God every day why Father made me marry her. She is so very, very *dull*. Whereas you, dear sisters, are more fun to be with than any other women in court! " He wheeled round to face me,

"Stop staring at me Kat! You look like Princess Mary. I could almost imagine she was watching us, and it spooks me." I looked down at the floor, muttering an apology. I had learnt to ignore people comparing me to Princess Mary. But the resemblance was real, I could see it. And somewhere, deep inside, I wondered if I shared a parent with Princess Mary. I could see the similarities between us from the cast of her eyes and the way she lifted her chin. Could the King have taken some servant girl and forgotten about it? But such thoughts were highly impudent. How could I, a servant, even imagine that the King was my father?

"Don't let him bully you, Kat," said Anne. "Although, yes, you do have a look of the King. Maybe another one of his mistresses that he loved so much?" Her voice took on an ironic tone.

"Oh no, my lady," I said quickly. "I am a foundling. No one knows who my father is."

"Yes, I know. But still, strange...." Anne mused, considering me carefully. "Go now Kat, we have no more need for you tonight. Go back to the Queen. She will be wanting her bedfellow." I bobbed a curtsey and left the chamber. As I went down the stairs, I could hear giggles and shouts. The Boleyn siblings were close, very close.

There was one other man that Lady Anne allowed near her. It was Sir Thomas Wyatt. A courtier who had grown up on an adjoining estate to the Boleyns, he knew her well. For him, a childhood friendship had grown into an unrequited love. And oh, how he let you know that he was in love! It wasn't enough that he would be mooning over Lady Anne on every occasion. He fancied himself a poet and would pass his scrawled endearments to her regularly. She would laugh at him, read the verse, and throw it on the fire. I thought then that she despised him, but later, I wasn't so sure. Maybe she burnt his poems, not because she disliked him, but because they were a record of a love affair. I don't know, but I remember reading one of his poems, which convinced me that they had loved each other.

> "When her loose gown from her shoulders did fall,
> And she me caught in her arms long and small;
> Therewithal sweetly did me kiss
> And softly said, "Dear heart, how like you this?"

Wyatt was a tall man with curling dark hair and a fashionably long beard. His brown eyes, which Lady Anne called "puppy dog eyes', were always trained upon her. Married some years ago, he wasn't happy in the match. Outwardly, Anne treated him with disdain, to which he would respond with ever more extravagant declarations of love. But I saw them together one evening, standing so close that they almost touched. Their dark eyes were locked on each other, and it was as if the hurly burly that was going on around them was completely stilled. Then I saw something that told me the truth. He had something, a white feather I think, on his black velvet coat, just below his shoulder. Lady Anne reached up, standing on tiptoes, and picked the feather off. Then she smoothed down the pile of the velvet, briefly touched his arm, and softly withdrew her hand. It was an act so tender, it made me realise that Lady Anne wasn't all she seemed.

Lady Anne Boleyn was the cleverest woman at court, well yes, unless you counted Queen Katherine. But Katherine couldn't match her quick fire repartee, her pin-sharp dance steps, and her fine high singing voice. Sir Thomas was besotted.

"Fie Sir Thomas, of what use is your verse? Does it teach us the words of our Lord Jesus Christ? Does it tell us the history of our people? Does it, mayhap, give us good recipes for swans' meat, for posset and jellies?"

"My lady, it tells of love, and love is the lifeblood of a

man," he replied. "Without love, no man is made, without love, no man can cast his arrows into the future."

"Sir Thomas, this woman can live very easily without love!" she replied sweetly. "What is love? I loved once, and it was foolish. I assure you; I can manage without that kind of love." I knew she was talking about Harry Percy, whom she had wanted to marry. But she hadn't been aristocratic enough to deserve a duke's son, so the King and the Cardinal had squashed their engagement. "I don't want your silly verses. I prefer to be reading God's word." But her eyes flashed so enticingly at Wyatt, that he wasn't put off.

"But love brings us to God. Saint Peter writes, 'Love covers a multitude of sins'," Wyatt said, pleased with himself. I smiled to myself. He couldn't trip Lady Anne up.

"Saint Peter also writes, 'I urge you as sojourners and exiles to abstain from the passions of the flesh, which wage war against your soul'," she replied tartly.

"Ah, but my lady, my passion for you is not simply of my flesh, but is made noble by being from my soul." He looked at her, and for a moment their eyes met.

There was a new lady in waiting in the Queen's household. A young girl, very quiet and shy. Her name was Jane Seymour. The Queen tried to build her confidence up by conversing with her and asking her about her family. But inevitably, she would hang her head and mumble. She had to find every word she said, so those words took a long time to leave her mouth. The Queen was kind as always, but Lady Anne Boleyn was privately scathing.

"Tis a mercy that Jane Seymour's life is so very boring, for otherwise we would die waiting for her to tell us about it!" Lady Boleyn and Lady Stafford both laughed, but I thought she was being cruel. Jane Seymour was not a beauty, like Mary Carey, nor a wit like Anne, and yet she was a pleasant, religious girl, and the Queen took to her straight away. I didn't feel jealous of her, I knew my place was in the Queen's bed with her at night. I was happy for Lady Jane to learn black work embroidery at the Queen's knee during the day. I was never skilled at needlework, and I am afraid to say, daughter, that I didn't care.

Queen Katherine was missing her daughter. At night, when she was preparing for bed, she would take out Princess Mary's letters, all kept in an oak casket with a lock and hinges made of silver.

"She is reading Justinius, Kat! History is good for a queen, and she tells me she is studying diligently. Oh I am so proud of her!" Queen Katherine paused and pressed the letter to her breast. "She will make a great queen, Kat, I know that. She has the royal blood of Isabella of Castile, my mother, and Elizabeth of York, Henry's mother. She is from a line of queens."

She opened the casket and replaced the letter.

"But my heart longs for her!" she said in an anguished whisper. "I want to hear her voice again, hold her little hand, and give her sweetmeats." The Queen was lonely, I knew that. Of course, she had her ladies, but many of them were themselves part of the power play of court and could not be trusted.

"At least I have my little Kat. Sweetheart, where go you in the afternoons? I hear you are with the Boleyn ladies."

"Yes, your Majesty, we like to sing together," I admitted, feeling a little guilty at deserting Queen Katherine for these joyful afternoons.

"And how is Lady Mary Carey?" Queen Katherine asked icily. "I hear the child has quickened in her belly." Queen Katherine knows everything, I thought. She knows that the child Lady Mary is carrying is the King's. And yet she can sit and discuss it without any emotion. That was what it took to be a Queen.

"She is well, Your Majesty. Her belly is showing now, and she is very happy."

"But she will, I think, not be entertaining his Majesty now?"

I was surprised. I didn't expect Queen Katherine to be as

direct as she had been. She was asking me if Henry still came to Lady Mary's bed.

"I mean, dear Kat, that a woman with child must rest. So she will not be able to take part in the late night revels that surround the King," she said, looking intently at me.

"Oh no, she tells me she is abed after supper and sleeps through till dawn," I averred. Queen Katherine looked pleased.

"Ah. Yes Kat, it is the lot of us women to bear the fruit of our adventures – she will be entering confinement soon." She paused and then spoke again: "Her sister, Lady Anne, she is quite a serious girl?"

"Oh yes, Your Majesty, and she is not wanting marriage, not after she was parted from Henry Percy."

"Yes, yes. A serious girl, and quite plain. The King may make music with her while Lady Mary is incapacitated. She will do him good."

We knelt together by her large oak bed and said our prayers. As always, the Queen prayed first for the King, and then for the Princess. Sometimes, at the end of a long list of requests she would add a little prayer for me, that I might be successful and make a good marriage.

I cared not for that. All I wanted was to stay at court with my dearest Queen.

CHAPTER

9

Queen Katherine was merry. It was autumn, and the leaves were falling from the oak trees that stood in the King's hunting park at Greenwich. The air was crisp and clear, and sometimes we ladies would accompany the hunt. Seated on white palfreys, with gowns of velvet, tipped with fur, the ladies were a glowing addition to the party. I was never on a palfrey, maybe following on a spare nag. But the days were full of gaiety and fun. Early starts, chases through the forest, and late afternoon returns to a hearty supper at the palace. The court was no longer in progress and had settled again at Greenwich Palace, one of the Queen's favourite places.

But it was more than sport that had brought the light to my dear Queen's eyes. Dancing through her chamber, waving a piece of paper, she paused to kiss me on top of my cap, skipping over to Maria, Lady Willoughby, embracing her in a flurry of red silken sleeves and rose oil.

"Princess Mary is to come to court! She tells me here; she has been commanded by the King!" Tears were streaming from her face as she looked again at the paper, almost afraid that the import of what Princess Mary had written might have changed.

"She will be here for Christmas! See here, she says that she will obey the King, her father, with all due speed. I shall be seeing her before the month is out." I looked across at the Queen and smiled at her joyousness. I knew that she had been asking the King to allow Princess Mary to come to court. She had tried persuasion, with honeyed words and rich wine. She had tried reason, referring to the need for the dynasty to show itself and its future. And finally, she had begged him on her knees. She liked to do that because she knew it made King Henry uncomfortable. While he thought that every subject owed him such obeisance, to have his mature, steely, queen abasing herself in front of him was embarrassing. However he had refused to commit himself, telling her he would have to consult with his privy council.

Then she had heard nothing. I felt for her as she had looked across at the King, day after day, looking for some sign from him. But he had said nothing. There was nothing like the close-ness between the two of them that there had been when I had first eavesdropped on the royal couple. Yes, they were together every day, for splendid meals, for dances and parties. But now he didn't drop into her chambers for a soothing word of advice very often. And those cosy times when they had sat together playing cards were long gone. It had taken a letter from Princess Mary to inform her that her wish had been granted.

I'd noticed the distance between them that existed, but I hadn't been particularly worried. They were King and Queen and would continue to be so, whether or not they were still close. Lady Mary Carey was no longer at court. She had retired to Suffolk to have her second child, a little boy called Henry.

"He takes the King's name," said Lady Elizabeth Boleyn, his grandmother. She never said it, but we all knew that this baby was sired by the King. Yes, he hadn't recognised either of his children by Lady Mary Carey, but they were acknowledged by William Carey, her ever-obliging husband, and thus scandal had been averted. Although Lady Mary was still in Suffolk, the whisper was that the King's eye had fallen elsewhere. But for the Queen, there was no humiliation, no usurpation of her place by the King's side. And so, matters had improved.

I was sent with the Queen's orders to the merchants who supplied her with fine fabrics. This Christmas she would be at her most magnificent. "And Princess Mary will need new gowns," the Queen said. "There is nothing of style in the Welsh Marches." I hurried through the outer chambers of the royal apartments and headed out to find a boat to take me upriver to London. My thoughts were interrupted suddenly.

"Mistress Kat, how goes it?" a handsome young man enquired. I started and turned to look at him. It was Will, taller and broader than the last time I had seen him, dressed in a fine black doublet and hose.

"Will! Why are you calling me mistress? We know each other too well for that, surely? What are you doing here anyway?" I looked up at him, at his curly dark hair, his brown eyes sparkling with fun, and his lean, tanned face. I couldn't help it, but I found myself admiring his muscled legs and his broad chest, so well shown off by the fashionable clothes he was wearing. Daughter, some may say I should not speak of these things to you, but Will is part of my story, and it is important that you know everything. This was the time when we both began to realise that things had changed between us. The way he looked at me, the warmth in his eyes, gave me a new and delicious feeling.

"You are a lady now, Kat, and I was paying you respects," he said. "I am here with Master Cromwell. He works for the Cardinal now. He has sent me to fetch some documents from his house. Are you going upriver?"

"Yes, I am," I said, "the Queen wishes to order some fabrics for Christmas gowns. She is in a hurry; she has just now learnt that Princess Mary is to be here for Christmas."

"Then let us go together," he said, steering me towards the steps where a skiff was anchored, the boatman sitting between the oars.

He held my waist as if I were precious, and then stepped in front of me onto the boat, handing me down beside him. This was strange from Will, my brother, my childhood companion. While he would have protected me with his life, he would never have treated me like fine-blown glass.

"Hey Will? What are you doing?" I asked, but he ignored my question.

"Westminster!" he said to the boatman as we settled ourselves at the stern of the boat.

"I'm glad I saw you. I've wanted to ask you something," he said. "I was planning to visit you now that you are back at Greenwich." He took my hand in his. His hand was warm, his nails clipped and clean, except for a couple of ink blots. I could smell the warm green scent of cedar as he sat beside me. The boatman rowed on his face impassive, the oars feathering the water with every stroke. On either side of us, royal London unfolded in all its majesty.

"Kat, we are not brother and sister," he said, "and it is right that we recognise that."

"But we are still brother and sister in spirit!" I cried, afraid that I would lose him again.

"No, we are not Kat. And I am glad that is the case." I looked at him, puzzled. Inside myself I had a small hope that he might be about to say something I'd hardly dared to think, and yet the sensible part of me dismissed that out of hand.

"Kat, the last few times we have met, I have... I have found myself having feelings for you."

"Feelings? We will always care for each other, Will." I had to keep my feet on the ground.

"More than that. No, different to that. You will always be in my heart Kat, that doesn't change. But as a sister? No." He shook his head, took a deep breath and looked into my eyes.

"Kat, I would like to pay court to you." He took my hand and started to gently trace patterns on my upturned palm.

"That's just not possible, Will! What about Tom, our

father? We were a family, brother and sister. He was our father. He can't suddenly change to see me as your sweetheart!"

"We must of course speak to my father," Will said calmly. "But he knows that we are not related. He will not stand in my way." He stroked my hand very gently, slowly moving his fingers up and just inside my sleeve. I gasped. This was something I had not expected, although I had maybe dared to dream about it.

"You are an idiot Will, what do you want with me?"

"I have seen you grow into a woman. You are quite beautiful." He spoke slowly and with emphasis.

"Beautiful!" I laughed scornfully.

"Yes, indeed. You are lissom, lovely, with your red gold hair!" He stared intently into my eyes. "I know how you survived when mother died, you were so brave. And you are clever, you have your own mind. I would give my all to have you to stand beside me through life."

"I am not interested in any man," I insisted. "I want to stay with the Queen."

He smiled at me, and his warm, dark eyes suddenly made me feel very strange.

"I will change your mind, Kat. I promise you." He spoke with a determination that I had not noticed before. "We can have a good life. I will be a lawyer, Master Cromwell says. You will have fine clothes, a good house, and a good name. You will no longer be a foundling."

That upset me. "No, I will always be a foundling until I discover who my parents were. Your kindness makes no difference to that Will."

He raised my hand to his lips and kissed it, "I am not being kind. I am being selfish. I want you Kat. It may take years. But it's you I want."

December came, and the court was fasting for the Advent season. No eggs or meat were eaten by us at this time, and in the Queen's chambers, prayer and contemplation replaced music. The Queen wore plain brown or grey gowns with an austere gable hood. And yet, while her face was solemn, in respect for this holy time, her eyes twinkled, and very often a smile would break through.

The household was frantic with preparations for the Christmas celebrations. The Queen held meetings with her Chamberlain and the cooks about the delicacies that would be prepared to feed the court and all the courtiers. There was to be peacock, roast boar, venison and hare. The cooks were planning pies of pigeons with dried apricots and mincemeat with candied oranges. For the first time this year, a strange new bird would grace the banquet table, a turkey. I saw one once, an ugly, large bird with a hanging chin. But, as the cooks promised, its size meant that it could be stuffed with chicken, partridge, and finally pigeon. Every day, sacks of dried fruits, nuts and spices were carried into the kitchen to make the sweetmeats and the pastries that were part of Christmas for us.

In the Queen's chambers, we were busy sewing. Most of the ladies were embroidering silk shirts with black work to give to the King for Christmas. They would hope he would, in turn, give them a pendant jewel, or a girdle embossed with precious stones. The Queen worked particularly hard. Her shirts for the King were beautifully detailed, with intricate patterning of flowers and fruits around the collars. She was proud of the fact that she still stitched her husband's shirts, no matter how grand she was.

Then there were visits of tailors and seamstresses, with new state gowns to inspect, some for the Queen, some for the Princess. Queen Katherine had decided she would wear a deep crimson velvet gown studded with yellow diamonds, with a cloth of gold petticoat underneath. For Mary, there would be a purple velvet gown, which was a match to her father's imperial robe. She would wear a rope of pearls, a golden crucifix, and a brooch of a Tudor rose, blooming out of a pomegranate, the twin badges of her father and mother. The ladies of the court were also considering their wardrobes and ordering new sleeves or fresh edgings of fur, to refresh past state gowns. For me, Queen Katherine had given me some fine woollen worsted, of an apple green, and the tailor had fashioned it into a gown that showed off my high breasts and small waist. Together with a sunny yellow kirtle and sleeves that were daintily edged with rabbit fur, I felt that I would be a fine lady this Christmastide.

"Maria, Elizabeth, Anne!" The Queen called out, beckoning for her ladies to come to the window. "See! It is the Messenger in advance of the Princess's arrival!" We all clustered around, peering to get a look.

"Quick Maria, fetch my tawny silk gown, and the black velvet hood. Kat, send a message to the King. We must be ready to greet the Princess. Tell the musicians to make ready. The trumpeters will be standing by." Ladies ran in different directions, some answering the Queen's commands, some straightening their own hair, and making sure their hoods were securely fastened. Only Anne Boleyn stood there, with her shapely finger to her mouth, as if contemplating the Christmas to come.

"Anne, come with me!" Lady Elizabeth Boleyn commanded her daughter. "We must put out the jewels for Her Majesty. Hurry now, we have maybe one hour until the Princess arrives."

Princess Mary would be making the last part of the journey by river. I slipped outside to a small hill just about the bank. The King's barge had already departed to meet her, with pennants flying and musicians playing. The landing stage was quiet without it as a crowd of courtiers assembled, rubbing their hands, their breath misty in the cold air. They talked to each other, subdued yet excited. Princess Mary had not been seen at court for eighteen months. Now, she would be nearly a woman, nearly ready to take hold of her position as the King's heir.

Eventually, the crowd spied the King's barge, edging its way along the misty river. The sound of distant cornets could be heard, playing martial music. Every now and then the gold-embossed decorations of the barge flashed as the sun penetrated the cloud.

Nearer to the palace, a flourish of trumpets played a fanfare. The King and Queen emerged, walking together, surrounded by their most eminent ladies and gentlemen to meet the Princess. The King looked impatiently towards the barge, making its way noisily along the river. The Queen looked calm and serene. But I knew what emotions were working underneath that mask of Majesty. As we had rushed to get ready, she had been both crying and laughing. She stripped down to her kirtle for us to lift the heavy state gown over her head, wiping the tears from her eyes and then jumping for joy in her stockinged feet.

But now, she was the Queen, and there was no hint of tears or laughter. She knew that everyone there would be watching her and her daughter. She knew she had to give no hint of weakness, of emotion. If the throne was to pass to her daughter, there must be no talk of women's emotionality or feebleness of spirit.

I looked down to the barge. I could see Princess Mary now, standing near the front of the barge. In a deep maroon velvet gown, topped by a cloak edged with black sable, she stood still and brave, a small figure flanked by the larger forms of her household courtiers. She was slim, but still low of stature. Her cheeks were pink in the cold, and her eyes were bright. How she must be looking forward to seeing her parents, I thought. But for her, like for all of them, her emotions would be hidden. I knew then that the days of us sharing our school books had long gone. She was destined to be Queen of England, while I... who knows? I was destined to be a serving maid for all of my life.

A couple of hours later, after all the speeches and the formal embraces, the Queen blew into her chambers, accompanied by the King and Princess Mary.

"Sweet Jesu, it is cold out there," Queen Katherine cried, pulling her gloves off and then handing me her cloak. "Your Majesty," she addressed the King, "will you deign to join us for some sweet wine and almonds to ward off the cold?" He had gone to stand in front of the fire, followed by his daughter. He turned.

"Yes, of course wife. Here, my princess, let me embrace you!" He held out his arms, and Princess Mary ran into them. He folded himself around her small figure, almost crushing her, and then standing back to look at her, before he clasped her again.

"My Mary, my princess! You are grown into a lioness!" he said, planting a kiss on top of her cap. She hugged him again and then turned to her mother.

"Mama," she cried, and her eyes brimmed with tears. The Queen's eyes were also wet. She bent and picked up her daughter, holding her as if she would never let her go.

"Mary, Mary, Mary, my lovely girl. I have missed you so much! I have prayed every night for you my little rose. Are they feeding you well in Ludlow? You look so small still." Indeed, Princess Mary would always be small. You would think that with her father so tall, she would take after him. But unlike me, she never grew. Still, she had a difficult time of it, growing up with the pressures put on her by her royal position.

Soon the family were settled by the fire, with crystal glasses of Hippocras in hand and eyes only for each other. Princess Mary had recovered from her tears and was soon telling her parents about the Lords of the Marches, her strict governess, the Countess of Salisbury, and the terrible weather.

"Oh that rain!" Queen Katherine sympathised. "I remember it so well. Day after day, in that grey old castle, with wind and rain all around. It was so miserable!" She laughed and took a sip of her wine. The King looked at her, and his eyes hardened. He never liked her talking about her time at Ludlow, as the young wife of his brother Prince Arthur.

"But my brother kept you merry, Katherine, did he not?" he said pointedly. She stopped laughing.

"Oh, we hardly saw each other! He was unwell for so much of that time, poor boy." She sighed. "I never knew that joy I have with you, dear husband."

King Henry looked at the floor. It was almost as if he wanted to say something, but couldn't quite bring himself to do so. For a moment he was silent.

"Yes indeed, Katherine. But too much about the past. For now, dear daughter, we prepare to welcome you for Christmas with much joy, laughter and song!"

Christmas Eve came, and vast branches of holly and garlands of ivy were brought into the apartments. Flowers were placed in all the apartments, and over spinning wheels and needlework boxes. There was to be no work for twelve days, except that which went towards the great feast of Christmas. Everywhere there was the sound of musicians tuning up, practising the songs and dances that they would be playing for all the great lords and ladies of the court. Every corner was filled with old friends catching up with news from the country and doings in the town. The rushes on the floor were fresh and fragrant with lavender, rosemary and chamomile. I loved Christmas at court, daughter, and that one was special. I look back on it now, daughter, and remember the happiness of that time, when no one was afraid and the future seemed secure.

Christmas Day and the great hall was jammed with people. The royal family sat at the top of the hall on a dais, surrounded by the greatest of their courtiers. King Henry wore the royal purple, embossed with rubies and lined with ermine. Queen Katherine was in crimson and gold, while Princess Mary echoed her father's colours. As they looked below at us, they must have seen a crowd of familiar and unfamiliar faces, all flushed with drinking good wine and whooping and waving at friends across the vast hall. Christmas was a time when the rigid decorum of the court was relaxed, and the hall was noisy with laughter and singing.

The King rose from his throne and took his daughter's hand. The hall fell silent. He led her down the steps of the dais to the head of the great hall. Motioning to the musicians, he led the tiny princess in a stately galliard, while the Queen watched, her face beaming with joy.

"Behold, my daughter, Princess Mary, and do homage to her!" the King boomed as the dance finished. Immediately all the gentlemen bowed, and the ladies curtseyed. This was Tudor power, the King and his heir, and no one could gainsay it. Princess Mary stood there, her red little face triumphant and determined. She knew, at this moment, that she was the future, and that whenever this vast, powerful King went to meet his god, it would be her who would take on his mantle.

Soon the general dancing started, with the tables being pushed back to the walls and the dishes of the Christmas banquet being replaced by flasks of wine and small bowls of dried fruit and nuts, marchpane confections and tarts of quince paste and almond. Queen Katherine retired to her chamber, which she often did when the official ceremonies were over. I knew I should go and join her, but I wanted to stay a bit longer and watch. The King's sister, Mary, who had married the Duke of Suffolk, was leading the floor, dancing first with her husband and then with George Boleyn. The King pulled Lady Elizabeth Boleyn up to dance while her husband looked on indulgently. John Skelton, the poet, was sitting in a corner with a full glass of wine and a quill, while Princess Mary sat with her governess, munching on a bowl of sugared almonds. She looked tired and like the small girl she really was. I noticed Lady Anne Boleyn leaving the hall. I guessed she might find the merriment boring and be going back to her chamber to read some of Thomas Wyatt's poetry.

The music was getting louder, and I felt a little tipsy, having drunk more wine than I normally had. I felt a little sick, and my head was spinning. My eyes blinked in the massed light of all the candles. To tell the truth, I wasn't used to the strong wine we were all drinking on that Christmas night. I left the great hall, trying to find a quiet place where I might compose myself before returning to the Queen's chambers.

I walked along through chamber after chamber, feeling giddy and a bit out of control. At last I came to a quieter part of the palace, where the candles did not blaze. Finding an alcove in the wall with a window that looked out over a small garden, I decided to sit for a minute while my head steadied.

I heard a soft, slow sigh. It was a woman, sounding as if she had found her heart's desire, and yet doubted it. Then a man's whisper, "My love, my love," low, urgent. Lovers. Of course, at Christmas, so many couples flirted, danced and even kissed under the mistletoe. I had seen it many times before at court. But this was more sober, and more meaningful than that. I drew back into the alcove, afraid that the couple would see me. Making myself as small as possible, I crouched into a ball and peeped out.

I could see the couple now, dark in the shadows. The woman was tall and slender. I could not see her face. It was held between the two large hands of the man, who had bent his lips to hers. The tall, broad man, who could take any woman he wished. The King. I knew at once that if I was caught, I would be in trouble. Freezing against the window, I waited, my heart beating.

I did not want to see what I saw, daughter. I did not want to see the King, my Queen's husband, whispering how much he loved this lady. While she kissed him ardently, she would not allow his hands to move beyond her shoulders.

"No, no, Your Majesty. I cannot," she whispered desperately. Well, she wasn't Mary Boleyn for sure. She had not returned to court after the birth of her son. This lady was not about to allow the King any liberties. And yet, every time she repulsed him, she gave a little sigh. Was that distaste, or suppressed desire? It seemed, as she kissed him back, that she was longing for him. I saw the pearls on the edge of her French hood, her white hands which she twined around his neck.

"I am not my sister, Your Majesty. I cannot be your mistress." Anne. Boleyn! How could it be her? She, who had so disapproved of her sister Mary, who had been so determined not to be any man's plaything? And yet, it was her, for I caught a glimpse of her face now in the candlelight. Her dark, intelligent eyes glowed, and there was a touch of a blush on her cheeks. But she was standing back now and raising her head to look at him.

"Your Majesty, I wish you Merry Christmas," she said formally and sunk into a deep curtsey.

"No, no, Anne, I am not your King, I am your servant, who would be your lover," he replied, his voice deeper and warmer than usual. He raised her up and made to kiss her again, but she pulled back.

"Your Majesty. Henry... you are not fair to me," she spoke calmly, and yet there was an edge to her voice. "I am in service to the Queen."

"The Queen will turn her face away, dear Anne. She is well used to doing so." I thought to myself how much dear Queen Katherine had suffered in doing exactly that, and I felt angry with him. I may be a strange woman, daughter, but it has never seemed to me to be right that a man can pleasure himself with any number of women, while us women are meant to be pure and chaste.

"Your Majesty, I do not want this. I do not want to be something the Queen turns her face from. I do not want to be an open secret at court, when all will talk about me behind my back. I tell you again, I am not my sister," Anne insisted.

"But you are one hundred times more bewitching, more intelligent than any other woman I know!" he protested, seizing her again in his arms. She resisted at first and then softened and pressed herself against him. For what seemed like an age they stayed in each other's arms, unable to move.

Finally, it was the King who pulled back. "I must bid my daughter goodnight, sweetheart. I would stay with you, but I cannot."

Immediately Anne swept to the floor in a deep curtsey.

"Your Majesty, goodnight." He motioned for her to rise

but was already walking across the chamber.

"Goodnight, sweet Anne. I shall see you at the joust in the morn," he threw back as he left the chamber. She stood still for a moment, tidying her hair and fixing her hood. Then she turned to leave the chamber. As she did, she saw me cowering in the alcove.

"Kat, what are you doing here? You should be with the Queen!" she accused me, her fierce eyes burning into me. I was a little scared but also angry. I am afraid to say daughter, that often my anger will get the upper hand, as it did on that night.

"You cannot talk about the Queen! You are betraying her, just as your sister did! You talk of being a chaste woman, but that is all lies. You are headed for the King's bed."

"Why Kat, you have claws," she said, amused. "But I tell you this Kat, be careful who you scratch. I have a long memory for those who do me harm." There was something in her voice that chilled me, and I felt a bit scared.

"Now, forget all of this. I do not wish the Queen harm. It was just a Christmas kiss, one of many tonight, I'll warrant. I am not headed for the King's bed, Kat. Why should I be? I will grace no one's bed but my husband's. I am not allowed to marry Percy, and Tom Wyatt is married already, so I shall die an old maid, just like you Kat!" She made a joke of it. It was well known among the Queen's ladies that I did not wish to marry.

"But, he wants you. And he is King. He will get his own way, I know it," I insisted.

"I tell you this Kat, and I tell you now. I will grace no man's bed except my husband's." She came up to me and took my face in her slim hand.

"Now, go to the Queen and warm her bed for her! She needs you Kat, her marriage bed is cold." She swept out towards the noise and the gaiety of the revels, leaving me standing alone and shivering.

CHAPTER 10

And so, Christmas rolled on in a blur of masques, jousts and feasting. Cardinal Wolsey had a play put on, which we all went to see. January the first was the time for gifts, and the Queen gave me a small, illuminated book of hours. In it there were all the prayers for every different time of day, the Saints' Days, and passages from the psalms. I loved particularly the page where my own dear Queen Katherine was pictured worshipping the Virgin Mother. Queen Katherine was magnificent, in scarlet and gold, while the Virgin's face was illuminated with a gold halo that seemed to shine over them both. I was overjoyed with it and threw myself into her arms to thank her. I treasured it then, as I do now, daughter. It is one of the few things I have to remind me of her.

I tried to put the embrace between the King and Anne Boleyn out of my mind. After all, if she was determined not to become his mistress, what harm could come of it? There were plenty of other willing women at court, should he want a romance. And I still hoped that one night we would hear his steps on the floor outside, and the Queen would turn me out of her bed, all in a hurry. It used to happen. Years ago, I spent many nights in the maids' dormitory while the King and

Queen slept together. But it hadn't happened for a long time now. The Queen, dignified as ever, had accepted it, although I knew she hoped that her husband would in time return. But the most important thing was that he had recognised Princess Mary as his heir. In time, she would make a suitable marriage, one where her husband could support her, and heirs could be born to the Tudor throne. Whether that marriage would be with a French or a Hapsburg prince, who could tell? It depended on the state of international affairs. Or maybe she would be matched with an English lord, who although her inferior, would prevent any fears of a foreign takeover. And, after all, she would always have the wisdom of her mother to guide her, and the power of her father to inspire her.

Princess Mary left for Ludlow just after Twelfth Night. The Queen wept bitterly in bed later but consoled herself. "My Mary will become a great queen," she told me. "The King knows that and has accepted it."

As the winter dragged to its close, the gales whistled around the palace walls, making the tapestry hangings in the Queen's chamber tremble in the draughts. Lent had started, and none kept it more strictly than Queen Katherine. Again, we ate no meat, no eggs or cheese. But this time there was not the glittering feast of Christmas to look forward to. Easter was quiet without Princess Mary. The King was distant, always courteous to Queen Katherine in public, but his mind seemed elsewhere. As for Lady Anne Boleyn, she continued to serve the Queen and showed no sign of any secrets to hide. She was at least as pious as the Queen during Mass, dutifully sinking to her silken knees to pray. I still visited her some afternoons, when we would sing together and read poetry. Her face came alive when she read out Wyatt's verses. Rather than being cold and forbidding, as she often was, she glowed. I thought Wyatt was too much concerned with displaying his feelings, but his poetry made Anne come alive.

"Who list her hunt, I put him out of doubt,
As well I may spend his time in vain.
And graven with diamonds in letters plain
There is written, her fair neck round about:

Noli me tangere, for Caesar's I am
And wild for to hold, though I seem tame."

Did Anne relish Wyatt's unrequited love? And did she consider herself to belong to the King? Surely that was just a fantasy. Here she was, a girl who had always been considered second to her sister in beauty, and she was now admired by at least two men, one of whom was the King? And yes, she saw herself as wild. She was no tame young lady to be played with and then discarded. I thought on these things, but I saw no sign of any liking between her and the King. I thought it pleased her to imagine that the King wanted her, but most likely his eye had alighted on a more conformable quarry.

At last, the lighter days came in, and the court became merry once more. In April, Will appeared in the Queen's presence chamber and asked her consent to escort me to the May Day revels. On hearing that he was training to become a lawyer, she smilingly gave consent. I was happy about this, not because I wanted my dear friend to become my lover, or anything embarrassing like that. No, I was just happy to see him again and spend a day with him. I wore my green gown again and twined sweet-smelling bluebells in my copper gold hair. Pinned to my gown I wore a small silver brooch, set with garnets. The Queen had given it me at Easter, and it was the first piece of jewellery that I had ever possessed.

Will met me at the palace gates, and we walked down together to the gardens beside the river, where there was dancing, singing, and games like blind man's buff. But Will wasn't looking at the revels. His eyes danced up and down me, taking in every detail of my May Day costume.

"By Jesu, I swear, I could not find a finer lady than you Kat, to spend my May Day with."

"Stop it! You're making me feel uncomfortable. I don't want any of that nonsense. Let's just do something together, like in the old days. Is Father free today?"

Will shook his head. "No, busy boiling sugar!" I looked at him, crestfallen. I had expected to be seeing the man I still considered my father today.

"But I have another treat for you, dear Kat. A debate so delicious, so dainty, that your sweet mind will love it. No, don't worry! No advances today, just discussion! Come, we are going up river!" He grabbed my hand and took me towards the landing stage, where the small boats waited for customers.

"Austin Friars!" Will said to the boatman, "I'm taking you to see where I live."

I looked doubtfully at him. "To Master Cromwell's house?" I was curious to see Will in his home surroundings but wasn't sure what he meant about a debate. Surely there was not much of interest there?

"Austin Friars, you know it. It is the Franciscan priory. Master Cromwell rents a house from them. It is a very fashionable part of London, you know. Erasmus lived there, and the ambassador to the Holy Roman Emperor has a house. It is so cosmopolitan, you see Italians, Flemish and even Africans on the streets around the house. Today, Master Cromwell is having a May Day dinner, and he told me to bring you. You will hear many interesting discussions at Master Cromwell's table!"

"I'll look stupid," I protested. "I'm just a maid servant." Will laughed at me.

"No, you won't," he assured me. "You are far from stupid. And Master Cromwell, he is a blacksmith's son. He has no care for status or gentility. He likes people who are clever and speak their mind."

When we got to Austin Friars, we disembarked and walked up to the house. It was close to the gateway to the Friary itself,

a little set back from the street. A goodly size, it was three sto-
reys tall, with a porch at the front leading into a large hall. I
was used to court apartments, with their luxury and decoration, but still, the hall impressed me. It was well proportioned,
with a blazing fire and tapestries showing religious scenes on
the wall. The long table was set ready for dinner, entwined
with green spring leaves and flowers. Groups of people were
starting to sit down, and some musicians at the end of the hall
were playing "The Merrie Month of May".

A stoutish man got up and came to meet us. After a moment
I realised it was Master Cromwell. He had put on weight since
I saw him at the Field of the Cloth of Gold, and his clothing
was better quality. He had on a black velvet doublet, slashed to
show a white linen shirt underneath and red hose.

"Mistress Kat, welcome!" He bowed courteously and I
swept him a deep curtsey. "You have grown since I last met
you. You were such a small girl then!" He smiled at me, and I
felt encouraged by him. Unlike so many others, I thought he
would not dismiss me as a mere serving maid.

"I told Will to bring you today. We will have a merry time
of it. We have my friend from Italy, John Calvacanti, we have
the ambassador Eustace Chapuys, and many others." He swept
his arm expansively around the room at the richly dressed
occupants. "But first you must meet my wife, my Elizabeth."
He beckoned to a small woman, dressed well in a blue velvet gown but with a simple coif on her head, much like my
mother had worn. She came up to us, and again, I curtseyed,
and Will bowed. She curtseyed herself, then took my hand.

"Mistress Kat, I have so much wanted to meet you. Will
tells me how clever you are. How you can read Latin and speak
French!" She smiled ruefully. "Now, my husband is a great linguist, but for myself, I am afraid all I can speak is the King's
English."

"You speak more sense in English than most do in any
other language, my dear," Cromwell said, smiling down at his

wife. "And we will be speaking in English today. I want to know, and you can tell me Kat, what are the fashions that the ladies of court most desire? I deal in cloth, as well as my clerking. I need to know what types and qualities of cloth I should import from Italy. What the ladies of the court wear today, the ladies of London will wear tomorrow, and by next year, even the ladies of York will be wearing them!"

Will spoke to his master and mistress. "I told Kat that we would be having a dainty debate today. She will be able to tell you all about the latest fashions."

"And maybe even a little of the latest news from the court?" asked Elizabeth Cromwell, a mischievous smile on her face. "Come sit by me, Mistress Kat, and Will can sit beside you. With my children being so young, I am so unaware of all the latest doings at court. I ask my husband, but will he spare the time to tell me how Princess Mary fares, or what the Queen is wearing this spring? He is a man, my dear!"

Dinner was held in the middle of the day, with the pale spring light pouring in through the glazed windows. Servants brought in dishes of roasted chicken, pheasant, and pork. There were salads of tender green leaves, the first of the season, and loaves of soft white bread. Afterwards, we ate creamy lemon posset with tiny, sweet biscuits. We drank a light, dry Italian wine with the scent of gooseberries. Looking down the table, I could see around forty people, and I could hear conversations in Italian, German and English. I spoke happily with Mistress Cromwell about the events at the court, and the fashions for this spring. I was then cross-questioned by Master Cromwell, who wanted exact details, and my estimation of the heaviness, the pile, the decoration of certain fabrics that were common at court. He might be working for Cardinal Wolsey now, but he did not see many of the court ladies during the course of his work, and I soon found out he was the kind of man who needed detail.

Occasionally, Will would take my hand and squeeze it. His

eyes were fixed on me whenever I looked. He was proud of me, I could tell. Mind you, he had always been proud of me, just as I had been proud of him. Feeling at ease, I held my own in the conversation, even joining in when it turned to religion. Master Cromwell had been working with Cardinal Wolsey to close some of the monasteries that were not serving God as they should, either because they were very small or because the monks had gotten used to an easy life.

"The Church needs reform," Master Cromwell said deliberately. "There's no doubt about it. And the Cardinal will use the money saved to pay for colleges for poor boys."

"What about poor girls?" I asked cheekily. He paused and chuckled. Will and Mistress Cromwell both smiled. "Why should there not be colleges for poor girls?" I asked. "I would have attended such a college, and maybe studied to become a lawyer!"

"Ah, Mistress Kat, you are well ahead of us!" Master Cromwell laughed. "But you would not want to be stuck in all day with smelly schoolboys! Not that I am against women's education. My daughters will be educated. But at home. At home, where they are safe, and respected."

"Ah, but Mistress Kat might become a lawyer one day, if she was able!" joked his wife. "Then she could take both you and Master Will on!"

"I am sure you could, Mistress Kat," Cromwell replied. "But for now, allow us men to learn. We will need much education to match the wit of women."

I was tired, and a little merry when Will took me back, and it seemed that all our old easiness together had returned. As he left me just outside the palace, I wrapped my arms around him.

"Hey, hold on! You know not what you do!" he admonished me. He felt so nice, and so hard and masculine I couldn't let go. He stood stiffly for a moment, and then he relented and put his arms around me. It felt as if I had come home, to a place where I never wanted to leave. Tenderly, tentatively, he bent his lips to mine and kissed me. His lips tasted sweet, and I loved the feeling of my smooth skin against his stubble. I felt like I'd never felt before, somehow wild and excited and scared all at the same time. I pushed myself against him, and he groaned in frustration.

He pulled back. "I'm not going to rush you Kat. Now go. The Queen will be waiting for you. Take my kiss with you." He kissed me once more and then pushed me away.

"Goodnight, sweet Kat. I will see you very soon."

In fact, I didn't see Will for several months. I knew that Master Cromwell worked him hard. The court swung into its summer patterns, moving between palaces, jousting, hunting and picnicking in the lush green parks owned by the King. At Windsor, the ladies, after months of shivering and pulling fur tippets around their throats, started to bemoan their hot, heavy gowns, and change their linen several times a day. Queen Katherine remained serene through all of this, she never seemed to sweat or look uncomfortable, no matter how thick and stiff her ornate gowns were. When there was no hunting, we passed the days walking in the hedged gardens, reading from sacred texts, and singing. Midsummer passed, and we moved into July. Now the King was also at Windsor, although he did not spend much time with the Queen.

"The King desires the Queen to attend him in his chamber!" The pageboy's voice broke the peace of the sleepy afternoon. The ladies were all playing cards, stopping occasionally to fan themselves. Suddenly, the household sprung into action. The Queen rose from her chair and smoothed out her skirts. At once everyone got up. Lady Maria Willoughby glanced at the Queen anxiously, while Lady Elizabeth Boleyn adjusted her girdle. Lady Anne Boleyn was holding her cards up as if she was about to read her future. Deliberately, she placed them down on the table. Two of the women hovered beside the Queen, checking that her hood was on straight, that no wisps of hair were escaping. Lady Anne Boleyn put down her cards deliberately on the table, one by one. I removed my apron and checked my cap. We were all going to follow the Queen to the King's chamber. Whatever this summons meant, we would be there to witness it.

Slowly and calmly the Queen processed through her chambers, her ladies and servants walking behind her. As she passed the outer rooms, conversations hushed, and courtiers bowed. I felt proud walking behind her, this great Queen of England, who commanded so much respect.

At last, we came to the great doors of the presence chamber. The Queen paused as the two guards flung them open and then bowed. Inside there was a great mell of people, but as they saw the Queen approaching, they moved to the sides of the chamber and let her move through, step by step. Lady Elizabeth Boleyn held her train, towering over the tiny Queen in front of her.

Queen Katherine walked to the end of the hall and processed towards the King's private chambers. Immediately, the trumpeters blew a fanfare, and she walked through into a room full of men. King Henry was seated under his cloth of estate, and there was a small group of men standing to his side. I noticed the Cardinal, the Archbishop of Canterbury and the Duke of Norfolk. The Queen curtseyed deeply to the King, and he rose and took her by the hand, leading her to the chair that was placed beside his. Lady Boleyn arranged her train and then stepped back to join the rest of us. This was a procedure that we all knew. It happened almost every day. The exact moment when the trumpets sounded, the entry of the Queen, all of this was calibrated exactly.

As the trumpeters ceased, the King held up his hand for silence. He looked troubled; his face creased with a frown. All conversations stilled, and all eyes were on him.

"Welcome," he said. "Madam, I thank you for your attendance. I have a great matter to inform you of. A very grave and difficult issue that has been concerning me. My conscience is troubled, and it is right that I share this with you all."

Queen Katherine leaned forward, looking at him sympathetically. Although they had become more distant with each other, he was her husband, and it was her place to support him.

"After extensive studies of the Bible and conversations with my confessor, I must tell you that a terrible mistake has come to light!" Cardinal Wolsey and the Archbishop whispered to each other, but the King raised his hand again, and they ceased. Uncharacteristically, he was looking down at the floor. His normal, confident glance had disappeared. He almost mumbled.

"I have doubts about the validity of my marriage." The Queen started up, I could see her face white with surprise. She gripped the handles of her chair and fixed her eyes even more intently upon him. He looked at her pleadingly, but she did not smile.

"These verses in the Bible have been brought to my attention by priests and scholars. They are from Leviticus. 'If a man shall take his brother's wife, it is an unclean thing – they shall be childless'." A gasp of amazement swept the chamber. I looked around at the ladies beside me, and they were absolutely taken aback. Meanwhile, King Henry painfully continued.

"Katherine, when you came to England, you came to wed my brother, Prince Arthur, which you did in great state and joy. You and my brother then lived as man and wife in Ludlow, until his sad death some months later. You are Arthur's wife, and therefore our marriage was not valid."

"Your Majesty," the Queen whispered. "You know I was never Arthur's wife fully. Why do you say otherwise?"

"How do I know Katherine? There are differing accounts of your wedding night, differing accounts that I have heard and marked full well."

"But Your Majesty, these were not true. I have many witnesses who can swear to my purity when I came to you. And, we had a dispensation from the Pope to marry, which specifically provided against those verses."

"Katherine, that dispensation could not cancel out those verses." King Henry was in his stride again now, speaking loudly and clearly so that we could all hear. "I am as distressed as you are, dear lady, to realise this. Would it were not for your previous marriage to my brother, I would choose no other wife but you! I grieve that your years of service now mean nothing because of the sham that was our marriage. You never were the Queen, my dear."

"Never? Not during all the dangers we faced together, all the love we shared, all the children I bore for you?" The Queen's voice was anguished. I felt the anger build inside me. How dare he put her through this? I hated him at that moment, more than I had hated anyone else. My dear sweet Queen Katherine, who had given him her life, to be treated like a halfpenny whore!

The King was kindly, patronising. "But my dear, we have not been blessed with children. Those you bore all died, except for Mary. Surely, you must see that this proves the verse to be correct."

"But we have a child. We have Princess Mary. Your child, whom you have been preparing to take the crown!" The Queen's voice rang out across the hall. King Henry answered her soothingly.

"She is a female child, my dear. I have said before, the English will never accept a female ruler. I tell you again, were it otherwise, you would always be my Queen. But, you have never been so because our marriage was invalid. My conscience has troubled me deeply on this issue. I can tell you, I have not slept for many nights. I have prayed that I might have read the verse wrongly, and that we could go back to the happy old times. But don't you see Katherine, those times were built on a lie?"

"Our marriage was no lie!" Katherine spoke passionately.

"Your Majesty, you know that! I have been a true wife to you these eighteen years. I have obeyed you, supported you, loved you, like no other!"

"Katherine, my dear, I have spoken to eminent scholars and priests about this matter. I have stayed long into the night debating with the Archbishop here, and the Cardinal. They both tell me that our so-called marriage was not valid." Cardinal Wolsey and the Archbishop both nodded uncomfortably to confirm this.

"So how have they, have you, given me the title, respect and legitimacy of being Queen? I did not notice these doubts when I led the troops against the Scots, or when I delivered a young son to Your Majesty?"

"A young son that did not live!" King Henry retorted.

"A young son who lived for seven weeks, until God took him for himself. He was a living child!" Queen Katherine's face crumpled, and she started to cry. I had never seen this before; she was so much a Queen that she would never normally expose her tears publicly. King Henry's eyes looked moist, and he stood up before her, holding his hand out to her as if to comfort her.

"You are shocked, Madam, as I was. And believe me Katherine, I would that it were any other way. I love you dearly, and I do not wish for your soul or mine to be in danger because of our adultery."

"Adultery!" Queen Katherine spat. "It is not me who has committed adultery, and you know that! You have had your mistresses, and I have turned a blind eye. You have dandled your bastards on your knee while you sent our daughter away! And always, through everything, I have been your wife. Your wife!"

"Katherine, this matter is difficult for both of us." The King spoke soothingly. "It needs to be decided in church law. I pray that my doubts are resolved. But until it has been debated by the great theologians and princes of the church, we cannot live as man and wife. Retire, dear Katherine. I will give you a grand country house with orchards and a park. You shall have everything you desire. Or, if you would rather, you could go to a nunnery and live quietly there. That might suit you better, the chance to lead a religious life?"

"A nunnery? I was called by God to the position of Queen and wife, not of nun!"

"Just while the matter is decided, dear Katherine." The King looked pleadingly at her. Queen Katherine rose, wiping the tears from her eyes, and curtseyed to him.

"My husband, my lord, I was destined to be by your side all of our lives, and that is what I will do. Excuse me, my lord, I have some shirts of yours that I need to finish."

I do not know how the Queen managed to leave with the same dignity and grace as she had entered. But she walked through the privy chamber and, stick erect, stepped down through the presence chamber, the courtiers, all bowing and curtseying to her, although some half-heartedly. She waited for the guards to open the doors and passed through them without a backward glance. Her ladies followed, most of them ashen faced. I noticed, though, that Anne Boleyn looked composed, and her mother had a small smile on her face. Had they known what was going to happen?

We processed slowly back through the state apartments, through the chambers, until we reached the Queen's quarters. It took a minute or two for us all to enter the chamber, before the doors were closed.

"Ai eee! Oh, sweet Virgin Mother, what have I done to deserve this?" The Queen was wailing, an animalistic sound that scared me. She kicked off her shoes, took her hood off and threw it to the floor. Then she limped to her big bed and lay on it weeping.

"What evil demon bewitched the King? Henry, who has loved me, who has fought for me, as I fought for him. Henry, who swore to love me forever? Does he not remember that the

Pope gave us that dispensation to wed? And he knew, he *knew*, I was pure when I came to him! How can he deny that? And what will become of Mary? Will he disinherit her?"

Lady Maria Willoughby lay down on the bed beside her, cradling her mistress's head in her arms. "Nothing will happen to Princess Mary. The King is in a miasma of doubt, his thoughts are troubling him. But we shall pray to our Virgin Mother, and that doubt will clear. He loves you Catalina. Hush now sweet lady. All is not lost. Your place in the King's heart is secure. We will get theologians to reassure him. He is a good son of the church. He will come round."

"A nunnery! A nunnery! He may as well wish me in my grave!" Queen Katherine cried. She was very pious, but we all knew she saw herself as a married woman, and a Queen. She was not going to allow those positions to be stolen from her.

CHAPTER 11

The next few months were quiet in the Queen's chambers. Lady Anne Boleyn moved out, into a suite of apartments that were very grand. As with Lady Mary's chamber, they were close to the King's chambers. Unlike Mary's though, they were large and airy, with windows looking out over the Thames. I heard that they were furnished with the finest tapestries and carpets on the walls, with the ceiling bosses carved with Anne's initials.

"Nothing but the best for my Anne," Lady Elizabeth Boleyn said. "The King has supervised all of the arrangements." She remained in the Queen's household, even though her own daughter was now acknowledged to be in a relationship with the King.

"You should see the fine velvets he has bought for her, and the jewellery. She is fit to be a queen, I can tell you that," she told Jane Seymour when they were sorting through the Queen's dresses.

"But, but, but, she will never be Queen," said Jane, rather boldly for her. "The King will never leave the Queen. He will realise that their marriage is valid, accordingly to the Holy Church, and it will all be alright again."

"Tell your daughter to get as many presents from the King as she can," said Lady Stafford. "For he will leave her, as he left her sister."

"Oh no, this is a much more serious affair," protested Lady Boleyn. "They are not intimate, for she will not allow it. They debate theology and write music together."

Lady Stafford gave me a look that said, "if you believe that, you'll believe anything." I bent my head to hide a smile and continued with my sewing. From what the servants said, I knew that the King and Anne were very much in love – but whether he had taken her to his bed, no one knew. It was a matter for debate on most mornings, when the court looked at the King and wondered if he had slept that night, and if not, why. But Anne's family maintained that the relationship had not been consummated, and would not be unless Anne was married to Henry. That seemed impossible at the time, so all debate tended to end there.

I had the chance to see Lady Anne's apartments that autumn. Will had a day off, and he met me outside the palace gates.

"Come, we're not going far today," he pulled at my arm and brought me back towards the palace. "This is interesting, you'll enjoy it."

We walked through the great hall, through chamber after chamber, until we reached what I knew were Anne Boleyn's apartments. He led me into a large hall, where a number of men and women had gathered together. I recognised Thomas Cromwell, who nodded at us both, and Thomas Wyatt. The further door opened, and George and Anne Boleyn entered, leading a man who was obviously a scholar with his long gown and ascetic face.

"Ladies and Gentlemen, we are fortunate here to have Hugh Latimer, the noted priest and scholar from the University of Cambridge to debate with us about the need for reform and rebirth within the church." It was Lady Anne Boleyn speaking while George listened approvingly. All of those present clapped their hands and settled themselves down to listen to the eminent scholar.

"He says that the church needs to become simpler and lose some of the ritual that hides God," Will whispered to me. "There's too many saints' days, and too many monks being paid to say prayers that might not work anyway."

"The Queen wouldn't agree with you," I cried. Several people turned round to look at me, and I modified my voice. "The Queen is the most religious woman I know! She is an example to everyone."

Will turned to me. "Kat, the Queen is a good woman. But the times are changing. She follows the old ways with a faithful heart, and I respect that. But now, we want there to be a simpler communication with God, and less of the corruption and indulgences shown by the church."

The debate was long, and I followed only some of it. Lady Anne Boleyn asked many questions of Latimer, and his answers were tightly argued and complex. I wanted to know what was wrong with the lovely saints' days? Why could the Queen not use the girdle of the Virgin Mary to keep her safe through labour?

But as Will explained to me later, too much power was invested in the hands of the church:

"Simple people, we can pray to God without asking a priest. Yes, they will always be there to lead the worship, but if I want to pray for Mother's soul, I can do that myself. I do not have to ask a priest to do it."

Daughter, now we are a Protestant nation, and these ideas are part of our identity. But then, even those small reforms were thought of as being revolutionary. Lady Anne Boleyn was only one of a number of people who favoured reform in the church. I knew that she encouraged scholars and theologians to come and debate with her and wondered if those views were getting back to the King.

As the meeting was drawing to a close and people were

standing up to leave, Lady Anne came over to me. Her face was glowing, and for the first time I could see that some might call her beautiful.

"Why, Mistress Kat, what do you here? You are welcome, of course, but does not the Queen require your services?"

"I am here with my friend Master Cooke, who works for Master Cromwell. The Queen has given me leave." I explained.

Will bowed to Lady Anne. "It has been an interesting discussion," he observed. "We have enjoyed it, your Ladyship."

"Good! Will you are welcome here, with your master. And Kat, I want you to come more often. You remember our singing afternoons? I miss your lute playing and your sweet voice. My brother is never in tune," she complained, turning her dazzling eyes upon her brother. He laughed and shrugged his shoulders.

"That is because I do not always sing to your tune sister," he said. "Beautiful though it may be." She laid her hand on his sleeve and gazed at him.

"I do not agree, Kat, what do you think? Surely a brother should be influenced by his sister in all things?" I looked at Will for a moment before giving a careful reply.

"Brothers should serve their sisters, my Lady. But then sisters must serve their brothers too." Will and I shared a smile at this. We'd had no more embraces since May Day, but the attraction between us was strong. And yet, and yet, I still could not forget that he had been my brother.

"What a very politic reply, Kat. 'Tis a shame you are only a serving maid, for you would do well at court with your skills."

"Thank you, my Lady," I blushed to the roots of my hair. In truth, I liked this new breed of people who were less obsessed with rank and privilege. I felt that they saw me for what I was rather than just my lowly position.

"I need you, Kat, in my household. I need your sweet voice, your lute, and your wonderful secretary handwriting!" Lady Anne was being imperious now. "Promise me, you will visit my chambers as you did. Sometime in the future, I may be able to offer you a position. How like you that?"

"Very much indeed, my lady," I answered clearly. I was already imagining being part of this glamorous set. I'd still serve the Queen, of course I would. But I would become more than a plaything, a comforter and a confidante. I would be able to be myself, whoever that was.

And so, for the next year, it went on. At night, I would be in the Queen's chambers, curled up in bed, watching over her while she slept. In the mornings we would attend Mass, and then there would be dinner at the middle of the day. After that I would slip off to Lady Anne's apartment, carrying sheet music and my lute, ready for several hours of singing, composing and dancing. Many of the younger ladies went there, and the afternoons were lively, with much laughter and teasing between them. They would discuss important matters like whether a lady should be cruel to her lover ("Of course she should," said Lady Anne, "she should put him to the test.") Sometimes there would be a cleric there, or a scholar, who would talk about how to reach God, or the political situation in Europe. It was so exciting for me, especially when Lady Anne asked me to sing. I had such a pure voice then, she said it touched her heart. I didn't see many signs of softness in her, but she lived so much behind a mask it was hard to tell. I sensed she was fragile, but also dangerous.

It didn't stop me being fascinated with her. I remember one afternoon when, unusually, we were alone. Anne spent the first half hour lecturing me about how I should braid my hair, and then cross questioning me about Will.

"So Kat, will you take him for your lover?" she asked bluntly. "He is a handsome fellow, no doubt of it, and he works for Master Cromwell."

"No, I will not," I swore. "I do not wish to marry."

Anne looked at me strangely and then said, "In that, Mistress Kat, you and I are together. Oh, I wanted to marry once, but I was prevented, and now I see how lucky I am."

"But surely, your Ladyship, you will marry sometime?" It was always easy to talk to her, and it felt at that moment that we were like sisters.

"To be subject to a man? No Kat, I do not wish that. Men are messy, difficult. I want to be my own mistress, not tied down to one man's whims. Look at Mary! Oh, she had a good time for a while, but now where is she? Stuck in the country with two small children and not one soul to talk to. I could not do that."

"But, even if you do not marry, the King...." I ventured, wondering at myself for asking this.

"I am not the King's mistress, if that is what you are wondering Kat. The King and I, we are kindred souls," she sighed. "But I have told his Majesty I will never be his mistress."

"So where does that leave you?" I asked. "Surely King Henry will not endure this platonic relationship forever?"

"He will have to," she said flatly. "For I will yield my maidenhead to no one but a husband. And as I do not intend to marry, he will have to endure."

I was puzzled. Surely, she did not mean that she would never marry? I realised that if she did want to marry the King, she had many hurdles to overcome, and maybe it felt safer to announce that she was not interested in matrimony.

"Maybe he will go back to the Queen," I said, "she misses him so much."

"Maybe he will." She shrugged her shoulders. "It depends if he is willing to pay the price." I looked into her deep black eyes. I did not know if, like me, she had truly decided marriage was not for her, or whether she had embarked on a dangerous game and wasn't sure where it would lead her. She knew that Queen Katherine was a clever, determined woman, as she was. And she was uncertain of her position at that time. She truly didn't know what the future would bring. Maybe the King would take her as his mistress. But Anne was determined that wouldn't happen, and King Henry wasn't a man to take a woman by force. Maybe they would remain platonic lovers, whose love was never consummated? Or maybe the King would simply get bored and move on. Anything was possible, and she knew it.

Daughter, people say that Anne Boleyn was hard, and so she was, on the surface. But she was vulnerable too. She wasn't from the grand old aristocracy, and she wasn't beautiful like her sister. She just had her wit, and her courage to drive her on. I could sympathise with that.

"Don't you feel bad for the Queen?" I asked. "She has given the King everything, and now he wants to just get rid of her, like a dirty towel."

"A country house is hardly a dirty towel, Kat!" Anne snapped. "The King will make her very comfortable. All she has to do is to agree that their marriage was not valid. She will be treated with all honour, and be comfortable for the rest of her life."

"She just wants to be his wife," I said, "like she's been for years."

"This is not my doing Kat," Anne rubbed her eyes. "The King makes his own decisions. He knows I will not give up my maidenhead except to my husband. But I would not force him to divorce her. If he feels the marriage is good, he may continue in it as long as they both live. But Kat, he wants me. And I have learned that the King is used to getting what he wants."

However, the time went by without any sign of the King getting what he wanted. It was all very strange. On public occasions and at Mass, the King was polite to Katherine. But privately he wasn't above threatening Queen Katherine, which made us ladies angry. He told her one evening that he believed she was scheming to get her nephew, the Holy Roman Emperor, involved. If she asked for his assistance, Henry told her she would be committing treason and face the consequences.

"But he is my nephew. He is concerned about his aunt!" Queen Katherine had protested.

"He may support you with his heart, but not his soldiery, is that clear? If you encourage him, you will never see your daughter again," he threatened. Queen Katherine blanched at this, and spoke intensely.

"I have served England for over twenty-five years, Your Majesty. I would do no harm to England. There will be no invasion, I can assure you of that. But please, I beg you, do not bar me from seeing Princess Mary, my jewel, the heir to your throne." She sank to her knees, imploring him. He looked impatiently at her and turned to go,

"You may see Mary at the moment. But do not try my patience, Madam, I am warning you!"

Will told me that Master Cromwell was now looking for Queen Katherine's old servants and the nobles who had witnessed her short marriage to Prince Arthur. They'd been told to search for anyone who might be able to testify that the marriage had indeed been consummated and that, therefore, Queen Katherine's marriage to King Henry was invalid.

"Poor lady," I said to Will. "To have people trailing through your private life, old men getting excited by sexual details. It isn't right, Will. She is too good for that!"

"She is a good woman, I'll acknowledge that," said Will. "But the King orders us to find evidence. That is what we have to do. The King has doubts about his marriage..."

"He wants a new wife!" I protested. Will held up his hand.

"Yes, that too, but the basis of this, the main issue, is the doubt about the validity of the marriage. And that is what has to be determined."

I knew that like me, Will had to obey orders, but I wasn't happy. I said goodnight to him rather snappishly and didn't embrace him as normal. I went back to the Queen's apartments in a depressed mood.

She was sitting in front of her dressing table with her hair down her back. I took up the ivory comb and started combing it, slowly, calmly, just as she liked. The ladies were tidying up the room, putting away the cards, the goblets, the lutes and mandolins.

"Will there be anything else, Your Majesty?" Lady Willoughby asked.

"Yes, ask the pageboy to bring some wine and two goblets, Maria. After that, you may go." The Queen, as always, a queen.

"Of course, Catalina." Lady Willoughby curtseyed and left the chamber. Moments later a servant came in with a tray, carrying a flagon of wine and two goblets. She placed it down on the table beside the Queen and left.

The Queen poured two glasses. "Come on Kat, drink with me. I need to talk tonight and tell you the tale of my first wedding. So many people doubt me now, and accuse me of lying, but I know the truth. Maria Willoughby knows it too, but no one else now. I want to tell you because you are my own sweet Kat, and you will never betray me."

I took a sip of my wine. It was sweet, probably German, I thought. I was quite good at identifying the different wines that were served at court.

"Your Majesty, tell me whatever you wish. I am here to listen."

"For tonight, do not use Your Majesty. Tonight, call me Catalina, as Maria does. Tonight, I am talking to you as a mother to a daughter, a sister to a sister."

"Of course, Your Ma.... Er Catalina," I said, amazed by this development. The Queen drank deeply of her wine and then started to talk.

"Do you know how old I was when I married Prince Arthur? I was thirteen, four years younger than you are now, Kat. Of course, that was by proxy, I was still in Spain, but from then on, I was considered his wife and referred to as the Princess of Wales. Oh, that windy and cold country! But apparently, such an honour to be a Prince or Princess of Wales, it signalled you were heir to the throne.

"I left Spain in 1501, at fifteen, never to see my homeland again! But it was exciting, the journey, travelling through

Spain, taking part in all the celebrations. I knew my marriage would seal the alliance between England and Spain, and that I would play a major part in ensuring peace between my birth country and the country I was to count as my home. Then we put to sea. Kat, it was a terrible sea journey. It took five days of storms before we reached the coast of England. Plymouth, it was, right down in the West Country. My first sight of England shrouded in mist and rain!

"I first saw Arthur as I travelled up towards London. He came down with his father to meet us, Henry was there too, only he was quite a lot younger than I. He was a talkative child who enjoyed being with me. I think we were fated to be together, even then. But of course, all eyes were on me and Arthur at this time.

"Arthur was tall and slim, with a sensitive face. I liked him from the first moment I met him. He was kind to me. We spoke Latin to each other, the only language we had in common, although at first it was difficult as we had different accents! Still, we were both young, and keen to learn. Like me, Prince Arthur was religious, and we celebrated Mass together the day after we first met. After that, there was the long journey to London, where we would be married.

"Oh, the parties we had in London! I was welcomed by the Queen Elizabeth of York, and her daughters. She was a kind woman and looked after me well. The night before the wedding, we danced and drank and sang until late. We had such fun together, and I felt I was already part of their family. Earlier in the day I had met the King's grandmother, Lady Margaret Beaufort. She was very pious, strict and stern. But I was used to Spanish ladies who were like that, so it didn't upset me.

"I got to bed late, and tossed and turned for a while until I finally dropped to sleep. Maria de Salinas, you know her, she is now Lady Willoughby, she slept with me. I wanted to wake her up and talk, but I didn't think that was fair. We all had a long day to come.

"My wedding dress! Oh, my wedding dress was so beautiful, Kat! It was white satin, as pure as snow, with the bodice fitting closely to my breasts, and the skirts billowing out over my farthingale. The English ladies were not used to farthingales, and I remember it occasioned much comment that I wore one. I had a gold circlet on my head, holding my veil in place. Kat, it was silk, with diamonds, pearls and gold sparkling through it. It was hard for me to see, but I felt I was in my own little heaven, surrounded by heavenly bodies. I was a romantic, and I loved Prince Arthur already.

"But it wasn't Prince Arthur who took me to the cathedral. Waiting for me at the palace door was nine-year-old Prince Henry, brimming with confidence and life as he took my hand. The Queen's sister, Lady Cecily, held my train as we walked into the great church of Saint Paul's.

"The crowds are out to greet you, sister," said Henry. I could see he was enjoying their attention, smiling, touching his cap, and exchanging pleasantries with the crowd.

"I trust I will be worthy of them," I answered solemnly, looking down at the ground so I didn't fall over my enormous skirts. Henry didn't answer. Instead, he was looking teasingly at a small child in the crowd who was being held out to him by its mother. He dropped my hand for an instant, darted over, and kissed the child before returning to my side. A cheer went up. Already, he was a favourite.

"He was more dignified when he walked me down the aisle, in place of my father. Through the veil I peered at Prince Arthur, standing in front of the Archbishop. He was wearing white satin too, with Tudor roses embroidered on his doublet. I moved to stand beside him, and a ghost of a smile crossed his face. He was a handsome lad, but not like King Henry. He had a thoughtful manner, and I remember he would speak slowly and deliberately. He was not a charmer, like Prince Henry. He was a thinker, and someone who always liked to weigh up his options before he made any decisions. I knew I could love him then, and Kat, I did love him, very much.

"The wedding took hours. First, there were the agreements read out about my dowry, and then the endowment that I would receive from King Henry VII to keep me and my household. Only after all the business was transacted did we take our vows and then process proceed around the church, showing ourselves to the crowds. At last, we were married.

"But we couldn't just enjoy ourselves like any merchant's son or seamstress's daughter might. We had the wedding banquet to sit through, and I was seated next to my Spanish Archbishop. We couldn't just dance and talk together and get to know about each other. We sat at different tables, two shining orbs that would later become one, or that was what the world expected.

"After some hours, my ladies came to fetch me and help me prepare. Maria was close to me as always. She was not married then, and neither of us knew what I could expect of a wedding night. The conception of an heir was important, but can you believe it Kat, I didn't know how that happened!

"My ladies undressed me and sponged me all over with rose water. Then they dropped a fine silk nightgown over my head, thin as mist. My hair was unpinned and combed until it shone. They rubbed creams and unguents into my feet, my hands and my legs. Finally, they helped me climb into the great bed and slip underneath the sheets, my heart pounding.

"Maria whispered to me, wishing me well, and told me to tell her how it was like tomorrow. I can remember smiling foolishly and telling her I was sure it would be interesting!

"She told me she wanted to know everything and planted a kiss on my forehead. We could hear the sound of music and men's voices coming from outside the room. The bridegroom was being escorted to the bridal chamber. As was tradition, his nobles and friends would accompany him, and watch us being bedded. He just had to get into the bed, I had been assured, and then they would leave us alone. At that point, our married life would start.

"When Arthur got in beside me he was trembling. He coughed, and I could see that his hands were trembling. I felt sorry for him then. All the men were crowding round, making rude jokes, while he sat at the far side of the bed from me, clutching at the sheets.

"Two priests were blessing the bed and sprinkling holy water on us while Prince Arthur's father, Henry VII, addressed his son, wishing him a happy married life and many children. The courtiers all crowded round, wishing him luck, telling him to be strong, and urging him to breathe fire into the Tudor dragon. Kat, he and I were just so shy. We just sat there, looking down at our hands, praying that all the people would leave! At last they did, and we had some blessed silence.

"After a minute I spoke. I asked him if he found me fair. I was clumsy, but I was trying to welcome him into my arms. He turned and looked at me from under his clouded eyes. He called me sweet Katharine and swore that he found me passing fair. I can remember he wanted to ask me something, but he was too shy to say it. At that moment we both laughed. He was a boy, Kat, just a boy.

"Then he plucked up the courage to suggest we both took off our nightgowns and look at each other. I agreed, and we both scrambled out from under the covers. I was shy, of course, but I knew that my husband should know my nakedness, and so I pulled the thin slip over my head, just as he emerged from his shift. He was thin, very thin and his chest had yet to broaden. But his arms were wiry and covered in a fine golden down of hair. He stared at me, looking me up and down as I lay on the bed.

"He told me I was beautiful and asked to touch me. He reached out a hand, and very gently, very hesitantly, started to caress my breasts. I cast my eyes downwards, and saw, for the first time, his genitals. His penis was small, Kat, and it

hung over his balls. I had never seen such a sight before Kat."
The Queen stopped suddenly, becoming aware of the private
nature of her conversation.

"I should not tell you really, you are still a maid, but oh
Kat, I need to talk to someone I can trust." Her voice was
hoarse with emotion.

I replied immediately, "But the dogs in the street. I have
seen them Your Majesty. I know more than you think!"

She laughed and poured us both some more wine.

"So you know a little. But you are a good girl, of that, I am
sure. I was a good girl. I was sheltered. We were not allowed
freedom to be with men as you are in the English court. I had
no idea of men Kat, no idea at all. To me, Prince Arthur was
the very model of a man, and I was destined to love him, so
that was that. Well, we hugged each other Kat, and I stroked
his hair, and then he climbed on top of me. I wasn't sure I liked
that, but I knew I had to do my duty, so I let him. He fumbled
for a bit, moving around on top of me, and I felt the hardness
of his young body, and the softness of his genitals. He was not
aroused Kat, and I didn't know that – how could I?

"We rolled around on top of the bed, embracing each
other, for some time. It was nice, but it was not married love
Kat. He never came inside me, never! After about half an hour,
he rolled off me, and told me we should sleep. I felt uncomfortable in my nakedness, so I reached out for my nightgown
and pulled it on again. He copied me, telling me he was cold.
And so we lay there side by side, not touching. He fell asleep
almost immediately, but I couldn't still my thoughts.

"So I wondered, was this what married people did? It
seemed bearable, but a bit embarrassing. And why hadn't I
felt the pain, and also the joy that women whispered about
behind their hands while playing cards in the afternoons?
Had I done something wrong? But Kat, I had submitted to my
husband's wishes, as a good Christian wife should. I decided
not to worry, and composed myself to sleep.

"The next morning, I was woken by the sound of Prince Arthur coughing. He sat up in our bed, his slim body shaking. I asked him if he was alright, and asked him if I could get him a drink. I thought his throat must be dry. I didn't know then that he already had the malady that killed him, and that every morning his body would be wracked by coughing.

"Kat, he left me then and stumbled to the door of our chamber. He almost fell through it into a crowd of his courtiers. I could hear them offering him some small ale, and after a while the coughing stopped. He said something, and they all laughed. I didn't know then Kat, but he had been boasting about being 'in Spain' during the night, which had made him thirsty. I was upset about that. I felt it wasn't fitting for him to joke about me. But I thought I had to bear it. I was a wife now and we were definitely married.

"It wasn't until later that day, when I spoke to one of my Spanish ladies, a married woman, that I learnt that what we had done was not the sexual union I had been expecting. Still, I thought, we had time, and as we got used to each other, things would happen. We had lots of parties after the wedding, and we made merry. But nothing happened when we shared a bed, and after a week Prince Arthur even stopped coming to my chamber.

"I wondered about him. Did he not find me pleasing? But I realised quite soon that he was not healthy like his brother. I think he was not strong enough to bed a woman, but he couldn't bring himself to admit it. So he told his courtiers that he had consummated the marriage. Can you imagine a Prince of Wales having to say that he was not fit enough to continue his dynasty? I was humiliated at the time, but I feel sorry for him now, Kat. In truth, I know and I will swear to Almighty God that I was only Prince Arthur's wife in name. My husband, the husband who took my maidenhead, is King Henry, the man who showed me the true delight of the marriage bed. And he will be my husband until the day I die."

CHAPTER

12

I was shocked by everything that had happened. By confiding in me, Queen Katherine had changed my picture of her. To me, she had been the Queen, the magnificent consort of King Henry Eighth, but confession had made her seem very vulnerable to me. In a way, she seemed more of a woman to me, and less of a Queen. I loved her, but I was no longer dazzled by her. She looked older now, and she complained of feeling stiff in the mornings.

Maria was constantly at the Queen's side now, watching over her like a concerned mother. Sometimes the Queen was as normal, but on other days, she did not bother to eat. It was always Maria who managed to get her to eat a little pottage or a sliver of chicken in cream.

It was good to escape the gloom of the Queen's household for the lively atmosphere I found at Anne Boleyn's chambers. Yes, I felt a little guilty about it, but the people who flocked around Anne were young, like me. They were full of new ideas, about religion, about poetry, about men and women. Lady Anne read the Bible in French. That was quite revolutionary then. It had always been in Latin so that the common people needed it to be interpreted by a priest. But now, there was a move to translate it into everyday language. Lady Anne let me read her French Bible. My French was good enough to understand every word. It was quite thrilling. I might be told by the priest that I should obey my betters, and always accept my place at the bottom of the hierarchy. But, reading the Bible, I understood that Jesus had no hierarchy. He was the Son of God, but he came to save us as an ordinary man. That released a spirit in me that I had long kept down. I was no longer willing to be humble and to fade into the background.

I was a good singer, and I knew it. Lady Anne knew it as well, and she encouraged me to sing in her chambers. I would accompany myself on the lute, and sometimes the virginals. Sometimes, I would be applauded by lords of the realm, great ladies and ministers of the King. That was quite something for the girl from nowhere! Will came occasionally to these afternoons, although he was very busy. I knew he was trying to trace servants and courtiers who had been with the Queen around the time of her wedding to Prince Arthur. The King was desperate to find evidence that Katherine and Arthur had been intimate, for then he could divorce Katherine. But so far, nothing had been found. The English courtiers that had attended the wedding were definite that Prince Arthur had consummated his marriage with Katherine, but then they would scarcely say otherwise.

Lady Anne did not talk of these matters. Her position was clear. She would not allow the King to make her his mistress. She would only be a wife, and if Henry was not in a position to make her his wife, then so be it. She would not yield, but nor would she scheme against Katherine. She was a religious woman, although in a totally different way to Queen Katherine.

One day, we were on our own in her chambers. The court had gone hunting, and she, unusually, had a headache. She asked me to stay with her and make her more comfortable. I sat on the side of the bed where she lay, straight and slim. I took a linen cloth, soaked it in a camomile infusion, wrung it out and applied it to her forehead. She breathed in the scent of the herb and started to relax.

"That is better Kat. Yes, do that again." I repeated the action, pressing the cloth gently against her hairline, leaving small tendrils of damp brown hair curling around her face.

"Kat, I have had discussions with the King over many months," she said. "He has tried every ruse, every game, to get me into his bed. It has made me so tense and my life so difficult." She sighed and turned her head to look into my eyes.

"Kat, I know you love Queen Katherine, and I respect you for that. She has been like a mother to you. I told you last Christmas that I was no threat to the Queen. I would not be the King's mistress, much as I admire and esteem him. But Kat, he has continued to press his suit, begging me to be his mistress, again and again. He told me he would be faithful to me alone, but I would not give in. I tell you Kat, it has been wearing! I would have happily retired from the court, but no, he would not allow it. He thought that one day I would yield. But he did not know me." She smiled. "As a child, I would fight with George or Mary. No matter how hard they hit me, I would not give in. They can tell you; I am obdurate."

"I know my lady; you told me once you didn't forgive a slight either." Anne laughed at my effrontery.

"Yes indeed Kat, I do not forget those who do me harm. But you have done me no harm. I like you well. That is why I want to talk with you now. Matters have changed. I need your good opinion, and so I must explain. As you know, the King and I have been at a stalemate, him pressing me while I resisted. But the King has shifted his position. He has asked me to be his wife." She looked at me, and there was a glint of excitement but also fear in her eyes. She knew she was moving onto a worldwide stage, where there was glory, but also no pity.

"But he can't marry you. He is married!" I protested.

"Kat, his marriage to the Queen is invalid, the Bible shows us so. Their souls are in danger by continuing with this farce!" Anne sat up on the bed, her face animated. "The King does not wish her to risk her soul any longer, he must act to bring it to an end. I wanted to ask you Kat. Do you think the Queen might change her mind? If she agreed to an annulment, it would be so much easier for her. She would be honoured by all, and the King would treat her as his sister."

"Lady Anne, she believes it is her destiny to live her life out as his wife and his Queen. She will not change that belief. She is... a little... like you."

She nodded, acknowledging the truth of what I had said.

"But Kat, could you not, for her own good, give her counsel that an annulment would be much the most pleasant way to resolve this problem?"

"My lady, I respect you, as you know. But did you know that the Cardinal and Thomas Cromwell are searching for blood-stained bridal sheets and asking around Europe for those who will testify she was intimate with Prince Arthur? Is that pleasant? This most Christian of ladies finds herself the subject of scandal mongers and gossips—is that fair?"

Anne flushed a little. "That is unfortunate, I will agree Kat. But it could all be avoided. None of this detail needs to be gone into. All she has to do is submit to the King's will. She says she is an obedient wife. Mayhap she needs to show some of that obedience now."

I got up from the bed. "My lady, I cannot do that. You know how strongly the Queen feels. She was pure when she came to King Henry's bed. She has told me that, and I believe her, absolutely. As you say, she has been like a mother to me. I cannot go against her in that way, even if it means making an enemy of you." I felt sad as I said this, as my time with Lady Anne was the best part of my life then. I was afraid that I had lost her and all the fun and brilliance that was around her.

"No, you will not make an enemy of me Kat. I do not ask

you to betray the Queen or to doubt her word. That is for others to do, in courts of law. I just ask that you consider my suggestion. You will see your Queen suffer, I am sure. That is not my doing. It is because she will not accept the King's will. If only she could be persuaded, she would avoid so much pain. I just ask you to consider that and remember it during the coming months."

It seemed like the world was turning on its axis. Lady Anne now had splendid rooms in the Tiltyard at Greenwich Palace and held court as if she was already queen. Everything I had known seemed about to change. The Pope was considering the King's petition for an annulment despite the Queen's opposition. It seemed as if everything had started to move very quickly.

In July the sweating sickness came. It was rife in Cardinal Wolsey's household and in parts of the court. It was an anxious time for me. I remembered how the woman who I'd thought was my mother had died within hours, with me sitting beside her. How could I forget the terrifying speed of that illness, which snatched people from life within hours? I was a tiny bereft child then, and somehow, I had wound up at Woking Palace, trying to find the woman who could tell me who my mother was. But I didn't find her, and instead I found a woman who became like my mother, although she was a Queen. My life had been changed forever by her.

King Henry decided to leave London, taking a small entourage with him.

"He is taking the Queen too!" Jane Seymour told me.

"The Queen?" I looked at her, wondering if she was mistaken. She nodded her head, and said very deliberately, "The King has asked the Queen to accompany him to the country, as normal." Then she smiled a secret smile that made her plain face look beautiful. "The Lady Anne Boleyn is to go to her family home, Hever Castle".

I was thunderstruck. Up until now, Lady Anne Boleyn had

been everywhere that the King had been. But now, now he was frightened he might catch the dreaded sweating sickness, what had he done? He had dismissed his mistress and opted for the safety and comfort of his faithful wife.

Queen Katherine was overjoyed. For once, she was unconcerned about the plague. She sang again in her chambers while her gowns were being packed. She made lists of the King's favourite foods to be sent ahead. She wrote long letters to Princess Mary, telling her that her father and mother were very happy.

"I must tell the King about how Mary is getting on with her studies," she said. "She has been learning about governance, and the rights and prerogatives of monarchs. Her tutor is very pleased with her." Then she almost ran into her chamber to choose some fetching pearls to wear when she was to dine with the King.

At Woking Palace, they dined together every night. King Henry was kind and courteous to Queen Katherine. He even pretended he was visiting her at night, although I knew the truth of that. His footsteps never sounded outside her chamber. But still, she was happy, even overjoyed when he joined her at Mass every morning.

"Now I have him to myself," she told me, "he will come back to the right path. He is a good man; I know him better than he knows himself."

The King and Queen enjoyed hunting. They took advantage of the long summer days to go out hunting stags.

I did not go with the hunt. The only servants who did were those connected with the hounds, the horses, or the bows and arrows. Queen Katherine had left instructions for us. She wanted me to find one of her favourite gowns, a deep green silk, shot through with gold. The kitchen had been told that the King and Queen would dine in her chamber that night, and were to prepare a separate and delicious banquet of venison, chicken and quails for them both. Fine wines were to be fetched from the cellar, and fresh beeswax candles were to be placed around the chamber.

In mid-afternoon the hunt returned, dragging a couple of stags and some game birds on hurdles behind them. They were all laughing, the Queen smiling at the King, who regarded her warmly. We rushed out to welcome them and offer them refreshment.

"You bring me luck, my Kate," the King said. "That stag, I nearly missed him. But you brought me your calmness, and that helped me aim. You are my Diana!" he said, comparing her to the goddess of the hunt. The Queen, a little stout, but erect, beamed at him. Her cheeks were pink after the exercise, and her eyes bright. For the first time in many months I saw her as she had been. The King jumped down from his horse and walked over to her, offering her his hand.

"Kate, let me help you." She took his hand as if it was something very precious, and allowed him to help her down.

"Thank you, Your Majesty," she said, and dropped him a deep curtsey. As she rose, she looked at him in the eyes. "Your Majesty, we have had a long day hunting. I will be dining in my chamber tonight. Would your Majesty do me the honour of joining me? It will be more relaxing and private than being in the great chamber?"

I gasped. She was trying to get him back, and it looked like she might have a chance.

"Why yes, my dear Kate. I would be pleased to do so. We can avoid being on show for once."

Queen Katherine curtseyed again and bustled into the palace, with her ladies and servants following her. She stood in her privy chamber while we eased her out of her gown and took off her hood. Then she shrugged off her shift and stood there naked. Her little stout body still had a grace about it, despite the stretch marks and rounded stomach. I brought a bowl of hot water scented with lavender, and a soft linen cloth, and sponged her face, breasts and inner thighs. We dried her with a towel and then pulled a fresh shift over her head. Then her kirtle, made of rich buttercup yellow, and her hose. Finally, her deep green gown, lacing it up as tightly as it would go on her thickening waist.

Queen Katherine sat there while we unbraided her hair and brushed it. It was still her crowning glory, red gold, shining and thick. The King had started to go grey, but Katherine's hair was still vibrant. I took the pins and made to braid it again, but she shook her head.

"No Kat, for tonight I will wear it loose. We will not be dining with the court. I do not need to cover my hair in front of my husband." From the jewels laid out in front of her, she chose a rope of pinkish pearls and a delicate tiara made of gold and emeralds.

"There!" she said, peering into her silver mirror. "Do I not look like a queen?"

"Indeed, you do, Your Majesty. You look beautiful!" I said, admiring her. She looked almost as she used to look, despite the lines around her eyes.

"I think the King will stay with me tonight," she confided. "Did I not say to you that he would return to me?" She bustled off to order that a fire of applewood be laid and lit in the hearth. "His Majesty hates being cold, and these summer evenings can get chilly." I watched her and hoped that she was right. She was so happy tonight, and she knew that it was her best chance of getting the King back. I was not so sure though.

King Henry arrived, also wearing green and bearing a rose in his hand.

"For you, sweet Kate, I picked it in the gardens." He bent down on one knee and presented her with it. Her eyes misted over as she took it from him and slowly breathed in its perfume. He stood up, with a little more effort than he had needed before and took her hand.

"Your Majesty, thank you," she said. "Shall we dine? The table is set."

"Kate, for tonight it is you and me. Call me Hal, as you used to." Her eyes opened and she nodded her head slowly.

"Of course, dear Hal. It is a long time since we spoke like this."

"Too long. Now let us eat." They moved towards the table and sat down. I was the only other person in the room, Queen Katherine had dismissed everyone else. I poured them both a goblet of wine. Their meal was set out on the table, on silver plates which glinted in the candlelight. I retreated towards the back of the chamber to enable them to dine in private. I heard low conversation and some laughing. King Henry was telling a story about the hunt, and as he did so, he laid his hand on Katherine's arm. She glanced down at it, smiled, and let it lie.

Finally, they both stood up. "Your Majesty, Hal.... Would you care for a nightcap before retiring? Maybe some hippocras?" Queen Katherine stood in front of him, looking up at him appealingly. A glance, was it of love, passed between them. "Kat, fetch some more wine!"

I moved to fetch the wine, but at the same moment there was a knock on the door. I rushed to go and open it. John the Messenger stood outside, his cap in his hand.

"Mistress Kat," he said. "How are you? It is a long time since I saw you."

"I am well, thank you," I answered coldly. "But busy. What is your message?" I did not wish to encourage him to have any ideas about me. He had been keen, but I was firmer than ever in my desire not to wed, and anyway, with Will around I did not need any more admirers.

Fortunately, he took the hint and immediately held out a letter.

"This is for the King. I was told that it was urgent and that he must receive it immediately. Otherwise I would not have disturbed you, Mistress Kat. I will stay here tonight. If the King wishes to reply I will be leaving in the morning."

"Thank you, John," I said, taking the letter. I shut the door gently and walked towards the King and Queen, still standing together by the fire.

"Your Majesty," I bobbed a curtsey. "The Messenger brought a letter for you. It is urgent he says."

The King turned to Queen Katherine. "My apologies, sweetheart, this will not take long." She smiled and nodded at him as he took the letter from me and broke its seal.

"It is the Boleyn seal," he said, and immediately the Queen's face fell. I could see her fighting to compose herself. I knew she was thinking that maybe it was just something routine, maybe about one of Mary's bastards. I knew she was praying it wasn't from Lady Anne.

The King scanned the letter, then sat down heavily. Queen Katherine, unable to help herself, demanded, "Is it from Anne?"

The King's face looked as if he had been knocked out at a tourney. "No, it is not from Anne," he said. "It is from her father."

"That need not concern you now, Your Grace. Stay and drink some wine with me." She put her hand on his sleeve to detain him and turned to me. "Kat, I told you to bring more wine!" I hurried out to the antechamber, where there was some wine on hand. I found a large flagon and went back into the privy chamber with it.

When I returned, the King was still sitting on the chair, his head in his hands. The Queen knelt in front of him, entreatingly.

"What is it, Your Grace? Do not let it spoil your evening. Come with me. Let us drink wine and then retire." He pushed her off brusquely.

"I will not be retiring with you, Madam," he said. "Do not forget that we have committed the sin of incest. I am trying, despite your wiles, to atone for that sin. I thought you were a good woman, but like all women, you look to tempt me to do wrong." His voice had completely changed now. It was harsh and cold.

"To do wrong? How so, Your Majesty? We are joined by God." Queen Katherine spoke impetuously, but maybe unwisely.

The King growled, with an anger that was frightening. "Madam, stop this charade! We can never lie again together, never commit that act again. It is damnation!"

"Hal, it is not damnation. It is my love for you and your love for me. Do not be afraid." Katherine spoke as if she was speaking to a child.

"Do not talk to me of love. If you loved me, you would release me. But instead you cannot bear to let go! I am kept a prisoner by my so-called wife!" His face was flushed red, and his hands were balled into fists.

"But your Majesty...." she attempted, but he cut her off.

"How many times do I have to tell you, Madam? You are not my wife. You never have been. I do not love you." He was so cold towards her that I felt uncomfortable. This time Queen Katherine retaliated, calling out,

"No, instead you hunger after that whore! Bed her and then forget her. That is all she is worth!"

"She is the woman I want to marry," King Henry said flatly. "But this letter brings grave news. She is very ill with the sweating sickness and like to die. I will never wed her, my heart's own true desire! And that is all your fault Katherine, your lying, and your delaying tactics. If it were not for you, Anne and I would have been married now. You have cost me the love of my life, do you know that? How does it feel to be destroying my happiness?"

The Queen stepped back; her face shocked as if she was winded. "I do not wish to destroy your happiness, Your Majesty. I want to bring you happiness within our marriage bed."

"Well, you never did! And now, and now..." the tears were starting to roll down King Henry's cheek. "Now, I have lost the only woman I have ever loved. You have brought me to the depths of despair. I hope that you are proud of yourself!"

The Queen flinched and turned to me. "Kat, leave us. I

must speak with the King alone." I scuttled out of the chamber and waited next door. They were talking for a while but then I heard raised voices, shouting and crying, but I could not hear what was said. After a moment, the door crashed open, and the King strode through, white-faced and angry. He left by the other door, his footsteps echoing on the stone floor.

After the King left, Queen Katherine sat by the dying fire, weeping. Her face, which had been glowing, now sagged. She looked like an old woman, her cheeks hollowed out, her skin sallow. I went up to her, hugged her, and tried to comfort her. But she brushed me off.

"Kat, not now. I am deeply wounded to the core of my soul. I am weary of this, so weary. I do not know if I can continue," she said in a small, defeated voice.

"Your Majesty, you can continue. We all love you. England loves you, I know that. Whenever I am in the city people talk of you."

She turned to me and said, "The King is misadvised Kat, but that will not always be the case. It is up to me to ensure he becomes well-advised instead." And with that she stood up, gathering her skirts around her.

"Come, Kat, let us retire to bed. Fetch my night shift, and then we shall say our prayers."

The next morning the Queen stayed in her chambers, hearing Mass privately. All hunts and jaunts outside were cancelled. The atmosphere was tense, with her sitting at her desk writing letters to her nephew, the Holy Roman Emperor, to the Pope, to Princess Mary. There were deep shadows under her eyes where she hadn't slept, but she had lost the defeated air she'd had the night before. This was a Queen preparing to fight.

Just before dinner, the guards outside opened the door and announced:

"The King to see you, your Majesty." King Henry strode in, his face grim and unsmiling. All of us ladies, including the Queen, curtseyed deeply.

"I need to speak with you, Madam," he said peremptorily. "Some details...." But then his face crumpled, and he sat down. Immediately, she sat beside him and put her hand on top of his.

"She's dying, Katherine, she's dying, and I can't bear it!" I was amazed at the man. I could not call him King because I had lost all respect for him. He comes to his wife, who he plans to divorce, for comfort! It was unbelievable.

The Queen stroked his face. "Sometimes the ways of God are hard to understand, my dear," she said softly. "I pray that you will receive God's grace and comfort."

"She was so lovely, so clever. You don't understand Katherine. She would argue with me like a man! She had no fear. I loved that about her. She wasn't one of these frightened little women without a thought in their heads. She was my equal, my beautiful equal!"

I could imagine what Katherine thought about these words, but she said nothing, continuing to stroke Henry's tear-stained face.

"She is near crisis point, I have heard, and they do not expect her to last the day. She may already be dead!" he sobbed. Katherine withdrew her hand and sat tall in her chair.

"Maybe you wish to ride to Hever – you may be there within a couple of days," she said icily. He did not notice her tone, however.

"Much as I dearly wish that, I cannot. My responsibilities as King mean I cannot put myself at risk. What would the country do without me?" Katherine nodded, and a small smile played around her lips. She had realised that much as Henry cared for Anne Boleyn, he was not willing to put himself in danger for her. That was deeply satisfying to Katherine, I could tell.

"Of course, Your Majesty. We all need you to be fit and healthy, to reign over us and protect us." Was there a hint of irony in her voice? If there was, he didn't get it.

"Thank you, Katherine. I know you understand the heavy

burden of Kingship. I wish there were more who respect the sacrifices I have to make. Now, you did not attend Mass this morning. I missed you. Can you assure me that you will be present at dinner?"

"Of course, Your Majesty. I shall be pleased to attend." The King nodded, satisfied, and got up to leave. I looked at Jane Seymour as we both rose from our curtseys.

"How can she do it?" I whispered. "After all he has done to her?" Jane looked at me reprovingly,

"He is the King. We must obey him, and the Queen knows that. She is a wise woman. All she needs to do is to bide her time, and he will come back to her. I am sure of that."

CHAPTER

13

But Anne Boleyn did not die, and now she was back. Having pulled through the sweating sickness, which had killed her brother-in-law and many other courtiers, she had spent the summer recuperating at Hever Castle. Now it was September, and she was back in her apartments at Greenwich Palace, which soon echoed with music, dancing and debate.

I stayed away for a week or so, but eventually I gave in to temptation and visited Anne with a basket of fresh peaches. And so, my visits started again. Queen Katherine knew that I was going, but she didn't stop me. I often wondered why. Maybe she liked to hear about what was going on with Anne and what mood she was in. And she was in no doubt that I loved her. It was just that Anne and her friends were more exciting to a young woman, and she probably guessed that. Her faithful ladies were mainly older, except for Jane Seymour (and nobody could say that she was lively and exciting). The Queen knew that I went only for entertainment, and that suited her well.

We heard that Cardinal Campeggio had arrived in London on the Pope's orders to adjudicate on the validity of the King and Queen's marriage. The Queen decided not to wait for the public hearing.

"Today I will see Campeggio," she told me. "He is ill in bed, poor man. This English climate is not good for the bones. So I will visit him. I know that he will listen to my case and concur with my wishes. The King is bewitched, he does not know what he is saying." I held out her fur-lined cloak for her to put on. She pulled on her gloves.

"Kat, my case will go to Rome, and then I will win back the King!" She tapped her foot on the floor in impatience as we waited to hear that her barge was ready. I knew that she thought she was at last going to be heard.

That evening, the Queen returned to her chambers, pulling off her gloves and cloak. We all curtseyed, and then I rushed to pick them up and put them away. Lady Maria Willoughby approached her solicitously.

"Would you like a glass of wine, your Majesty? We have some Spanish wine today."

"The warm, sweet wine of Spain! How different from the thin, bitter stuff we get in England!" Katherine said angrily. "Why was it ever my destiny to leave my beloved Spain? The people are cold here, cold and irreligious. My case must go to Rome, it will not be decided here."

"I thought Cardinal Campeggio would have listened sympathetically to you Madam," Lady Jane Seymour said. "He is a prince of the church, and you are our rightful Queen." Like Queen Katherine, she had no doubts about the excesses of the Catholic Church.

"Listened? He did not listen! He simply talked... and talked... and talked!" the Queen said. "I arrived there; I was kind. I kissed his ring. The poor man was in bed, and I enquired after his health. That was about the last thing I said!"

"So what happened then?" I asked. My voice probably didn't hide the fact I was very curious.

"He paints this picture to me. A convent converted to a palace with gardens and a hunting park. My having guardianship of Princess Mary, who will live a few miles away. A reasonable income to live on and a large household. Maybe even going to celebrate Christmas with the King and..." she spat out the word "his whore! A convent Kat, and the pity in men's eyes! I was not made for that, and I told him so.'

"So you replied to him fully?" I queried, thinking that Queen Katherine had managed, after all, to say her piece.

"Indeed I told him!" she bridled. "I also said that he had no business to bully a poor foreign woman on her own in a strange country, and that the only fair way to decide this is for the case to go to the Pope in Rome."

"What did he say to that?" I asked.

"He would not say a thing! A court is to be convened next month. To try the King and myself for incest. Incest! That insults me, as a woman, as a wife and as a Queen! I am a sinner, as we all are, but I am not the incestuous woman that these men are painting me as."

"They are insolent, those Cardinals," Maria Willoughby cried out. "How dare they insult you like that?"

"But it sounds quite nice, don't you think?" I said tentatively. "To be out of all of this trouble, to see Princess Mary when you want. Might that be better than you think?"

"Kat, Kat, you traitor! How can you say these things?" Maria Willoughby cried out in anger. She made towards me as if to cuff me around the ears. The Queen raised her hand.

"No, no, leave her be, Maria. She has no understanding. How can she? She is not royal. She does not have the blood of kings running through her veins." Katherine was contemptuous.

"I'm so sorry, your Majesty! I just thought it might be easier...." my voice trailed off into silence.

"Child, you are not royal, you cannot understand what it is to be born to a destiny. I was born to be a Queen. I was told I was going to be Queen of England when I was three. That is a holy destiny for me. I was picked by God to serve the English people, and, above all, the English King. I can no more lay aside that duty than I can lay aside my daughter or my faith.

Don't you see, what the King wants is impossible? And if I agree to it, then I am going against God's will, and my husband, and the Holy Church." She reached out her hand to me. I kissed it, but I was raging. Again, the Queen was insisting that I was just a servant. While I accepted my position, I was unhappy that she thought it made me less than her.

In November, we moved to the new residence at Bridewell, where the chambers were comfortable and well-appointed. However, the palace lacked a chapel, and therefore the Queen had to traverse a long open gallery to walk above the street from her chambers to the church of the Dominican Friars. Every morning she would proceed that way to Mass with all her ladies and servants following her. Londoners knew she made this journey, and there were always a few people in the street looking up to see if they could see her. Over a few days, the numbers grew. Queen Katherine would wave graciously to them as she walked, the smile on her face showing that she was heartened.

The crowds continued to grow, and one morning an old woman called out to the Queen. "God bless Your Majesty!" This was echoed by others in the crowd, "God bless Your Majesty! Our Queen, may you win your case." A few young men started chanting, "Win your case, win your case, win your case!" The crowd took up the cry, and Katherine paused her progress and peered out to see the faces below her. She stood there for a moment, basking in the warmth of the crowd. Then, ever the Queen, she continued walking along the gallery. Just before she vanished from view, the old woman cried out again, "God help England if you don't. Our country will go to ruin without you!" The crowd cheered her to the rafters.

We were near the end of the gallery when the Queen turned to us and said, "So, the people love me."

"Of course we do," I said. "Everyone loves you!"

"Maybe I am not a friendless foreigner after all," she murmured and led us all down the staircase to the church.

Christmas passed, and the King and Queen held it in grand state. But Princess Mary was not present. The King did not come to the Queen's private rooms, and Lady Anne Boleyn was holding her own court a few hundred yards away. So it was a cold, miserable time, and nobody enjoyed it much. The King still ate with the Queen and attended Mass sometimes with her. But he was doing that to convince the Pope that his doubts about his marriage were based on theological worries, not the lust for another woman. Anne was only a minute away from the King's rooms, and they spent many hours writing poems and playing music together. Often some of the ladies would be in the room, sewing or playing cards, acting as the King's chaperones, for it was his reputation that he wished to protect.

Time dragged on with Queen Katherine writing pleading letters to the Pope, Lady Anne becoming more and more impatient, and the King's advisers searching through Europe for witnesses who might swear that Katherine was lying when she said she'd not had sex with Prince Arthur. I knew though that she was telling the truth. Her late-night confession to me about their wedding night and the naivety of two teenagers who didn't manage to do the deed, rang very true with me.

Will and I met with Tom, the man I had thought was my father. We went to an inn together near London Bridge. Tom was greying now, and his face was lined. He was pleased to see us, but I could tell he was a bit in awe of our fine clothes and educated accents. As we approached him, already waiting at the table, he stood up and doffed his cap.

"No need for that, Father," Will walked over and embraced him. I noticed Will was taller than him now, and broader in the shoulders. I paused for a moment, standing behind Will, and Tom looked a little hesitantly at me. How should he treat me, who was a daughter once but now was no longer family? But our hearts told us we were still father and daughter, and without thinking we both hugged each other deeply.

When we were settled with our ale and a hearty meat pasty each, we talked about the King's Great Matter. Will spoke as Cromwell's man, "She was a good Queen, Father, but she has had her time. The King needs a male heir, otherwise we have chaos."

"Who says a woman ruler would bring chaos?" I said sharply.

Daughter, you know that at that time no one had experience of a Queen ruling England successfully. But I was determined to defend the Queen and Princess Mary.

"I did my lessons with Princess Mary. She is sharp and clever. She may make a great Queen," I said.

"May?" Will queried. "Don't forget, Kat, that only fifty years ago we were in the middle of a bloody civil war between powerful men. No woman could handle that, and we could fall back into major conflict."

Tom looked down into his ale. "I know the King wants a son, and I can understand that. But it doesn't seem fair to the old Queen to my mind. All of this business trying to prove she had sex before she married the King. What does it matter now?"

"It matters because Queen Katherine is fighting the King all the way. I'm following orders and I am searching for servants who were in her household, who can tell us the answer. I don't wish to do it, Father, but the King's hand has been forced. Queen Katherine has been offered an honourable and comfortable retirement at a convent, but she won't take it. She isn't close to the King anymore, and they do not have marital relations. She is sitting there, blocking him from getting a son. And the King isn't getting any younger. He wants to watch over his son as he grows, train him to be a King."

I chimed in. "I love Queen Katherine, but I think it would be better for everyone if she did go to a convent. Lady Anne has new ideas, and she loves music, poetry, studying the Bible. I think she will be good for the King, and for England."

Tom shook his head and said, "Well, I will have to disagree with you both then. My view is that we have a good Queen who has given us much, and we should not discard her. But then, there is nothing any of us can do, either way!"

"That is true enough," Will agreed, glad to have found common ground. "Father, the reason I wanted to meet was not to discuss the King, but to tell you something."

Tom took a sip of his ale and looked at Will. "Go on."

"Father, I am walking out with Kat. I would like to court her. She is not convinced, I must admit! She has a foolish idea that she doesn't want to marry. But I am going to change her mind. I wanted you to know father, so that when she does change her mind, it isn't a shock."

"What do you think about this Kat?" asked Tom, "not too keen on our Will then?" I laughed self-consciously.

"I love you and Will more than anyone in the world, except perhaps the Queen. But I don't want to marry. I want to stay in royal service all my life, not be tied to a nursery of scream- ing babies. Also, it feels strange, that we were once brother and sister. I know we are not brother and sister, but I cannot get into that new way of thinking."

"That is why I need time to convince her," said Will. "And if she doesn't want me in the end, I will accept it and remain her best friend for life." I reached over and squeezed his hand. He really was my best friend, and I was so blessed to have him.

"Well, you both have my blessing, whatever you decide to do," Tom finished his ale. "Time for another one, my dears?"

CHAPTER 14

The Legantine Court was fixed for 21st June at Blackfriars. Although the Queen had objected to the court, saying that the case should be tried in Rome, she was due to appear. The two Cardinals, the bishops, and the King would all be listening to what she said and trying to find ways to undermine her.

That morning she dressed as every inch a queen. First a fine silk shift, with seed pearls at the neck and wrists. Then a kirtle of green brocade, embroidered with small pink pomegranates sparkling with rubies. Overall, a gown of creamy white velvet shot through with diamonds and silver. Her hood was also white velvet, with a black veil hanging behind. She wore a long golden chain with a large ivory crucifix. Around her waist, she wore a golden girdle, from which a cloud of enamelled Tudor roses hung. We all knew the symbolism of her costume. The green and white was the Tudor livery, the pomegranates her own personal badge, and the Tudor roses spoke of the peace the Tudors had brought to England. The crucifix signified her piety, and her determination to follow what she saw as God's will.

We were all following her to the court. She wanted us all to be standing behind her. She was so brave, but she needed our support. Yes, I thought she was wrong, but I loved her so much, I couldn't deny her that. As we got to the court building, we could see the crowds gathered outside. This was a public court, and some would be admitted. After all, it wasn't every day that a King and Queen were tried in front of the Pope's representatives for incest! Of course, we knew that they wouldn't be punished. The issue that had to be decided was whether their marriage was legal and in accordance with God's teaching. The crowd cheered as she entered, but she didn't turn and wave. She was aware that the King was inside, and that he would see any such action on her part as inciting rebellion.

We all squeezed into the hall. I saw Will standing in the public gallery and waved to him, but the crush was too great for us to stand next to each other. At the far end of the hall, on a raised dais were two chairs, decorated in cloth of gold where the two Cardinals sat, Wolsey and Campeggio, behind a large oak table. Two large oak chairs stood on either side, facing each other, both covered by cloth of gold canopies. To the side, squeezed in tightly, were the English bishops, many talking quietly to each other. The noise hushed as the King and Queen entered and took their places.

Cardinal Wolsey signalled to the King to speak. He rose, magnificent in his red velvet and gold robe, his square hands be-ringed and sparkling.

"Thank you, your Eminences. We are here, in this court, not because I do not love this lady," he gestured towards Queen Katherine, who lowered her head and stared at the floor.

"Oh no, if it were my choice, why I would wed her again. I love her above all others. But it has become clear to me, through a study of the Bible, that the laws of God were against our marriage. A man may not lie with his brother's widow, it is there clearly in Leviticus. For all of those years when we lived comfortably together, we were committing a grave sin, the sin of incest. I fear for our souls that when we come to judgement, we will be damned for all eternity." Queen Katherine tightened her hands into small fists and would not meet his eye.

"The only way we can be absolved is by bringing this sham of a marriage to an end," King Henry said sincerely. "In that, I care not only for myself, but for Katherine also." He had to appear as if he regretted what had happened. But the lies made me boil with anger. We all knew that he cared only to marry Anne Boleyn, and thus to bed her.

The King sat down, looking around him, smiling at those he recognised in the crowd. Then Cardinal Wolsey spoke. He said that he had been concerned about the Queen's assertion that the court was not impartial. Man to man, he appealed to King Henry to assure her that it was completely fair. The King stood up again and spoke directly to Queen Katherine,

"Madam, do not trouble yourself with this. I know that this court is impartial. In fact, my Lord Cardinal, you are so impartial that you are somewhat hard on me," he said with a little smirk. Wolsey inclined his head in thanks, and Campeggio smiled. These men were united in patronising the woman who stood against them. Whatever you might think about Queen Katherine, this wasn't fair. She was fighting for her beliefs in a situation where anyone could see that the odds were stacked against her.

Queen Katherine was called to speak. She paused for a moment, then rose from her chair, smoothing out her skirts. Without saying a word, she walked across to where the King was seated and knelt in front of him. There was a shocked gasp from the crowd. What was she going to do?

"Sir, I beseech you for all the love that hath been between us, and for the love of God, let me have some justice!"

King Henry reached out a hand to her. "Stand, Katherine," he whispered, but she remained kneeling. She went on to beg him for compassion, for mercy on her, a poor foreigner alone and with no friends.

"Alas! Sir, wherein have I offended you, or what occasion of displeasure have I deserved?" She spoke with passion, as if to a lover. King Henry shifted uncomfortably on his seat. She went on, talking about how she had always conformed to his desires, had done everything to make him happy, and had born him many children. "Although it hath pleased God to call them out of this world, which hath been no default in me." I felt myself start to cry, as I could see her eyes well up with tears. Even King Henry looked a little emotional. He again tried to raise her up, but she shook him off. Now she was going to show what a fighter she was. She looked up at him and spoke directly to him.

"You know, my Lord, that when I came to you in the marriage bed, I was a maid. You took my virginity. You are the best witness to that, and you know in your heart I tell the truth. I put it to your conscience, can you solemnly swear that I was not a maid when you and I were married?"

King Henry cleared his throat, deeply embarrassed. He, who was so careful about his immortal soul, would not wish to lie about this matter. So why, I wondered did he say nothing? Queen Katherine moved on to talk about her father, King Ferdinand, and Henry's father, King Henry VII. Why did they both agree to the marriage unless they were sure that it was legal? She was like a lawyer on that day, marshalling all her arguments one after another, and each one made King Henry look even worse. At last she seemed to be coming to an end:

"Finally, Sir, as my lord and master, who can dispose of me as you will, I beg you to give me permission to write to the Holy Father in Rome so that I can defend my name and my conscience to him?" She raised her face and fixed her eyes on the King, a picture of wifely submission. He coughed and wiped his face with a handkerchief.

"Why yes, of course, Madam," he spluttered. "You are free to write to the Holy Father at any time. Now please do get up!" She reached out to him to help her up, which he reluctantly did. She then took a step back and curtseyed deeply to him. Then she turned on her heel and walked down towards the crowd, holding out her arm to her receiver general, Griffin Richards. He took it, and they walked together through the crowds towards the great doors.

"Katherine, Queen of England, come into the court!" a court official called after her. Richards paused and said she'd been called back. A decent man, he wasn't quite sure what to do,

Queen Katherine half turned and said in a loud, clear voice, "On, on! It makes no matter, for it is no impartial court for me, therefore I will not tarry. Go on!"

After she left, there was a flurry of ladies trying to get into line to follow her. We were all looking at each other, and in many eyes, I saw respect for her courage. She had shown those men that she was more than their equal. What was it that Will said about the rule of women leading to chaos? I knew that if this woman had ever had the chance to be a ruling queen, there would have been no chaos, only courage and determination.

Queen Katherine went no more to the trial, while it dragged on through the summer. She had written to the Pope begging him to bring the case back to Rome, where he himself could decide it. Will told me that the Pope wanted to delay the whole thing. He was in the middle of a conflict between the Holy Roman Empire and the French, and his decision depended on who he was most afraid of. He was hoping that Katherine might die and thus solve the problem. Katherine did think that she might be killed if she continued to resist, but she had no intention of dying in her bed. Every night she prayed that the missive would come soon from the Pope, that would give her what she hoped was an impartial hearing. But the court in Blackfriars was due to come to a decision. Was this the end for her? Would she lose her case before she even had the chance to take it to Rome?

Cardinal Campeggio thought of a way out of the impending crisis. In late July, Roman courts take a holiday because of harvest time. Therefore, as the court in Blackfriars was essentially a court of Rome, it would also take a holiday. Queen

Katherine breathed a sigh of relief, while Lady Anne fretted, and the King stormed. A few weeks later, word came from Rome that Queen Katherine's appeal had been granted, and the whole process would be moving there.

Cardinal Campeggio was glad to be going home, but Cardinal Wolsey was worried. After years of being the King's fixer, his administrator and friend, he was now feeling the cold wind of his disapproval. Lady Anne Boleyn pressed King Henry to punish Wolsey for the failure of the Legatine Court, and that autumn he was accused of the crime of praemunire, putting the laws of Rome above those of England. He pleaded guilty and had his house in London and his property taken from him. However, he was allowed to go and live quietly at his house in Esher.

Queen Katherine started to show some sympathy for him. She had never liked him, but now he had fallen foul of Anne Boleyn, she found some fellow feeling with him.

"Poor man," she said. "Losing everything because he is a Prince of the Church? It is not right. He obeys the Pope, as we all must do. I shall send him some apples with a short note."

After months of coldness, the King announced that he would have dinner with the Queen at Greenwich Palace on St Andrew's Day. I wondered if her hopes would be raised by his message. But no, she had learnt her lesson.

"I do not hope anymore," she said. "I simply do what is right." She dressed magnificently as always in blue sarcenet with pearls, but she did not smile. When he arrived in her apartments, she rose to welcome him, curtseyed, and escorted him to the table.

"You are welcome here, Sir, on this St Andrew's night," she said. "Would that you had come sooner." Her voice was icy as she continued.

"Why is it, Your Majesty, that you no longer visit me? At bed or board, I am alone. Where are you Sir?" King Henry finished his mouthful of venison and wiped his fingers on his napkin.

"Affairs of state, Katherine. I have so many papers to read, so much to do now that Wolsey has, er, left. You know, my dear, the lot of a King is not an easy one."

"And does the Lady Anne Boleyn help you with your 'state affairs'?" the Queen asked sarcastically. "What role exactly does the concubine play?" This was not something she would have said a few years ago, being so careful to please Henry, to make him feel he was the best man in the world. But now she was angry, and after weeks of being ignored, she was going to speak. King Henry stood up and pushed his large face into hers.

"Do not speak in that foul manner, Madam. It does not do you favours. The Lady Anne does indeed discuss many matters with me. She is intelligent and can argue like a man." He sighed. "Something which you, Madam, seem unable to do."

"I am your *wife* Henry, not your friend, or your adviser, or even your mistress. All I ask from you is that you treat me as your wife. I have not seen you for weeks!"

He was really angry now. "I do not know what you have to complain about! You have your own household! You can do exactly as you wish! You can hunt, pray, sing, do everything you love with no trouble from me. You say I do not visit you, in bed or at board. That is true, and you know the reason for it. It is because our marriage is not legitimate, Madam, and I would be persisting in sin if I did so!" He walked swiftly towards the door and paused before leaving. "One day, Madam, I hope you will find yourself capable of understanding a simple Bible verse. That is all I ask of you! Until then, you will not see me." He slammed the door as he went, leaving Queen Katherine weeping.

Lady Anne's family continued to prosper. In early December, the King made her father Earl of Wiltshire and Ormond. Apparently, at the celebration feast, Lady Anne sat in the Queen's place and acted as if she already wore the crown. The Queen heard about it the next day and again spent many hours in tears. But then, a few days later, the King was pleasant again. I don't know whether Lady Anne had hurt his feelings somehow, but he announced a few days later that he would be spending Christmas at Greenwich with the Queen and Princess Mary. What kind of game was he playing? Was he doing the same to Lady Anne, one day pleasant, the next day casting her out? I did not know. I hated him for what he was doing to both women. It was strange, people said that they were very different, and they were. But in their loyalty, their intelligence and their piety, they had a lot in common.

Princess Mary was a young woman now, still short in stature, but with an earnest, pretty face and a confidence about her that made us all love her. I did wonder if she remembered our days together as children, but she never said anything to me. She was pleasant, but serious, and our encounters now were much more businesslike.

"Kat, fetch me my sewing, I left it behind," or "Kat, will you sing with us? We need another voice." That was alright with me. I did not love her; it was her mother that I loved.

The palace was decorated with holly and ivy, and the air was thick with the scents of Christmas, cinnamon, cloves, sage and oranges. The royal family attended chapel on Christmas Morning and sang the old carols that we all loved: Personent Hodie, the Boar's Head Carol, and Gaudete.

The King and Queen feasted together, with Princess Mary sitting between them. In the candlelight, they looked the happiest of families, both parents smiling as Princess Mary told them about her studies and her fondness for dancing. And yes, there was dancing that Christmas; it was full merry, with the King dancing with his sister and the Queen dancing with us ladies. Anne Boleyn was nowhere to be seen; her apartments were empty. I wondered what she was doing. Had she gone back to Hever Castle? Maybe she was trying to force the King into action by ignoring him.

I was too busy with my own life to care much. Thomas

Cromwell's wife Elizabeth had died earlier in the year, the sweating sickness again, and Will and I offered to help out at Christmas. Thomas Cromwell was morose and withdrawn, but his three children, Gregory, Anne and Grace, needed entertainment. We were able to put on plays with them and take them out to play in the heavy snow. Elizabeth Cromwell's sister Joan was there with her husband, as was Cromwell's nephew, Richard. They were a welcoming family, and I loved the children.

Mainly, though, the time was a special one for Will and me. Early one morning we walked along by the icy river, muffled up in our woollen cloaks. We talked about the King's Great Matter from different perspectives. We talked about the Bible, and how exciting it was to be able to read it. But most of all, we spoke about ourselves. As we spoke, our breath hung mistily in the air and merged into the fog.

"I love Queen Katherine, and I want to protect her, but it's so much more exciting with Lady Anne. And she has promised me she will give me work in her chambers if I will leave the Queen. But I can't do that, Will, I really can't."

He looked at me searchingly, and then nodded. "I know Kat, you are loyal. But you may find that it is no longer possible to be loyal to Katherine. We do not know what will happen. She may not be with us for much longer." Fear rushed through my heart. Surely the Queen could not be in danger?

"Do you think she will be killed by the King?" I asked anxiously. He laughed.

"No, no, the King does not kill anyone. If it were to happen, it would be by another's hand. Whether that be an assassin or an executioner, the King would be careful to stay at arm's length."

"Would Cromwell do it?" I wondered. "Now Wolsey is not in power, it might be a way for him to progress." I liked Thomas Cromwell, and he had always been pleasant to me. But I had heard that he was a man who had few scruples when dealing with people who got in his way.

"My master is a lawyer, not an assassin," Will answered, smiling. "He knows how to handle himself, yes, and he was a soldier, but he will not kill in a dark alley nowadays." He shook his head.

"No, Kat, he will not kill the Queen, nor arrange for her to die. What he will do is find a way out for the King. A new way of looking at the law, differing opinions. He will get rid of the Queen, do not doubt that Kat, but he will do it legally. Even if he has to change the law to do so." Will took my hand and stared into my face.

"And then Kat, what will you do? Be stuck with an old woman in a crumbling castle somewhere? There will be prayers aplenty, but no singing and dancing, no writing poetry or playing cards. You cannot do that."

"I'm not sure," I said. "I like Lady Anne, but she can be sharp. I am not sure if she would be kind."

"Lady Anne is a woman who believes in her destiny. She will be sharp to those who stand in her way. But you wouldn't do that. She loves your voice; she likes to sing with you. You would be a musician. She would be a good mistress to you." Will spoke the truth, I knew that. He would not advise me to work for the Lady Anne if he thought that any harm would come to me.

"I'm not sure...." I mused. "It is a difficult decision."

Will sighed, frustrated. After a moment, he spoke up. "Then don't do either. Marry me!" He turned his head to one side and looked at me, his eyes teasing. I felt I loved him so much at that time. He was the person who had been close to me since I was a baby. But did I want him as a husband?

"I will be a lawyer soon. You will have a good life. You would be free to do as you wished Kat. I would never see myself as your master. You could visit your Queen, go and sing for Lady Anne, do whatever you pleased." He made a convincing case for it, but I shook my head.

"No, Will, I do not wish to get married. Not ever." I shivered in the bitter cold breeze.

He shrugged his shoulders. "Well, at least Kat, let me keep you warm." He enfolded me in his arms, and I felt the warmth of him, the safe strength of his arms. He smelled of rosemary soap. I was entranced by him and raised my face to his.

Slowly, gently, he put his lips on mine. I felt the soft scratchiness of his beard against my chin, sending shocks of excitement through me. This was not the Will I had remembered, but a different Will. He was a man, and for the first time I felt that I was a woman. My nipples hardened under my shift as I felt his muscled chest against them. I returned his kiss ardently, pressing my body against his. I clung to him, feeling excitement and desire, but also fear. But was it Will I was afraid of, or was it life without Queen Katherine? I didn't know.

I pulled away from him regretfully. "Will, I'm not sure," I said. "I cannot leave the Queen now, and who knows what will happen in the future?"

"Well, well, Kat. I can wait for you, and I will. You will not get rid of me, you know that?"

I laughed. "Yes, you are like a bad penny. You will always turn up!" I looked at him earnestly.

"I know that, and I am glad of it," I said softly. His eyes lit up, and he let out a slow whistle.

"So be it, Mistress Kat. Now, we have to devise some New Year's revels for the children. Do you have any ideas?"

Master Cromwell went into the court on New Year's Day, mainly to show his face. With Wolsey's fall, it was important that he continued to remind the King of his presence and his services. It was the day for giving gifts, and the courtiers would all vie with each other as to whose was most appreciated by the King.

When Cromwell returned, he sat by the fire, telling us and the others about the day. He had given the King a bolt of red velvet, shot through with gold threads. It would be enough for his tailor to make him a sizeable coat. In return, the King gave him a silver goblet:

"From which to drink your Italian wines, Cromwell," he'd jested. "I know you like that green wine from the north." He did not mention Cromwell's wife, and nor did any of the courtiers. Cromwell was useful, he did the King's bidding. He was not an equal, and the events of his family were of no interest to them.

"I do not care. Those people are the powerful ones, the players. Why should they care for me? I must just be of service to them, that is all. I do not care for them either. It is the people here, my people, that I care for. We are the ordinary people who marry for love and work to feed our families. We may work for the grandees, but our hearts are free." He looked sad as he said this, and I knew he was remembering his wife. Elizabeth had died very quickly, just like the woman I remembered as my mother. She had risen in the morning, well and merry. But by the evening she was dead, and her funeral procession was winding its way towards the graveyard.

"The Queen asked for you, Kat," Cromwell said. "She asked when you would be back at court, as she misses you. I told her that you had been helping with the children, and she smiled and told me you were a good girl. I think, though, that you will need to return tomorrow." My heart sank. I had been hoping for more time with Will, but I knew that the Queen needed me, and Cromwell probably wanted Will to return to work. It could not be helped.

"How was the King with the Queen?" I asked Cromwell. He looked at me consideringly.

"The Queen will be happier without him," Cromwell said bracingly. "He treats her with this exaggerated courtesy, but he doesn't listen to what she says. All the time he is fidgeting, looking for messengers at the gate. He is desperate to hear from Lady Anne."

"So, she was not there?" I asked.

"She has not shown her face all Christmas. He is desperate to hear from her. I heard that he had sent her a very expensive New Year present. So far, not a word out of her!" He laughed ironically. "She is made of steel, that one. Strange, isn't it, that the greatest King in Christendom is bested by two women? I could never say this at court, but they are the only people who are not afraid of him and see him for what he is. It is a delight to watch!!" He smiled, and for a moment I saw that he had forgotten his grief. He loved the intrigue, the power play of the court, and it had kept him going through this dark time.

God takes those whom he most loves. Later that year, Will told me that Cromwell's daughters, Grace and Anne, had also died from the sweating sickness. I remembered how much they meant to him and grieved for him in his terrible loss. The Queen, God bless her, sent him a handwritten note of sympathy. Yes, he was an enemy, but she understood what it was like to lose children, and her feelings for him were heartfelt. He had responded with a brief visit to her, his eyes wet with tears.

"I saw your daughters once," the Queen remarked gently. "You brought them into the court one day to see the Christmas revels two years ago. They were beautiful girls with such lovely manners."

Cromwell nodded mutely, his hands clutching his cap.

"It is hard, is it not, when God claims them for Himself?" she mused. "I have the comfort of knowing, as I am sure you know, that I will see my babies again, when I join them in the arms of God. I pray that you will also have that reward."

"It is my fervent hope, Your Majesty," Cromwell said, giving her the title that he was determined to take from her. She nodded and sighed deeply.

"Thank you for your visit, Master Cromwell. I may not see you again, in which case I wish you well, and godspeed." And she dismissed him, with a regretful but determined wave of her hand.

CHAPTER

15

The Queen was reading to us from "The Education of a Christian Woman" by the Spanish scholar Juan Luis Vives. She would read a passage in Spanish, and then translate it quickly for the benefit of those who did not speak the language. It was late in the afternoon, and even Lady Maria Willoughby was looking slightly sleepy. I glanced over at Lady Jane Seymour. She was listening intently, nodding every now and then. Like Queen Katherine, she was a very religious woman, and she took these readings very seriously.

The quiet rhythm of the Queen's voice was broken by a disturbance just outside the chamber, men's voices talking loudly. After a moment, the doors opened, and Will strode past the guards. He took off his cap, bowed deeply to the Queen, and then to all the ladies.

"My apologies, Your Majesty, for disturbing your afternoon. I come with urgent news for Mistress Kat. May I speak with her for a moment?" The Queen looked at him for a moment, then nodded.

"I remember you, Master Cooke. You have been paying court to Mistress Kat. Yes, speak. But do not take too long!"

"Thank you, Your Majesty," he said. "May we withdraw to the antechamber?"

"Yes indeed." The Queen motioned for me to get up, and I curtseyed to her and then hurried over to Will. We both paid our respects again, and then walked through the doors into the next chamber. There were two guards standing there, but they paid no attention to us. Will led me to a window seat, looking out over the gardens.

"Kat, I have news!" He grabbed my hand. "Kat, we have found your laundress, Meg. My aunt."

"What? Where is she?" I cried, "Can I see her?" I couldn't wait for him to answer. "How did you find her, Will? Is she well?"

Will held up his hand. "One thing at a time, Kat. I'll tell you everything. You know that I have been looking for former servants of Queen Katherine on the directions of Master Cromwell?" I nodded impatiently.

"He wants to find anyone who can remember whether Prince Arthur and Princess Katherine consummated their marriage," Will continued. "I've spoken to so many people! Mostly, they just didn't know, had heard gossip, but nothing more. But then I found a chambermaid who worked for the Prince and Princess when they were just married."

"And?" I was desperate to hear the story.

"She knew nothing, just like the others. But she did say that there was a laundress who had washed the sheets of the bridal bed, and that maybe she might know something. So then I asked her if she could tell me where this laundress was. I was disappointed when she told me that the woman had moved to deepest Sussex, having married a farmer. I wondered if it was worth going all that way to be told much the same as I had been told already. But then I heard her name. It was Meg Skinner. Skinner was my mother's name before she married. This Meg is her sister and our lost laundress!"

"So what has she got to say, Will? Does she know what

happened to me?" I clutched at him in excitement. One of the guards glanced at us disapprovingly, and Will detached my hand from his doublet.

"Hold on, Kat, I haven't seen her yet! She lives in East Lavant, at the foot of the Sussex downs. It is too far for a day's journey, and Master Cromwell keeps me busy. But he has agreed that I should go next week and will make arrangements for my travel."

"But that's wonderful!" I said. "What will you ask her? Will you write it all down so that I can read what she says?"

He shook his head decisively. "No, I will not Kat! You are coming with me to speak with her yourself!"

"But how can I?" I asked. "The Queen will not release me to go into the wilds of the countryside with you!"

"Leave the Queen to me. I can handle her," Will said optimistically. "She has too much on her mind to worry about what you are doing in just one week away."

"We can do it in that time?" I asked. I had never travelled as far as Sussex.

"Yes, it will be easy. We will go down, stopping at Woking Palace. Master Cromwell has arranged a room for me there – he has said we are on government business. Then we can ride to Guildford the next day and stay at an inn. We will then come over the downs and down to East Lavant on the third day. We will have plenty of time."

I was carried away by his excitement. At last, I would find out about the mystery of my birth. What is more, Will and I could speak to Meg about the woman who was his mother and had brought me up. I did wonder about the arrangements for us to ride together, but I decided to leave it all to him. It would be sweet to spend a week with him, riding through the highways of England in midsummer. Life had suddenly become rather interesting.

Will pulled me back into the Queen's chamber. He bowed, and I curtseyed as Queen Katherine looked at me questioningly.

"So, Mistress Kat? What news do you have?"

I spoke up clearly, looking into her eyes. "Your Majesty, Master Cooke has found a woman who may know the secret of my birth."

The Queen's face lit up. She knew how much it had grieved me not to know where I came from.

"That is excellent news, Mistress Kat. So when will you see this woman?"

Will interrupted. "Your Majesty, she does not live in London but in Sussex. It will take a week to reach her and then return."

"And so, how will she go?" the Queen enquired, wrinkling her brow. I could tell that she was not convinced so far. Will took a deep breath and composed his face to look sensible.

"Your Majesty, I will be travelling with Master Cromwell's stablehand to manage the horses. He will be bringing his wife with him to act as a chaperone. I promise you that Mistress Kat will come to no harm. If you could allow her to come, it will answer the questions that have haunted her all her life." Will looked imploringly at Queen Katherine. She stared at him and then smiled enigmatically.

"I can understand that Master Cooke. So many of us have questions from the past that will not let us go! Very well. She may go. Kat, you must say your prayers, behave with all due modesty, and make sure you are back within the week. Master Cooke, I will entrust you with my maid Kat. Do not break my trust! " And with a wave of her hand, she dismissed Will and returned to reading aloud. Lady Willoughby sighed slightly and settled back down to her sewing.

We were set to leave the following Monday. I was busy washing myself some clean shifts and coifs, finding hose and riding boots. On the morning I was due to leave, the Queen pressed a purse into my hand.

"For you Kat. You may have some expenses." She folded my hand over the purse and then took something out of her pocket. "Here, this is to protect you, my Kat, whatever you may encounter." It was a golden crucifix, inlaid with pearls, at the end of some rosary beads.

"Oh no, your Majesty. I could not take that!" The rosary would have cost more than most ordinary people earned in a year.

"Yes you can, my Kat. It is just a trinket. It was from my mother, Queen Isabella."

I cried out, "I cannot take that if it is from your mother."

"Kat, I have many rosaries from my mother. Confirmation, birthdays, saints' days. What is important is that she loved me, and this rosary will carry my love for you. Now, let me give it to you." She leant forward and pressed it into my hand. I opened my palm, I kissed it and then pushed it down into my pouch. Her eyes filled with tears, and she put her arms around me. For a moment I clung onto her, this woman who had rescued me when I was nothing. But then she pulled back and held out her hand. I kissed it and sank a deep curtsey.

One of the cooks gave me some homemade bread and a big hunk of cheese. He also popped a handful of sugared almonds into my saddlebag. "I know you like them, Mistress Kat," he smiled. "Now off you go, and godspeed."

I saw Will by the gatehouse, holding two horses, one tall and midnight black, and one a rich bay. He looked tall and very handsome in his black doublet and cloak. He helped me up into the saddle of the bay, jumped onto his horse, and then we set off.

"Where is the stablehand and his wife?" I asked. "Are we meeting them on the road?"

Will looked a bit sheepish and then admitted, "Kat, they are not coming. I said that to reassure the Queen. We didn't need them anyway. I can manage the horses."

"But I have no chaperone!" I snapped. "What will I do? Where will I sleep on my own with no woman to accompany me?"

"We can sleep together," Will said, "just as we used to. We can say we are man and wife."

I was furious. "You have tricked me, Will! What will you do when we are alone together? Try to beat down my defences? Try to get me drunk and bed me?"

Will slowed his horse down and held out his hand to hold my horse's bridle. "No Kat, I am not going to do that. I promise you. I have told you again and again that all of this rests on you. If you do not wish anything to happen, then it will not happen. I swear on my mother's life, I will not do anything to cozen you into bed." He sounded so sincere that my anger subsided a little. But I would not let him see that. I took up my reins and kicked the horse gently to start walking again. He followed on, a couple of paces behind.

We went like that, not talking, up into London and then through the city, bustling with street vendors, preachers and merchants going about their business. It was already getting warm, and the stink of excrement, old meat and sour vegetables filled the air. Although my face remained severe, I was glad I was leaving all of this behind to get out into the countryside for a few days.

After we left London, we travelled through a small village called Wimbledon. There was an inn where we stopped for lunch. We sat outside with tankards of ale, eating our cheese and bread. There was one fine old manor in the village and a few small thatched cottages. Otherwise, there were pastures, where goats and cows grazed, and some large enclosed spaces where the sheep nibbled at the turf. The air smelt sweet, and I felt my spirits rise. This might be quite fun after all, I thought. I turned to Will and tapped him on the shoulder.

"That was very ungentlemanly of you, Will Cooke, and you know it!"

He caught the lightness of my voice and laughed. "I never claimed to be a gentleman, Kat. You know me. You know where we came from. I am no gentleman!" He took my hand, and his voice became serious.

"But I swear I will respect you, Mistress Kat, as no gentleman ever could. For they believe that anyone of ordinary birth is not worthy of respect. And I believe that everyone is worthy of respect, as we are all made by God. And you, my Kat, are the one that I respect and love above all others." I gazed at him, feeling my heart beating against my bodice.

"Oh, Will, what would I do without you? You are my best friend." He smiled at me, and I felt the warmth flood my heart.

We continued our ride, travelling the highway that I remembered going along with the messenger John all those years ago. I remembered the pain and uncertainty of that time, and again blessed Queen Katherine for taking me into her household. I hadn't known if I would see Will ever again at that time, but here we were riding out together in the middle of a new adventure. What would Meg tell me? Would I be pleased, or would I wish that I had never asked her? All of that was to come. Right now, it was my feelings about Will that were distracting me. He looked so handsome nowadays, and yes, my heart did quicken when I saw him. Also, I knew that he was absolutely on my side and that I could trust him with my life. So what was it that was holding me back?

We got to Woking Palace by nightfall. Will led our two horses into the stables, and arranged with the stablehand to feed and water them. Then we walked on to the house. It was strange to see the stately building almost deserted, except for a handful of servants looking after it. The state rooms were aired and cleaned regularly. Sometimes vagabonds squatted in empty palaces, and men were needed to throw them out. We were met by a tall, thin gentleman, who introduced himself: "Master Wilton, the resident steward, at your service." We were assigned a large room in the servants' quarters, with around twenty pallet beds in it.

"When the King is in residence, his guards sleep here," the steward said, "but you won't be disturbed tonight." He looked across at me, my head bowed, trying to look respectable. "What about her? Will she be alright?"

"Yes, of course," Will reassured him. "She is my wife. I will be here to protect her. Can you fetch us some bedding and something to eat?"

The man nodded and said, "My wife can find you some blankets. If you need us, we are living in the rooms next to the kitchen. Come to the kitchen when you are ready, and you can have some food."

A few moments later, a large round woman bustled in with an armful of blankets and a couple of pillows.

"Here you are, my dears," she said. "Make yourselves comfortable, and then come down to the kitchen. I have some hot pottage on the fire, and some meat pies in the oven. You will be hungry after your travelling!"

We walked through the palace courtyard to get to the kitchen. I remembered hiding in the stables, which was where I'd first seen the King and Queen. Will and I looked in, and the smell of the horses and the straw took me back to that time immediately. Now those buildings were nearly empty, with the exception of a couple of old workhorses and our own two animals, who were by now happily munching away at some sweet hay.

"This was where I first saw the Queen," I told Will. "I was hiding behind that door there. She was talking with the King."

"You must have been amazed," he smiled. "Such grand people!"

"Oh, I was. I thought they were like gods at first. Both of them so good looking, and so lively! They were different then."

"Yes," Will nodded. "I remember the Field of Cloth of Gold. That was the first time I saw them. They put on a magnificent show. But the years have not been kind to the queen, poor lady."

"So you do have some sympathy with her?" I pounced on him.

"Of course I do. Who could not have sympathy with her? But that doesn't mean that she is right."

On this I was silent. I thought like Will, that the deal that had been offered to the Queen was enough for her to live in state and comfort, with a King's gratitude to sustain her. But she wouldn't budge. While I loved her dearly, there were times I wanted to give her a good shake.

The kitchen wasn't in use. Instead, the Wiltons were using a chamber off it, normally used for baking. The oven was on, and there was a small fire burning. I felt myself suddenly relaxing in the heat and drew closer to the fire.

"Welcome, welcome," the Steward said. "I am so glad to see you. Now, we can hear all the news from the court. I can assure you, my wife is most interested in what the Queen and the Princess are doing."

We hungrily ate the pottage, with large hunks of bread washed down by big tankards of ale. Mistress Wilton asked many questions about the King's Great Matter, which we answered vaguely, saying that we were only servants. Then Master Wilton and Will started a conversation about the King's new horses. They were good company, and it was late before we walked back to the dormitory to sleep.

It was a pretty cheerless place, without the buzzing of people around, but Will and I lay fully clothed on neighbouring pallets, with a couple of blankets draped over us both. It was chilly and uncomfortable, but strangely I felt safer than I had done for years. I was pleased to note that Will still didn't snore.

I can remember, daughter, sleeping outside the Queen's chamber while the King was with her, and by God, he snored terribly! I was surprised she ever got any sleep.

We got up early, had a wash and some breakfast, and set off on our way. Our next stop was to be Guildford. We stopped for some bread and cheese at midday and arrived late in the afternoon. Guildford was a pretty little town, with a fine Guildhall and a Cathedral. When we arrived, it was market day, and Will stopped by a pedlar and looked at his wares. He was selling cheap jewellery, the kind that farm lads bought for their lasses. Will selected a small brass ring and paid for it. He held it out to me.

"Will you marry me, Kat?" he joked. "Now we have slept together, we might be considered man and wife anyway." Seeing me blush, he smiled very wickedly.

I shook my head vigorously. "No, I won't, Master Cooke, and no, we are not man and wife at all!"

He laughed but still held the ring out to me. "It would be a good idea to wear this. Then, when I say we are married, there will be no awkward questions. I wouldn't want to leave you to sleep in the stables!"

I took the ring and slid it onto my finger. It fitted well, and I held out my hand to admire it.

"I like this well," I admitted, turning it round. "Will, did you know this is my first ring!"

"And not your last, Kat. Of that, I am sure." Will would not let go of the subject of marriage. Time and again he brought it up, so often that I snapped at him sometimes. However, he was very good about keeping his word. He did not try to pressure me into intimacy, even when we were lying close together in a small fourposter bed at the end of the day. We were at the Angel, an old inn on the High Street, and I appreciated the comfort of the feather bed after the hard pallets of the night before. We'd lain there not touching, except for our fingertips. It felt, though, that all of the warmth of his body passed into me through his fingers. Our breathing was in harmony, and I felt my heart was beating to the same time as his.

"Goodnight, darling Kat," he said, leaning over and kissing my hand.

"Goodnight Will." I lay there, not moving, but feeling as if I was bathed in happiness.

The next day's journey was to bring us to the village of East Lavant, on the edge of Chichester. The highway started to climb upwards. We were making our way into the Downs, the rolling hills that formed a high green ridge before slowly

sloping down to the sea. The lanes were edged with cow parsley and daisies, and the fields were full of golden wheat. As
we climbed up, there were flocks of sheep grazing on the
short, scented grass. The air was clear, and the sun sparkled
on the small streams that made their way downwards. Will
and I spurred our mounts onwards, looking at each other frequently, talking and singing as we went.

We stopped beside a stream that flowed cleanly over a bed
of flint. The water was like glass, and we bent over to drink
it. I had never tasted water so good. It had the scents of all
the grasses that grew around it and was cold on the tongue.
We sat down and opened the bundles that the Angel Inn had
given us this morning. Hard dark bread and creamy sheep's
milk cheese. It was simple food, but we ate like kings that day,
feeling that we had everything in life that we would ever need.

After he had eaten, Will lay down on the short, springy
turf and closed his eyes. The sunlight was warm, and within
a few minutes he had fallen asleep. I turned to look at him, to
examine every inch of him.

He was wearing his black doublet and hose, both quite
tight-fitting. His legs, I could see, were well-muscled, but his
hips were narrow. I watched his chest going up and down and
looked at the small curls of dark hair that showed around his
neck, just at the hem of the shift he wore. He had a dark beard
now, well-trimmed and oiled. His lips were red, like a girl's,
and they parted slightly as he slept.

I leant over him, ever so carefully, and gave him a kiss. I
could hear the larks singing and the buzz of the bees all around
us. His lips tasted of salt and barley. I wanted to taste more,
and so I kissed him again. He stirred, and his arm brushed
against mine. His eyes opened wide with surprise, and then he
smiled and relaxed.

I kissed him again, pressing myself down on him. Then he
sat up, throwing his arms around me, and started to kiss me.
This was passionate, wild kissing unlike anything I'd known

before. He grabbed my coif and pulled it off. My red hair tumbled down my back, and he took a handful of it and pressed it to his lips.

"Beautiful Kat," he said, guiding my face again towards his and giving me another long kiss. My chin felt sore against his beard, but it felt like the most delicious soreness in the world. I kissed him back eagerly, opening my lips to him and feeling his tongue moving inside my mouth. This was what I had feared since I was a little girl, to be at the mercy of a man like this. But now it felt absolutely right, absolutely full of life, absolutely what I was designed to do.

I kissed the side of Will's neck, beside his ear, and he groaned. I was not used to men. I thought he might be in pain, but no, he was in ecstasy. I moved to unbutton his doublet, wanting to feel the hard chest beneath it.

Will stopped my hand.

"No, Kat, not now." He pushed me off gently and held out my coif to me.

"Braid your hair again, Kat and put this on." I obeyed but felt as if he had rejected me.

"You do not find me pleasing?" I asked, tears in my eyes. He groaned again.

"Kat, I find you utterly pleasing! I love you and want you for my wife. But I will not take you like some farm girl in a meadow. I will marry you and make you my wife so that all can see. Can I believe now that you might accept me?"

I looked long and hard at him, considering him. Then I did up the ties of my coif and spoke quickly. "Yes, I will take you, Will Cooke. Just give me some time to get used to the idea."

He planted a tender kiss on my cheek. "I will give you time, Kat. I know now that you will be mine very soon. Now, we must get on to East Lavant. There is an inn there that we can stay at."

We got back on our horses, and they climbed steadily uphill, their breath coming heavily. We paused when we got to the top of the hill to admire the view of the green grasslands sloping down towards the coast.

"See, over there! That is the sea," Will told me. He knew of such things, having travelled with Cromwell, but me, I'd only seen the sea once before. It was hard to make out much, the heat haze shimmered, and all I could see was a line of intense blue merging into the sky.

"I wish I could go there!" I cried. Now I felt I wanted to experience life, see things I'd never seen before, travel and learn.

"We haven't time now, but we will go together one day, I promise. See, though, here, it is East Lavant, just below us." Will pointed just below us. Nestled in the lee of the downs was a small settlement of thatched wattle and daub houses next to a grey Norman church.

"Is that where she is?" I asked, hardly daring to believe we'd found her.

"Yes, she lives there, in one of those houses." We went downhill through the winding lane, the horses picking up speed now in anticipation of a drink of water, some sweet hay, and a rest. After about half an hour, we arrived there. There was a small inn at the side of the road, where we stopped. Will arranged for us to have a room, and we took the horses to the stables. Then we sat down in the parlour, drinking ale and talking to the innkeeper, who had a broad country accent.

"We're looking for a woman who used to work at court. Her name is Meg. We were told she'd married a farmer down here." Will looked enquiringly at the innkeeper, who took a gulp of his ale and said:

"So why ye askin'?"

Will explained that Meg was his aunt, and he needed to find her to tell her about his mother's death.

"So, what's she got to do with it?" the innkeeper asked, looking at me suspiciously.

"She's my wife," Will said airily, waving a hand at me. I smiled and put my hand to my face, showing off the cheap wedding ring.

"Women! Nothing but trouble!" said the innkeeper, shaking his head. "See what's happening in London? Two queens

215

fighting over one king, just like a catfight!"

I sat up straight and said angrily, "No sir, it is not the women at fault, but the man." Will hushed me.

"Excuse my wife, she has a mind of her own!" he joked. "So tell me, master, is there a Meg from London that lives in this village or nearby?"

"Aye, she lives in the farmhouse down the road. But I should say she lived there. She died last month."

I couldn't help myself. "Oh no, this is not fair. God is against me, I swear it!" I wailed. Tears sprang into my eyes, and I thumped the table with my fist. After all this time, all this searching, just at the moment when we had found her, she died. I felt that all my hopes of finding out about my past had been dashed.

The innkeeper looked puzzled. "Mistress, you are sore unhappy for a woman you have never met," he observed.

"She wanted my aunt's blessing on our marriage," Will interrupted. "With my mother having died, it is... it was... important."

"Well, you can go down and speak to her husband if you like. He was with her to the end. Took it hard, he did. But I guess he'll find another one before the year is out."

We made our way down the path to the farmhouse, set back a little from the highway. It was surrounded with flowers and beds of herbs and vegetables. Meg must have been a good gardener, I thought. What a change from living in the royal court, slaving away in the laundries.

We knocked on the door, and after a few moments it was opened by an elderly man with long grey whiskers.

"Can I help you?" he asked, in a way that suggested that was the last thing he wanted to do.

"We're looking for Meg," I said. "We think she lived here."

"Aye, that she did. Until last month, that is. She died. She's in the churchyard now," he said, waving vaguely in the direction of the church. He took out a handkerchief and wiped his eyes. "God rest her soul; I miss her every day."

"I am sorry for your loss," Will responded politely. "Of course, you will miss her very much."

"Oh yes, and the chickens don't get fed by themselves, and the parsley is running to seed. I have a girl that cooks for me, but she's no good. This place needs a good woman to work it. When I met Meg, I knew she was the one for me. A hard worker and strong. My first wife died five years ago, and Meg just took her place. She was a good woman, and a good wife."

I thought this was an unromantic view of marriage, so very different from the songs and poems that I was used to at the court. But the farmer was obviously fond of Meg, and sad at her loss.

"She just took sick one day. She'd cut her hand in the garden, and it went bad. She kept on applying poultices, but it wouldn't clear. Then, one day, she said she felt ill. She was hot, and said her whole body was aching." A tear escaped from the farmer's eye and trickled down his nose. He wiped at it furiously with the handkerchief.

"I sat with her," he said. "She was raving and crying out. She was burning hot, and I tried to cool her with a wet cloth, but it was no good. She was dead by nightfall." He looked down at the ground, trying to compose himself.

"She was my aunt," Will said. "The sister of my mother, Joan. That is why we came down here to see her."

The farmer nodded. "Oh aye, she talked about a sister in London. They'd argued, she'd said."

"My mother would have wanted to make peace, I know that," said Will. "Did you know that Meg and another woman brought her a baby to care for? My mother would have wanted to tell Meg that everything had been fine."

"Oh, the baby!" the farmer cried out in recognition. "She raved about that on her last day. She kept on saying she had to find the baby. I thought she was out of her mind with the fever you know."

"Was the baby hers?" Will asked gently. "She was a single woman then, without a husband to support her." The farmer shook his head.

"Oh no, Master, Meg had no babies. She told me that herself. And she had none of the marks of childbirth on her, not like my first wife. When I married her she was past all that, but she'd been working at the court all those years. She'd been happy as she was."

"So when she was raving, at the end, did she say anything about the baby? Anything at all that might give a clue about who its parents were?" I asked, trying to keep the desperation out of my voice. Surely, surely, there must be something that she had said in her last hours?

"What's so important about the baby?" the farmer asked. "Why do you want to know?" He looked us up and down suspiciously. I glanced at Will, and he nodded.

Taking a deep breath, I turned to the farmer and said, "I was that baby. My name is Kat, and for many years I thought that Joan was my mother. But then I was told that I was a foundling. Meg and the midwife, Mistress Stabb, had brought me to Joan very quietly in the middle of the night. I just want to find out who my parents were, and now it looks like I never will."

The old man looked at me thoughtfully, nodding his head up and down. Then he got up and went to a chest at the back of the room and opened it. He took out a linen package and brought it over to us.

"By God's wounds, Mistress, I have told no one about this. I did not want to bring trouble down on my Meg. But I believe your story, and now she is gone, she cannot be harmed." He set the package down on the table and unwrapped it carefully. Inside, there was a fine cambric handkerchief edged with lace. In one corner was a Tudor rose, surmounted by a coronet, all embroidered in gold. Will and I gasped. This handkerchief bore the personal emblem of the royal family. We both knew them. No one, apart from them, would have possessed such a thing.

"She showed this to me when she first came here. She told me it was the King's, but I don't know, I'm a simple man. She said it had been tucked in the wrappings of the baby... of you, Mistress, when she took you. I was afraid she would be charged with stealing, so we didn't show anyone. We didn't even talk of it. That was, until the day she died." He hesitated, the emotion coming through his voice.

"Mistress, you must not act on this," he said, "it may well be just imaginings. But on the day she died, she kept on trying to say something. Yes, she was screaming and shouting, but every now and then she would calm down and say, 'Husband, this you must know.' I asked her what I should know. What was of such import when she was dying?" Will and I were all ears now, concentrating on what the old man said. It was like torture when he paused for a moment to catch his breath.

"Mistress, you must not act on this" he said, "it may well be just imaginings. But on the day she died, she kept on trying to say something. Yes, she was screaming and shouting, but every now and then she would calm down and say, "husband, this you must know." I asked her what I should know, what was of such import when she was dying?" Will and I were all ears now, concentrating on what the old man said. It was like torture when he paused for a moment to catch his breath.

"Then she said, and this was it, "she is the King's child". That was it, "She is the King's child". Nothing else. She was failing by then and she tried to say more, but she couldn't. But it's clear Mistress, that you are the King's child, for why else would you have had that handkerchief tucked into your wrappings? Here Mistress, this is for you." He carefully wrapped up the handkerchief and placed it into my hand.

"Is this true?" I asked, twisting the linen in my hands. I could hardly breathe for the shock.

"Aye Mistress, it is true, that I swear. And you have a look of the King about you, now I come to think of it! I saw him once when I was in London. Such a man!"

That night at the inn, Will and I sat up in bed trying to absorb what had been said. I knew that for many years people had said that I looked like the King, but this had been in jest. Now, I believed that I was a King's daughter. But by whom? That was still a mystery. Probably some small servant girl, who had been over-awed by him, and given him her body once or twice. He would have lost interest then, and moved on. And for her, what happened? She must have been very frightened. Did she give the baby to Meg so that she could continue working? Or had she already been dismissed?

"Poor girl, her life was destroyed," I said tearily. "She was taken advantage of."

"You don't know that Kat. She may have left and got married, and be very happy." Will was measured, and it annoyed me.

"But you see, how women are used by men, and then thrown aside, like this poor girl? I hate being a woman Will. I hate being at the mercy of men, especially men like the King! I have seen how he treats his women, and these are royal women, noble women, and still he abuses them! I am not proud that he is my father. In fact, I hate him. He has ruined so many lives, and he does not care."

"He cares for Anne Boleyn," said Will. He lay down and turned his head as if to sleep.

"Now he does. See what will happen in a few years time. I hate him!" Will reached over and patted my arm, and then shut his eyes. But I couldn't sleep. Angry and upset, I lay rigid in the bed, until at last I could see the dawn through the window.

Chapter

16

Our journey back to London was a miserable one. The fine weather had broken and it rained constantly. Every night we were having to dry our clothes in front of the fire, and towel our hair dry. We didn't speak much. It seemed that everything had been said, and we were both deep in our own thoughts. I was raging against the unfairness of men, and as for Will, he was impossible to read. I didn't know what he was thinking. I feared that he was thinking I was too much trouble to wed. He was an ambitious man, who wanted to get on. Being saddled with a King's bastard for a wife might not be politically advantageous. Of course, nobody knew at the moment. But what if they found out? I didn't know, but the court was a cruel place, where people were forced out because of their connections with one side or another. Was he willing to take that risk?

Will and I agreed that we could not tell anyone about Meg's last message. I knew that Queen Katherine was hurt by the attention King Henry had paid to his bastard son. If she knew I was also his bastard, what would she think of me? I didn't want to incur her anger. Also, there was no guarantee that the King would recognise me as his. After all, what did I have? A servant girl's story, and a royal handkerchief. I might even be accused of stealing. Best to forget that wild improbable story! I put the whole week in Sussex to the back of my mind, and tried not to think of it.

I couldn't help the thoughts of Will though. We had been so close during that journey through the green hills. I had felt for a moment, that I maybe could, maybe would, one day, become his wife. But the discovery of my parenthood had turned me against marriage again. Why should I put myself under the authority of any man, even one that I adored? Queen Katherine was the highest in the land, but still she was subject to the King's whims, infidelities and cruelties. I wanted none of it. I was resolved to stay a maid, and stay with the Queen. I saw Will quite often, and he was friendly, but a bit reserved. I wondered whether we would ever be close again, as we had been. Sometimes I feared that Will might find a maid that he liked, and leave me behind. But if that happened, I would have to accept it, and let him go on his way. It wasn't fair to keep him hanging on.

Queen Katherine asked me what had happened in Sussex.

"Did you find out who your mother was?" she asked, "I have been praying for you Kat."

I answered truthfully, "No your Majesty, the woman had just died, and her story with her."

"Oh my dear Kat, I am so sorry. But remember you will always have a home with me, until you get married." I nodded and returned to my sewing.

"Will Cooke, now he is a coming man," the Queen observed. "Training to be a lawyer. He would be a good match for you Kat. Would you like me to have a word with Master Cromwell?"

"Thank you, your Majesty, but not now. I am not ready to wed." The Queen shrugged her shoulders.

"So be it, but there will come a time Kat, when you must."

It was quiet and sombre that autumn in the Queen's

household. We heard that Wolsey had been arrested for treason. He was in York, and started the long journey back to
London under guard.

"Treason? What treason? The Cardinal has been for the
King at every turn. He has intrigued against me, but not the
King." The Queen was at first surprised by what had hap-
pened, but later she learnt more.

"He is accused of treason for advising the King to treat me
with respect! Of course, he advises that if the King does not
treat me properly, the Pope may have to excommunicate him.
That is a simple fact, and Wolsey knows it. I cannot believe it
Kat! He and his bullies spent years trying to force me to go
into a nunnery, and now, because he may have said a word in
my favour, he is a traitor! The world is strange indeed, Kat."

The Queen was getting frightened now. Before she had
always believed that there were limits to what the King could
do to her. He had loved her for nearly twenty years, they'd
had many children together. As a chivalrous king, he would
not, could not, physically harm her. But now he had turned
on Wolsey, his oldest friend and supporter. Why should he
not turn on her? She knew that she was protected to some
extent by being the aunt of the Holy Roman Emperor. But she
also knew that she would never ask him to invade or do any
harm to England or the English people. Henry knew that. And
in the contest between the great Kings of Europe, one ageing
Queen was not worth a full-scale war. Her case was still in
Rome, awaiting the Pope's verdict, but very little seemed to
be happening.

She was still the same gracious Queen that I knew for
much of the time. She loved sewing, and I would read to her as
she embroidered altar cloths and sacred vestments. I noticed
she was no longer sewing the King's shirts.

"Kat, the Lady Anne was angry with the King," she said,
smiling ironically. "She heard that he had requested me to
make more shirts for him, and she roasted him alive! Poor

man, he is not used to being treated like that!" I thought that it was exactly what he deserved, but Queen Katherine would never say something like that. As far as she was concerned, King Henry was her husband and she owed him her respect.

News came that Wolsey had died on the way down to London. He had refused to eat and, already ill, had turned his head to the wall and given up. He knew what was coming and could not bear it. The Tower of London and a traitor's death. Not that he was afraid of death, but to be cast out by the King was more than he could bear. The Queen arranged for special masses to be said for his soul.

"He was not my friend, but he was a faithful servant to the King, and as such, I honour him. Soon, Kat, all of those who speak for me will face what Wolsey faced. I fear that."

"Surely not, your Majesty," I reassured, but I was not certain.

The Queen was worried about Princess Mary. She wrote saying that she was suffering from terrible stomach pains. Much worse than the pains she got normally with her courses. Queen Katherine wrote back immediately, with remedies that might help, prayers and the promise of a visit from a trusted apothecary. It was so hard for her to be away from her daughter, she cried at night sometimes, and hugged me to her as if I could somehow take away the pain.

I still visited the Lady Anne to play music with her, maybe once a week. She had a group of young courtiers who liked to compose and play music. I was included because of my singing voice, which, Lady Anne said, was unusually pure. It was exhilarating for me to be able to sing and lose myself in the beautiful songs I was singing. It was then I started to write simple songs, sometimes with accompaniments for the lute, the virginals or the flute. They would all make a fuss of me as if I were a pet dog, almost patting me on the head. Actually, Lady Anne already had a dog called Purkoy, who, alongside me, was petted by all. He had this habit of putting his head to one side as if he was asking a question, which was why she had given him his name, from the French word pourquoi.

I loved it in Lady Anne's chambers. I loved hearing the poetry, the extravagant declarations of love, and the harmony of the singing voices. I loved the religious debate and how that spilled into wider discussions about education, the role of women, and the rights of common people.

The young courtiers went there now. Her brother George was there all the time. He and the Lady Anne were almost inseparable. I also saw Thomas Wyatt, Henry Norris, and William Brereton. Thomas Cromwell came occasionally and brought Will with him, which meant we had a chance to talk sometimes.

Increasingly, the King would visit and join in with the singing. Sometimes he would help with the composition of a new song or poem. He often ate with Lady Anne in the afternoons while we entertained them. We didn't discuss politics so much when he was there. I think we were all aware that it was a risky topic, best left to those close to the King.

It was April time when the King came to Lady Anne's chambers waving a letter in his be-ringed hand.

"My lady, I have heard from Princess Mary. She talks of wanting to visit me. I am minded to agree, I have not seen her for many months." He looked down at the letter, rereading it to himself.

Lady Anne took the letter from his hand. "What does she have to say? Why should she see you? She is just a bastard?" Inwardly, I flinched at that term. That was just what I was. But surely Princess Mary could not be made illegitimate? Lady Anne did not like Princess Mary, I knew that. But she could be cruel. I told myself that this was because she felt so insecure in herself, and that once she and the King were married, it would cease.

"Don't be a fool, Henry! See here, she says that she wishes to be with her mother, and you at Greenwich Palace! You must refuse her! It is just a game of playing happy families. Once you are all together, they will conspire to change your mind. Henry, you must not let them deceive you like this. You are too soft on them. This is all her mother's doing, and you know she is always outwitting you. Do not give in to their wiles. Tell her she stays where she is."

We were all embarrassed by this. To see the King, our lord, being scolded by a woman in front of the massed courtiers was unprecedented. Yes, the Queen had sometimes been angry with him, but always in private. In public, she had behaved with the utmost civility and obedience. Yet here was Lady Anne, talking to him as if he was a naughty schoolboy. He even bowed his head and looked ashamed, which I had never seen before.

Maybe he was tiring of Anne, though, because a few days later he came to the Queen's chambers to dine. As always, the Queen welcomed him with great ceremony, and ordered his favourite foods and wines. It was a private occasion, with just us chamber women in attendance. The pair talked quietly, even laughing occasionally. It seemed like they were in harmony at last.

"Do you remember when Mary told the French Ambassador she wanted to kiss him?" the Queen asked. "She thought he was the Dauphin." King Henry smiled at the memory.

"Yes, she was always forward for her age, Mary. Clever like me, and like you Katherine. And with my Tudor colouring! She is a good girl."

"Sir, she wrote to me recently," the Queen said hesitantly. She knew he would probably snap at her, but she was a mother, and she wanted to see her daughter. "She would like so much to see us both. She misses you, Sir, and she needs her father and mother's love. What if she were to come to Greenwich for a few weeks? She would be a help to me, and a pleasure to you."

The King's face became less amiable. He set his wine goblet down deliberately and spoke roughly.

"If you want to see your daughter, Madam, you can see her elsewhere! You will not see her with me!"

The Queen bowed her head. "In that case, Sir, I will not see her. I would not go without my husband."

"Husband! When will you get it into your head I am not your husband?" He snapped. "Don't try any of your tricks on me, Madam. I am wise to them. You want us to be a family. But we were never a family, understand that! You may visit your daughter whenever you wish, but it will be without me!" He got up, threw his napkin on the table, and left the room. The Queen took her napkin, smoothed it out, and also left the room in total silence. I followed her into the next chamber, where she was sitting with her head in her hands. She looked up at me, and spoke bitterly,

"It was her, Anne Boleyn, that made him do this. My Henry would never have refused me this! He loves Princess Mary; she is his blood! That woman has bewitched him! So what can I do, Kat? What can I do?" I looked down at the floor.

I believed now that Anne Boleyn would become Queen. So how to protect Queen Katherine? How to make sure she would be treated with dignity? How to stop these terrible scenes with the King, where she was always rejected most cruelly?

I took a deep breath. She would not like what I was going to say, but maybe I could at least make her think.

"Your Majesty, my Queen. You will always be England's Queen, and all will respect you as such. But maybe it is the time to retire to a convent? You would be allowed to take your ladies; we wouldn't leave you! You would be treated with dignity and respect, just as you deserve. I say this because I love you, and I don't want you to suffer. Please, your Majesty, I beg you!" I knelt down in front of her, my hands clasped as if in prayer.

She looked down at me. I was expecting anger, but there was only coldness.

"You cannot love me, Kat, if you expect me to make a bargain with that whore. I have told you many times that I am married in the eyes of God to my husband, King Henry."

"But he doesn't love you anymore!" I cried out. "Stop pretending he will come back to you some time. He won't! He has cast you aside, as he has cast others aside!"

"Ah, so now Kat, you are comparing me with Bessie Blount or Lady Mary Carey. Just a discarded mistress to be married on or retired. How can you even imagine I am like them? You can have no respect for me if you do this, even though you pretend to love me." Her eyes were stony as she looked down on me.

"I do love you, your Majesty. You have meant everything to me," I said quietly. "I just wish that you would leave this poisonous place. Go to the country, visit your friends. Be happy with Princess Mary. It would be easier for her without having to pick sides between you and the King."

"You cannot love me. You stand there and abuse the King, who is god's anointed ruler and has ruled over all of us for many years with fairness and justice! You cast doubt on my sacred destiny to be a queen. You deny the meaning of the solemn marriage and coronation oaths. You do not understand me Kat!"

The truth was, I didn't understand her. I didn't understand why she still fought for the King after how he had treated her. I didn't understand why she couldn't just take the easier path for everyone, including herself and her daughter. And although I had royal blood, I had not been brought up to revere the man who was my father. Indeed, I hated him for what he had done to Queen Katherine, and to the poor serving maid, whoever she was, who had given birth to me.

"I am sorry, your Majesty. I did not mean to cause you pain. You are right, I don't understand you. But I still love you."

Queen Katherine sighed. "Yes Kat, I know that. I love you too. But I am too old-fashioned for you now. You are young. You want to be part of the new court that is growing up around Lady Anne. You would be better in her household."

"No, your Majesty, I want to stay with you," I insisted.

Queen Katherine shook her head. "Kat, you have been visiting the Lady Anne for a long time now. I know that she would like you in her household."

"But I don't want to go!" I cried. "I beg you, do not dismiss me!" I clutched at the hem of her gown as if it might have magic properties, as if by touching it I could somehow change her mind.

"You enjoy being with the Lady Anne, no? She flatters your singing; she treats you as a lady and not a servant. You have your future with her, my dear. I would not hold you back." She leant down and gently detached my hand from her gown.

"Kat, you are young and talented. Go with the other young people. My fight will only hold you back, my dear. It is time to let go." With that, she gathered her skirts about her and left me alone in the chamber, my future suddenly up in the air.

That night, I was in the maids' dormitory for the first time in many months. Of course I didn't sleep, after what had happened. The Queen did not wish to see me, and the ladies in waiting were cool. No one would question the Queen's decision to fight on, even if they could see she would lose the battle. Yes, she might persuade the Pope to support her, but the discussions that went on around the court were increasingly along the lines of "If he won't do it, then we shall just have to do it for ourselves." After all, not everywhere in Europe was under the Pope's sway nowadays. The reformers were talking about setting up an English church ruled by English people under the command of the English King. Five years ago, it would have seemed revolutionary, but now it was one of the choices that the King could make.

I got up early and packed a bag with my belongings. Some shifts, some coifs, a couple of good gowns. My silver cup and the brooch the Queen had given me. A rosary, a couple of books about the Scriptures, and my much-loved Book of Hours. I opened it up, and a bookmark fell out that she had embroidered for me. I sat on the floor clutching it, and the tears flowed down my face. I thought about going back and begging the Queen to change her mind. But I knew that she had made her decision, and she was not a woman to waver. She knew I had no appetite for the fight that was to come. And, to be honest, a part of me was relieved. I did want to spend more time with Lady Anne, and the glamorous courtiers who surrounded her. I did want to be there when all of the new ideas were debated. If I had stayed with Queen Katherine, I would have felt that I was being left behind.

I picked up the bag, took one long last look around the chambers that had been my home for so long and walked away.

I didn't go directly to Lady Anne's chambers. Instead, I made my way to the administrative offices in the palace, where Thomas Cromwell and Will were often to be found. Will was on his own in his small chamber, chewing on a hunk of dry bread, and reading a grubby, much thumbed manuscript.

"Kat!" He jumped up when he saw me and moved a pile of books from a chair. "Sit down dear Kat. What brings you here?"

"I knew this was where you worked sometimes. I hoped I might catch you," I said, starting to shake with emotion.

"Kat, you will always catch me! But what is the matter?" Concerned, he raised me from the chair and wrapped his arms around me. And it was then that the dam broke. All of the feelings I'd had over the last couple of years suddenly came to the surface. I cried out,

"The Queen has told me to leave." And with that I started to bawl, feeling the deep grief of being rejected by a woman I had considered as a second mother.

Will held me for a moment and then passed me a handkerchief. His face was concerned as he said, "What happened

Kat? The Queen loves you; she would not tell you to go."

My words tumbled out in a tearful flood: "I tried to persuade her to retire into a nunnery. It was because I love her Will. I didn't want her to suffer anymore. And I was scared!"

"Scared?" Will queried, looking troubled.

"The Queen thinks she might go the same way as Cardinal Wolsey. She thinks she will be a martyr Will. And I just don't understand why she doesn't just give up! It isn't worth risking her life for."

Will looked thoughtful. "It is not in her nature to give up," he said. "Some might call it stubbornness; others might say she has principles. It is not up to me to judge. But it is the ordinary people that will suffer when the Kingdom divides, King against Queen, Evangelicals against the Pope."

"That is why I tried to persuade her Will, and that is why she made me leave. She's told me to find employment with Lady Anne. But just now I feel as if my world has ended. I cannot bear it that she has rejected me, my heart hurts so much." I put the handkerchief to my eyes and howled. For a few moments, I was like a wild animal in pain, unreachable in my agony.

Will waited until I started to quieten down and took both of my hands in his. They felt warm and strong, and I clasped onto them as if I was drowning. Slowly, the tears stopped, although I was still shuddering like a small child recovering from a tantrum. He spoke calmly and clearly.

"She hasn't rejected you Kat. I am sure you will see more of Queen Katherine. But she is hurting badly, and in her mind, you have rejected her. Yes, it was for her sake, and you genuinely want for her to be happy. But In her mind, that puts you with those who would bully and denigrate her. She is very wounded." I pulled away.

"But Will, so you have sympathy for her? I thought you wanted her to retire to a convent?" I asked. He smiled ruefully.

"Indeed I do Kat. But I would not be human if I did not

feel sorry for her and have some admiration for her courage. And I know she is important to you, and so she is important to me." This calmed me a little, and I took a deep breath. Now I had to decide what to do next.

"So, I suppose I'll go to the Lady Anne, and ask her to take me on," I said, wondering what the outcome would be. Yes, she had oft-times said she'd like me to join her household, but had she been serious?

"You could always marry me!" Will teased, his smiling eyes showing he wasn't serious. Then he sighed, and he looked down for a moment, "No, I know Kat, you don't want to ever marry. But here's a plan. Come back with me to Master Cromwell's house tonight. You can sleep with the maidservants there. You can have a couple of days to think about things, maybe ask Master Cromwell for his advice. Then we can send a letter to the Lady Anne, asking for employment. She likes you, I know. She will welcome you. And then, I will be able to see you almost every day. Don't groan Kat, I will not get in your way. It will just be good to have you in the new court, next to the Lady Anne."

CHAPTER

17

Cromwell took me to one side. I had been staying at his house for a few weeks, making myself useful, helping with the constant washing, cooking and mending that such a household occasioned. He had been amiable with me, but I had not spoken with him much. He was still grieving the loss of his wife and two daughters. This sweating sickness was a terrible curse upon us all. It would take anyone, no matter how high or low.

"Mistress Kat," he said formally. "I understand that you have applied to work for the Lady Anne."

"Yes indeed, Master Cromwell," I replied. "She is expecting me to start soon."

"Remember you always have a home here, Kat," he smiled at me. "I think ere long you may be living here in a different capacity? Will is a fine lad you know, and he will make a good living once he has his articles." I blushed and looked down at the floor. To many people my desire not to marry seemed very strange. But anyway, now that the Queen no longer wanted me, my motivation to stay single wasn't quite as strong. So I said nothing.

"Be that as it may Kat. I invite you to my house whenever

you wish to come, whenever you have a holiday, or Mistress Anne is away."

"Thank you, Master Cromwell," I said, smiling at him. He was a very kindly gentleman. But then he said something which surprised me.

"And you can tell me all about the court around Lady Anne. Who does she see? What books does she read? I know you are a clever woman Kat; she will talk to you." All at once, his eyes, which had always been so warm and friendly, had become calculating. I stared at him. What did he want? Why did he want this information if he and Lady Anne were allies?

"Just the gossip, Kat, just the gossip," he said reassuringly. "I like to hear from the women's point of view."

I started working for Lady Anne just before Christmas of that year. She had been glad to take me on, to entertain her ladies and do a few light chores. It was very different from being with Queen Katherine. I found myself on duty for much longer, always in demand to sing, or play the lute. But I loved it. Who wouldn't enjoy singing in front of the grandest people in England? I was also allowed to be present when Lady Anne and her brother George composed songs together, with my suggestions being taken seriously, and even sometimes copied.

I was there when they discussed the corruption of the church, and how it would be better for England if we could break away from Rome. I said nothing but concentrated on the sewing in my lap. Lady Anne had started sewing the King's shirts for him, but she was not as neat as Queen Katherine had been, and I was often called upon to restitch a seam. Lady Anne's household stayed up late at night, and it was often gone midnight when I stretched out on my pallet in the ante-chamber. I slept in the next-door chamber to Lady Anne, with the other ladies. But at night, Anne, most definitely, slept alone.

Christmas at Greenwich Palace was observed lavishly, and the King and Queen were on public display for every celebration. It was so strange for me to see her up there, blazing with jewels, smiling graciously at the King and acknowledging the cheers of the crowds. It was as if we were back ten years, when they were happy together, and he was still visiting her chamber for love, rather than arguments.

What was different for me was that I no longer had that intimate time with the Queen, at the end of the evening, when I would comb her hair, we would say our prayers and talk. Looking at her there, surrounded by ladies, with every courtier bowing as she passed, I realised that she must be very lonely.

Lady Anne did not attend these large events. She was not going to demean herself by having to curtsey to the Queen in front of hundreds of watching eyes. Instead, she ate in her chamber. After the official banquets many of the courtiers moved over to her apartment in the Tiltyard, and there would be music and dancing past midnight. It was quite different from the official celebrations. It was louder, and more vibrant, and very glamorous. Exciting, new, and rather dangerous. The King rarely attended. When he wished to see the Lady Anne, he would send for her, and she would leave the party going on in her absence. Henry was not really part of this new generation, the young people who wanted change. He had just fallen in love with someone who was.

George Boleyn was now Lord Rochford, but he was still as familiar as he had been before. Unhappily married, he would flirt with every woman present, even the servant maids like me. He and I got on well together, as he would often try out his latest musical composition on me, as Lady Anne was so often absent.

"Hey Kat, come with me," he ordered. "I need some help on a chorus, I can't make it work." We were both standing at the edge of Anne's presence chamber, watching the dancing going on in front of us. They were dancing the Salterello, a fast Italian dance, which had recently arrived at the court. All the dancers stepped up to each other, then sprung into the air with exhilarating whoops of joy. Catching each other as they landed, they linked hands, and then spun each other round in a whirl of silk skirts and velvet robes.

"I want to watch the dancing," I protested. "I don't know this dance."

"Don't be boring Kat. You can watch the dancing any-time. But this is your only chance to make a song with me." His merry brown eyes smiled at me enticingly. He was a very handsome young man, with a fine figure, well shown off by his close-fitting blue doublet and hose. He beckoned me per-suasively:

"Come on Kat, I'll bring us some wine. We can go to Anne's chamber; we won't be disturbed there." I shrugged my shoul-ders.

"Oh, alright then. But I'm only staying a few minutes. Will is coming tonight, and I want to see him."

George laughed. "So, is he your young man, this Will?" he said in a tone that suggested that was a laughable idea.

"No, we are just friends. He works for Thomas Cromwell. He's training to be a lawyer."

"Men and women cannot be friends. He will want more. Kat do not worry, I will get you back within twenty minutes. Now come with me!" He held out his hand and led me away from the Presence Chamber. Turning back as we left, I caught sight of Will entering by the main door.

"Hold on, there's Will!" I cried out to George. But he was pulling me away.

"You'll be back in twenty minutes, now be a good girl and come with me," he ordered. He was not above using his exalted status to get what he wanted. We walked through sev-eral chambers, each one richly furnished with tapestries and rich carpets, with bowls of fruit and silver goblets standing on side tables and oak settles placed beside blazing fires. The air smelled of pine, spices, and all the scents of Christmas. Beeswax candles burned in sconces, creating pools of glowing, honey-scented light.

"Here, Kat, come into Anne's chamber," said George. "Come and sit with me beside the fire."

It was hot beside the fire, and he was so close to me that I could have reached out and touched his face without moving. I could smell the scent of his fresh linen and the sandalwood oil that was on his hair. I felt uncomfortable.

"So where's this song then? Have you written it down?" I asked, inching away from him.

He sprang up. "Have some wine first Kat. Let me fetch you a goblet. Anne keeps good wines here, much better than in the Presence Chamber!" He went over to the table and poured wine for us both.

"Here, Kat," he said, offering me a goblet. "Let us drink to my sister, who will be Queen of England within the year! If you play your cards right Kat, you will benefit as we all will do." I drank some of the wine. It tasted of raisins and honey.

"I will serve Lady Anne as well as I can," I said. "I am a hard worker, she knows that."

"Ah, but will you serve me, Kat?" George asked silkily. "You are a fine-looking woman, Kat, but you are causing me trouble. You are far too distracting for me. I am an important man, that cannot happen." He took my face in his hands and bent his lips to mine. I felt the wiriness of his beard against me. He started to push inside my mouth with his tongue; his lips felt very wet, and his tongue was intrusive.

I pulled back, disgusted. He restrained me with his arms.

"No, my lord. Get off me!" I tried to push him off, but he was very strong and pinned me down. I twisted my face away from him and cried out. "I do not want this! I thought we were going to talk about a composition."

"You are very naive Kat," he panted. "Why would a women go off with a man to a bedchamber if she didn't want something from him? Come on now, you want me! It would be nice, wouldn't it, to have a lord as your lover?"

I managed to wriggle out of his grasp and stood up, but he

grabbed me again and tried to drag me to the bed. I twisted out of his grip and ran to the door. He followed me but stopped as I reached the outer chamber, where a couple of gentlemen were sitting at a table playing cards. I strode through the chamber, bobbing to the gentlemen and making for the outer door. Chamber after chamber I went through, retracing the steps George and I had taken just a few minutes earlier. As I neared the Presence Chamber, I realised that I was safe, and I started to tremble. Tears came into my eyes as I realised what might have happened.

George Boleyn, Lord Rochford, had just tried to rape me. He had tried to take me for sex against my will. This was in spite of the fact that he knew me. He knew I was close to the Lady Anne. That didn't matter to him. I was just a musician, a servant maid, to be taken whenever he wanted. I wondered if that was what had happened to my mother. Had she been raped by the King when she was going about her duties, maybe cleaning and tidying or bringing wine and sweet biscuits? Had she been unable to stop him because, as a serving maid, her job was to obey? I felt the hate mount inside me. These men, these noblemen who used women as easily as they used a handkerchief, I despised them!

I wondered what would happen with Lord George. Would he complain about me to Lady Anne? He could not tell her what had happened, but he might make up some story about me being rude or unwilling? I didn't know. I hadn't realised it until then, but working for Queen Katherine, I was so protected. No man would dare to trouble one of Queen Katherine's maids, for she would have gone straight to the King. It was a bitter irony that this majestic King would have agreed with the Queen on this and punished the man responsible. He was proud that his court was one where decency and morality were observed. And yet, he had mistresses, he had illegitimate children. He had taken advantage of a servant girl, I was sure of that. I was glad that he didn't come often to Lady Anne's chambers, as I hated the very sight of him.

When I got back into the Presence Chamber the dancing was in full swing. I looked for Will but couldn't see him. He wasn't in the group of men who stood by the fire drinking and watching the dancers. I hoped desperately that he hadn't left already. I so much wanted to talk to him, to get his reassurance after George Boleyn's assault on me. I strained my eyes, trying to find his familiar figure amongst the crowds.

Then I saw him, deep in the middle of the dance. He was smiling and laughing, talking loudly to his partner, who was flushed and rosy with the exercise. Lady Madge Shelton, one of Lady Anne's ladies. One of the most beautiful women at court, who was always with a crowd of admirers around her. And now, she was dancing with Will, and he looked like he was enjoying himself. I told myself that I was just friends with Will. I had told him many times I would not marry. So I should be pleased that he was enjoying the company of a pretty woman. But I wasn't pleased at all. I wanted desperately for the dance to stop, and to be able to go over and talk with him, take him away from her arms.

"You're not being fair," I told myself. But I couldn't help it. I was jealous. The dancing went on and on, with one dance blending into another. And throughout it all, Will and Lady Madge danced on with their eyes trained on each other.

At last, they stopped, he bowed to her and went on his way. I pushed my way through the crowds to his side, my breathing short with anxiety.

"Will! I was looking for you!" I panted. "Did you not see me at the side?"

He looked at me coolly and responded, "I saw you Kat, but you were with the Lord Rochford. I would not wish to interrupt your private conversation together." He said the word "conversation" as if it was something dirty on the bottom of his shoe. I cringed, bright red with embarrassment.

"But no matter, Kat. I found a good companion in Lady

Shelton. I did not know how much pleasure I would find in ladies' company. You are right, marriage is not for you. I did not miss you." He bowed and walked away. I tried to go after him, but he was walking too quickly, and it was difficult to push my way through the crowd.

"Will!" I called out, causing some courtiers to turn round and stare at me. He did not answer, but left the chamber and walked into the darkness. I stood there, thinking that these glamorous, stylish people who were all around me were looking at me and laughing inside. A mere musician, a servant, and I had got above myself and my station. They were all talking about me behind their hands, I could tell.

That night, it was as if the sky had fallen in on me. Will had obviously thought I had an assignation with George Boleyn. But he hadn't given me the chance to explain! That really hurt. And then he had found it easy enough to forget me and enjoy the pleasant company of Madge Shelton. Maybe I should just accept it. After all, that was what I had wanted, wasn't it, to be single and in royal service? And that was what I had. Of course, Lady Anne was not yet Queen, but there was no doubt now that she would be. And I would be one of the new servants she brought with her. A singer and a musician, I would flourish at her court. And yet, and yet, that brought me no comfort. In the space of a couple of months I had lost Queen Katherine, and now Will. I felt friendless.

I'll be honest, I shed a few tears that night. All around me the maids slumbered, and yet I could not rid myself of the pain I felt. At last, as the dawn was breaking, I decided to make a plan. I was not going to sit and worry but take affairs into my own hands. I would speak to Lady Anne about her brother. She might then dismiss me, but that was surely better than waiting for him to get rid of me. Then, if I could, I would explain everything to Will. I would say that I had been naive but that nothing had happened, nor ever would. I hoped that he would understand and become my friend again. If that was all that happened, it would be enough.

Lady Anne slept late the next morning. Madge Shelton told me she had been up until after midnight composing sonnets with the King.

"They sit and talk for hours," she said. "Sometimes it is religion, sometimes music, sometimes even architecture! She gets him to think about the new ideas that he hadn't considered before. I tell you Kat, she will bring much good to England."

Lady Anne had me playing the lute while her ladies dressed her. Today she was wearing a deep green silk gown with long sleeves that draped over her white hands. The gown was shot through with tiny sapphires, giving the impression of the sea as she moved. She wore, as she usually did, a sleek French hood, edged with pearls, that showed off a part of her shining dark hair. I wanted desperately to speak to her, but there were people all around. At last though, she was ready, and she dismissed everyone except for me.

"So you enjoyed the dancing last night Kat?" she asked. I noticed that her manner was now more imperious than it had ever been before.

"Yes, my lady," I answered. "But there was one thing...." She nodded.

"George. I wondered if you would say something."

"You know, madam?" I was amazed. I knew the court was full of spies, but how had she found out so quickly?

"He visited me last night after the King had left. He told me he had tried to bed you but that you had pushed him away." Her voice was cold, as if she disliked me. I braced myself for bad news.

"I am sorry, madam; I did not know what to do." I excused myself. But inside I was thinking that it was George who needed to apologise, not me. Lady Anne waved away my apology.

"You did the right thing Kat. But you should not have gone off with him without a chaperone. As a woman you must guard your honour. Look at my sister Mary, the laughing stock of the court – you cannot afford for that to happen to you!"

"Yes, my lady, I thought he just wanted to discuss music with me. I wouldn't have gone if I'd known what was in his mind."

Lady Anne frowned, and then admitted, "I was very angry with George last night. He is like a little boy, he cannot get enough sweetmeats! Kat, if you wish to progress in court, you will avoid any compromising situations. You have no family behind you, no royal connections...."

If only she knew, I thought. But she would never know. It would be a secret forever. Lady Anne continued to talk:

"You have real talent Kat, the ability to become a great musician and singer. I order you to concentrate on that and speak with my brother only in company."

"Yes, my lady, I will," I agreed and bobbed a curtsey.

"He will have a sore head this morning," she observed drily. "Too much wine, and then a stern rebuke. Not what he was looking for!"

Lady Anne was in good spirits this spring. There was a new cleric in town, a Thomas Cramner, whose opinion was that the King should retain control over the church within his kingdom. King Henry, having read William Tyndale's book, "The Obedience of a Christian Man", took to the idea enthusiastically. At last, they could see a way out. Rather than wait for years for the Pope's ruling, if Henry was in fact the head of the English church, then he could enable that church to give him the annulment he desired. There was a sense that things at last were moving.

I saw Will often in passing, but he never had time to stop. He was always busy on Thomas Cromwell's business, and when I went to the Cromwell house, he was never there. I yearned to explain what had happened that night with George to him, but I could never catch him alone.

Lady Anne caught me looking sad one afternoon and

demanded to know what was the matter. Tears filled my eyes, and I broke down. She wasn't the kind to be motherly and sympathetic, but she did reach out a hand to me.

"Don't cry Kat. Surely it is not too bad," she said, with the optimism of one who was about to have her own dreams come true.

"It is, it is," I sobbed. "Will Cooke will no longer speak to me! He saw me going off with your brother that night and thinks I allowed him to bed me. You know I didn't! I keep trying to explain it to him, but he never has time to listen." I mopped at my face with a handkerchief.

"So... you are interested in Will Cooke?" Anne asked. "I thought you had said you would never marry."

"I miss him so much, my lady. I don't want to marry him, well not yet. But I cannot bear to be enemies with him."

Lady Anne pursed her lips.

"Leave him to me," she said. "I will speak with him. We will sort him out, don't worry. I cannot have my lutanist crying while she plays! And yes, you can marry if you wish, but don't go and do it until I allow you! Now go and fetch my mirror. I have an unfortunate spot that I need to cover."

It took a few weeks, but Lady Anne was as good as her word. It was late afternoon, and a small group of courtiers were playing cards with her. There was her brother George, Henry Norris, and William Brereton among others. I was singing, something I would do for hours on end to entertain her. The door opened, and a footman came in, followed by Will. He looked severe and business-like in his black doublet and hose. I thought he had never looked more handsome. He glanced at me sourly, before bowing to the company.

"You sent for me, my lady?" he said questioningly.

"Yes, indeed Will. Now, I have heard that you are a clever young man, and I know you work for Master Cromwell. So you are on our side. But what are you doing making my musician Kat so miserable? She is like a silly girl who hasn't been given the sweetmeats she wants. I cannot bear it; she is so depressing! You must help me here, Master Cooke."

Will glanced at me, and then at George.

"I did not think that Mistress Kat was interested in me, my lady. She showed interest in other gentlemen, far beyond my station."

"George!" snapped Lady Anne. "This is your fault! Now, will you explain to Master Cooke what you were doing with his sweetheart last Christmas?"

Lord George Boleyn looked bored and threw his cards down on the table. He drawled out his reply.

"It is quite simple, sister, and you know it. I wanted Mistress Kat's assistance with a composition I was writing. She has a quite unusual talent, particularly for one with no noble background. And that's it. We were sitting maybe too close, and she misunderstood me. But my sister has told me that I should not have compromised her in the way I did. Master Cooke, do not be anxious. Nothing occurred, nor would it have!"

Will looked quite shocked by this, his face working to control his emotions.

After a moment, he bowed and said, "Thank you, my lord, for explaining the situation. That eases my mind." He turned and bowed to Lady Anne and then looked at me. Our eyes met.

"I must go. Master Cromwell has many communications with the European universities that I must read and reply to. I bid you good afternoon." He bowed again and turned and left.

Lord George Boleyn laughed and then picked up his cards. He turned to his sister and said, "And now, sister, may we get on with our game? We have sorted out the servants' romance, and so let us continue with the important things in life." The company laughed, and I flushed with embarrassment.

Lady Anne raised her eyebrows and then remarked, "Well, I did my best. Now Kat, give us some more music! Something cheerful please."

I cleared my throat and started to play the lute. I don't

know how I managed to hit the notes. Lady Anne had done what she promised. But it hadn't had the effect I'd hoped for. Obviously, Will was not interested in me anymore, and I felt like weeping.

"Come on, Kat, you sound like a wet Wednesday!" said George. "Be merry girl! Your reputation is cleared, and so, for your mistress's sake, give us a smile!"

CHAPTER

18

It was July, and the court was at Windsor Castle. Still, there was the King in his apartments, the Queen in hers, and Lady Anne in separate, very grand quarters. The days were full of jousts, masques and hunting. Sometimes the King and Queen went to Mass together, more often they did not. When the Queen was in the main hall, Lady Anne was not there. When the Queen was not in the great hall, Lady Anne sat in her place, as if she was already crowned.

I felt very sorry for Queen Katherine, although I only saw her at a distance. We were not in London, so Will was not around. I had seen him a couple of times since Lady Anne had spoken to him, and he had been friendly, but not effusive. He had shown no wish to speak with me privately, or to have anything other than the briefest of contacts.

I tried not to think of him. I was working harder than I had ever done before. I would be on duty most afternoons, entertaining the ladies as they sewed or played cards. On days when there were jousting, I got an hour or so off to watch the knights. It was a risky business, and I understood that Lady Anne did not want the King to continue with it. He was in his forties now, and jousting was really a game for a young man.

I imagined having a man in full armour, hurtling at me on a two-ton steed with a sharp pointed lance in his hand. The game was to land a blow on him before he did it to you. I was glad that women and common people did not engage in this sport, as it was prohibitively expensive. Thank god it was only young noblemen, desperate to prove their virility, that took part. I did not like the thought of Will in that situation at all.

One morning, I was woken up by a maid servant. King Henry and Lady Anne had already left to go hunting, on their way to Chertsey Abbey. The rest of their households were to follow on immediately.

I asked, "What about the Queen, is she to come too?" The maid servant shook her head.

"No, she is to stay here. The King sent her a message. She looked to see if he had gone, but he didn't even say goodbye!"

And so we packed up everything belonging to Lady Anne and loaded it into the wagons. We didn't see Queen Katherine at all. Her servants were going about their business as usual. There were no wagons being packed for her. Every now and then, I saw groups whispering in corners, asking each other what was going on. Lady Jane Seymour passed me on her way to the stables.

"The Queen will ride this afternoon," she told me. "The horses must be prepared."

"Where is she going?" I asked. "Surely she is not going to try to go to Chertsey?"

Lady Jane shook her head sadly, "No, poor lady. She has been weeping all morning, and she refuses to eat or drink. We suggested she went for a ride to clear her head, and she said she would think about it. So we will get the horses ready and then persuade her to take the air."

"How is she? Is she alright?" I asked anxiously.

Lady Jane looked at me and then said pointedly, "Why should you care? You were never on her side."

I was stung by her remark, and protested, "Oh I was, my

lady! I just tried to persuade her to avoid all this pain."

Lady Jane looked long at me and then softened a bit. "You may be right, Kat," she said, "but you did not know the Queen. She will never, ever give up the role that God has called her to. No matter what the pain, she will always see herself as Queen, and King Henry's wife."

The summer passed pleasantly enough, with masques and music and jousting. I did not go on the hunting parties, but that meant I had more time to practice my lute, and my songs. I was writing more songs but hadn't played them to anyone yet. If only Will had been around, he would have listened.

I did have one visitor. John the Messenger came to find me after delivering a message for King Henry from the Queen. He was respectful, as always, and told me that he was now married to a blacksmith's daughter, who was expecting their baby. I congratulated him and breathed a sigh of relief. He had been kind to me, and I liked him, but I was glad he had dropped the idea of courting me. However, I was keen to talk.

"How does the Queen?" I asked him. "Did you see her when you were at Windsor?"

"Yes, indeed I did," he said. "She is well. Princess Mary is staying at Windsor, and they spend every minute of the day together. After a long separation, this is what every mother wants."

I nodded, agreeing with him. If the King had now broken with her, that meant that she and Princess Mary could spend some time alone together. I was sure that this was what they both needed and hoped that the King would allow it to continue. I'm sad to say, daughter, that later on the King stopped any further visits from Princess Mary, and that summer was the last time mother and daughter saw each other. But that was in the future, and for the time being they were happy together.

A thought came into my head.

"Do you remember that woman who booked my passage

with you when you took me to Woking Palace?" I asked, wondering if Mistress Stabb was still at the same address.

"Indeed I do," he answered. "The midwife, who people accuse of being a witch. She left that house where you used to live. She's living now with her sister in Southwark, I forget where. She is getting on in years now, and her sister looks after her. They have a pie shop."

I sighed. I had hoped that she was maybe still in the same house. She had refused to tell me my history three times before, but I'd thought that maybe she might have changed her mind. But I couldn't find her now. How many pie shops were there in Southwark? And when would I have the time to go and search? Now that I was one of Lady Anne's musicians, I scarcely had a day off. In Queen Katherine's household, I had held a privileged place, with duties so vague that I could more or less do as I pleased. It was very different now.

We went back to London at the end of the summer and moved into Greenwich Palace. Lady Anne had moved into the Queen's apartments, which had been refurbished especially for her. I heard that the King had told Queen Katherine to leave Windsor Castle and move to a smaller place called The More. It now seemed just a matter of time before the powerful men decided that her marriage had never been. I felt desperately sorry for her and wished I could comfort her. But again I felt that if she had given in to the King, it would be better for her. And she, of course, could not forgive me for thinking that.

I started to see Will again, now we were back in London. At first it was just in passing, as he hurried about his business for Thomas Cromwell, but one morning he stopped and asked me if we could talk. We went to a window seat, looking out over the courtyard, and sat together.

"I wanted to apologise, Kat. I doubted you. I thought that you were impressed with George Boleyn. I thought now you know you are the King's daughter; you would be setting your sights higher than me. And then I got very jealous and could not bear to think of you being with him. He is a reprobate Kat, and not to be trusted."

"I know that now," I assured him. "He did try to rape me; it was worse than he said. But I got away, and then Lady Anne told him he was not to trouble me further."

"He tried to rape you?" Will's face flushed with anger. "If I had known, I would have fought him!"

"Will, you know that would end badly for you!" Our voices were raised, and a couple of passing courtiers looked curiously at us. "Don't even consider fighting him. I got away. No harm done!" I sounded angry, but inside I could feel the relief flooding through me. I hadn't lost Will after all.

I still had to check though. "I thought you liked Madge Shelton," I queried, a little archly.

"Indeed I do," Will smiled. "She is a very pleasant lady. But unfortunately, I have my heart set on the guttersnipe that I grew up with!"

I looked at him and smiled, feeling happy for the first time in many months. He took my hand in his and brought it to his lips.

"Kat, will you stop all your doubts now, and marry me? I love you deeply, you know that. When I thought you were lost to me, it was hard to carry on. I couldn't bear the thought of going through life without you. I know that you are the King's child, however secret that is, and I know that if the King ever accepted you, you could marry much higher than me. But never more loving. And no one else can give you a truer heart."

I paused for a moment, and then the words rushed out, "Yes, I will!"

He started in surprise, and then his face cracked with an enormous grin. Quickly, I qualified my acceptance. "But give me a few months more in Lady Anne's service. I will be sorry to leave it all behind."

Will smiled at me and waved his hand. "You do not need

to leave it all behind, Kat. You can continue as a musician in the court, and if we have children, why then we can get a nurse for the children. The grand ladies do it all the time."

"I could do that?" I found it hard to comprehend such an unusual arrangement. What man wishes for his wife to be away from the household working? But then, Will had a point. The grand ladies did it and took it for granted that their children would be reared by wet-nurses. If they could, why not me?

"Why not you, Kat?" he said quickly, "You and me, we were always different. I got to know you as the amazing person that you are. I wasn't dazzled by your beauty..."

"Thanks very much!" I laughed. He held up his hand to still me.

"... although that beauty grows yet more wonderful every day. And Kat, I am not beguiled by your wealth, and nor are you beguiled by mine. But we fit together Kat, we always will."

That hour with him was enchanted. The sun shone on us as confessions of our love and hopes tumbled out of each other. My eyes did not move from his face, and nor did his from mine.

We decided to announce our betrothal at Christmas and get married the following Spring. That would give me enough time to get around the idea of being a married woman, and Will enough time to find lodgings for us both.

In private, Lady Anne was growing restive.

"Again, we wait! How can it take so long for the King to declare himself head of the church? It is his church after all? My youth is passing, Kat," she said one day when I was playing to her as she lay on her bed. "What if my fertile years are gone? I could not bear to be childless." She looked wistfully out of the window, where some small children were playing in the fallen leaves. "And to be childless to the King... well, that would be... dangerous."

She looked afraid then, like a deer facing its hunters. She knew how much rested on her ability to bear sons. King Henry loved her, that was true. But she had to give him sons. I wondered how often this was on her mind, and whether it might hold her back. But she had come too far now to withdraw, especially now when her crown was coming into view.

"My lady, that will not happen. Your mother and your sister were both fertile into their later years. You will be the same. You will have a tableful of sons soon, all needing to be fed!" She smiled distractedly at me and waved for me to carry on playing.

"You are lucky Kat, that you do not have these matters to concern you. Your father never despaired of having a son. If he had daughters, he would marry them and bring their husbands into the business."

"Lady Anne, I do not know who my father is," I said quietly. "He may not have known who I was even."

She grimaced and waved for me to carry on. "Well in that case he never had the worry, did he?" she said, closing the subject.

November came, and with it cold mists and frosty mornings. The court was chilly in the corridors, and the draughts came in from every window. One afternoon I was singing with some of Anne's ladies when Will was announced. The singing stopped as he came in, bowed to Lady Anne and to the rest of the company, and then spoke to Lady Anne.

"My lady, I need to speak with Mistress Cooke on an urgent matter. Would you excuse her for a few minutes?"

Lady Anne looked annoyed. "We were in the middle of this roundel," she said irritably. "I cannot easily spare my musician."

Will bowed again and tried to persuade her. "It is just for a few minutes, my Lady. My master Thomas Cromwell has sent me on this occasion. He would be most pleased if you were to allow Mistress Kat to speak with me."

"Very well," Lady Anne said. "What is it they say? Whatever Master Cromwell wants, Master Cromwell gets?"

She looked a little mollified. She knew that Cromwell was working night and day to ensure that she could marry the King, and so she could afford to go a few minutes without music to meet his request.

I curtseyed and joined Will, both of us leaving quickly before she had a chance to change her mind. Once we were out of the chamber, he took me through many chambers and stairways to the office where he worked. It was dusty and dark compared with the rest of the palace and piled up with books, files and manuscripts.

"Sit down, Kat," he said, gesturing me to a chair. "Have some wine," pouring goblets of wine for both of us. "I think this is important. He picked up an old file that was on the desk and sat down next to me. He opened it and brought out an old document that looked like it had been written some time before.

"Last year, an old woman came to Austin Friars, Master Cromwell's house," he said. "She asked for me by name, but I was away from the house. She said to the maid that she had an important document for my sister. Well, the maid told her that I did not have a sister. Of course, Kat, they know you as my friend and not my sister. The maid told her to leave, at which the old woman became tearful. She begged the maid to take the document, saying she had to grant the wish of a dying woman. She stood there crying, and at last the maid took the document, mainly to get rid of her. The old woman thanked her profusely and went on her way. The maid was busy and put the document on a desk in the office for me to see when I returned. As it happened, I did not return for several days, and before I came back the document had been filed away. The maid forgot about it, and I was never told about it. And so, it sat in a back file, where we put everything that isn't current, but might be useful." He paused and took a drink of wine before he continued. I started to tremble.

"So Kat, yesterday I was looking for a list of university dons who support the King. I knew I had it somewhere but couldn't find it. In desperation, I opened this old file and found this document."

I started to tremble. What was written on this grubby piece of paper? He put it into my hands. "See it is addressed to you, Mistress Kat Cooke, care of her brother." I stared at it. The handwriting was spidery, not a good secretary hand at all. But my name was clearly there.

"Have you read this?" I asked Will.

He nodded. "I didn't want to bring you over if it was nothing. But I saw very soon that it is very important. Here, read it." He handed me the document, and I started to read.

The inscription on the outside was as he'd said, "To Mistress Kat Cooke, care of her brother." I started to read. Daughter, I have copied it for you, exactly as I read it. This is the account of what happened on the night when I was born:

"I am entrusting this letter to my sister, Mistress Elphick, in the hope that she will find you, Mistress Cooke. I am near death, and I cannot go to my grave without telling you the truth about your birth. I am sorry that I did not tell you earlier. It was true, I was concerned for your safety, but I was also concerned for my own safety. My story could be used by enemies of the King to make the succession to the throne insecure. I was afraid I would be implicated in something for which I would be punished severely. I have done wrong, but nothing was designed to harm the Tudors. It is important that you understand that, and that you respect my dying wish to leave this matter undisturbed. If it ever comes out, it could harm so many people, and even the monarchy itself.

"I have worked as a midwife for thirty years now, and I have delivered many, many healthy babies. But I have never before or since encountered a birth like the one I attended on 31st January, 1510. It was in the middle of the night, about one or two, when I was woken by loud knocking at my door. It was a messenger from the court. He told me that the Queen had gone into labour prematurely, and that the royal midwife was not in London. He asked me urgently to go and help the Queen.

"Of course, I got dressed, picked up my midwife's bag, and hastened away with the messenger. I had not been in the royal court before, but I was confident of my ability as a midwife. When it comes to labour, a Queen is no different from an ordinary maid.

"When I arrived at the palace, I was taken swiftly through many richly decorated chambers, until at last I reached the Queen's birthing room. She was lying on a pallet bed, with a couple of ladies sitting beside her, holding her hand as she cried out. I could see that she was labouring hard, and that the babe was due to arrive soon. I took the place of the ladies and felt her belly as she had contractions. I told her to breathe through it, to bring the air into her lungs. A doctor arrived, but he was content to allow me to manage the labour. Doctors do not have the knowledge of birth that us midwives do.

"The Queen was in a lot of pain, but after each contraction she gave me small triumphant smiles. 'I will be a mother tonight, god willing,' she told me. I remember that, I remember the hope that filled her and made her brave. I answered her that yes, God willing, she would be a mother by that night. I did not add that the baby was very early, from the size of her belly, around seven months. It would need many prayers to help it survive.

"As the contractions grew closer and closer together, the Queen became restless, calling out to God and the Virgin Mary and clutching at her holy girdle. The pain was almost too much for her, but she was getting the instinctive need to push the baby out in spite of it. I propped her half up with pillows, with her legs parted in front of her. I could see the baby's head crowning in the birth canal. I told her just two more pushes, then she would have her baby. She pushed once and let out a terrible cry of pain. I told her to wait for a moment until the next contraction, and then she was to push with all her might.

"With an unearthly scream, the Queen pushed, and I was able to guide the baby out into the world. It was a little girl, perfectly formed, but she was dead. Her chest was not moving and she didn't cry. I did what I always do, I sucked out the baby's airways and rubbed hard on her chest. But still it didn't move.

"The doctor, hovering, came and put his hand on the tiny child. "Your Majesty, the child is dead," he said sombrely. "May God rest her soul."

"The Queen broke down and started a terrible keening, the grief was bursting out of her. The doctor reached for his silver scissors, cut the cord, and waved to me. He told me to take the babe away and that he would examine the Queen.

"I took the little dead girl, wrapped her in some linen and took her into the next door chamber, where I laid her upon the table. Shortly, her little body would be disposed of. The doctor called me back into the room. He took me aside and whispered to me that the Queen was still pregnant, that there was another baby inside her. He had felt her belly, and it was still firm.

"He told me to help the Queen to bed, where she must rest. During all of this the Queen was in a storm of grief, wailing and hugging herself. Her ladies stood helpless, unable to help in the face of this misery, none of them listening to the frantic conversations between me and the doctor.

"Even now, I remember the words that the doctor said to Queen Katherine, 'Your Majesty, do not distress yourself, there is another babe in your womb.'

"The Queen looked dazed, as if she could not quite understand what was going on. She kept on saying, 'Another baby? Another baby?' as if she couldn't believe it. The doctor was very matter-of-fact when he answered,

"'Your Majesty, you were carrying twins. There is every sign that the second baby will be well. You must rest now, madam. Drink some honey and eggs for strength, and say your prayers from your bed.'

"'So I am still with child?' she asked.

"'Yes, indeed Madam, and there is every chance that it will be a healthy boy. But you must rest now.' He swept out of the chamber, leaving me to deliver the placenta. The Queen was very pale and quiet, but not crying anymore. I washed her, put her into a clean night shift, and helped her into the great state bed. Then the ladies tended to her, bringing her spiced ale and sponging her face with lavender water.

"I took the bloody sheets from the pallet bed into the next chamber and tidied away the signs of birth. I remember the King came to visit his wife, we all curtseyed. I had never seen either the King or Queen before, and it was strange to see them in such a situation. The King was consoling the Queen and told her that she must rest until the next baby came. He said that he had announced that one baby was dead, too early born to live, but the other babe was still safely in her womb. The court would be praying for the Queen, and for the son that she was carrying.

"There were no prayers for the baby that had died. She had not been christened, so she would go to limbo, where unbaptised babies stayed for all eternity. People don't like to think about that, it makes them uneasy – what kind of God is it that excludes innocents from heaven? But I am just an ordinary woman. I am no scholar, so I don't understand.

"The King stayed for about an hour and then left, instructing the Queen to sleep. I went into the next chamber and called for a laundress to collect the bloody linen that I had taken in there. That was when Meg came to the door, curtseying to me and hurrying over to take the piles of cloth.

"It was then that we heard a little snuffling sound from the table, almost like a little puppy. The handkerchief that had been covering the dead baby moved slightly. I ran over to the table and pulled the handkerchief off. The little girl was struggling to breathe. Each breath was an effort, but she was alive.

"Meg couldn't believe it. She kept saying, 'The babe lives, the babe lives!' I had no time to wonder. This baby had to be saved. I cleared her airways again and started to gently massage her tiny heart. She was no bigger than a child's doll. Slowly, her breathing started to become regular, and her colour became pink. I knew I must keep her warm, it was very cold in the ante chamber, so I wrapped her in the handkerchief and then my cloak.

"It was then that I made the mistake that has haunted me for the rest of my life. I know I should have gone back into the Queen and told her that the baby was alive, but then she had already been pronounced dead. The whole of the court would know by now. Anyway, she probably wouldn't last the night, she wasn't well. If I told the truth, I could get into serious trouble for missing the signs of life in the baby. I don't know how that happened, I really don't. I am sure that the babe was dead when she was delivered. Somehow, being in that cold room for a couple of hours had brought her back to life.

"So then I knew I had to decide what to do with the baby. Meg agreed that we couldn't tell the Queen. But this baby needed milk, and a mother's warmth, immediately. I wondered if I could find a wet-nurse for her who had no connection with the court. Then Meg told me that her sister had just had a baby boy that very day. Meg could bring the baby to her to be fed alongside the little boy. Meg told me her sister was a good woman, the wife of a cook, and she would be pleased to take care of the baby for a few weeks, until it was decided what to do.

"So it was that we left the palace with the baby girl wrapped up and in my midwife's bag. I told the servants that I had arranged for the burial of the little girl in an unmarked grave, and that the body had already gone.

"Mistress Kat, that little girl was you. You are the legitimate daughter of King Henry and Queen Katherine, born in 1510. This will seem extraordinary to you, but I swear on the

Bible that it is the truth. This has been my secret, and Meg's for many years. Then Meg died, and it was just my secret. Now it will become yours. You will never be able to claim your heritage. You would not be believed. The King and Queen would not accept an older daughter for Princess Mary, it would be too complicated. Now, if you had been a boy, it might have been different.

"So, Mistress Kat, you spent your first few months safe in Joan's arms, drinking her milk and sleeping in a crib together with baby Will. Joan never knew where you had come from, just that Meg had found you. Meg took the royal handkerchief that you were wrapped in before she handed you over to Joan, and we agreed never to talk about it again.

"When you were weaned, I talked with Joan about finding you another home, but she loved you by then, and she didn't want to give you up. I could see that you would have a happy childhood with her, and so I let things be. You may not be living as a Princess, but I can tell you that you were happier than any Princess could be. But then the sweating sickness came and took Joan, and you were left on your own. I knew I had to get you to Meg to take care of you. She was the only person who knew your history. I thought she was still with the court and so I sent you there – what I didn't know was that she had got married.

"Joan thought I was a bad influence on you both. She thought I was a witch. I wouldn't say a witch, I would say a wise woman. I'm afraid I used to tease her sometimes because she would get so annoyed. I could sometimes see the future, and it's true that people used to visit me to look into the pictures in the fire, but I have never put a spell on anyone! I could see part of your future, but what I knew was your past, and the effect it might have on you.

"Now I am near death, I realise it was wrong to hide this from you, that you have a right to know. It will not make your life easier, but, god willing, it will help you to understand where you came from. I had hoped to find you at Queen Katherine's court, but you were no longer in attendance there.

Signed Agnes Stabb, 5th August 1531."

I put the document down on the table and started to weep. All those years of not knowing, of believing I was the result of a servant girl getting into trouble. All that time I thought that the King had seduced and then deserted my mother. And it wasn't true. I was a child the King and Queen had wanted, had prayed for, but had thought was dead. How my life would have been different if I'd taken my first breath in the birthing chamber instead of in the antechamber, next to a pile of dirty linen! Princess Mary would have been my younger sister, and I would have been the heir. I thought for a moment what that might mean, and realised I was glad that life had been denied me. The court was a dangerous and volatile place for the main players, and I was happiest on the sidelines.

Will stood over me as I mopped my face with my handkerchief.

"But what happened to the other baby?" I asked. "The one that was still in the Queen's womb? Why is there no royal child of around my age?"

"There was no other baby Kat, the doctor was wrong," Will answered. "And some months later the Queen had to admit it, much to her sorrow."

I cried out at the thought of all Queen Katherine had suffered, and the pain it had caused her. I wanted to hold her in my arms and comfort her, tell her that she had another daughter who had lived.

"Here, Kat, drink some wine," he gestured to the goblet, and I picked it up and sipped. It felt warm and comforting. I looked over at Will and saw that he had got down on one knee. He took my hand in his and kissed it, his face looking very serious.

"I must say this to you, you may have changed your mind about getting married, but I will be yours forever. Princess

Katherine Tudor, I, William Cooke, do become your liege man of life and limb and of earthly worship. I swear that I will be faithful and bear true allegiance to you for all of my life, so help me God."

CHAPTER

19

I looked at Will, kneeling there, and I knew straight away what I must do. At last there was no doubt in my mind. I knew where I came from, and now I knew where I was going.

"None of that, Will," I said, raising him up. "We are equals, you and I. I may have been born in a palace, but I was brought up alongside you. You have been my constant friend, my companion and my love. Ever since I found out that I was not your sister, I have been lost, trying to find out who I am. Now, at last, I know. And praise Jesu, I realise that it does not matter. Will, we must get married! We don't need to tell anyone yet, but I want you to be my husband. There is something I have to do, and I want you to do it with me."

Will was staring down at me, a dawning light in his eyes. He took me in his arms and kissed me, a long, hard kiss that had a depth of longing in it. He paused, "So, you still want to marry me?" he asked, "Even though I am so far below you?"

"Will, you and me, neither of us are below. We walk together." I kissed him back, twining my arms around his neck. I pressed up against him, feeling his desire for me. I knew that he couldn't do anything, and I enjoyed teasing him, just a little.

"Watch it madam," he said, "you won't get away with this when you are my wife." The determination in his voice made me shiver. I wondered what our wedding night would be like. At last I would know what it was like to be a woman, to have the love of a man. I had learnt at court that this love was the most powerful force a woman could experience. How would it take me, who all my life had declared my intention to remain single?

"I'll do as I please," I laughed.

Will chuckled, a strangely satisfied sound. "Ah, my love, you will do as you please, and so, wife, you will please me."

We heard footsteps outside, and the door swung open. Master Cromwell stepped inside, casting a shrewd look at me and Will. He looked more solid than before, and his clothes were richer. He was becoming a powerful man, and I wondered if he would be displeased by our embrace. But he was in a good mood and looking forward to a large dinner.

"I am sorry to disturb you young lovers," he smiled. "Mistress Kat, have you finally agreed to marry this reprobate? If so, he is a lucky man." He saw the document on the table and picked it up. He scanned it quickly and then looked straight at us.

"What's here? Has this just come in?" Now, he wasn't the friendly master but the man of business, always needing to know what was going on. Even his voice was harder.

"No, that's mine..." I said vainly, "I was asking Will about it. It is of no importance." But Cromwell continued to read it. His eyes widened in surprise as he took in the matter of the document. He looked at me and then whistled.

"Well, Mistress Kat," he said curtly. "It seems that you are not as you appear. What a surprising confession. How long have you known about this?"

I looked down at the floor and said, "Only today...."

Will interjected, "It is only now, Master Cromwell. We have had clues about Kat's identity before, but it was just today, when we read this, that we knew the whole story."

"And how did this document come to be in my office?" Cromwell asked, staring at Will.

"It was sent here for me, but you know the office boys, they put it away, and I haven't seen it till today." Will was respectful of his master, but not afraid. I told myself I must be brave and trust this man. He was said to be ruthless, but also a good master and kind to those around him. There was nothing for it. I had to tell him the whole story.

Once I had finished, Cromwell looked thoughtfully at me and made a mocking bow.

"Well, well, Mistress Kat, or should I say Princess?" He smiled, and it wasn't an entirely friendly smile. "You realise, of course, that this can never come out? People remember the pretenders to Henry the Seventh's throne, Lambert Simnel and Perkin Warbeck. They will say you are a liar, or they may even use you to challenge the succession. Have you got that ambition Kat? You would end up with your head on the block. You don't want that, do you? Let us forget this. Marry your Will, and I will look after you both."

He moved quickly over to the fire, holding my document, tore it into four pieces and threw it into the flames. I watched it burn, the only evidence of my true identity.

Dismayed, I turned to Cromwell, "How can I go back to being a foundling when I know my parentage?" I cried out. "I didn't ask to be the child of the King and Queen. I would have been happy to be the daughter of a weaver or a baker. But don't you see, it is important to me to belong somewhere, to someone?"

Cromwell smiled frostily, "You will belong to Will, who is a fine fellow with a great future ahead of him. That is, if he is sensible."

"But I can't just forget all this! It makes a difference to me!"

Will intervened, putting his arm around my shoulder. "Sweetheart, you won't have to forget it. I won't let you. We just need to keep it to ourselves."

I understood he was trying to calm me, but my sense of injustice was too great. "I've been waiting for this for years, you know that. And now, I have to hide it! I don't know if I can."

Cromwell frowned and turned his heavy head towards me. "You are not going to tell the King," he growled. "It will be the worse for you if you do."

Will tightened his grasp around my shoulder, and I gasped, taken aback by Cromwell's harshness.

"Sir, you should not threaten this lady. If you will, you will make an enemy of me." And then I realised. Will would put himself at risk to defend me. It might have been ridiculous to challenge the most powerful man at court. But it made me realise that he was really on my side.

Cromwell commented wryly, "I would not make war with you, Will. I may come off worse." He laughed. "Come on you two. I am here to look after you."

I sensed he understood that I had been shocked and became avuncular.

"Kat, the King is in love. He wants babies with Lady Anne Boleyn. Everything he does is with that in mind. Anyone who stands in the way must be dealt with. For example, Princess Mary is an inconvenience. What will he do with her? Will she no longer be the heir? Will she be declared illegitimate if his marriage to Katherine is annulled?"

He laid his hand on my shoulder and said quietly, "Would the King welcome yet another inconvenience? It might be different if you were a boy, but another girl out of Katherine of Aragon? He would send you to a faraway nunnery, where you would coincidentally fall out of a tower to your death. He is not going to allow anyone to stand in his way, Kat."

Will stood up to face his master. "I will not allow anyone to harm Kat, sir, not anyone!"

Cromwell laughed in his face. "Will, I would not harm your Kat, but there are others who will if her identity becomes public. Fortunately, now that the document has burnt, there is no evidence to back up the story, and it becomes an alehouse tale, a song that lasts for a summer and then dies."

I nodded; I realised the truth in what he said. Looking at Will, I could see what he was offering me, and it was very good indeed. To love and be loved by an honest man and to bear his children. I could understand that if I were to declare myself as a lost Tudor princess, the outlook for me would be bleak indeed. Far better to stay quiet and make a life with Will. Besides, I wanted to continue working as a musician, I wanted to work for Lady Anne at the court. Her patronage was important to me, and her household was always vibrant, exciting and challenging.

And so I accepted the situation and went back to my work as a musician. Lady Anne was getting evermore demanding. She wanted music, then she wanted quiet. She wanted to dance, then she wanted to read. All those in her household suffered.

I had to inform her that I would be getting married. It was important to pick the right time and place. I waited until she was resting one afternoon, after dinner. I played a light country dance as she listened, tapping her fingers on the arm of her chair.

As I finished, I lay down my lute. "I think I will play that song at my wedding, my lady."

Anne started up immediately. "What wedding Kat? What on earth are you talking about?"

"Will Cooke has asked me to marry him. We hope to marry in the Spring."

Anne stood up, strode over to me and stuck her face in mine. I could see the lines starting to form around her eyes.

"You hope to marry? You hope? Why should you marry? You must stay with me. I cannot have my musicians getting married."

"My lady, I would still work for you, if that was acceptable."

Anne looked at me suspiciously. "Why would it be acceptable? Why should everyone marry except for me? You hope to marry, I hope to marry. Why should you be rewarded with a wedding ring when I am not?"

Her fists clenched; she was in an aggressive mood. I stepped back, not wanting to have my hair pulled. When she was in full sail, Anne was a dangerous vessel.

But I felt sorry for her too. How long had she waited for the King, yearned for him and I had just made it a lot worse? Here was her musician just casually informing her that she was going to marry. No wonder her temper got the better of her.

Being Anne, though, the temper passed. She wept copiously, then kissed my cheek and gave me her blessing, "On strict condition that you return to me. I will not lose you!"

"You will not lose me, my lady, I promise."

We got married a couple of months later at Austin Friars church with Will's father, Tom, and Thomas Cromwell as witnesses. I wore my best green gown, with the silver brooch that Queen Katherine had given me pinned to it, and carried a bouquet of rosemary, bay and ivy leaves. I walked down the aisle on my own to meet the man I would love for the rest of my life. I was a little late, and I saw Will looking anxious as he stood at the altar. I felt a moment of pure joy as I saw his face.

"Well met, my love," he said as I reached him, "no last-minute doubts?"

I reached out and touched his hand, "No doubts at all. You are my life."

That night we sat in the great hall of Thomas Cromwell's house at Austin Friars, with all of his household. We were toasted and cheered by the company, with many speeches and good wishes. The wine flowed and Joan, Cromwell's sister-in law, had made special spiced meat pies for our wedding feast. I didn't eat much, as I was both nervous and excited at the same time. Will was sitting next to me, and I felt his warmth and the strength of his body as he put his arm around me. I wanted him, but at the same time I felt a bit scared. I knew what belonging to a man meant, that the most private parts of my body and my life were open to him. I prayed that he would be kind, and then I laughed at myself, for I knew that Will was always kind. Looking at his dear face I knew that I had made the right choice, for he was the man that made me complete. From our poor beginnings, where we lived in a tenement, to our lives now, when he was training to become a lawyer and I was a court musician, we had come on a long journey together. He was the only person I wanted to continue that journey with.

Thomas Cromwell led us up to a chamber where esteemed visitors like Eustace Chapuys sometimes slept. It was a fair size, with tapestries covering every wall. Candles glowed in all the sconces, casting golden lights on the large oak bed. A fire of applewood burnt in the hearth, giving off sweet woody scents.

"May God bless your wedding night," Cromwell said, smiling as he softly closed the door. Will and I stood there and looked at each other. I saw how slender he was, and how the hair on his head curled tightly at the nape of his neck. He looked at me as if he was seeing me in a dream.

"Kat, you are so beautiful. My darling wife, come here, let me undress you." I went to him, and he started unlacing my bodice. His fingers were strong, capable. I reached up to him to help him out of his doublet as he managed at last to remove my gown. For a moment he shivered and clasped me to him.

"Come to bed Kat," he said, leading me to the high old bed. We were both in smocks and hose now, like two children in their night shifts. We were quiet, undemonstrative, as if we were dreaming. But then, as we lay on the bed together, the excitement started to build. He was looking at me strangely, his eyes alight, and I felt prickles of desire deep inside. We clung to each other, kissing and licking and biting each other's faces, necks and hair. He smelt of juniper and salt. I will always think of my wedding night when I smell juniper, even now.

And so we became naked, under the candlelight. I gasped at how beautiful he was, with his narrow hips, broad shoulders and well-muscled chest. He in turn was entranced by me, by my white skin, my pink nipples and my rich red-gold hair, which tumbled down my back. For a moment, we stared at each other, not wanting this moment to pass. But then we embraced each other, crying and laughing before he moved on top of me. And so, we became man and wife, one flesh, the dark and the fair entwined together. It hurt a little, but he was considerate and soothed me until it suddenly became delightful. I responded to him, cleaving unto him, not wanting to let him go.

As he finished, he cried out, "My princess, my princess!" and it was my turn to comfort him, to soothe him in his moment of vulnerability. I cradled him like a child, holding his head to my breasts and stroking his long, dark curls.

I don't know how long we lay there like that, it seemed like an eternity, suspended between heaven and earth, unwilling to move. Eventually we slept, curled up close together, as we had done when we were children. But this was so different now. I knew now that he completed me, and I him. We could never be parted.

Married life suited us both. We lived at Cromwell's house at Austin Friars, with both of us sleeping over at court occasionally. Cromwell had become once more our friend, and he made sure that Will and I were welcomed. He was rarely at home, being almost on call at court. So we spent many hours in our chamber, discovering and loving each other.

I discovered a hunger in myself, for my lovemaking with Will. I lived for our nights together, and the touch of his hand thrilled me. He showed himself to be a kind husband, buying me small gifts, the sugared almonds I loved, a new silk kerchief, some fine leather shoes. We lived in a blissful haze, the two of us. We continued to work, to converse with others. But all that mattered was each other.

My courses continued to come. I was a little disappointed, but I wasn't quite yet ready to be a mother. Will was patient and told me that God would bless us with a child in time. Truthfully, I was relieved. I wanted to continue in Lady Anne's household without the encumbrance of a baby.

One night, after we had made love, I suddenly felt myself weeping. Wil embraced me and did his best to comfort me, but I was overtaken by longing. I was happy, so happy, but I wanted to share my happiness with my mother, Queen Katherine of Aragon.

I started to think of her, cast out of the court with a few loyal ladies. She wasn't seeing the King, and the whole purpose of her life was gone. She had been deserted by so many. That included me, I now recognised. I had left this woman, who had loved me so much, for the Lady Anne, with all her temper tantrums and cruel tongue. I wished now that I hadn't been so harsh and wanted desperately to tell her I was sorry. I wanted to thank her for all her love and tell her the amazing secret of my birth. Maybe it would help her, in her sorrow, to know that she had another daughter who loved her dearly?

Will stroked my hair. He loved my hair, my red Tudor hair as he described it.

"What is the matter, my love? I hate for you to be unhappy. Tell me what troubles you?"

"Will, I'm sorry, I must see my mother. I long to see her. She may be angry, she may cry at the thought of the baby she lost. But I have to tell her, do you understand? I want to go to visit her with you and tell her everything. When she sees us together, she will know I'm alright, and she will have nothing to regret."

Will propped himself up on his elbow and regarded me steadily. "Will she want to see us?" he asked doubtfully.

"She may not! She may not forgive me. But I have to try. I have heard she is unwell, and I fear for her. I just want, just once, to call her my mother and embrace her as the woman who gave birth to me. I want to smell the rose oil in her hair and feel the softness of her hands. Just once more, Will, I promise you."

"Mistress Stabb asked you to keep the secret of your birth, for your own safety. Can we trust the Queen with this?" Will did not know the Queen as I did.

"One thing I know, Will, the Queen is the straightest, most honourable woman I know. I would trust her with my life."

"But what if she wants to bring you to live with her? Say you are some kind of royal bastard and introduce you at court?"

I shook my head. "No, she loves Princess Mary too much to do that. She knows that acknowledging me would threaten the Princess. Of course, she will never recognise me publicly. She used to hate the way that the King brought his bastards to court. She would do nothing to harm Mary. But why deny her the joy of recognising who I am? If we tell her we are married, she will only be happy for us."

Will looked gloomy. "We will have to tell Cromwell," he said. "It's not going to be easy. But if it's that important to you, I'll fight your corner."

We waited until one Sunday when Cromwell was sitting by the fire enjoying a fine Hippocras. He looked up as we came into the room and sat beside him.

"I want to see my mother," I said. "I want to see the Queen and tell her my story."

Cromwell frowned. "What good will that do? She will not believe you. She will never accept anyone in front of Mary."

"I think she will believe me," I cried passionately. "I was with her for ten years, and we loved each other. She will be happy for me."

"She will not disinherit Mary," Cromwell said flatly, as if that was the end of the matter.

"I know she will not, and I would not expect her to do

so! I believe it would give her great joy to know that she has another surviving child. We can keep the matter secret. I can visit her as an old servant."

"Hmm," said Cromwell, "that would be much easier if she would agree to retire to a pleasant country manor away from court. She could have as many visitors as she wished."

I pushed my advantage: "Yes, it would be so easy if she were not surrounded by guards and courtiers. I could walk with her and play for her. We could sew shirts together. Her life would be so much better. I could maybe even try to persuade her once more."

Cromwell smiled, "That would be a miracle indeed," he said. "Very well, you may visit with Will. I will arrange it with the Lady Anne. We can tell her that you are trying once more to persuade the Queen to soften. Anne will agree, even though it is unlikely." I smiled triumphantly at Will, who reached over and clasped my hand.

Cromwell raised his voice: "But if this ever gets out, I will disown the pair of you. You must be very careful indeed. You know the fate of the pretenders to the Tudor throne? You will both be executed for treason, no matter how innocent your intentions. So, Will, are you willing to take that risk?"

I held my breath. I knew that Will had his doubts about my longing to see my mother.

"Master, I thank you. I will take that risk, for my wife's sake. I believe that the Queen will be discreet, as will we."

Cromwell nodded. "Yes, you are right, she is a woman you can trust," he conceded, "but you are both fools. Here, have some hippocras."

We set out for The More, the house where Queen Katherine lived, in early March. Thomas Cromwell had fixed it for me to be away for a couple of weeks, assuring the Lady Anne that this was a last-ditch attempt to get Queen Katherine to change her mind. She hadn't believed him, and had shrugged her shoulders dismissively,

"Why should she be successful when every priest and scholar has not?" she had said contemptuously. "Still, it will do no harm. Let her try!"

Later, when Will and I were on our own, I lamented the fact that the letter from Mistress Stabb had been burnt. "It was my only evidence, and it set out what happened so well! I don't think the Queen will believe me."

Will grinned and reached into an inner pocket on his doublet. "One of the first things Master Cromwell taught me was to always take a copy!" he said. "Here it is, word for word, Mistress Stabb's letter. All the details are here. I knew that we couldn't risk losing them."

"Will, you are a genius! But will you get into trouble? What if Master Cromwell finds out?"

He smiled reassuringly at me. "Why would that happen? We will keep this document safe and show it to no one except the Queen. After that, we will hide it, and no one will be the wiser."

So, still newly married, we set off on our way. We were muffled against the cold with warm cloaks and gloves, the horses saddled up and carrying bags with clean linen and my book of hours, bread with spiced ham, and bottles of water. On my finger was the cheap ring that Will had bought last summer, when we were playing at being man and wife. But now it was for real.

The More was a palace in Rickmansworth, about thirty miles from London. We planned to ride to an inn, where we would stay the night before visiting the Queen on the next day. It had been dark for a couple of hours when we arrived, our horses stamping with the cold, and our breath hanging frostily in the air. The inn was warm though, and welcoming. After some pottage washed down with ale, we enjoyed the delights of being a married couple in a chamber with a warm fire, sweet, scented rushes, and a comfortable bed. But in the middle of the night I woke and lay there watching Will's chest rising and falling peacefully under the covers. My mind wasn't easy. I dreaded Queen Katherine's reaction. Would she send me away? And what would she say after learning about my birth? I longed for her to take me in her arms. Would her love for me remain strong? I thought it would. But she might just as well reject me with a justified revulsion.

Next morning Will saddled up the horses and we rode the short distance to The More. As we rode up the drive, I could see that it was indeed a palace. There were clipped gardens all around it, with bare orchards and kitchen gardens. The main building was brick-fronted, in the latest style, with then many smaller buildings around it, some of them linked together by long passageways. Will told me it had once belonged to Cardinal Wolsey but was now the property of the King. I was glad to see that Queen Katherine was still living as a queen, with all the style and dignity she was entitled to.

We rode up to the gatehouse, where we were stopped by two guards.

"Who goes there?" one asked, looking at us suspiciously. Will answered, in his best lawyer's authoritative voice:

"We bring messages from Thomas Cromwell. You are ordered to admit us!"

The guard grimaced. "The Princess Dowager is not always inclined to follow Cromwell's orders," he said. "But wait here. I will send to the main house and ask if I should admit you."

I interrupted, "Tell the Queen that Mistress Kat is here, with important news. She will want to hear from me."

The guard shrugged. "Didn't you know we aren't supposed to call her the Queen anymore? But no matter. Now wait here." He beckoned another guard to take his place and set off for the main building.

We waited, sitting on our horses, for what seemed like hours, but was probably only about forty minutes. I looked across at Will, and he smiled at me. It was true, he was completely on my side. At last the guard returned.

"The Princess Dowager will see you both, in the Presence Chamber. Leave your horses at the stables. Come with me."

We followed him on horseback until we reached the stables, where a stablehand took the bridles of both our horses and brought them inside, next to a manger full of hay. They snuffled in pleasure and struck their feet against the stone.

We dismounted, and walked past the gardens and the orchards, and into the main house. As with most palaces, the Presence Chamber was next to the entrance. The guard ushered us in, bowed, and closed the massive oak door.

The Queen was sitting on a dais, resplendent in court dress, and blazing with jewels. She was surrounded by ladies. I could see Lady Maria Willoughby, and Lady Jane Seymour both near the front. They looked at me as if I was an unpleasant rat that had scuttled in from the courtyard. I curtseyed, and Will removed his cap and bowed deeply.

"Stand!" the Queen said shortly. She was not going to make us get on our knees, although she might have wanted to. "So, you bring a message from Master Cromwell? Of what concern is that to me? Master Cromwell and I have had many conversations, and in the last years in very few of them have we agreed!"

"Your Majesty," I said, my voice cracking with emotion. "I need to speak with you alone. I have news that I must share with you."

"You can speak in front of my ladies," the Queen said, gesturing at them all. Lady Jane Seymour looked down her nose at me.

"Your Majesty, I beg you. One last kindness. Then if you wish I will never see you again. But your Majesty, I will never forget what you did for me, how you helped me and cared for me. For the sake of that little maid that you took in so long ago, please listen to me."

Queen Katherine looked thoughtful, then nodded her head. "Very well, you can come with me to my privy chamber.

Just you Kat! Not Will. He must wait here." She got up from her chair, and stepped down from the dais, making her way towards the entrance to the private apartments.

I looked at Will, and he nodded at me, as if to say, "you go, I will wait for you." I went over to her and followed her out.

We walked together through several antechambers, the Queen a little breathless. I felt a great pang as I remembered the many times I had accompanied her to her bedroom, carrying her train, smelling the rose oil that she always used. It was as if she sensed this, as she turned to me and said, "Just like old times Kat, do you remember?"

"Indeed I do your Majesty. How could I ever forget your kindness to me?"

She looked at me and sighed deeply. "Come Kat. Come and drink some wine with me." We were in her bedroom now, where a couple of maids were tidying up. She waved them away, sending them to get wine and sweet biscuits. Then she sat down and gestured to me to sit also.

"So, what is it that Master Cromwell wishes to tell me?" There was still a touch of imperiousness in her voice.

"He wishes to tell you nothing, Madam," I said hurriedly. "He knows the real reason for my visit, and he said I was taking a message so that Lady Anne would allow me to go. He said I was to try to persuade you to retire, but he knows that is not what I am going to do." I didn't think he would exactly put it like that, but it was true that he hadn't expected anything from my visit.

"So what are you going to do Kat?" the Queen asked, looking searchingly into my face. Her eyes, once so bright blue, had faded.

"Madam, your Majesty... it is so difficult to know where to start. You know, when you took me in, I was a foundling, I did not know who my parents were. In the last few months, I have found out where I come from, and who gave birth to me. Madam... I believe that you are my mother."

Queen Katherine's face froze, and she stared at me, looking me up and down. "You are lying girl. You cannot be my baby," she hissed. "My babies all died. How dare you insult me in this way? You, of all people, who know how I have wept for them?" She turned away from me and bowed her head. Then she turned back and gave me a long, long look. I reached out to her and took her hands in mine. She let them rest there.

"Madam, look at me! Look at my hair, the same colour as yours, look at my skin, milky white like yours, look at my hands, they are small like yours." I released one of her hands and held mine against it. They were identical.

She registered this, but then cried out, "How can it be?" she said. "My babies all died. Kat, I can see you have a look about you, almost a Tudor look, but you cannot be mine."

Slowly, hesitantly, I told her my story, referring to the document which I had in my pocket. As she listened, the tears began to fall. I showed her the handkerchief, with its royal crest.

"I was wrapped in that," I said quietly. She took it and held it up to her face.

"That is the King's," she said. "I used to take something of his into the birthing chamber to feel close to him. I remember, I couldn't find it later."

She started to look at me with a gathering belief in her eyes, pulling the handkerchief through her fingers again and again. When I came to the part where I was left for dead in the antechamber, she called out in pain.

"Aieee! They left you to die! I was told you were dead! Kat, I was told you were dead! They promised me that I was carrying another baby. Don't worry about that girl, they said. She is dead, think about the son that you are still carrying. Only they were wrong. I was carrying nothing! If only I had known, while I was mourning you, you were struggling for breath in the next room! I cannot forgive this. Where is the midwife, Mistress Stabb?"

"Madam, she is dead now. She said she had never come across a case like it. I was born lifeless, she was certain of that. But somehow, in that cold room, the breath came into my body. She was afraid that she would be blamed, or that someone would say a live baby had been smuggled into the birthing chamber."

"But you were my child Kat, and you were stolen from me!"

The Queen, my mother was struggling with the enormity of what had happened. She, who had been taunted with her inability to bear live children, who had been made to feel inadequate, had in fact born three live children, Princess Mary, Prince Henry, who died at two months, and me. I could feel the anger stirring in her, as she clenched her fists, and cried out:

"Lord Jesu, what have I done to deserve this? I was a good wife, a good mother. But always they were taking that away from me. Just as they took you away from me!"

I tried to comfort her. "Madam, it wasn't the King, or his ministers that took me away. It was just a frightened midwife, who didn't know what to do. She found me a good home, I had a happy childhood."

"Only to be left at the age of eight with no one to care for you!" she retorted, shuddering and crying without restraint.

"But that was the sweating sickness madam, no one's fault. And Mistress Stabb did her best to send me to the court."

My mother paused for a moment and took a breath. Then she reached for the handkerchief to mop her face. She stopped though and dropped it on her lap. It was too precious. So she dried her tears with her fists, like a little girl.

She looked at me seriously, and I could see her becoming a Queen again.

"Kat, this must never come out," she said. "Princess Mary has been brought up to be the heir. I cannot have her position threatened."

Despite myself, I felt a twinge of jealousy. She would

always defend Mary, not me. But I pushed the feeling down.

"It never will, I promise you," I swore. "It is enough for me to know that you are my mother. I never wanted to be royal. Your life is too hard for me, all the time with your heart at other people's disposal. I want to live an ordinary life, with people I love, that's all."

"It will not be an ordinary life with the Lady Anne," said my mother, musingly. "But you must never tell her your secret Kat. You would be in danger."

"I will not tell her mother. I will work for her, but I will never be close to her as I am to you." I flung my arms around her, feeling her stout little heart beating. This was my mother. My story. And it meant so much.

"I'm so sorry mother, I shouldn't have gone to work for Lady Anne. I was young, and it was exciting, but I hurt you, and I beg your forgiveness."

She pulled back from me and looked into my eyes. "Kat, there is nothing to forgive. I should never have let you go. The court is a dangerous place for a young woman on her own. How will you manage?"

"I am married now," I told her. "I have a husband who I love."

She nodded and remembered who I had come with. "Will Cooke," she said, looking pleased. "I remember. A likeable young man, although he works for my enemy, Cromwell. Still," she shrugged, "I hear he is a good employer. So Will is a fine prospect. But my dear, you should have had a Prince! Your true destiny has been stolen from you. Are you not angry?"

"No, I am not. For years I felt lost, because I didn't know where I came from. But now I know the story, I am content. Will has been my life for years now, and I could marry no one but him."

A look of peace came over her face. As I had thought, she was reassured by my marriage. But I didn't want to let go.

"Mother, I don't want to lose you now." I clasped her

hand. "I would like to visit you sometimes. Would you allow that? I would come as an old servant. We could walk in your gardens."

My mother's face looked very sad. "You may visit whenever you want, my dear Kat. But I cannot tell you how long I will be allowed visitors. The King is already threatening to move me. But let us trust in God my dear girl. For now, though, there is something I can do for you. I can still instruct my Chamberlain to pay you a pension, as one of my servants who has left my service. I will do that this afternoon. That will help you both afford a house. You do not want to live at court my dear."

I pulled away from her, "Mother, I didn't come here to get money! I came here because I had to see you, and tell you my story. We have been so close, and now I understand why. That's what brought me here!"

My mother put her arm around me again. "Kat do not deny me that one mother's pleasure, of providing for my child. I have done so little for you...."

I interrupted, "That isn't true! You took me in as a girl, and you cared for me like a mother, even though I was a foundling. You taught me to read and write, to sew a fine seam. You taught me French and Latin and started me playing the lute! Most of all though, you loved me, and I will never forget that."

"My dear, I do love you, and I will provide for you, as is only right."

She sighed and started to talk about those early days. We spoke of the King, when he was young and handsome, we spoke of Christmases and Easters. We spoke of the Field of Cloth of Gold. Her voice became lighter, and her eyes were glowing. For the first time in years, I remembered how much fun it had been. We laughed together, picturing King Henry, and how he had loved to surprise her by bursting in, disguised as an outlaw, or a pirate, or even a bishop. He was like a boy then, and he loved her dearly.

The light was starting to fade when she collected herself.

"My ladies will be wondering where I am," she said. "And Kat, you must join your husband. But before you go, please take this." She pulled a sapphire ring, surrounded by diamonds and set in gold off her finger. "Take this my dear, in case we never meet again. It will remind you that you are very precious to me. I will remember you every night in my prayers."

"But Mother, we will meet again, surely?"

She hushed me, and looked sadly at me. "Now it must be your Majesty," she said. "And yes, you may come Kat, whenever you wish. But I must say goodbye now. I fear that extra restrictions will be placed upon me. For your sake and mine, we should not hope too much to meet again, my darling girl." I took the ring and put it in my pouch. I could not wear it in public, but maybe when Will and I were alone.

"Come and kiss me Kat," she said softly, "and never forget that I love you, my daughter." I smelt her smell of rose oil as my lips touched her soft skin. I tried to fix this moment in my mind, so that I could remember it for the rest of my life. She took my face in her hands and kissed me on both cheeks, and then my lips.

"Never forget," she whispered, standing back from me.

She walked with me back into her Presence Chamber, where her ladies were looking bored. Will was standing there awkwardly. He glanced at me with questioning eyes and hurried over to where I stood.

"Good day Mistress Kat! God Speed." She waved me away and turned to the women.

"How far have you got with that embroidery?" she asked as the women held up their work for her to inspect. She was no longer looking at us as I curtseyed, and Will bowed. We were dismissed. Holding hands, we made our way to the door, and our new life together.

Alice, I did see Queen Katherine, once more, before she died. Poor lady, she resisted King Henry to the end, and her exile became more and more like imprisonment. Her friends were barred from visiting her, and her daughter Princess Mary kept from her. It was only through the bravery of Lady Maria Willoughby that we went to her on her deathbed, but that's another story. Thinking of it all now I am sorry about my differences with Princess Mary. But when you think of what she went through, being barred from her mother's love, it wasn't surprising she was sour. Punished for loving her mother, she was harshly treated by Lady Anne Boleyn. That was forgivable maybe for Anne, she had no reason to love Mary. But King Henry's actions towards Princess Mary were cruel. His love, pride and acceptance replaced by rejection and insults was outright inhuman. It was that which crushed her.

We remained based at court. Will was advancing fast in Cromwell's service and would shortly qualify as a lawyer. I continued to work for Lady Anne. I have many stories to tell you, Alice, about her reign as Queen, but I like to remember her just as she was about to realise her great ambition, to be Queen. I can see her now, exultant, when she finally knew she would become Queen:

"Do you know what the King told me last week? He said that near the end of the year, we are going to France, on a state visit. I will be accorded all honours, as a queen. I will sit beside him, and the French King, lead the English ladies, and wear the Queen's jewels! That gives me hope Kat. He is determined to make me his wife. He would not take me to the French court as his consort if he did not intend to marry me. A few months Kat, and then I will be crowned."

She looked beautiful at that time, with her black eyes shining, and her hair a glossy brown. At last everything was coming right for her.

"Do you remember, Kat, how I told you I would go to no man's bed, except as his wife? You didn't believe me then. No one did. But I meant it. I did not think the King would pursue me the way he has. I was angry with him for wanting to take me to his bed and then discard me, just as he did with my sister. I thought that he would lose interest and allow me to marry someone else. Or maybe be a single woman, working for reform in the church."

Daughter, of one thing I am sure. Lady Anne was completely sincere in this. At the beginning, she was not playing a game. She sincerely believed in a faith that wasn't dictated by old men in golden capes. At the same time, she was determined she would be no man's mistress. She was an individual, and she wasn't going to play anyone's game.

But now things were different. Anne poured herself a cup of small ale. She was abstemious in nature, unlike her sister she did not drink wine until the evenings. She continued:

"But Kat, the King did not lose interest. It took a while, but he started to believe me. He could have forced me to be his mistress, but he didn't. Why was that? I realised he wanted my approval, my love even. I am different to all the other women. I do not agree with everything he says. He cannot take me for granted. And so, and so, he found himself loving me. It was then he realised that he could only have me as his wife."

She sighed and took a sip of the ale. "But once we both knew that, others became involved. I am carrying the flag for reform, and I know it. If I fail, so does the reformed church! And then, there is my family, Boleyns and Howards. They were amazed that I might become queen at first. But now, they plot endlessly to bring that about. Through me, they can stand at the right hand of the King."

She put her cup down and stared at the floor. "So you see Kat, it is not about him and me anymore. It is about power, and my heart has very little to do with that." She said this so flatly that I felt a great stab of sympathy for her. She, such an individualist, was now the standard bearer for forces that were much greater than her.

"But you love him, my lady, don't you?" I asked.

Daughter, you know that my tongue has always come into action before my brain. I should not have asked her that, it was not my place. But she was in a reflective mood, and she didn't seem to mind.

"Of course I love him. I have loved him for years now. Why else would I wait for him so long?" She picked up her skirts and made to walk to her presence chamber. I followed her, carrying my lute.

And that was the tragedy of Anne. She did love King Henry, and she believed he loved her. She wasn't a courtier, chopping and changing as the winds at switched direction. He'd fallen in love with her as a woman who was determined, brave and clever. She said what she meant, sometimes screamed it. Like Katherine of Aragon, she wouldn't abandon her beliefs to creep around the King. And in the end, it was that which did for her.

Of course, if she'd had a son, she would have been fine. She and Henry would have had enormous rows, and he would have spent more time with his mistresses. But, as the mother of a prince, she would have been safe. It was her bad luck that she only had a daughter. I often wish she had known that her daughter, who now rules us, is one of the most glorious monarchs in Europe.

And so, in one of the most disgusting acts of his monarchy, the King instructed Cromwell to get rid of her. A case was constructed against her, accusing her of adultery. That was laughable! Anne was not an easy woman, but the one thing no one could deny was that she stuck by her principles. She and Katherine, both broken by a King who loved and then loathed them.

I continued in service at the court. As I've told you, I served all of Henry's Queens. Your father Will, and I, survived our storms. Looking back now, with you working at court for Queen Elizabeth and Roger making his way in the world, I can say that Will was a good father to you both, and a good husband to me. We were both ordinary people, and our lives were dictated by the whims of the powerful. But finally, we were made for each other. I never wished to be a Princess, or even a Queen. I had so much more than them. Remember this, my dearest daughter. Keep our secret close, and know where your treasure lies.

Additional note from Kat:

Alice, I had intended to keep these documents from you until I died. But as you grew to adulthood, you would ask questions, and I could never satisfy you with vague answers.

Will thought that I should tell you: "Kat, she must know about her grandparents. As it is, she knows about Tom and Joan, my mother, but she has no idea about where she came from on your side." We were walking in the orchard, enjoying the sweet spring air, and the blush pink blossom.

"It is a great thing to bear," I said. "I think she would be better off without the knowledge just now."

Will looked quizzically at me. "But you weren't content not to know. What makes you think she will be? Why are you ashamed of where you came from?" he asked. "You, who are the most beautiful, cleverest, and most entirely good of King Henry's offspring?" Once I would have gone bright red at his comments, but now I just laughed.

"Will, you are very good with the honeyed words, particularly when you want something."

He gave me a long look, and I felt his eyes moving over me. "You know what I want from you Kat, and will always want. Tonight, when we are on our own, in our marriage bed, I will ask you once more to be my lover. And you, unless you are unwell, will gently and generously accede to my request."

He pushed me up against the trunk of an old apple tree and took my face in his hands. Slowly, he started to kiss me. It wasn't urgent now, as it had been when we were younger. But it was still intensely sweet, feeling his hard lips on mine, and then his tongue moving into me. God help me, a middle-aged woman, but I could not resist him, and I wantonly pressed my body against his. That was it, Alice, when you find your true love, it never goes. You can fall in love many times, but to love, to really love a man, and for him to love you, that is something that is a possession through time. I know, up until judgement day, it will be Will for me, and me for Will.

And so it was that he persuaded me to let you read the first of these documents, setting out the secret of your birth. I called you in to the parlour and gestured to you to sit beside me. It was a sunny day, with light pouring in through our glass casement windows.

"Alice, I know that you have had questions about my, and hence your, origins. I would like you to read this. It sets out exactly what happened."

You looked at me for a moment, then picked up the papers. "So this is the answer to the mystery, mother?"

"Yes, indeed it is."

I sat quietly while you read through the document. Like me, you were a quick reader, and I noticed with some amusement that you skimmed through sections that did not affect you. After a couple of hours, you laid it down.

"I didn't think it would be like this," you said, and looked out of the window, blinking in the sunlight.

"I didn't either," I replied.

"So, if you had been recognised, it would have been you on the throne now?"

I smiled, still finding this incredible. "But I wasn't recognised, not before it was much too late."

"I could have been a princess," you mused, "married to a French or a Spanish prince."

"Yes, that might have happened. But Alice, if I had been recognised as King Henry's daughter, I would not have been allowed to marry your father. Our family would not have existed."

You looked at me and smiled.

"I would never want to be without you as my mother," you said.

Dear girl, then you leaned forward and kissed me. What a blessing it is to have a husband and children, and I thank God for the fate that gifted me with you all, and not a crown.

ABOUT ATMOSPHERE PRESS

Founded in 2015, Atmosphere Press was built on the principles of Honesty, Transparency, Professionalism, Kindness, and Making Your Book Awesome. As an ethical and author-friendly hybrid press, we stay true to that founding mission today.

If you're a reader, enter our giveaway for a free book here:

SCAN TO ENTER
BOOK GIVEAWAY

If you're a writer, submit your manuscript for consideration here:

SCAN TO SUBMIT
MANUSCRIPT

And always feel free to visit Atmosphere Press and our authors online at atmospherepress.com. See you there soon!

ABOUT THE AUTHOR

CAROLINE WILLCOCKS has worked in the theatre, freelance journalism and charities. Now she combines being a solution focussed therapist with writing about the Tudors and Stuarts. She also has a successful podcast called *Tudor and Stuart Fairytales*. Her two adult children are happily married, and she hopes she doesn't embarrass them too much. She loves to travel and has visited many countries, including Syria, Iraq, Kosovo, India and the United States.

She lives in the idyllic county of Herefordshire in the UK with her beloved husband, dog and two cats. Recently she discovered she is a direct descendant of Edward III.

Printed in Great Britain
by Amazon

48966291R00169